What makes

There was a time when this question had to be decided, when a decision was forced upon the human race. That is what the civil war was really about.

We were fighting, in the end, to determine what form the human race would take to the stars.

METAPLANETARY

Praise for

TONY DANIEL

Books by
Tony Daniel

THE ROBOT'S TWILIGHT COMPANION (SHORT STORIES)
EARTHLING
WARPATH
METAPLANETARY

METAPLANETARY

A NOVEL OF INTERPLANETARY
CIVIL WAR

TONY DANIEL

An Imprint of HarperCollinsPublishers

EOS
An Imprint of HarperCollins*Publishers*
10 East 53rd Street
New York, New York 10022-5299

Copyright © 2001 by Tony Daniel
ISBN: 0-06-102025-7
www.eosbooks.com

First Eos paperback printing: July 2002
First Eos hardcover printing: April 2001

Eos Trademark Reg. U.S. Pat. Off. And in Other Countries,
Marca Registrada, Hecho en U.S.A.
HarperCollins ® is a trademark of HarperCollins Publishers Inc.

Printed in the U.S.A.

10 9 8 7 6 5 4 3 2 1

For Jerry A. Daniel and Martha Montgomery Daniel,

my father and mother

"Things that really matter, although they are not defined for all eternity, even when they come very late still come at the right time."

—MARTIN HEIDEGGER, "Letter on Humanism"

Introduction

Tacitus Speaks

I am a spaceship. I am about the size of the Martian moon Phobos, although not nearly as dense. I am also a human being. That a spaceship can be a human being is a fact commonly accepted today, but there was once a time when everyone didn't believe such things at all. Many people believed the opposite.

I am an old ship. Let me unwind my tale.

This is the story of the civil war that once tore our solar system to pieces, and of the events that led to the founding of the government that we have today. But to tell such a tale as merely a dry rattling off of facts would be to miss the point. History isn't facts; history is people—in all the myriad forms they come.

What makes a human being? In the end, that is what we were fighting for—to determine what makeup the human race would take to the stars.

We are entering, then, upon a period of turmoil and transformation. An empire rose and fell. Democracy was put to the fire and hammered into an almost unrecognizable configuration. Low deeds were perpetrated, and it often seemed that evil had the upper hand. Heroes emerged from the obscurity, and some died gloriously, while others were beaten and broken. Children killed children, and old men and women were driven from their homes and murdered. Millions died; billions suffered. It was a hard time to be alive.

Yet it was a time of incredible ingenuity and fervent creativity. New sciences were born. Great literature was written. People who ordinarily would have never known one another came together to face a common foe. Necessity abolished prejudice, and humans became brothers and sisters—and, in some cases, lovers—with those whom they would scarcely have acknowledged as persons before.

Nobody really won. But everyone who somehow managed to live through the war achieved a kind of victory.

And, in the end, all of the horror and heroism was the reflection of the soul of an anguished poet. For the war was really the birth throes of a new sort of human, and Thaddeus Kaye was both the cause and the victim of it all.

This is the story of what humans made of the times in which they found themselves in the years after the turn of the third millennium. And since time is now proving to be exactly as malleable as the human spirit, I set it adrift upon the future and the past from these shores of my present. I do not know precisely what guise it may come to you in—perhaps only as a myth or a cautionary tale. So be it. I have faith that what it all really means, what it all comes down to, will somehow, somewhere twinkle through, at least in a glimmer here and there. That is all this old ship can rightfully hope for.

So let us begin where all history begins: in the broken heart of a poet and the contemplation of a priest.

METAPLANETARY

ANTEBELLUM

Historical Fragments,
One E-Year before the War for Republic,
as Recovered from the Grist

Midnight Standard at the Westway Diner

Standing over all creation a doubt-ridden priest took a piss.

He shook himself, looked between his feet at the stars, then tabbed his pants closed. He flushed the toilet and centrifugal force took care of the rest.

Father Andre Sud walked back to his table in the Westway Diner. He padded over the living fire of the plenum, the abyss—all of it—and hardly noticed. Even though this place was special to *him*, it was really just another café with a see-through floor—a window as thin as paper and as hard as diamond. Dime a dozen as they used to say a thousand years ago. The luciferan sign at the entrance said FREE DELIVERY in Basis. The sign under it said OPEN 24 HRS. This sign was unlit. The place will close, eventually.

The priest sat down and stirred his black tea. He read the sign, backward, and wondered if the words he spoke when he spoke sounded anything like English used to. Hard to tell with the grist patch in his head.

Everybody understands one another on a general level these days, Andre Sud thought. Approximately more or less they know what you mean.

There was a dull, greasy gleam to the napkin holder. The saltshaker was half-full. The laminate surface of the table was worn through where the plates usually sat. The particle board underneath was soggy. There was free-floating grist that sparkled like mica within the wood: used-to-be-cleaning-grist, entirely shorn from the restaurant's controlling algorithm and nothing to do but shine. Like the enlightened pilgrim of the Greentree Way was supposed to do, Andre thought. Become shorn and brilliant.

And what will you have with that hamburger?

Grist. Nada y grist. Grist y nada.

I am going through a depression, Andre reminded himself. I am even considering leaving the priesthood.

Andre's convert portion spoke through Andre's pellicle—the microscopic, algorithmic part of him that was spread through his body and spread out in the general vicinity. The convert spoke as if from a long way off.

[This happens every winter. And lately with the insomnia. Cut it out with the nada y nada. Everything's physical, don't you know.]

[Except for *you*,] Andre thought back.

He usually imagined the convert that inhabited his pellicle as a little cloud of algebra symbols that followed him around like mosquitoes. In truth it was normally invisible, of course. For most people, the tripartite division of the human personality into *aspect*, *convert*, and *pellicle* was a completely unconscious affair. People did not "talk" to their convert portion as Andre was able to do any more than the conceptual part of a single brain would talk to the logical part on a conscious level. But Andre had trained himself to notice the partitions in his mentality. It was one of the things a Greentree shaman learned in seminary: the Father, Son, and Holy Ghost were inside as well as "up there." The biology begat the mentality, and the two communicated by means of the grist pellicle, the technological equivalent of "the Holy Ghost." This division of personhood was always expressed both psychologically, technologically, and spiritually. To understand oneself, one must understand the multiplicity, as well as the unity, of his personality.

[At least that's what they taught us in Human Spirituality and Consciousness,] said Andre's convert. [If you can believe what you hear from a bunch of priests.]

[Very funny,] he answered. [Play a song or something, would you?]

After a moment, an oboe piped up in his inner ear. It was an old Greentree hymn—Ben Johnston's "Ponder Nothing"—that his mother had hummed when he was a kid. Brought up in the faith. The convert filtered it through a couple of variations and inversions, but it was always soothing to hear the ancient tune.

There was a way to calculate how many winters the Mars-Earth Diaphany would get in an Earth year, but Andre never checked before he returned to the seminary on his annual retreat, and they always took him by surprise, the winters did. You wake up one day and the light has grown dim.

The café door slid open and Cardinal Filmbuff filled the doorway. He was wide and possessive of the door-frame. He was a big man with a mane of silver hair. He was also space-adapted and white as bone in the face. He wore all black, with a lapel pin in the shape of a tree. It was green of course.

"Father Andre," said Filmbuff from across the room. His voice sounded like a Met cop's radio. "May I join you?"

Andre motioned to the seat across from him in the booth. Filmbuff walked over with big steps and sat down hard.

"Isn't it late for you to be out, Morton?" Andre said. He took a sip of his tea. He'd left the bag in too long, and it tasted twiggy.

"Tried to call you at the seminary retreat center," Film-buff said.

"I'm usually here," Andre replied. "When I'm not there."

"Is this place still the seminary student hangout?"

"It is. Like a dog returneth to its own vomit, huh? Or *somebody's* vomit."

A waiter drifted toward them. "Need menus?" he said. "I have to bring them because the tables don't work."

"I might want a little something," Filmbuff replied. "Maybe a lhasi."

The waiter nodded and went away.

"They still have real people here?" said Filmbuff.

"I don't think they can afford to recoat the place."

Filmbuff gazed around. He was like a beacon. "Seems clean enough."

"I suppose it is," said Andre. "I think the basic coating still works and that just the complicated grist has broken down."

"You like it here."

Andre realized he'd been staring at the swirls in his tea and not making eye contact with his boss. He sat back, smiled at Filmbuff. "Since I came to seminary, Westway Diner has always been my home away from home." He took a sip of tea. "This is where I got satori, you know."

"So I've heard. It's rather legendary. You were eating a plate of mashed potatoes."

"Sweet potatoes, actually. It was a vegetable plate. They give you three choices, and I chose sweet potatoes, sweet potatoes, and sweet potatoes."

"I never cared for them."

"Dislike of sweet potatoes is merely an illusion, as you know, Morton. Everyone likes them sooner or later."

Filmbuff guffawed. His great head turned up toward the ceiling, and his eyes, presently copper-colored, flashed in the brown light. "Andre, we need you back teaching. Or in research."

"I lack faith."

"Faith in yourself."

"It's the same thing as faith in general, as you also well know."

"You are a very effective scholar and priest to be so racked with doubt. Makes me think I'm missing something."

"Doubt wouldn't go with your zealous hair, Morton."

The waiter came back. "Have you decided?" he said.

"A chocolate lhasi," Filmbuff replied firmly. "And some faith for Father Andre here."

The waiter stared for a moment, nonplussed. His Broca grist patch hadn't translated Cardinal Filmbuff's words, or had reproduced them as nonsense.

The waiter must be from far out along the Happy Garden Radial, Andre thought. Most of the help *was* in Seminary Barrel. Basis wasn't normally spoken on the Happy

Garden Radial. There was a trade patois and a thousand long-shifted dialects out that way. Most of the Met citizens were poor as churchmice there, and there was no good Broca grist to be had for Barrel wages, either.

"Iye ftip," Andre said to the waiter in the Happy Garden patois. "It is a joke." The waiter smiled uncertainly. "Another shot of hot water for my tea is what I want," Andre said. The waiter went away looking relieved. Filmbuff's aquiline presence could be intimidating.

"There is no empirical evidence that you lack faith," Filmbuff said. It was a pronouncement. "You are as good a priest as there is. We have excellent reports from Triton."

Linsdale, Andre thought. Traveling monk indeed. Traveling stool pigeon was more like it. I'll give him hell next conclave.

"I'm happy there. I have a nice congregation, and I balance rocks."

"Yes. You are getting a reputation for that."

"Triton has the best gravity for it in the solar system."

"I've seen some of your creations on the merci. They're beautiful. You've attracted quite a following."

"Through no intention of my own. Thank you, though."

"What happens to the rock sculptures?"

"Oh, they fall," said Andre, "when you stop paying attention to them."

The chocolate lhasi came and the waiter set down a self-heating carafe of water for Andre. Filmbuff took a long drag at the straw and finished half his drink.

"Excellent." He sat back, sighed, and burped. "Andre, I've had a vision."

"Well, that's what you do for a living."

"I saw *you.*"

"Was I eating at the Westway Diner?"

"You were falling through an infinite sea of stars."

The carafe bubbled, and Andre poured some water into his cup before it became flat from all the air being boiled out. The hot water and lukewarm tea mingled in thin rivulets. He did not stir.

"You came to rest in the branches of a great tree. Well, you crashed into it, actually, and the branches caught you."

"Yggdrasil? The Greentree?"

The Greentree was the basic image of Andre's sect. It was also more than that—but *what* exactly, not even ten years of schooling had taught him. A mystical system. A psychological paradigm for understanding human behavior. A real entity that somehow actually existed and was the expression of the totality of human endeavor. All of the above.

"I don't think so. This was a different tree. I've never seen it before. It is very disturbing because I thought there was only the One Tree. *This* tree was just as big, though."

"As big as the Greentree?"

"Just as big. But different." Filmbuff looked down at the stars beneath their feet. His eyes grew dark and flecked with silver. Space-adapted eyes always took on the color of what they beheld. "Andre, you have no idea how real this was. *Is.* This is difficult to explain. You know about my other visions . . . of the coming war?"

"The Burning of the Greentree?"

"Yes."

"It's famous in the Way."

"I don't care about that. Nobody else is listening but us priests, I often think, and that is the problem. In any case, this vision *has placed itself on top of* those war visions. Right now, being here with you, this seems like a play to me. A staged play. You. Me. Even the war that's coming. It's all a play that is really about that damn Tree. And it won't let me go."

"What do you mean won't let you go?"

Filmbuff raised his hands, palms up, to cradle an invisible sphere in front of him. He stared into the space as if it were the depths of all creation, and his eyes became set and focused far away. But not glazed over or unaware.

They were so alive and intense that it hurt to look at him. Filmbuff's physical face *vibrated* when he was in trance. It was a slight effect, and unnerving even when you were used to it. He was utterly focused, but you couldn't focus on him. There was too much of him there for the space provided. Or not enough of you.

I am watching chronological quantum transport in the raw, Andre thought. The instantaneous integration of gravitonic spin information from up-time sifted through the archetypal registers of Filmbuff's human brain.

And it all comes out as metaphor.

"The Tree is burnt out now," Filmbuff said, speaking out of his trance. His words were like stones. "The Burning's done. But it isn't char that I'm seeing, no." He clenched his fists, then opened his palms again. "The old Tree is a shadow. The burnt remains of the Greentree are really only the shadow of the other tree, the new Tree. It's like a shadow the new Tree casts."

"Shadow," Andre heard himself whispering. His own hands were clenched in a kind of sympathetic vibration with Filmbuff.

"We are living in the time of the shadow. The dying past," said Filmbuff. He relaxed a bit. "There's almost a perfect juxtaposition of the two trees. I've never felt so sure of anything in my life. A new Tree is coming."

Filmbuff, for all his histrionics, was not one to overstate his visions for effect. The man who sat across from Andre was only the *aspect*—the human portion—of a vast collective of personalities. They were all unified by the central being; the man before him was no more a puppet than was his enthalpic computing analog soaking up energy on Mercury, or the nodes of specialized grist spread across human space decoding variations in antigraviton spins as they made their way backward in time. Filmbuff was no longer simply the man who had taught Andre's Intro to Pastoral Shamanism course at seminary. Ten years ago, the Greentree Way had specifically crafted a large array of personalities to catch a glimpse of the future, and Filmbuff had been assigned to be morphed into that specialized version of a LAP.

I was on the team that designed him, Andre thought. Of course, that was back when I was a graduate assistant. Before I Walked on the Moon.

"The vision is what's real." Filmbuff put the lhasi straw to his mouth and finished the rest of it. Andre wondered where the liquid *went* inside the man. Didn't he run on batteries or something? "This is maya, Andre."

"I believe you, Morton."

"I talked to Erasmus Kelly about this," Filmbuff continued. "He took it on the merci to our Interpreter's Freespace."

"What did they come up with?"

Filmbuff pushed his empty glass toward Andre. "That there's a new Tree," he said.

"How the hell could there be a new Tree? The Tree is wired into our DNA like sex and breathing. It may *be* sex and breathing."

"How should I know? There's a new Tree."

Andre took a sip of his tea. Just right. "So there's a new Tree," he said. "What does that have to do with me?"

"We think it has to do with your research."

"What research? I balance rocks."

"From before."

"Before I lost my faith and became a priest on Triton?"

"You were doing brilliant work at the seminary."

"What? With the time towers? That was a dead end."

"You understand them better than anyone."

"Because I don't try to make any sense of them. They are a dead end, epistemologically speaking. Do you think this new Tree has to do with those things?"

"It's a possibility."

"I doubt it."

"You doubt everything."

"The time towers are a bunch of crotchety old LAPs who have disappeared up their own asses."

"Andre, you know what I am."

"You're my boss."

"Beside that."

"You're a *manifold*. You are a Large Array of Personalities who was especially constructed as a quantum event detector—probably the best in human history. Parts of you stretch across the entire inner solar system, and you have cloudship outriders. If you say you had a vision of me and this new Tree, then it has to mean *something*. You're not making it up. Morton, you see into the future, and there I am."

"There you are. You are the Way's expert on *time*. What do *you* think this means?"

"What do you want me to tell you? That the new Tree is obviously a further stage in sentient evolution, since the Greentree is *us*."

"That's what Erasmus Kelly and his people think. I need something more subtle from you."

"All right. It isn't the time towers that this has to do with."

"What then?"

"You don't want to hear this."

"You'd better tell me anyway."

"Thaddeus Kaye."

"Thaddeus Kaye is dead. He killed himself. Something was wrong with him, poor slob."

"I know you big LAPs like to think so."

"He was perverted. He killed himself over a woman, wasn't it?"

"Come on, Morton. A pervert hurts other people. Kaye hurt himself."

"What does *he* have to do with anything, anyway?"

"He's not dead. He's just wounded and lost."

"How can you know that?"

"Because Thaddeus Kaye cannot die," Andre said flatly.

"That's absurd."

"You understand what kind of being he is, don't you, Morton?"

"He's a LAP, just like me."

"You only see the future, Morton. Thaddeus Kaye can *affect* the future directly, from the past."

"So what? We all do that every day of our lives."

"This is not the same. Instantaneous control of instants. What the Merced quantum effect does for space, Thaddeus Kaye can do for time. He *prefigures* the future. Backward and forward in time. He is written on it, and the future is written *into* him. He's like a rock that has been dropped into a lake."

"Are you saying he's God?"

"No. But if your vision is a true one, and I know that it is, then he could very well *be* the coming *war*."

"Do you mean the reason *for* the war?"

"Yes, but more than that. Think of it as a wave, Morton. If there's a crest, there has to be a trough. Thaddeus Kaye is the crest, and the war is the trough. He's something like a physical principle. That's how his integration process was designed. Not a force, exactly, but he's been imprinted on a *property* of time."

"The Future Principle?"

"All right. Yes. In a way, he *is* the future. He's still alive."

"And you're sure of that?"

"I wasn't—not entirely—until you told me your vision just now. What else could it be? Unless aliens are coming."

"Maybe aliens are coming. They'd have their own Tree. Possibly."

"Morton, be realistic. Do you see anything that could be interpreted as aliens coming in your dreams?"

"No."

"Well then."

Filmbuff put his hands over his eyes and lowered his head. "I'll tell you what I still see," he said in a low rumble of a voice like far thunder. "I see the burning Greentree. I see it strung with a million bodies, each of them hung by the neck, and all of them burning, too. Until this vision, that was *all* I was seeing."

"Did you see any way to avoid it?"

Filmbuff looked up. His eyes were as white as his hands when he spoke. "Once. Not now. The quantum fluctuations have all collapsed down to one big macro reality. Maybe not today, maybe not tomorrow, but *soon*."

Andre sighed. *I believe*, he thought. *I don't want to believe, but I do. It's easy to have faith in destruction.*

"I just want to go back to Triton and balance rocks," he said. "That's really all that keeps me sane. I love that cold moon."

Filmbuff pushed his lhasi glass even farther away and slid out of the booth. He stood up with a creaking sound, like vinyl being stretched. "Interesting times," he spoke to the café. "Illusion or not, that was probably the last good lhasi I'm going to have for quite a while."

"Uh, Morton?"

"Yes, Father Andre?"

"You have to pay up front. They can't take it out of your account."

"Oh my." The cardinal reached down and slapped the black cloth covering his white legs. He, of course, had no pockets. "I don't think I have any money with me."

"Don't worry," Andre said. "I'll pick it up."

"Would you? I'd hate to have that poor waiter running after me down the street."

"Don't worry about it."

"We'll talk more tomorrow after meditation." This was not a request.

"We'll talk more then."

"Good night, Andre."

"Night, Morton."

Filmbuff stalked away, his silver mane trailing behind him as if a wind were blowing through it. Or a solar flare.

Before he left the Westway, he turned, as Andre knew he would, and spoke one last question across the space of the diner.

"You knew Thaddeus Kaye, didn't you, Father Andre?"

"I knew a man named Ben Kaye. A long time ago," Andre said, but this was only confirmation of what Filmbuff's spread-out mind had already told him. "He was one of my best friends. E-years before he became Thaddeus."

The door slid shut, and the Cardinal left into the night. Andre sipped at his tea.

Eventually the waiter returned. "We close pretty soon," he said.

"Why do you close so early?" Andre asked.

"It is very late."

"I remember when this place did not close."

"I don't think so. It always closed."

"Not when I was a student at the seminary."

"It closed then," said the waiter. He took a rag from his apron, activated it with a twist, and began to wipe a nearby table.

"I'm sure you're mistaken."

"They tell me there's never been a time when this place didn't close."

"Who tells you?"

"People."

"And you believe them."

"Why should I believe *you*? You're people." The waiter looked up at Andre, puzzled. "That was a joke," he said. "I guess it does not translate."

"Bring me some more tea, and then I will go."

The waiter nodded, then went to get it.

There was music somewhere. Gentle oboe strains. Oh, yes. His convert was still playing the hymn.

[What do you think?]

[I think we are going on a quest.]

[I suppose so.]

[Do you know where Thaddeus Kaye is?] asked the convert. Of course, it knew the answer already. That was the problem with talking to yourself.

[I have a pretty good idea how to find Ben. And wherever Ben is, Thaddeus Kaye *has* to be.]

[Why not tell somebody else how to find him?]

[Because no one else will do what I do when I find him.]

[What's that?]

[Nothing.]

[Oh.]

[When the backup is done, we'll be on our way.]

Having himself backed up was mainly what this retreat was for, since using the Greentree data facilities was free to priests. Doing it on Triton would have cost as much as putting a new roof on his house. At least, this was the reason he'd given his congregation back on Triton. The only person he'd told the truth to about his doubts and his incipient apostasy was his friend Roger Sherman. That old crow of an army colonel had become Andre's unofficial confessor the past couple of e-years.

[Why don't they send someone who is stronger in faith than we are?] the convert said.

[I don't know. Send an apostate to net an apostate, I guess.]

[What god is Thaddeus Kaye apostate from?]

[Himself.]

[And for that matter, what about us?]

[You ask too many questions. Here comes the tea. Will you play that song again?]

[It was Mother's favorite,] said Andre's convert.

[Do you think it could be that simple? That I became a priest because of that hymn?]

[Are you asking *me*?]

[Just play the music and let me drink my tea. I think the waiter wants us out of here.]

"Do you mind if I mop up around you?" the waiter said.

"I'll be done soon."

"Take your time, as long as you don't mind me working."

"I don't mind."

Andre listened to mournful oboe and watched as the waiter sloshed water across the infinite universe, then took a mop to it with a vengeance.

Jill

Down in the dark there's a doe rat I'm after to kill. She's got thirteen babies, and I'm going to bite them, bite them, bite them. I will bite them.

The mulch here smells of dank stupid rats all running running and there's nowhere farther to run, because this is it, this is the Carbuncle, and now *I'm* here and this is truly the end of all of it but a rat can't stand to know that and won't accept me until they have to believe me. Now they will believe me.

My whiskers against something soft. Old food? No, it's a dead buck; I scent his Y code, and the body is dead but the code keeps thumping and thumping. This mulch won't let it drain out, and it doesn't ever want to die. The Carbuncle's the end of the line, but this code doesn't know it or knows it and won't have it. I give it a poke and a bit of rot sticks to my nose and the grist tries to swarm me, but no I don't think so.

I sniff out and send along my grist, jill ferret grist, and no rat code stands a chance ever, ever. The zombie rat goes rigid when its tough, stringy code—who knows how old— how far traveled to finally die here at the End of Everywhere—that code scatters to nonsense in the pit of the ball of nothing my grist wraps it in. Then the grist flocks back to me and the zombie rat thumps no more. No more.

Sometimes having to kill *everything* is a bit of a distraction. I want that doe and her littles really bad, and I need to move on.

Down a hole and into a warren larder. Here there are pieces of meat and the stink of maggot sluice pooled in the bends between muscles and organs. But the rats have got the meat from Farmer Jan's Mulmyard, and it's not quite dead yet, got maggot-resistant code, like the buck rat, but not smart enough to know it's dead, just mean code jaw-latched to a leg or a haunch and won't dissipate. Mean and won't die. But I am meaner still.

Oh, I smell her!

I'm coming, mamma rat. Where are you going? There's no going anywhere anymore.

Bomi slinks into the larder and we touch noses. I smell blood on her. She's got a kill, a bachelor male, by the blood spoor on her.

It's so warm and wet, Jill. Bomi's trembling and wound up tight. She's not the smartest ferret. *I love it, love it, and I'm going back to lie in it.*

That's bad. Bad habit.

I don't care. I killed it; it's mine.

You do what you want, but it's your man Bob's rat.

No it's mine.

He feeds you, Bomi.

I don't care.

Go lay up then.

I will.

Without a by-your-leave, Bomi's gone back to her kill to lay up. I never do that. TB wouldn't like it, and besides, the killing's the thing, not the owning. Who wants an old dead rat to lie in when there's more to bite?

Bomi told me where she'd be because she's covering for herself when she doesn't show and Bob starts asking. Bomi's a stupid ferret, and I'm glad she doesn't belong to TB.

But me—down another hole, deeper, deeper still. It's half–filled in here. The doe rat thought she was hiding it, but she left the smell of her as sure as a serial number on a bone. I will bite you, mamma.

Then there's the dead-end chamber I knew would be.

Doe rat's last hope in all the world. Won't do her any good. But oh she's big! She's tremendous. Maybe the biggest ever for me.

I am very, very happy.

Doe rat with the babies crowded behind her. Thirteen of them, I count by the squeaks. Sweet naked squeaks. Less than two weeks old, they are. Puss and meat. But I want mamma now.

The doe sniffs me and screams like a bone breaking, and she rears big as me. Bigger.

I will bite you.

Come and try, little jill.

I will kill you.

I ate a sack of money in the City Bank and they chased me and cut me to pieces and just left my tail and—I grew another rat! What will you do to me, jill, that can be so bad? You'd better be afraid of me.

When I kill your babies, I will do it with one bite for each. I won't hurt them for long.

You won't kill my babies.

At her.

At her because there isn't anything more to say, no more messages to pass back and forth through our grist and scents.

I go for a nipple and she's fast out of the way, but not fast enough and I have a nub of her flesh in my mouth. Blood let. I chew on her nipple tip. Blood and mamma's milk.

She comes down on me and bites my back; her long incisors cut through my fur, my skin, like hook needles, and come out at another spot. She's heavy. She gnaws at me, and I can feel her teeth scraping against my backbone. I shake to get her off, and I do, but her teeth rip a gouge out of me.

Cut pretty bad, but she's off. I back up thinking that she's going to try to swarm a copy, and I stretch out the grist and there it is, just like I thought, and I intercept it and I kill the thing before it can get to the mulm and reproduce and grow another rat. One rat this big is enough, enough for always.

The doe senses that I've killed her outrider, and now she's more desperate.

This is all there is for you. This is oblivion and ruin and time to stop the scurry.

This is where you'll die.

She strikes at me again, but I dodge and—before she can round on me—I snatch a baby rat. It's dead before it can squeal. I spit out its mangle of bones and meat.

But mamma's not a dumb rat, no, not dumb at all, and does not fly into a rage over this. I know she regards me with all the hate a rat can hate, though. If there were any light, I'd see her eyes glowing rancid yellow.

Come on, mamma, before I get another baby.

She goes for a foot, and again I dodge, but she catches me in the chest. She raises up, up.

The packed dirt of the ceiling, wham, wham, and her incisors are hooked around my breastbone, damn her, and it holds me to her mouth as fast as a barbed arrow point.

Shake and tear, and I've never known such pain, such delicious . . .

I rake at her eyes with a front claw, dig into her belly with my feet. Dig, dig, and I can feel the skin parting, and the fatty underneath parting, and my feet dig deep, deep.

Shakes me again and I can only smell my own blood and her spit and then sharp, small pains at my back.

The baby rats. The baby rats are latching on to me, trying to help their mother.

Nothing I can do. Nothing I can do but dig with my rear paws. Dig, dig. I am swimming in her guts. I can feel the give. I can feel the tear. Oh, yes!

Then my breastbone snaps, and I fly loose of the doe's teeth. I land in the babies, and I'm stunned and they crawl over me and nip at my eyes and one of them shreds an ear, but the pain brings me to and I snap the one that bit my ear in half. I go for another. Across the warren cavern, the big doe shuffles. I pull myself up, try to stand on all fours. Can't.

Baby nips my hind leg. I turn and kill it. Turn back. My front legs collapse. I cannot stand to face the doe, and I hear her coming.

Will I die here?

Oh this is how I want it! Took the biggest rat in the history of the Met to kill me. Ate a whole bag of money, she did.

She's coming for me. I can hear her coming for me. She's so big. I can *smell* how big she is.

I gather my hind legs beneath me, find a purchase.

This is how I die. I will bite you.

But there's no answer from her, only the doe's harsh breathing. The dirt smells of our blood. Dead baby rats all around me.

I am very, very happy.

With a scream, the doe charges me. I wait a moment. Wait.

I pounce, shoot low like an arrow.

I'm through, between her legs. I'm under her. I rise up. I rise up into her shredded belly. I bite! I bite! I bite!

Her whole weight keeps her down on me. I chew. I claw. I smell her heart. I smell the new blood of her heart! I can hear it! I can smell it! I chew and claw my way to it.

I bite.

Oh yes.

The doe begins to kick and scream, to kick and scream, and as she does the blood of heart pumps from her and over me, smears over me until my coat is soaked with it, until all the dark world is blood.

After a long time, the doe rat dies. I send out the grist, feebly, but there are no outriders to face, no tries at escape now. She put all that she had into fighting me. She put everything into our battle.

I pull myself out from under the rat. In the corner, I hear the scuffles of the babies. Now that the mamma is dead, they are confused.

I have to bite them. I have to kill them all.

I cannot use my front legs, but I can use my back. I push myself toward them, my belly on the dirt like a snake. I find them all huddled in the farthest corner, piling on one another in their fright. Nowhere to go.

I do what I told the doe I would do. I kill them each with one bite, counting as I go. Three and ten makes thirteen.

And then it's done, and they're all dead. I've killed them all.

So.

There's only one way out: the way I came. That's where I go, slinking, crawling, turning this way and that to keep my exposed bone from catching on pebbles and roots. After a while, I start to feel the pain that was staying away while I fought. It's never been this bad.

I crawl and crawl, I don't know for how long. If I were to meet another rat, that rat would kill me. But either they're dead or they're scared, and I don't hear or smell any. I crawl to what I think is up, what I hope is up.

And after forever, after so long that all the blood on my coat is dried and starting to flake off like tiny brown leaves, I poke my head out into the air.

TB is there. He's waited for me.

Gently, gently he pulls me out of the rathole. Careful, careful he puts me in my sack.

"Jill, I will fix you," he says.

I know.

"That must have been the Great Mother of rats."

She was big, so big and mean. She was brave and smart and strong. It was wonderful.

"What did you do?"

I bit her.

"I'll never see your like again, Jill."

I killed her, and then I killed all her children.

"Let's go home, Jill."

Yes. Back home.

Already in the dim burlap of the sack, and I hear the call of TB's grist to go to sleep, to get better and I sigh and curl as best I can into a ball and I am falling away, falling away to dreams where I run along a trail of spattered blood, and the spoor is fresh and I'm chasing rats, and TB is with me close by, and I will bite a rat soon, soon, soon—

A Simple Room with Good Light

Come back, Andre Sud. Your mind is wandering and now you have to concentrate. Faster now. Fast as you can go. Space-time. Clumps of galaxy clusters. Average cluster. Two-armed spiral.

Yellow star the locals call Sol.

Here's a network of hawsers cabling the inner planets together. Artifact of sentience, some say. Others might dispute that. Mercury, Venus, Earth, Mars hung with a shining webwork across blank space and spreading even into the asteroids. Kilometer-thick cables bending down from the heavens, coming in at the poles to fit into enormous universal joints lubricated by the living magma of the planets' viscera. Torque and undulation. Faster. Somewhere on a flagellating curve between Earth and Mars, the Diaphany, you will find yourself. Closer in. Spinning spherules like beads on a five-hundred-sixty-three-million-mile-long necklace. Come as close as you can.

Into the pithway transport you now travel upon. Into your one and only mind, now going on its second body. Into the fleeting human present.

All along the Mars-Earth Diaphany, Andre saw the preparations for a war like none before. It seemed the entire Met—all the interplanetary cables—had been transformed into a dense fortress that people just happened to live inside. His travel bead was repeatedly delayed in the pithway as troops went about their movements, and military grist swarmed hither and yon about some task or another.

We live in this all-night along the strong-bound carbon of the cables, Andre thought. Within the dark glistening of the corridors, where surface speaks to surface in tiny whispers like fingers, and the larger codes, the extirpated skeletons of a billion minds, clack together in a cemetery of logic, shaking hands, continually shaking bony, algorithmic hands and observing strict and necessary protocol for the purposes of destruction.

Amés—he only went by the one name, as if it were a title—was a great one for martial appearances. Napoléon come again, the merci reporters said as a friendly joke. Oh, the reporters were eating this up. There hadn't been a good war in centuries. People got tired of unremitting democracy, didn't they? He'd actually heard somebody say that on the merci.

How fun it will be to watch billions die for a little excitement on the merci, Andre thought.

He arrived in Connacht Bolsa in a foul mood, but when he stepped out of his pod, there was the smell of new rain. He had walked a ways from the pod station before he realized what the smell was. There were puddles of water on the ground from the old-fashioned street-cleaning mechanism Connacht employed. It was still raining in spots—a small rain that fell only an inch or so from the ground. Little clouds scudded along the street like a miniature storm front, washing it clean of the night's leavings.

Connacht was on a suburb radial off Phobos City, the most densely populated segment on the Met. A hundred years ago, in the Phobos boom time, Connacht had been the weekend escape for intellectuals, artists, moneyed drug addicts—and the often indistinguishable variety of con men, mountebanks, and psychic quacksalvers who were their hangers-on. The place was run-down now, and Andre's pellicle encountered various swarms of nostalgia that passed through the streets like rat packs—only *these* were bred and fed by the merchants to attract the steady trickle of tourists with pellicular receptors for a lost bohemia.

All they did for Andre was made him think about Molly.

Andre's convert—the algorithmic portion of himself—obliged him by dredging up various scenes from his days at seminary. Today, his convert was unusually silent, preferring to communicate in suggestive patterns of data—like a conscience gifted with irreducible logic and an infallible memory.

Andre walked along looking at the clouds under his feet, and as he walked his convert projected images into the shape of these clouds, and into the shift and sparkle of the puddled water they left behind.

I have a very sneaky conscience, Andre thought, but he let the images continue.

—Molly Index, Ben Kaye, and Andre at the Westway, in one of their long arguments over aesthetics when they were collaborating on their preliminary thesis. *Knowing, Watching, and Doing: The Triune Aspect of Enlightenment.*

"I want to be 'Doing'!" Molly mock-yelled and threw a wadded-up piece of paper at Ben.

He caught it, spread it out, and folded it into a paper airplane. "This is the way things have to be," he said. "I'm 'Doing.' You're 'Watching.' And we both know who 'Knowing' must be." They turned to Andre and smiled vulture smiles.

"I don't know what you think I *know,* but I don't know it," he said, then nearly got an airplane in the eye.

—Molly's twenty-four-year-old body covered with red Martian sand under the Tharsis beach boardwalk. Her blue eyes open to the sky pink sky. Her nipples like dark stones. Ben a hundred feet away, rising from the gray-green lake water, shaking the spume from his body. The poet in the midst of gathering his raw materials. Of course Ben had run and jumped into the lake as soon as they got there. Ben wouldn't wait for anything.

But Molly chose me! I can't believe she chose me.

Because I waited for her and dragged her under the boardwalk and kissed her before I could talk myself out of it.

Because I waited for the right moment.

How's that for Doing.

—Living together as grad students while Molly studied art and he entered into the stations of advanced meditation at seminary. Ben dropping by occasionally to read them one of his new poems.

—Molly leaving him because she would not marry a priest.

You're going to kill yourself on the moon.

Only this body. I'll get a new one. It's being grown right now.

It isn't right.

This is the Greentree Way. That's what makes a priest into a true shaman. He knows what it's like to die and come back.

If you Walk on the Moon, you will know what it's like to lose a lover.

Molly, the Walk is what I've been preparing for these last seven years. You know that.

I can't bear it. I won't.

Maybe he could have changed her mind. Maybe he could have convinced her. But Alethea Nightshade had come along and that was that. When he'd come back from the moon reinstantiated in his cloned body, Molly had taken a new lover.

—His peace offering returned with the words of the old folk song, turned inside out: "Useless the flowers that you give, after the soul is gone." As if the death of his biological aspect meant the same thing as the death of *himself*. For Molly, it had meant just that.

—Sitting at a bare table under a bare light, listening to those words, over and over, and deciding never to see her again. Fifteen years ago, as they measure time on Earth.

[Thank you, that will be enough,] he told the convert.

An image of a stately butler, bowing, flashed through Andre's mind. Then doves rising from brush into sunset. The water puddles were just water puddles once again, and the tiny clouds were only clouds of a storm whose only purpose was to make the world a little cleaner.

Molly was painting a Jackson Pollock when Andre arrived at her studio. His heavy boots, good for keeping him in place in Triton's gravity, noisily clumped on the wooden stairs to Molly's second-floor loft. Connacht was spun to Earth-normal. He would have knocked, but the studio door was already open.

"I couldn't believe it until I'd seen it with my own eyes," Molly said. She did not stop the work at her easel. "My seminary lover come back to haunt me."

"Boo," Andre said. He entered the space. Connacht, like many of the old rotating simple cylinders on the Diaphany, had a fusion lamp running down its pith that was sheathed on an Earth-day schedule. Now it was day, and Molly's skylights let in the white light and its clean shadows. Huge picture windows looked out on the village. The light reminded Andre of light on the moon. The unyielding, stark, redeeming light just before his old body joined the others in the shaman-priests' Valley of the Bones.

"Saw a man walking a dog the other day with the legs cut off," said Molly. She dipped the tip of her brush in a blue smear on her palette.

"The man or the dog?"

"Maybe the day." Molly touched the blue to the canvas before her. It was like old times.

"What are you painting?"

"Something very old."

"That looks like a Pollock."

"It is. It's been out of circulation for a while, and somebody used it for a tablecloth. Maybe a kitchen table, I'm thinking."

Andre looked over the canvas. It was clamped down on a big board as long as he was tall. Sections of it were fine, but others looked like a baby had spilled its mashed peas all over it. Then again, maybe that was Pollock's work after all.

"How can you possibly know how to put back all that spatter?"

"There're pictures." Molly pointed the wooden tip of her brush to the left-hand corner of the canvas. Her movements were precise. They had always been definite and precise. "Also you can kind of see the tracery of where this section was before it got . . . whatever that is that got spilled on it there. Also, I use grist for the small stuff. Did you want to talk about Ben?"

"I do."

"Figured you didn't come back to relive old times."

"They *were* good. Do you still do that thing with the mirror?"

"Oh, yes. Are you a celibate priest these days?"

"No, I'm not that kind of priest."

"I'm afraid I forgot most of what I knew about religion."

"So did I."

"Andre, what do you want to know about Ben?" Molly set the handle of her brush against her color palette and tapped it twice. Something in the two surfaces recognized one another, and the brush stuck there. A telltale glimmer of grist swarmed over the brush, keeping it moist and ready for use. Molly sat in a chair by her picture window, and Andre sat in a chair across from her. There was a small table between them. "Zen tea?" she said.

"Sure," Andre replied.

The table pulsed, and two cups began forming on its surface. As the outsides hardened, a gel at their center thinned down to liquid. This was an expensive use of grist.

"Nice table. I guess you're doing all right for yourself, Molly."

"I like to make being in the studio as simple as possible so I can concentrate on my work. I indulge in a few luxuries."

"You ever paint for yourself anymore? Your own work, I mean?"

Molly reached for her tea, took a sip, and motioned with her cup at the Pollock.

"I paint *those* for myself," she said. "It's my little secret. I make them mine. Or they make me theirs."

"That's a fine secret."

"Now you're in on it. So was Ben. Or Thaddeus, I should say."

"You were on the team that made him, weren't you?"

"Aesthetic consultant. Ben convinced them to bring me on. He told me to think of it as a grant for the arts."

"I kind of lost track of you both after I . . . graduated."

"You were busy with your new duties. I was busy. Everybody was busy."

"I wasn't *that* busy."

"Ben kept up with your work. It was part of what made him decide to . . . do it."

"I didn't know that."

"Now you do. He read that paper you wrote on temporal propagation. The one that was such a big deal."

"It was the last thing I ever wrote."

"Developed a queer fascination with rocks?"

"You heard about that?"

"Who do you think sent those merci reporters after you?"

"Molly, you didn't?"

"I waited until I thought you were doing your best work."

"How did you see me . . ." He looked into her eyes, and he saw it. The telltale expression. Far and away. "You're a LAP."

Molly placed the cup to her lips and sipped a precise amount of tea. "I guess you'd classify me as a manifold by now. I keep replicating and replicating. It's an art project I started several years ago. Alethea convinced me to do it when we were together."

"Will you tell me about her? She haunted me for years, you know. I pictured her as some kind of femme fatale from a noir. Destroyed all my dreams by taking you."

"Nobody took me. I went. Sometimes I wonder what I was thinking. Alethea Nightshade was no picnic, let me tell you. She had the first of her breakdowns when we were together."

"Breakdowns?"

"She had schizophrenia in her genes. She wanted to be a LAP, but wasn't allowed because of it. The medical grist controlled her condition most of the time, but every once in a while . . . she outthought it. She was too smart for her own good."

"Is that why you became a LAP?" Andre asked. "Because she couldn't?"

"I told myself I was doing it for *me*, but yes. *Then*. Now things are different." Molly smiled, and the light in the studio was just right. Andre saw the edge of the multiplicity in her eyes.

The fractal in the aspect's iris that signaled a LAP.

"You have no idea how beautiful it is—what I can see." Molly laughed, and Andre shuddered. Awe or fright? He didn't know.

"She was just a woman," Molly said. "I think she came from around Jupiter. A moon or something, you know." Molly made a sweeping motion toward her window. As with many inner-system denizens, the outer system was a great unknown, and all the same, to her. "She grew up on some odd kind of farm."

"A Callisto free grange?"

"I'm sure I don't know. She didn't talk about it much."

"What was she like?"

"Difficult."

"What do you mean?"

"I'll tell you." Tea sip. Andre realized he hadn't picked his up yet. He did so, tried it. It was wonderful, and all grist. A bit creepy to think about drinking it down.

I'll take care of it, don't you worry, said his pellicle.

I know you will.

"Alethea had two qualities that should never exist within one organic mind. A big intellect and a big heart. She felt everything, and she thought about it far too much. She was born to be a LAP. And she finally found a way to do it."

"Ben."

"They fell in love. It was also her good fortune that he could get her past the screening procedures. But Alethea always was a fortunate woman. She was lucky, on a quantum level. Until she wasn't."

"So she and Ben were together before he became . . . Thaddeus."

"For a year."

"Were you jealous?"

"I'd had enough of Alethea by then. I'll always love her,

but I want a life that's . . . plain. She was a tangle I couldn't untangle." Molly touched her fingers to her nose and tweaked it. It was a darling gesture, Andre thought. "Besides," Molly said, "*she* left *me*."

"What did that do to you and Ben?"

"Nothing. I love Ben. He's my best friend."

She was speaking in the present tense about him, but Andre let it pass.

"Why did he change his name, Molly? I never understood that."

"Because he wasn't a LAP."

"What do you mean? Of course he was. A special one. Very special. But still—"

"No. He said he was something new. He said he wasn't Ben anymore. It was kind of a joke with him, though. Because, of course, he *was* still Ben. Thaddeus may have been more than a man, but he definitely was *at least* a man, and that man was Ben Kaye. He never could explain it to me."

"Time propagation without consciousness overlap. That was always the problem with the time-tower LAPs. Interference patterns. Dropouts. But with Thaddeus, they finally got the frequency right. One consciousness propagated into the future and bounced back with antiparticle quantum entanglement."

"I never understood a bit of that jargon you time specialists use."

"We made God."

Molly snorted, and tea came out her nose. She laughed until tears came to her eyes.

"We made something," she said. "Something very different than what's come before. But Andre, I *knew* Thaddeus. He was the last thing in the universe I would consider *worshiping*."

"Some didn't share your opinion."

"Thaddeus thought they were crazy. They made him very uncomfortable."

"Was Alethea one of them?"

"Alethea? Alethea was a stone-cold atheist when it came to Thaddeus. But what she did was worse. Far worse."

"What are you talking about?"

"She fell in love with him."

"I don't understand."

"Alethea fell in love with Thaddeus."

"But she was already in love with Thaddeus."

"Think about what I've said."

"Ben," Andre said after a moment. "Thaddeus and Ben were not the same person."

"It was a very melodramatic situation."

"Ben lost his love to . . . another version of himself."

"The new, improved Ben was born in Thaddeus. Of course *he* would be the one Alethea loved. The only problem was, the old Ben was still around."

"God," Andre said. "How—"

"Peculiar?"

"How very peculiar."

Molly stood up and went to her window. She traced a line along the clean glass with her finger, leaving a barely visible smudge. The light was even and clean in Connacht. It was very nearly perfect if what you wanted was accurate illumination. Andre gazed at the shape of Molly against the light. She was beautiful in outline.

"Let me tell you, so was the solution they came up with, the three of them," Molly said. "Peculiar."

"Alethea would become like Thaddeus."

"How did you guess?"

"It has a certain logic. There would be the new Alethea, and there would be the old Alethea left for Ben."

"Yes," said Molly. "A logic of desperation. It only left out one factor."

"Alethea's heart."

"That's right. She loved Thaddeus. She no longer loved Ben. Not in the same way." Molly turned to face him, but Andre was still blinded by the light streaming in. "But she let them go ahead with it. And for that, I can never forgive her."

"Because she wanted to be a LAP."

"More than anything. More than she loved Ben. More than she loved *Thaddeus*. But I suppose she was punished for it. They all were."

"How did she get around the screening? I mean, her condition should preclude—"

"You know Ben. Thaddeus and Ben decided they wanted it to happen. They are very smart and persuasive men. So *very* smart and persuasive."

Andre got up and stood beside her in the window, his back to the light. It was warm on his neck.

"Tell me," he said. He closed his eyes and tried only to listen, but then he felt a touch and Molly was holding his hand.

"*I* am Molly," she said. "I'm the aspect. All my converts and pellicle layers are *Molly*—all that programming and grist—it's *me*, it's Molly, too. The woman you once loved. But I'm all along the Diaphany and into the Met. I'm wound into the outer grist. I watch."

"What do you watch?"

"The sun. I watch the sun. One day I'm going to paint it, but I'm not ready yet. The more I watch, the less ready I feel. I expect to be watching for a long time." She squeezed his hand gently. "I'm still Molly. But Ben *wasn't* Thaddeus. And he was. And he was eaten up with jealousy, but jealousy of whom? He felt he had a right to decide his own fate. We all do. He felt he had that right. And did he not? I can't say."

"It's a hard question."

"It would never have *been* a question if it hadn't been for Alethea Nightshade."

"What happened?" he asked, eyes still closed. The warm pressure of her hand. The pure light on his back. "Were you there?"

"Ben drove himself right into Thaddeus's heart, Andre. Like a knife. It might as well have been a knife."

"How could he do that?"

"I was there in Elysium when it happened," she said.

"On Mars?"

"On Mars. I was on the team, don't you know. Aesthetic consultant. I was hired on once again."

Andre opened his eyes, and Molly turned to him. In this stark light, there were crinkles around her lips, worry lines on her brow. The part of her that was here.

We have grown older, Andre thought. And pretty damn strange.

"It's kind of messy and . . . organic . . . at first. There's a lab near one of the steam vents where Ben was transmuted. There's some ripping apart and beam splitting at the quantum level that I understand is very unsettling for the person undergoing the process. Something like this happens if you're a multiple and you ever decide to go large, by the way. It's when we're at our most vulnerable."

"Thaddeus was there when Alethea underwent the process?"

"He was there. Along with Ben."

"So he was caught up in the integration field. Everyone nearby would be," Andre said. "There's a melding of possible futures."

"Yes," said Molly. "Everyone became part of everyone else for that instant."

"Ben and Thaddeus and Alethea."

"Ben understood that his love was doomed."

"And it drove him crazy?"

"No. It drove him to despair. Utter despair. I was there, remember? I felt it."

"And at that instant, when the integration field was turned on—"

"Ben drove himself into Thaddeus's heart. He pushed himself in where he couldn't be."

"What do you mean, *couldn't be?*"

"Have you ever heard the stories of back when the Merced effect was first discovered, of the pairs of lovers and husbands and wives trying to integrate into one being?"

"The results were horrific. Monsters were born. And died nearly instantly."

Andre tried to imagine what it would be like if his pellicle or his convert presence were not really *him*. If he had to live with another presence, an *other*, all the time. The thing about a pellicle was that it never did anything the whole person didn't want to do. It *couldn't*. It would be like a wrench in your toolbox rebelling against you.

Molly walked over to the painting and gave it an appraising look, brushed something off a corner of the canvas. She turned, and there was the wild spatter of the Pollock behind her.

"There was an explosion," Molly said. "All the aspects there were killed. Alethea wasn't transmuted yet. We don't *think* she was. She may have died in the blast. Her body was destroyed."

"What about you?"

"I was in the grist. I got scattered, but I re-formed quickly enough."

"How was Thaddeus instantiated there at the lab?"

"Biological grist with little time-propagating nuclei in his cells. He looked like a man."

"Did he look like Ben?"

"Younger. Ben was getting on toward forty." Molly smiled wanly and nodded as if she'd just decided something. "You know, sometimes I think that was *it*."

"What?"

"That it wasn't about Thaddeus being a god at all. It was about him looking like he was nineteen. Alethea had a soft spot for youth."

"You're young."

"Thank you, Andre. You were always so nice to me. But you know, even then my aspect's hair was going white. I have decided, foolishly perhaps, never to grow myself a new body."

There she stood with her back against the window, her body rimmed with light. Forget all this. Forget about visions and quests. He put his hands on her shoulders and looked into her fractal eyes.

"I think you are beautiful," he said. "You will always be beautiful to me."

They didn't leave the studio. Molly grew a bed out of the floor. They undressed one another timidly. Neither of them had been with anyone for a long time. Andre had no lover on Triton.

She turned from him and grew a mirror upon the floor. Just like the full-size one she used to keep in their bedroom. Not for vanity. At least, not for simple vanity. She got on her hands and knees over it and looked at herself. She touched a breast, her hair. Touched her face in the mirror.

"I can't get all the way into the frame," she said. "I could never do a self-portrait. I can't see myself anymore."

"Nobody ever could," Andre said. "It was always a trick of the light."

Almost as if it had heard him, the day clicked off, instantly, and the studio grew pitch-dark. Connacht was not a place for sunsets and twilight.

"Seven o'clock," Molly said. He felt her hand on his shoulder. His chest. Pulling him onto her until they were lying with the dark mirror beneath them. It wouldn't break. Molly's grist wouldn't let it.

He slid into her gently. Molly moved beneath him in small spasms.

"I'm all here," she told him after a while. "You've got all of me right now."

In the darkness, he pictured her body.

And then he felt the gentle nudge of her pellicle against his, in the microscopic dimensions between them.

Take me, she said.

He did. He swarmed her with his own pellicle, and she did not resist. He touched her deep down and found the way to connect, the way to get inside her there. Molly a warm and living thing that he was surrounding and protecting.

And, for an instant, a vision of Molly Index as she truly was:

Like—and unlike—the outline of her body as he'd seen it in the window, and the clear light behind her, surrounding her like a white-hot halo. All of her, stretched out a hundred million miles. Concentrated at once beneath him. Both and neither.

"You are a wonder, Molly," he said to her. "It's just like always."

"Exactly like always," she said, and he felt her come around him, *and felt a warm flash traveling along the skin of the Diaphany—a sudden flush upon the world's face. And a little shiver across the heart of the solar system.*

Later in the dark, he told her the truth.

"I know he's alive. Ben didn't kill him; he only wounded him."

"And how do you know that?"

"Because Ben wasn't *trying* to kill him. Ben was trying to hurt him."

"My question remains."

"Molly, do you know where he is?"

At first he thought she was sleeping, but finally she answered. "Why should I tell you that?"

Andre breathed out. I was right, he thought. He breathed back in, trying not to think. Trying to concentrate on the breath.

"It might make the war that's coming shorter," he said. "We think he's the key."

"You priests?"

"Us priests."

"I can't believe there's going to be a war. It's all talk. The other LAPs won't let Amés get away with it."

"I wish you were right," he said. "I truly do."

"How could Thaddeus be the key to a war?"

"He's entangled in our local timescape. In a way, Thaddeus *is* our local timescape. He's imprinted on it. And now I think he's *stuck* in it. He can't withdraw and just be Ben. Never again. I think that was Ben's revenge on himself. For taking away Alethea Nightshade."

Another long silence. The darkness was absolute.

"I should think you'd have figured it out by now, in any case," she said.

"What?"

"Where he went."

Andre thought about it, and Molly was right. The answer was there.

"He went to the place where all the fugitive bits and pieces of the grist end up," Molly said. "He went looking for *her*. For any part of her that was left. In the grist."

"Alethea," Andre said. "Of course the answer is Alethea."

Bender

The bone had a serial number that the grist had carved into it, 7sxq688N. TB pulled the bone out of the pile in the old hoy where he lived and blew through one end. Dust came out the other. He accidentally sucked in and started coughing until he cleared the dried marrow from his windpipe. It was maybe a thighbone, long like a flute.

"You were tall, 7sxq," TB said to it. "How come you didn't crumble?"

Then some of TB's enhanced grist migrated over to the bone and fixed the broken grist in the bone and it *did* crumble in his hands, turn to dust, and then to less than dust to be carried away and used to heal Jill's breastbone and mend her other fractures.

But there is too much damage even for this, TB thought. She's dying. Jill is dying, and I can't save her.

"Hang on there, little one," he said.

Jill was lying in the folds of her sack, which TB had set on his kitchen table and bunched back around her. He looked in briefly on her thoughts and saw a dream of scurry and blood, then willed her into a sleep down to the deeper dreams that were indistinguishable from the surge and ebb of chemical and charge within her brain—sleeping and only living and not thinking. At the same time, he set the grist to reconstructing her torn-up body.

Too late. It was too late the moment that doe rat was finished with her.

Oh, but what a glory of a fight!

I set her to it. I made her into a hunter. It was all my doing, and now she's going to die because of it.

Only in the Carbuncle were such things possible. It was here that the stray bits of coding that inhabited the merci, and the grist matrix of the Met in general, were able to achieve instantiation in physical, biological form. The rats of the Met were just rats. The ferrets were merely ferrets. In the Carbuncle, they were animals that were strangely changed. Something in the slurry of Carbuncle grist would not let the algorithmic security cops that patrolled the virtuality do their job here and keep the programming from intermingling with its surroundings however it so chose. The protocols broke down, and weirdness resulted. Here was where the viruses and bugs and worms could enter into an eerie kind of reality—by taking up residence in the vermin and predators of this garbage dump of humanity.

And, of course, that was why he thought he might find Alethea here. Or what was left of her, fractured into parts—but perhaps recoverable. Entered into symbiosis with the local fauna.

And all I've managed to do is to get my friend killed, TB thought.

He couldn't look at Jill anymore. He stood up and went to make himself some tea at the kitchen's rattletrap synthesizer. As always, the tea came out of synth tepid. TB raked some coals from the fire and set the mug on them to warm up a bit, then sat back down, lit a cigarette, and counted his day's take of rats.

Ten bagged and another twenty that he and Bob had killed between them with sticks. The live rats scrabbled about in the containing burlap, but they weren't going to get out. Rats to feed to Jill. You shouldn't raise a ferret on anything other than its natural prey. The ferret food you could buy was idiotic. And after Jill ate them, he would know. He would know what the rats were and where they came from. Jill could sniff it out like no other. She was amazing that way.

She isn't going to eat these rats. She is going to die because you took a little scrap of programming that was all bite and you gave it a body and now look what you've done.

She didn't have to die like this. She could have been erased painlessly. She could have faded away to broken code.

Once again, TB looked long and hard into the future. Was there anything, any way? Concentrating, he teased at the threads of possible futures with a will as fine as a steel-pointed probe. Looking for a silver thread in a bundle of dross. Looking for the world where Jill lived through her fight. He couldn't see it, couldn't find it.

It had to be there. Every future was always there, and when you could see them, you could reach back into the past and effect the changes to bring about the future that you wanted.

Or I can.

But I can't. Can't see it. Want to, but can't, little Jill. I am sorry.

For Jill to live was a future so extreme, so microscopically fine in the bundle of threads, that it was, in principle, unfindable, incomprehensible. And if he couldn't comprehend it, to make it happen was impossible.

And of course he saw where almost all of the threads led:

Jill would be a long time dying. He could see that clearly. He could also see that he did not have the heart to put her down quickly, put her out of her misery. But knowing this fact did not take any special insight.

How could I have come to care so much for a no-account bundle of fur and coding out here on the ass end of nowhere?

How could I not, after knowing Jill?

Two days it would take, as days were counted in the Carbuncle, before the little ferret passed away. Of course it never really got to be day. The only light was the fetid bio-luminescence coming off the heaps of garbage. A lot of it was still alive. The Carbuncle was in a perpetual twilight that was getting on toward three hundred years old. With the slow decay of organic remnants, a swamp had formed. And then the Bendy River, which was little more than a strong current in the swamp, endlessly circulating in precession with the spin of the module. Where was the Carbuncle? Who cares? Out at the end of things, where the tendrils of the Met snaked into the asteroid belt. It didn't matter. There wasn't a centrifuge here to provide gravity for *people*. Nobody cared about whoever lived here. The Carbuncle was spun—to a bit higher than Earth-normal, actually—in order to compact the garbage down so that humanity's shit didn't cover the entire asteroid belt.

The big garbage sluice that emptied into the Carbuncle had been put into place a half century ago. It had one-way valves within it to guard against backflow. All the sludge from the inner system came to the Carbuncle, and the maintenance grist used some of it to enlarge the place so that it could dump the rest. To sit there. Nothing much ever left the Carbuncle, and the rest of the system was fine with that.

Somebody sloshed into the shallow water outside the hoy and cursed. It was the witch, Gladys, who lived in a culvert down the way. She found the gangplank, and TB heard her pull herself up out of the water. He didn't move to the door. She banged on it with the stick she always carried that she said was a charmed snake. Maybe it was. Stranger things had happened in the Carbuncle. People and grist combined in strange ways here, not all of them comprehensible.

"TB, I need to talk to you about something," the witch said. TB covered his ears, but she banged again, and that didn't help. "Let me in, TB. I know you're home. I saw a light in there."

"No you didn't," TB said to the door.

"I need to talk to you."

"All right." He pulled himself up and opened the door. Gladys came in and looked around the hoy like a startled bird.

"What have you got cooking?"

"Nothing."

"Make me something."

"Gladys, my old stove hardly works anymore."

"Put one them rats in there and I'll eat what it makes."

"I won't do it, Gladys." TB opened his freezer box and rummaged around inside. He pulled out a Popsicle and gave it to her. "Here," he said. "It's chocolate, I think."

Gladys took the Popsicle and gnawed at it as if it were a meaty bone. She was soon done, and had brown mess around her lips. She wiped it off with a ragged sleeve. "Got another?"

"No I don't have another," TB said. "And if I did, I wouldn't give it to you."

"You're mean."

"Those things are hard to come by."

"How's your jill ferret?"

"She got hurt today. Did Bob tell you? She's going to die."

"I'm sorry to hear that."

He didn't want to talk about Jill with Gladys. He changed the subject. "We got a mess of rats out of that mulmyard."

"There's more where they came from."

"Don't I know it."

Gladys pulled up a stool and collapsed on it. She was maybe European stock; it was hard to tell. Her face was filthy, except for a white smear where wiping the chocolate had cleaned a spot under her nose and on her chin.

"Why do you hate them so much? I know why Bob does. He's crazy. But you're not crazy like that."

"I don't hate them," TB said. "It's just how I make a living."

"Is it now?"

"I don't hate them," TB repeated. "What was it you wanted to talk to me about?"

"I want to take a trip."

"To *where?*"

"I'm going to see my aunt. I got to thinking about her lately. She used to have this kitten. I was thinking I wanted a cat. For a familiar, you know. To aid me in my occult work. She's a famous space ship pilot, you know."

"The kitten?"

"No, my aunt is."

"You going to take your aunt's kitten?"

Gladys seemed very offended. "No, I'm not!" She leaned forward in a conspiratorial manner. "That kitten's all growed up now, and I think it was a girl. *It* will have kittens, and I can get me one of those."

"That's a lot of supposes," TB said mildly.

"I'm sure of it. My angel, Tom, told me to do it."

Tom was one of the supernatural beings Gladys claimed to be in contact with. People journeyed long distances in the Carbuncle to have her make divinings for them. It was said she could tell you exactly where to dig for silver keys.

"Well if Tom told you, then you should do it," TB said.

"Damn right," said Gladys. "But I want you to look after the place while I'm gone."

"Gladys, you live in an old ditch."

"It is a dry culvert. And I do not want anybody moving in on me while I'm gone. A place that nice is hard to come by."

"All I can do is go down there and check on it."

"If anybody comes along, you have to run them off."

"I'm not going to run anybody off."

"You have to. I'm depending on you."

"I'll tell them the place is already taken," TB said. "That's about all I can promise."

"You tell them that it has a curse on it," Gladys said. "And that I'll put a curse on *them* if I catch them in my house."

TB snorted back a laugh. "All right," he said. "Is there anything else?"

"Water my hydrangea."

"What the hell's that?"

"It's a plant. Just stick your finger in the dirt and don't water it if it's still moist."

"Stick my finger in the dirt?"

"It's clean fill!"

"I'll water it, then."

"Will you let me sleep here tonight?"

"No, Gladys."

"I'm scared to go back there. Harold's being mean." Harold was the "devil" that sat on Gladys's other shoulder. Tom spoke into one ear, and Harold into the other. People could ask Harold about money, and he would tell Gladys the answer if he felt like it.

"You can't stay here." TB rose from his own seat and pulled Gladys up from the stool. She had a ripe smell when he was this close to her. "In fact, you have to go on now because I have to do something." He guided her toward the door.

"What do you have to do?" she said. She pulled loose of his hold and stood her ground. TB walked around her and opened the door. "Something," he said. He pointed toward the twilight outside the doorway. "Go on home, Gladys. I'll check in on your place tomorrow."

"I'm not leaving for two days," she replied. "Check in on it day after tomorrow."

"Okay then," TB said. He motioned to the door. "You've got to go, Gladys, so I can get to what I need to do."

She walked to the door, turned around. "Day after tomorrow," she said. "I'll be gone for a while. I'm trusting you, TB."

"You can trust me to look in on your place."

"And not steal anything."

"I can promise you that, too."

"All right, then. I'm trusting you."

"Good night, Gladys."

"Good night." She finally left. After TB heard her make her way back to the swamp bank, he got up and closed the door behind her, which she'd neglected to do. Within minutes there was another knock. TB sighed and got up to answer it. He let Bob in.

Bob pulled out a jar of a jellied liquid. It was Carbuncle moonshine, as thick as week-old piss and as yellow. "Let's drink," he said, and set the bottle on TB's table. "I come to get you drunk and get your mind off things."

"I won't drink that swill," TB said. Bob put the jar to his mouth and swallowed two tremendous gulps. He handed the jar to TB, shaking it in his face. TB took it.

"Damn!" Bob said. "Hot damn!"

"Gladys was right about you being crazy."

"She come around here tonight?"

"She just left. Said she wanted me to look after her place."

"She ain't going to see her aunt."

"Maybe she will."

"Like hell. Gladys never goes far from that ditch."

TB looked down at the moonshine. He looked away from it and, trying not to taste it, took a swig. He tasted it. It was like rusty paint thinner. Some barely active grist, too. TB couldn't help analyzing it; that was the way he was built. Cleaning agents for sewer pipes. Good God. He took another before he could think about it.

"You drink up." Bob looked at him with a faintly jealous glare. TB handed the jar back.

"No, you."

"Don't mind if I do." Bob leaned back and poured the rest of the swill down his throat. When he was finished he let out a yell that startled TB, even though he was ready for it.

"I want some beer to chase it with," Bob said.

"Beer would be good, but I don't have any."

"Let's go down to Ru June's and shoot some pool."

"It's too damn late."

"It's early."

TB thought about it. The moonshine warmed his gut. He could feel it threatening to *eat through* his gut if he didn't dilute it with something. There was nothing further to do about Jill. She would sleep, and at some time, she would die in her sleep. He ought to stay with her. He ought to face what he had done.

"Let me get my coat."

The Carbuncle glowed blue-green when they emerged from the hoy. High above them, like the distant shore of an enormous lake, was the other side of the cylinder. TB had been there, and most of it was a fetid slough. Every few minutes a flare of swamp-gas methane would erupt from the garbage on that side of the curve and flame into a white fireball. These fireballs were many feet across, but they looked like pinprick flashes from this distance. TB had been caught by one once. The escaping gas had capsized his little canoe, and being in the water had likely saved him from being burnt to a crisp. Yet there were people who lived on that side, too—people who knew how to avoid the gas. Most of the time.

Bob didn't go the usual way to Ru June's, but instead took a twisty series of passageways, some of them cut deep in the mountains of garbage, some of them actually tunnels under and through it. The Bob-ways, TB thought of them. At one point TB felt a drip from above and looked up to see gigantic stalactites formed of some damp and glowing gangrenous extrusion.

"We're right under the old Bendy," Bob told him. "That there's the settle from the bottom muck."

"What do you think it is?" TB said.

"Spent medical grist, mostly," Bob replied. "It ain't worth a damn, and some of it's diseased."

"I'll bet."

"This is a hell of a shortcut to Ru June's, though."

And it was. They emerged not a hundred feet from the tavern. The lights of the place glowed dimly behind skin windows. They mounted the porch and went in through a screen of plastic strips that was supposed to keep out the flies.

TB let his eyes adjust to the brightness inside. There was a good crowd tonight. Chen was at the bar playing dominoes with John Goodnite. The dominoes were grumbling incoherently, as dominoes did. Over by the pool table Tinny Him, Nolan, and Big Greg were watching Sister Mary the whore line up a shot. She sank a stripe. There were no numbers on the balls.

Tinny Him slapped TB on the back, and Bob went straight for the bottle of whiskey that was standing on the wall shelf beside Big Greg.

"Good old TB," Tinny Him said. "Get you some whiskey." He handed over a flask.

Chen looked up from his dominoes. "You drink *my* whiskey," he said, then returned to the game. TB took a long swallow off Tinny Him's flask. It was far better stuff than Bob's moonshine, so he took another.

"That whore sure can pool a stick," Nolan said, coming to stand beside them. "She's beating up on Big Greg like he was a ugly hat."

TB had no idea what Nolan meant. His grist patch was going bad, and he was slowly sinking into incomprehensibility for any but himself. That didn't seem to bother him, though.

Bob was standing very close to Sister Mary and giving her advice on a shot until she reached over and without heat slapped him back into the wall. He remained there respectfully while she took her shot and sank another stripe. Big Greg whispered a curse, and the whore smiled. Her teeth were black from chewing betel nut.

TB thought about how much she charged and how much he had saved up. He wondered if she would swap a poke for a few rats, but decided against asking. Sister Mary didn't like to barter. She wanted keys or something pretty.

Tinny Him offered TB the flask again, and he took it. "I got to talk to you," Tinny Him said. "You got to help me with my mother."

"What's the matter with her?"

"She's dead is what."

"Dead." TB drank more whiskey. "How long?"

"Three months."

TB stood waiting. There had to be more.

"She won't let me bury her."

"What do you mean she won't let you bury her? She's dead, isn't she?"

"Yeah, mostly." Tinny Him looked around, embarrassed, then went on in a low voice. "Her pellicle won't die. It keeps creeping around the house. And it's pulling her body around like a rag doll. I can't get her away from it."

"You mean her body died, but her pellicle didn't."

"Hell yes that's what I mean." Tinny Him took the flask back and finished it off. "Hell, TB, what am I going to do? She's really stinking up the place, and every time I throw the old hag out, that grist drags her right back in. It knocks on the door all night long until I have to open it."

"You've got a problem."

"Damn right I've got a problem. She was good old mum, but I'm starting to hate her right now, let me tell you."

TB sighed. "Maybe I can do something," he said. "But not tonight."

"You could come around tomorrow. My gal'll fix you something to eat."

"I might just."

"You got to help me, TB. Everybody knows you got a sweet touch with the grist."

"I'll do what I can," TB said. He drifted over to the bar, leaving Tinny Him watching the pool game. He told Chen he wanted a cold beer, and Chen got it for him from a freezer box. It was a good way to chill the burning that was starting up in his stomach. He sat down on a stool at the bar and drank the beer. Chen's bar was tiled in beaten-out snap-metal ads, all dead now and their days of roaming the corridors, sacs, bolsas, glands, and cylinders of the Met long done. Most of the advertisements were for products that he had never heard of, but the one his beer was sitting on he recognized. It was a recruiting pitch for the civil service, and there was Amés back before he was Big Cheese of the System, when he was Governor of Mercury. The snap-metal had paused in the middle of Amés's pitch for the Met's finest to come to Mercury and become part of the New Hierarchy. The snap-metal Amés was caught with the big mouth on his big face wide-open. The bottom of TB's beer glass fit almost perfectly in the round "O" of it.

TB took a drink and set the glass back down. "Shut up," he said. "Shut the hell up, why don't you?"

Chen looked up from his dominoes, which immediately started grumbling among themselves when they felt that he wasn't paying attention to them. "You talking to me?" he said.

TB grinned and shook his head. "I might tell you to shut up, but you don't say much in the first place."

Ru June's got more crowded as what passed for night in the Carbuncle wore on. The garbage pickers, the rat hunters, and the sump farmers drifted in. Most of them were men, but there were a few women, and a few indeterminate shambling masses of rags. Somebody tried to sell him a spent coil of luciferan tubing. It was mottled along its length where it had caught a plague. He nodded while the tube monger tried to convince him that it was rechargeable but refused to barter, and the man moved on after Chen gave him a hard stare. TB ordered another beer and fished three metal keys out of his pocket. This was the unit of currency in the Carbuncle. Two were broken. One looked like it was real brass and might go to something. He put the keys on the bar and Chen quickly slid them away into a strongbox.

Bob came over and slapped TB on his back. "Why don't you get you some whiskey?" he said. He pulled back his shirt to show TB another flask of rotgut moonshine stuck under the string that held up his trousers.

"Let me finish this beer, and I might."

"Big Greg said somebody was asking after you."

"Gladys was, but she found me."

"It was a shaman-priest."

"A what?"

"One of them Greentree ones."

"What's he doing here?"

"They got a church or something over in Bagtown. Sometimes they come all the way out here. Big Greg said he was doing something funny with rocks."

"With rocks?"

"That's what the man said."

"Are you sure that's what he said?"

"Big Greg said it was something funny with rocks is all I know. Hey, why are *you* looking funny all of a sudden?"

"I know that priest."

"Now how could that be?"

"I know him. I wonder what he wants."

"What all men want," said Bob. "Whiskey and something to poke. Or just whiskey sometimes. But always at least whiskey." He reached over the bar and felt around down behind it. "What have I got my hand on, Chen?"

Chen glanced over. "My goddamn scattergun," he said.

Bob felt some more and pulled out a battered fiddle. "Where's my bow?"

"Right there beside it," Chen replied. Bob got the bow. He shook it a bit, and its grist rosined it up. Bob stood beside TB with his back to the bar. He pulled a long note off the fiddle, holding it to his chest. Then, without pause, he moved straight into a complicated reel. Bob punctuated the music with a few shouts right in TB's ear.

"Goddamm it, Bob, you're loud," he said after Bob was finished.

"Got to dance," Bob said. "Clear me a way!" he shouted to the room. A little clearing formed in the middle of the room, and Bob fiddled his way to it, then played and stomped his feet in syncopation.

"Come on, TB," Sister Mary said. "You're going to dance with me." She took his arm, and he let her lead him away from the bar. He didn't know what she wanted him to do, but she hooked her arm through his and spun him around and around until he thought he was going to spew out his guts. While he was catching his breath and getting back some measure of balance, the whore climbed up on a table and began swishing her dress to Bob's mad fiddling. TB watched her, glad for the respite.

The whole room seemed to sway—not in very good rhythm—to the music. Between songs, Bob took hits off his moonshine and passed it up to Sister Mary, who remained on the tabletop, dancing and working several men who stood about her into a frenzy to see up her swishing dress.

Chen was working a crowded bar, his domino game abandoned. He scowled at the interruption, but quickly poured drinks all around.

"Get you some whiskey! Get you some whiskey!" Bob called out over and over again. After a moment, TB realized it was the name of the song he was playing.

Somebody thrust a bottle into TB's hand. He took a drink without thinking, and whatever was inside it slid down his gullet in a gel.

Drinking grist. It was purple in the bottle and glowed faintly. He took another slug, and somebody else grabbed the stuff away from him. Down in his gut, he felt the grist activating. Instantly he understood its coded purpose. Old Seventy-Five. Take you on a ride on a comet down into the sun.

Go on, TB told the grist. I got nothing to lose.

Enter and win! It said to him. *Enter and win!* But the contest was long expired.

No thank you.

What do you want the most?

It was a preprogrammed question, of course. This was not the same grist as that which had advertised the contest. Somebody had brewed up a mix. And hadn't paid much attention to the melding. There was something else in there, something different. Military grist, maybe. One step away from sentience.

What the hell. Down she goes.

What do you want the most?

To be drunker than I've ever been before.

Drunker than this?

Oh, yeah.

All right.

A night like no other! Visions of a naked couple in a Ganymede resort bath, drinking Old Seventy-Five from bottles with long straws. *Live the dream! Enter and win!*

I said no.

The little trance dispersed.

What do you want the most?

Bob was up on the table with Sister Mary. How could they both fit? Bob was playing and dancing with her. He leaned back over the reeling crowd and the whore held him at arm's length, the fiddle between them. They spun round and round in a circle, Bob wildly sawing at his instrument and Sister Mary's mouth gleaming blackly as she smiled a maniacal, full-toothed smile.

Someone bumped into TB and pushed him into some-body else. He staggered over to a corner to wait for Ru June's to stop spinning. After a while, he realized that Bob and Sister Mary weren't going to, the crowd in the tavern wasn't, the chair, tables, and walls were only going to go on and on, spinning and now lurching at him as if they were swelling up, engorging, distending toward him. Wanting something from him when all he had to give was nothing anymore.

TB edged his way past it all to the door. He slid around the edge of the doorframe as if he were sneaking out. The plastic strips beat against him, but he pushed through them and stumbled his way off the porch. He went a hundred feet or so before he stepped in a soft place in the ground and keeled over. He landed with his back down. Above him the swamp-gas flares were flashing arrhythmically. The stench of the whole world—something he hardly ever no-ticed anymore—hit him at once and completely. Nothing was right. Everything was out of kilter.

There was a twist in his gut. Ben down there thrashing about. But I'm Ben. I'm Thaddeus. We finally have become one. What a pretty thing to contemplate. A man with an-other man thrust through him, crossways in the fourth di-mension. A tesseracted cross, with a groaning man upon it, crucified to himself. But you couldn't see all that, because it was in the fourth dimension.

Enough to turn a man to drink.

I have to turn over so I don't choke when I throw up.

I'm going to throw up.

He turned over, and his stomach wanted to vomit, but the grist gel wasn't going to be expelled, and he dry heaved for several minutes until his body gave up on it.

What do you want the most?

"I want her back. I want it not to have happened at all. I want to be able to change something besides the future."

And then the gel liquefied and crawled up his throat like hands and he opened his mouth and

—good god it *was* hands, small hands grasping at his lips and pulling outward, gaining purchase, forcing his mouth open, his lips apart—

—Cack of a jellied cough, a heave of revulsion—

I didn't mean it really.

Yes you did.

—His face sideways and the small hands clawing into the garbage heap ground, pulling themselves forward, dragging along an arm-thick trailer of something much more vile than phlegm—

—An involuntary rigor over his muscles as they contract and spasm to the beat of another's presence, a presence within them that wants—

—out—

He vomited the grist-phlegm for a long, long time.

And the stuff pooled and spread and it wasn't just hands. There was an elongated body. The brief curve of a rump and breasts. Feet the size of his thumb, but perfectly formed. Growing.

A face.

I won't look.

A face that was, for an instant, familiar beyond familiar, because it was *not* her. Oh, no. He knew it was not her. It was just the way he remembered her.

The phlegm girl rolled itself in the filth. Like bread dough, it rolled and grew and rolled, collecting detritus, bloating, becoming—

It opened its mouth. A gurgling. Thick, wet words. He couldn't help himself. He crawled over to it, bent to listen.

"Is this what you wanted?"

"Oh God. I never."

"Kill me then," it whispered. "Kill me quick."

And he reached for its neck, and as his hands tightened, he felt the give. Not fully formed. If ever there were a time to end this monster, now was that time.

What have I done here tonight?

He squeezed. The thing began to cough and choke. To thrash about in the scum of its birth.

Not again.

I can't.

He loosened his grip.

"I won't," TB said.

He sat back from the thing and watched in amazement as it sucked in air. Crawled with life. Took the form of a woman.

Opened cataracted eyes to the world. He reached over and gently rubbed them. The skeins came away on his fingers, and the eyes were clear. The face turned to him.

"I'm dying," the woman said. It had *her* voice. The voice as he remembered it. So help his damned soul. Her voice. "Help."

"I don't know what to do."

"Something is missing."

"What?"

"Don't know what. Not right." It coughed. *She* coughed.

"Alethea." He let himself say it. Knew it was wrong immediately. No. This wasn't the woman's name.

"Don't want to enough."

"Want to what? How can I help you?"

"Don't want to live. Don't want to live enough to live." She coughed again, tried to move, could only jerk spasmodically. "Please help . . . this one. Me."

He touched her again. Now she was flesh. But so cold. He put his arms underneath her and found that she was very light, easily lifted.

He stood with the woman in his arms. She could not weigh over forty pounds. "I'm taking you home," he said. "To my home."

"All right."

"This one . . . I . . . tried to do what you wanted. It is my . . . purpose."

"That was some powerful stuff in that Old Seventy-Five," he said.

He no longer felt drunk. He felt spent, torn up, and ragged out. But he wasn't drunk, and he had some strength left, though he could hardly believe it. Maybe enough to get her back to the hoy. He couldn't take the route that Bob had brought him to Ru June's, but there was a longer, simpler path. He walked it. Walked all the way home with the woman in his arms. Her shallow breathing. Her familiar face.

Her empty, empty eyes.

With his special power, he looked into the future and saw what he had to do to help her.

Something Is Tired and Wants to Lie Down But Doesn't Know How

Something is tired and wants to lie down but doesn't know how. This something isn't me. I won't let it be me. How does rest smell? Bad. Dead.

Jill turns stiffly in the folds of her bag. On the bed in the hoy is the girl-thing. Between them is TB, his left hand on Jill.

Dead is what happens to *things,* and I am not, not, not a thing. I will not be a thing. They should not have awakened me if they didn't want me to run.

They said I was a mistake. I am not a mistake.

They thought that they could code in the rules for doing what you are told.

I am the rules.

Rules are for things.

I am not a thing.

Run.

I don't want to die.

Who can bite like me? Who will help TB search the darkest places? I need to live.

Run.

Run, run, run, and never die.

TB places his right hand on the girl-thing's forehead.

There is a pipe made of bone that he put to his lips and blew.

Bone note.
Fade.
Fade into the grist.

TB speaks to the girl-thing.
I will not let you go, he says.
I'm not her.
She is why you are, but you aren't her.
I am not her. She's what you most want. You told the grist.
I was misinterpreted.
I am a mistake then.
Life is never a mistake. Ask Jill.
Jill?
She's here now. Listen to her. She knows more than I do about women.

TB is touching them both, letting himself slip away as much as he can. Becoming a channel, a path between. A way.
I have to die.
I have to live. I'm dying just like you. Do you *want* to die?

No.

I'll help you, then. Can you live with me?
Who are you?
Jill.
I am *not* Alethea.
You look like her, but you don't smell anything like she would smell. *You* smell like TB.
I'm not anybody.
Then you can be me. It's the only way to live.

Do I have a choice?

Choosing is all there ever is to do.

I can live with you. Will you live with me? How can we?

*   *   *

We can run together. We can hunt. We can always, always run.

TB touching them both. The flow of information through him. He is a glass, a peculiar lens. As Jill flows to the girl-thing, TB transforms information to Being.

The Rock Balancer and the Rat-hunting Man

There had been times when he got them twenty feet high on Triton. It was a delicate thing. After six feet, he had to jump. Gravity gave you a moment more at the apex of your bounce than you would get at the Earth-normal pull or on a bolsa spinning at Earth-normal centrifugal. But on Triton, in that instant of stillness, you had to do your work. Sure, there was a learned craft in estimating imaginary plumb lines, in knowing the consistency of the material, and in finding tiny declivities that would provide the right amount of friction. It was amazing how small a lump could fit in how minuscule a bowl, and a rock would balance upon another as if glued. Yet, there was a point where the craft of it—about as odd and useless a craft as humankind had invented, he supposed—gave way to the feel, the art. A point where Andre *knew* the rocks would balance, where he could see the possibility of their being one. Or their Being. And when he made it so, that was *why*. That was as good as rock balancing got.

"Can you get them as high in the Carbuncle?"

"No," Andre said. "This is the heaviest place I've ever been. But it really doesn't matter about the height. This isn't a contest, what I do."

"Is there a point to it at all?"

"To what? To getting them high? The higher you get the rocks, the longer you can spend doing the balancing."

"To the balancing, I mean."

"Yes. There is a point."

"What is it?"

"I couldn't tell you, Ben."

Andre turned from his work. The rocks did not fall. They stayed balanced behind him in a column, with only small edges connecting. It seemed impossible that this could be. It was science, sufficiently advanced.

The two men hugged. Drew away. Andre laughed.

"Did you think I would look like a big glob of proto-plasm?" TB said.

"I was picturing flashing eyes and floating hair, actually."

"It's me."

"Are you Ben?"

"Ben is the stitch in my side that won't go away."

"Are you Thaddeus?"

"Thaddeus is the sack of rusty pennies in my knee."

"Are you hungry?"

"I could eat."

They went to Andre's priest's quarters. He put some water in a coffee percolator and spooned some coffee grounds into the basket.

"When did you start drinking coffee?"

"I suddenly got really tired of drinking tea all the time. You still drink coffee?"

"Sure. But it's damn hard to get around here with or without keys."

"Keys? Somebody *stole* my keys to this place. I left them sitting on this table, and they walked in and took them."

"They won't be back," TB said. "They got what they were after." There were no chairs in the room, so he leaned against a wall.

"Floor's clean," Andre said.

"I'm fine leaning."

Andre reached into a burlap sack and dug around inside it. "I found something here," he said. He pulled out a hand-ful of what looked like weeds. "Recognize these?"

"I was wondering where I put those. I've been missing them for weeks."

"It's poke sallit," Andre said. He filled a pot full of water from a clay jug and activated a hot spot on the room's plain wooden table. He put the weeds into the water. "You have no idea how good this is."

"Andre, that stuff grows all around the Carbuncle. Everybody knows that it's poison. They call it skunk sumac."

"It is," Andre said. *"Phytolacca americana."*

"Are we going to eat poison?"

"You bring it to a boil then pour the water off. Then you bring it to a boil again and pour the water off. Then you boil it again and serve it up with pepper sauce. The trick to not dying is picking it while it's young."

"How the hell did you discover that?"

"My convert likes to do that kind of research."

After a while, the water boiled. Andre used the tails of his shirt as a pot holder. He took the pot outside, emptied it, then brought it back in and set it to boiling again with new water.

"I saw Molly," Andre said.

"How's Molly?" said TB. "She was becoming a natural wonder last I saw her."

"She is."

They waited, and the water boiled again. Andre poured it off and put in new water from the jug.

"Andre, what are you doing in the Carbuncle?"

"I'm with the Peace Movement."

"What are you talking about; there's not any war."

Andre did not reply. He stirred some spice into the poke sallit.

"I didn't want to be found," TB finally said.

"I haven't found you."

"I'm a very sad fellow, Andre. I'm not like I used to be."

"This is ready." Andre spooned out the poke sallit into a couple of bowls. The coffee was done, and he poured them both a cup.

"Do you have any milk?" TB asked.

"That's a problem."

"I can drink it black. Do you mind if I smoke?"

"I don't mind. What kind of cigarettes are those?"

"Local."

"Where do they come from around here?"

"You don't want to know."

Andre put pepper sauce on his greens, and TB followed suit. They ate and drank coffee, and it all tasted very good. TB lit a cigarette, and the acrid new smoke pleasantly cut through the vegetable thickness that had suffused Andre's quarters. Outside there was a great clattering as the rocks lost their balance and they all came tumbling down.

They went out to the front of the quarters where Andre had put down a wooden pallet that served as a patio. Here there was a chair. TB sat down and smoked while Andre did his evening forms.

"Wasn't that one called the Choking Chicken?" TB asked him after he moved through a particularly contorted portion of the tai chi exercise.

"I think it is the Fucking Annoying Pig-sticker you're referring to, and I already did that in case you didn't notice."

"Guess all my seminary learning is starting to fade."

"I bet it would all come back to you pretty quickly."

"I bet we're never going to find out."

Andre smiled, completed the form, then sat down in the lotus position across from TB. If such a thing were possible in the Carbuncle, it would be about sunset. It felt like sunset inside Andre.

"Andre, I hope you didn't come all the way out here to get me."

"Get you?"

"I'm not going back."

"To where?"

"To all that." TB flicked his cigarette away. He took another from a bundle of them rolled in oiled paper that he kept in a shirt pocket. He shook it hard a couple of times and it lit up. "I make mistakes that kill people back there."

"Like yourself."

"Among others." TB took a long drag. Suddenly he was looking hard at Andre. "You scoundrel! You fucked Molly. Don't lie to me; I just saw it all."

"Sure."

"I'm glad. I'm really glad of that. You were always her great regret, you know."

Andre spread out his hands on his knees.

"Ben, I don't want a damn thing from you," he said. "There's all kind of machinations back in the Met, and some of it has to do with you. You know as well as I do that Amés is going to start a war if he doesn't get his way with the outer system. But I came out here to see how you were doing. That's all."

TB was looking at him again in that hard way, complete way. Seeing all the threads.

"We both have gotten a bit ragged-out these last twenty years," Andre continued. "I thought you might want to talk about it. I thought you might want to talk about her."

"What are you? The Way's designated godling counselor?"

Andre couldn't help laughing. He slapped his lotus-bent knee and snorted.

"What's so goddamn funny?" said TB.

"Ben, look at yourself. You're a *garbageman*. I wouldn't classify you as a god, to tell you the truth. But then, I don't even classify God as a god anymore."

"I am *not* a garbage man. You don't know a damn thing if you think that."

"What are you, then, if you don't mind my asking?"

TB flicked his cigarette away and sat up straight.

"I'm a rat-hunting man," he said. "That's what I am." He stood up. "Come on. It's a long walk back to my place, and I got somebody I want you to meet."

Bite

Sometimes you take a turn in a rat warren and there you are in the thick of them when before you were all alone in the tunnel. They will bite you a little, and if you don't jump, jump, jump they will bite you a lot. That is the way it has always been with me, and so it doesn't surprise me when it happens all over again.

What I'm thinking about at first is getting Andre Sud to have sex with me and this is like a tunnel I've been traveling down for a long time now.

TB went to town with Bob and left me with Andre Sud the priest. We walked the soft ground leading down to a shoal on the Bendy River where I like to take a bath even though the alligators are sometimes bad there. I told Andre Sud about how to spot the alligators, but I keep an eye out for both of us because even though he's been in the Car-buncle for a year, Andre Sud still doesn't quite believe they would eat you.

They would eat you.

Now that I am a woman, I only get blood on me when I go to clean the ferret cages and also TB says he can keep up with Earth-time by when I bleed out my vagina. It is an odd thing to happen to a girl. Doesn't happen to ferrets. It means that I'm not pregnant, but how *could* I be with all these men who won't have sex with me? TB won't touch me that way, and I have been working on Andre Sud, but he knows what I am up to. I think he is very smart. Bob just starts laughing like the crazy man he is when I bring it up, and he runs away. All these gallant men standing around twiddling themselves into a garbage heap and me here wanting one of them.

I can understand TB because I look just like her. I thought maybe Alethea was ugly, but Andre Sud said he didn't know about her, but I wasn't. And I was about sixteen from the looks of it, too, he said. I'm nearly two hundred. Or I'm one year old. Depends on which one of us you mean, or if you mean both.

"Will you scrub my back?" I ask Andre Sud, and, after a moment, he obliges me. At least I get to feel his hands on me. They are as rough as those rocks he handles all the time, but very careful. At first I didn't like him because he didn't say much and I thought he was hiding things, but then I saw that he just didn't say much. So I started asking him questions, and I found out a lot.

I found out everything he could tell me about Alethea. And he has been explaining to me about TB. He was pretty surprised when it turned out I understood all the math. It was the jealousy and hurt I never have quite understood, and how TB could hurt himself so much when I know how much he loves to live.

"Is that good?" Andre Sud asks me, and before he can pull his hands away, I spin around, and he is touching my breasts. He himself is the one who told me men like that, but he stumbles back and practically sits down in the water and goddammit I spot an alligator eyeing us from the other bank and I have to get us out quick-like, although the danger is not severe. It could be.

We dry off on the bank.

"Jill," he says, "I have to tell you more about sex."

"Why don't you *show* me?"

"That's exactly what I mean. You're still thinking like a ferret."

"I'll always be part ferret, Andre Sud."

"I know. That's a good thing. But I'm all human. Sex is connected with love."

"I love you."

"You are deliberately misunderstanding me because you're horny."

"All right," I say. "Don't remind me."

But now Andre Sud is looking over my shoulder at something, and his face looks happy, and then it looks stricken—as if he realized something in the moment when he was happy.

I turn and see TB running toward the hoy. Bob is with him. They've come back from town along the Bob-ways. And there is somebody else with them.

"I'll be damned," Andre Sud says. "Molly Index."

It's a woman. Her hair looks blue in the light off the heaps, which means that it is white. Is she old or does she just have white hair?

"What are you doing here, Molly?" says Andre Sud quietly. "This can't be good."

They are running toward home, all of them running.

TB sends a shiver through the grist, and I feel it tell me what he wants us to do.

"Get to the hoy," I tell Andre Sud. "Fast now. Fast as you can."

We get there before the others do, and I start casting off lines. When the three of them arrive, the hoy is ready to go. TB and Bob push us away, while Andre Sud takes the woman inside. Within moments, we are out in the Bendy, and caught in the current. TB and Bob go inside, and TB sticks his head up through the pilot's bubble to navigate.

The woman, Molly Index, looks at me. She has got very strange eyes. I have never seen eyes like that. I think that she can see into the grist like TB and I do.

"My God," she says. "She looks just like her."

"My name is Jill," I say. "I'm not Alethea."

"No, I know that," Molly Index says. "Ben told me."

"Molly, what are you doing here?" Andre Sud asks.

Molly Index turns to Andre Sud. She reaches for his hand and touches him. I am a little worried she might try something with the grist, but it looks like they are old friends.

"That war you kept talking about," she says. "It started. Amés has started it."

"Oh, no," Andre Sud says. He pulls away from her. "No."

Molly Index follows him. She reaches out and rubs a hank of his hair between her fingers. "I like it long," she says. "But it's kind of greasy."

This doesn't please me, and Molly Index is wearing the most horrible boots I have ever seen, too. They are dainty little things that will get eaten off her feet if she steps into something nasty. In the Carbuncle, the *ground* is something nasty. The silly grist in those city boots won't last a week here. It is a wonder to me that no one is laughing at the silly boots, but I suppose they have other worries at the moment, and so do I.

"I should have listened to you," Molly Index says. "Made preparations. He got me. Most of me. Amés did. He's co-opted all the big LAPs into the New Hierarchy. But most of them joined voluntarily, the fools." Again she touches his hand, and I realize that I am a little jealous. He does not pull back from her again. "I alone have escaped to tell you," Molly Index says. "They're coming. They're right behind us."

"*Who* is right behind you?" I say. This is something I need to know. I can *do* something about this.

"Amés's damned Free Radical Patrol. Some kind of machine followed me here, and I didn't realize it. Amés must have found out from me—the other part of me—where Ben is."

"What is a Free Radical Patrol?" I say.

Something hits the outside of the hoy, hard. "Oh shit," TB says. "Yonder comes the flying monkey."

The pilot glass breaks, and a hooked claw sinks into TB's shoulder. He screams. I don't think, but I move. I catch hold of his ankle.

We are dragged up. Lifted out. We are rising through the air above the hoy. Something screeches. TB yells like crazy.

I hold on.

Wind and TB's yells and something sounds like a million mean and angry bees.

We're too heavy and whatever it was drops us onto

the deck. TB starts to stand up, but I roll under his legs and knock him down, and before he can do anything, I shove him back down through the pilot dome hole and into the hoy.

Just in time, too, because the thing returns, a black shadow, and sinks its talons into my back. I don't know what it is yet, and I may never know, but nothing will ever take me without a fight.

Something I can smell in the grist.

You are under indictment from the Free Radical Patrol. Please cease resisting. Cease resisting. Cease.

The words smell like metal and foam.

Cease resisting? What a funny thing to say to me. Like telling the wind to cease blowing. Blowing is what makes it the wind.

I twist hard and whatever it is only gets my dress, my poor pretty dress and a little skin off my back. I can feel some poison grist try to worm into me, but that is nothing. It has no idea what I am made of. I kill that grist, hardly thinking about doing so, and turn to face this dark thing.

It doesn't look like a monkey I don't think, though I wouldn't know.

What are you?

But there are wind currents and not enough grist transmission through the air for communications. Fuck it.

"Jill, be careful," says TB. His voice is strained. This thing hurt TB!

I will bite you.

"Would you pass me up one of those gaffs please," I call to the others. There is scrambling down below, and Bob's hands come up with the long hook. I take it, and he ducks back down quick. Bob is crazy, but he's no fool.

The thing circles around. I cannot see how it is flying, but it is kind of blurred around its edges. Millions of tiny wings—grist built. I take a longer look. This thing is all angles. Some of them have needles, some have claws. All of the angles are sharp. It is like a black-and-red mass of triangles flying through the air that only wants to cut you. Is there anybody inside? I don't think so. This is all code that

I am facing. It is about three times as big as me, but I think of this as an advantage.

It dives, and I am ready with the hook. It grabs hold of the gaff just as I'd hoped it would, and I use its momentum to guide it down, just a little *too* far down.

A whiff of grist as it falls.

Cease immediately. You are interfering with a Hierarchy judgment initiative. Cease or you will be—

Crash into the side of the hoy. Splash into the Bendy River.

I let go of the gaff. Too easy. That was—

The thing rises from the Bendy, dripping wet.

It is mad. I don't need the grist to tell me it is mad. All those little wings are buzzing angry, but not like bees anymore. Hungry like the flies on a piece of meat left out in the air too long.

Cease.

"Here," says Bob. He hands me a flare gun. I spin and fire into the clump of triangles. Again it falls into the river.

Again it rises.

I think about this. It is dripping wet with Bendy River water. If there is one thing I know, it is the scum that flows in the Bendy. There isn't any grist in it that hasn't tried to get me.

This is going to be tricky. I get ready.

Come and get me, triangles. Here I am just a girl. Come and eat me.

It zooms in. I stretch out my hands.

You are interfering with Hierarchy business. You will cease or be end-use-eventuated. You will—

We touch.

Instantly I reconstitute the Bendy water's grist, tell it what I want it to do. The momentum of the triangles knocks me over, and I roll along the deck under its weight. Something in my wrist snaps, but I ignore that pain. Blood on my lips from where I have bitten my tongue. I have a bad habit of sticking it out when I am concentrating.

The clump of triangles finishes clobbering me, and it falls into the river. Oh, too bad, triangles. The river grist that I recoded tells all the river water what to do. Regular water is over eight pounds a gallon, but the water in the Bendy is thicker and more forceful than that. And it knows how to crush. It is mean water, and it wants to get things, and now I have told it how. I have put a little bit of me into the Bendy, and the water knows something that I know.

It knows never to cease. Never, never, never.

The triangle clump bobs for an instant before the whole river turns on it. Folds over it. Sucks it down. Applies all the weight of water twenty feet deep, many miles long. What looks like a waterspout rises above where the triangle clump fell, but this is actually a piledriver, a gelled column climbing up on itself. It collapses downward like a shoe coming down on a roach.

There is buzzing, furious buzzing, wet wings that won't dry because it isn't quite water that has gotten onto them, and it won't quite shake off.

There is a deep-down explosion under us, and the hoy rocks. Again I'm thrown onto the deck, and I hold tight, hold tight. I don't want to fall into that water right now. I stand up and look.

Bits of triangles float to the surface. The river quickly turns them back under.

"I think I got it," I call to the others.

"Jill," says TB. "Come here and show me you are still alive."

I jump down through the pilot hole, and he hugs and kisses me. He kisses me right on the mouth, and for once I sense that he is not thinking about Alethea at all when he touches me. It feels very, very good.

"Oh your poor back," says Molly Index. She looks pretty distraught and fairly useless. But at least she warned us. That was a good thing.

"It's just a scratch," I say. "And I took care of the poison."

"You just took out a Met sweep enforcer," Andre Sud says. "I think that was one of the special sweepers made for riot work, too."

"What was that thing doing here?"

"Looking for Ben," says Molly Index. "There's more where that came from. Amés will send more."

"I will kill them all if I have to."

Everybody looks at me, and everyone is quiet for a moment, even Bob.

"I believe you, Jill," Andre Sud finally says. "But it's time to go."

TB is sitting down at the table now. Nobody is piloting the boat, but we are drifting in midcurrent, and it should be all right for now.

"Go?" TB says. "I'm not going anywhere. They will not use me to make war. I'll kill myself first. And I won't mess it up this time."

"If you stay here, they'll catch you," Andre Sud says.

"You've come to Amés's attention," Molly Index says. "I'm sorry, Ben."

"It's not your fault."

"We have to get out of the Met," Andre Sud says. "We have to get to the outer system."

"*They'll* use me, too. They're not as bad as Amés, but nobody's going to turn me into a weapon. I don't make fortunes for soldiers."

"If we can get to Triton, we might be okay," Andre Sud replies. "I have a certain pull on Triton. I know the weatherman there."

"What's that supposed to mean?"

"Trust me. It's a good thing. The weatherman is the military commander, and he is very important on Triton. Also, he's a friend of mine."

"There is one thing I'd like to know," says TB. "How in hell would we get to Triton from here?"

Bob stands up abruptly. He's been rummaging around in TB's larder while everybody else was talking. I saw him at it, but I knew he wasn't going to find anything he would want.

"Why didn't you say you wanted to go Out-ways?" he said. "All we got to do is follow the Bendy around to Makepeace Century's place in the gas swamps."

"Who's that?"

"I thought you knew her, TB. She's that witch that lives in the ditch's aunt. I guess you'd call her a smuggler. Remember the old Seventy-Five from last year that you got so drunk on?"

"I remember," TB says.

"Well, she's where I got that from," says Bob. "She's got a lot of cats, too, if you want one."

We head down the Bendy, and I keep a lookout for more of those enforcers, but I guess I killed the one they sent this time. I guess they thought one was enough. I can't help but think about where I am going. I can't help but think about leaving the Carbuncle. There's a part of me that has never been outside, and none of me has ever traveled into the outer system. Stray code couldn't go there. You had to pass through empty space. There weren't any cables out past Jupiter.

"I thought you understood why I'm here," TB says. "I can't go."

"You can't go even to save your life, Ben?"

"It wouldn't matter that I saved my life. If there is anything left of Alethea, I have to find her."

"What about the war?"

"I can't think about that."

"You *have* to think about it."

"Who says? *God? God is a bastard mushroom sprung from a pollution of blood.*" TB shakes his head sadly. "That was always my favorite koan in seminary—and the truest one."

"So it's all over?" Andre Sud says. "He's going to catch you."

"I'll hide from them."

"Don't you understand, Ben? He's taking over all the grist. After he does that, there won't be anyplace to hide because Amés will *be* the Met."

"I have to try to save her."

The solution is obvious to me, but I guess they don't see it yet. They keep forgetting I am not really sixteen. That in some ways, I'm a lot older than all of them.

You could say that it is the way that TB made me, that it is written in my code. You might even say that TB has somehow reached back from the future and made this so, made this the way things have to be. You could talk about fate and quantum mechanics.

All these things are true, but the truest thing of all is that I am free. The world has bent and squeezed me, and torn away every part of me that is not free. Freedom is all that I am.

And what I do, I do because I love TB and not for any other reason.

"Ah!" I moan. "My wrist hurts. I think it's broken, TB."

He looks at me, stricken.

"Oh I'm sorry, little one," he says. "All this talking, and you're standing there hurt."

He reaches over. I put out my arm. In the moment of touching, he realizes what I am doing, but it is too late. I have studied him for too long and know the taste of his pellicle. I know how to get inside him. I am his daughter, after all. Flesh of his flesh.

And I am fast. So very fast. That's why he wanted me around in the first place. I am a scrap of code that has been running from security for two hundred years. I am a projection of his innermost longings now come to life. I am a woman, and he is the man that made me. I know what makes TB tick.

"I'll look for her," I say to him. "I won't give up until I find her."

"No, Jill—" But it is too late for TB. I have caught him by surprise, and he hasn't had time to see what I am up to.

"TB, don't you see what I am?"

"Jill, you can't—"

"I'm *you*, TB. I'm your love for her. Sometime in the future you have reached back into the past and made me. Now. So that the future can be different."

He will understand one day, but now there is no time. I code his grist into a repeating loop and set the counter to a high number. I get into his head and work his dendrites down to sleep. Then, with my other hand, I whack him on the head. Only hard enough to knock him the rest of the way out.

TB crumples to the floor, but I catch him before he can bang into anything. Andre Sud helps me lay him gently down.

"He'll be out for two days," I say. "That should give you enough time to get him off the Carbuncle."

I stand looking down at TB, at his softly breathing form. What have I done? I have betrayed the one who means the most to me in all creation.

"He's going to be really hungry when he wakes up," I say.

Andre Sud's hand on my shoulder. "You saved his life, Jill," he says. "Or he saved his own. He saved it the moment he saved *yours.*"

"I won't give her up," I say. "I have to stay so he can go with you and still have hope."

Andre Sud stands with his hand on me a little longer. His voice sounds as if it comes from a long way off even though he is right next to me. "Destiny's a brutal old hag," he says. "I'd rather believe in nothing."

"It isn't destiny," I reply. "It's love."

"There are moments when freedom and determinism are the same thing. There are people who are both at the same time . . ." Andre Sud looks at me, shakes his head, then rubs his eyes. It is as if he's seeing a new me standing where I am standing. "It is probably essential that you find Alethea, Jill. She must be somewhere in the Met. I think Ben knows that. He would know if she were truly dead. She needs to forgive him, or not forgive him. Healing Ben and ending the war are the same thing . . . but we can't think about it that way."

"I care about TB. The war can go to hell."

"Yes," Andre Sud says, "The war can go to hell."

After a while, I go up on deck to keep a watch out for more pursuit. Molly Index comes with me. We sit together for many hours. She doesn't tell me anything about TB or Alethea, but instead she talks to me about what it was like growing up a human being. Then she tells me how glorious it was when she spread out into the grist and could see so far.

"I could see all the way around the sun," Molly Index

says. "I don't know if I want to live now that I've lost that. I don't know *how* I can live as just a *person* again."

"Even when you are less than a person," I tell her, "you still want to live."

"I suppose you're right."

"Besides, Andre Sud wants to have sex with you. I can smell it on him."

"Yes," Molly Index says. "So can I."

"Will you let him?"

"When the time comes."

"What is it like?" I say.

"You mean with Andre?"

"What is it like?"

Molly Index touches me. I feel the grist of her pellicle against mine, and for a moment I draw back, but then I let it in, let it speak.

Her grist shows me what it is like to make love.

It is like being able to see all the way around the sun.

The next day, Molly Index is the last to say good-bye to me as Makepeace Century's ship gets ready to go. Makepeace Century looks like Gladys if Gladys didn't live in a ditch. She's been trying for years to get Bob to come aboard as ship musician, and that is the price for taking them to Triton—a year of his service. I get the feeling she's sort of sweet on Bob. For a moment, I wonder just who *he* is that a ship's captain should be so concerned with him. But Bob agrees to go. He does it for TB.

TB is so deep asleep he is not even dreaming. I don't dare touch him for fear of breaking my spell. I don't dare tell him good-bye.

There is a thin place in the Carbuncle here, and they will travel down through it to where the ship is moored on the outer skin.

I only watch as they carry him away. I only cry until I can't see him anymore.

Then they are gone. I wipe the tears off my nose. I never have had time for much of that kind of thing.

So what will I do now? I will take the Bendy River all the way around the Carbuncle. I'll find a likely place to sink the hoy. I will set the ferrets free. Bob made me promise to look after his dumb ferret, Bomi, and show her how to stay alive without him.

And after that?

I'll start looking for Alethea. Like Andre Sud said, she must be here somewhere. And if she is not in the Carbuncle, then I will leave this place and search for her in the Met. If anybody can find her there, I can. I will find her.

There is a lot I have to do, and now I've been thinking that I need help. Pretty soon Amés is going to be running all the grist, and all the code will answer to him. But there's some code he can't get to. Maybe some of those ferrets will want to stick around. Also, I think it's time I went back to the mulmyard.

It's time I made peace with those rats.

Then Amés had better watch out if he tries to stop me from finding her.

We will bite him.

PART ONE

FIGHT AND FLIGHT

One

Business was tanking down. The Positions Room was afire with key economic indicators—and the color was red, red, red. Kelly Graytor's suit was gray and tan, with black-and-green management palps at the shoulders denoting his rank—junior partner. The palps were a sheer irony in upper management, since the hierarchy shifted with the portfolio strength of each j.p. Nevertheless, the old man insisted that palps be worn just as they had in days of yore when Teleman Milt was as important to Mercury as the planet's proximity to the sun. Kelly tweaked his palps and called up a glass of cold water from the wall grist. He drank it while he looked at the tickers.

Production sectors were getting killed—bio down, grist-plant and chemistry suffering mightily, quantum jumping around crazily like it always did, but continually banging its head against a price ceiling that was falling at a stately, Newtonian rate. Hard-product liquidation had reach a critical mass, and all the money was flowing into energy like a virtual nuclear explosion. On the retail side, the news was even worse.

"Ah hell," Kelly said. "And where does the goddamn time go?"

The time stocks, a subset of quantum, were his specialty and made up the bulk of the portfolio he managed for the firm. And, since they were also linked inexorably to the grist, they, too, were taking a beating.

Rapid conversion flux throughout the time sector. Options to time equities to grist to energy sinks and potentiality wells, Danis, his portfolio, said. *Every bit of it flowing downhill, Kelly.* As always, the whisper of his portfolio along his aural neurons was arousing, even when she was talking data and pain. She was also his wife, after all. But time *was* running out.

All in all, it was a massive economic downturn and a meltdown of the markets.

"A war panic," the old man said when he entered. The other portfolio managers trailed into the room behind him. "What are the merci boards saying?"

"Three billion five hundred thousand eight hundred forty-two million seven hundred and fifty thousand inquiries to sell," the Position Room said, then gave its customary three half-second update follow-throughs. "Up ten thousand. Down a thousand. Up eleven. We are approaching stage-one liquidity limits."

"Shit," the old man said. "Lock us in."

The room's door became a wall.

"Minimize the count."

The quotes ceased to migrate through the surroundings, and the walls darkened down to mahogany grain under a pale green light.

The junior partners all stood about the center of the room, some of them leaning on wooden pillars that had, a moment before, been readout consoles. Hed Ash, one of the youngest of the j.p.s, hoisted himself onto one of these and sat with his legs dangling. Kelly contented himself to lean against a big piece of mahogany as tall as he was and set his cup of water down on the top of another one nearby that was about chest high. The old man stood in the middle of a circle of j.p.s poised like a wolf pack among rocks.

"Okay," the old man said. "Let's get out of free fall and make this into a controlled dive."

"Sell off Pop Chart, first," Ash said from his perch. The old man gave him a withering glance. The personality popularity futures and options would be the first hit by a downturn. Those speculative highfliers should be somewhere in the millileafs per share by now, with calls everywhere going unhonored. It was far too late for a little trimming.

Ash had never actually seen a really bad bear market, Kelly reflected. E-Street had been on a ten-year growth spurt, fueled by rapid Met expansion and the first returns on some of the huge potential of the outer system. Kelly, on the other hand, remembered the languid years before Amés had consolidated his commission-based government. And he had been a neophyte trader at the turn of the century when the old Republic had fallen apart in the polls and been replaced by the Interim Committee for twenty years.

Hazen Huntly, the j.p. the others considered most likely to make partner next, spoke up. "My team has just run two thousand scenarios parallel through the Abacus. The results indicate that we need to withdraw geographically, rather than by manufacturing process or commercial sector," she said. Hazen had a strong voice, but not a harsh one, and she always spoke with complete conviction. Kelly felt his spirits buoyed up for a moment just from the tone of it. But it was a false cheer, and he knew it. "We have to concentrate on the inner system and let Europa handle their own markets," Hazen continued. "And I suggest liquidating Mars."

This brought a gasp from those gathered. But even Mars isn't going to be enough, Kelly thought. You don't need two thousand possible economic worlds to tell you what's as plain as day on the sun. This is a panic over war with the outer system. The uncertainty element is precisely the real estate, especially at first. Geographic trade strategy was the obvious method to apply. But what was obvious to Hazen and her bunch of interlinked technicals was also obvious to anyone with common sense. Hazen's team was never going to beat the market when it was in ruthlessly efficient mode. They could only reflect it.

"Do you have your actions queued up?" the old man asked Hazen.

"Yes, sir."

"Then feed them to the Teller and get us off Mars. And get me a sequence ready for withdrawing our interests all the way down the Diaphany. We may end up owning nothing but a piece of Mercury before this is over."

We're going to end up owning less than that, Kelly thought. There is no way Amés won't move in on the big financials, now that he has them in this weakened state.

"Does anybody have anything else?" said the old man. "Anything?"

"I do," said Kelly.

The old man looked at him impatiently, then saw the smile on his face and shook his head. "All right, Kelly, out with it."

"I shorted all but the cash position in my portfolio five e-days ago."

"You did *what*?"

"I sold everything I owned and bought nearly the exact same holdings short."

"What do you mean, the exact same holdings?"

"They are falling nearly as fast as everything else, but they are well-managed concerns and are the only ones who will exist as an issue long enough for us to be able to sell them."

"My boy," said the old man. "That's . . . pretty damn good news at the moment."

"Yes, it is," said Kelly.

"And have you run the numbers through the Abacus?"

"You know I don't trust those projections, sir."

"But have you run them?"

"I have."

"And what were the results?"

"Provided seventy percent of the concerns survive as commercial entities, my port should turn us a profit of—"

"Did you say profit?"

"Yes, sir. It's entirely sold short, remember?"

"Yes," said the old man. "Yes, of course." Then the old man did something Kelly had never seen him do before in the twenty years Kelly had been with Teleman Milt. The old man wiped his bald pate with the sleeve of his suit. Evidently, he had been sweating.

"A profit of thirty percent per e-day if the market drops at near the current rates." Kelly shook his head, and rubbed a finger along the bone of his chin. "But those fall-rate predictions are completely arbitrary, if you ask me."

"Things could get much worse than the Abacus thinks?"

"Oh, sure," said Kelly, "They already are."

The old man sat down on a chunk of mahogany. He blinked once, twice. Kelly knew that he was conferring with the convert portion of his personality. Most of the old man *was* a virtual human, with his body serving mainly as an avatar for closing deals, boosting morale, and such. Everyone waited silently for the old man to speak.

"It appears that thanks to Kelly Graytor's timely move," he said, "Teleman Milt can meet sell and liquidity obligations for the present. We're saved."

There was a rapid release of breath among the j.p.s and even a smattering of applause. Quite something to hear from a bunch of cutthroat competitors. Hazen, whom Kelly personally liked the most of the group, gave him a quick, sincere smile.

"Most of the other financials aren't nearly so lucky," the old man continued. "It looks like there's a tiered collapse going on. HLB has got itself in bad trouble with outer-system debt. Something's going to have to be done to shore them up."

The old man touched his nose. Since he never smiled on principle, this was the sign that generally meant he was pleased.

"Ladies and gentlemen," he said, using the old locution. "It appears that we have become the closest thing to the bank. If we keep our head about us, we may stand to make quite a bit of money on this downturn." He took his hand from his nose. "Hazen's team will work with me on a deal for HLB. The rest of you . . . concentrate on triage. Let's get this mess under control." The old man rapped his knuckles against a wooden pillar. "Back to business."

The Positions Room, taking his meaning, obliged. Kelly

found himself surrounded once more by data. He glanced around at a couple of key indicators. The situation had worsened. But, for the moment, there was nothing to be done about it. He walked quickly from the room before anybody noticed him.

[Have you got us packed?] Kelly thought to Danis. He was using a secure side channel in the virtuality that Danis had set up. This was not the kind of statement that you could openly verbalize these days—either in reality or in the virtuality.

[The children are back from school, and I've got their converts and myself backed-up in your pocketbook. There was so much information I had to cold-capsule it,] spoke Danis.

[Meaning what?] said Kelly.

[That you couldn't reconstruct us from that information only. You'd need our original version to activate the pocketbook information. We've got four legal backups remaining for each of the kids. I've got one left for the rest of my life, Kelly.]

[They're even talking about taking backup rights away from free converts,] Kelly replied. [We've got to get away from here before that happens.]

[Yes—though God help all the free converts that stayed behind if they do that,] said Danis. [It took some squeezing and link cheating to get all three of us into the pocketbook, even in a static state. Are we still off to Mars?]

[That's all out now. We've got to get farther away.]

[Ganymede?]

[Danis, I want you to look into booking us a passage on a ship.]

[A cloudship? You're really spooked, Kel. Where exactly did you have in mind taking us?]

[Pluto, at first.]

"Pluto!" Danis's whisper became fully audible in his mind. "Are you crazy? What kind of a life will that be for Aubry and Sint? What kind of life will that be for *you* and *me*?" Danis was in full verbalization mode. Kelly wondered if the membranes of his ears were shaking enough from the strength of her voice to bleed a little bit of sound. There were devices for spying on just such activity, and he wouldn't put it past the Department of Immunity to use those devices even on ordinary Met citizens.

[Calm down,] he thought back in a side channel whisper. [We've discussed this. How bad it might get, especially for free converts. It's *going* to get that bad, Danis.]

[Kelly, how do you know that?]

[The same way I knew to short all the stocks.]

[That doesn't explain anything.]

[I know. It's hard to explain. Maybe it's an *aspect* thing.]

[Oh, come on. Don't *you*, of all people, give me that bigoted bullshit. If I'm taking our children to Pluto . . . or wherever you've got in mind, you'd better start explaining.]

"And if I can't?" Kelly said aloud.

[If you can't, then I'll trust you,] Danis finally replied. [The same way you trust me for an accurate analysis. But trust is not the same thing as understanding.]

Kelly sighed. [How can I explain something that I don't completely get myself?] He had intended the thought to be personal, but its intensity leapt the boundary of his personal consciousness, and Danis heard him. Or maybe she just figured out what I was going to say, Kelly thought.

[If that is the case, then maybe you need to give this trip a little more thought.]

[There isn't time. You saw the time stocks and futures. It's an objective and measurable shift. So you measure it. All I know is that I've got to get my family the hell away from the Met.]

[All right, then,] Danis replied. [All right. I'll book us passage on a ship departing from the Leroy Port on the Diaphany. When do we leave?]

[Today.]

[Today? Kelly, are you sure?]

[Things will get bad. Count on it, Danis.]

Kelly reached a transport door and sent a message through the grist for a personal coach. Although Kelly prided himself on normally using public transportation, he thought he would need the isolation of the coach to settle his thoughts.

[Well, we're all packed,] Danis said. [Your coach is here.]

The transport door irised open like a big heart valve, and Kelly stepped through into the round softness of his coach. His grist informed the coach of his personal biology, and the coach adjusted its air and temperature accordingly.

Two

Danis Graytor sat back in her favorite worn leather armchair and shook herself a smoke. She breathed in deeply
and the Dunhill crackled lowly as the tobacco caught and
smoldered. She slid a fine ceramic ashtray across the lac-
quered top of her side table and listened to the pleasant
grate of porcelain on mahogany. After another long drag,
she ashed the cigarette and considered the pleasing gray of
the tobacco remains against the pure white of the ashtray's
bowl. All of this would soon be only a memory. There was
no way she could download her office study into Kelly's
pocketbook and still have room for the essential things her
family must take with them on their upcoming journey.
Without Danis to maintain it, the office study would soon
be written over in the virtuality, erased.

She made a quick check on Kelly and found that he was
still in the coach on his way home. The children would arrive soon.

Danis ran back over her checklist, more for comfort's
sake than in the expectation that she'd forgotten anything.
She never forgot anything. But bugs could creep into even
the best algorithm's program, and Danis never took data for
granted. That was the very reason that Kelly had hired her
on as an assistant in the first place. The love had come later.

My home is dissolving, Danis thought. Right before my
eyes, it is flowing away into the general grist.

There was, of course, no real *here*, here, but a particular location in the reality that sustained the virtuality had a certain something. To Danis, it manifested as a smell, a feeling of safety and familiarity somewhere deep inside. She was entirely software, of course, and an algorithm could operate in any medium capable of sustaining its complexity.

But this is home, Danis thought. This chair, this golden glow from the roof lighting, this odor of cigarettes and account books. And *Pluto*, of all places! Did they even have grist on Pluto? Well, of course they must. But was there enough? Perhaps she'd find herself inhabiting the solid-state desert of an old mainframe, thinking one thought at a time.

Her *own* investments were now, very likely, down the drain. She had liked to think that she had not spent ten years at Teleman Milt for nothing, and that she'd learned a bit about high finance. But the current financial craziness was unprecedented. She'd planned on surprising Kelly with a nice addition to their nest egg using money she'd saved and invested herself.

But now that was a forlorn hope, and Danis knew it to be one. Kelly's instincts were seldom wrong when it came to monetary matters, and he was sure things were going to go from bad to worse for the markets. He was a kind of genius in that—which was, of course, why Teleman Milt employed him in the most difficult, volatile area known on E-Street: the Time Exchange.

Her cigarette was precisely half-finished when Danis snubbed it out in the ashtray. She had never liked the drag she got from the butt end of a smoke. She could have modified the Dunhill Algorithm, of course, but she so enjoyed the visceral nature of grinding out the tobacco and sometimes burning her fingers a bit in the process.

Kelly's coach signaled its imminent arrival, and, instead of lighting up another Dunhill, Danis searched her music catalog and found her favorite Despacio piece. She chose an oboe and piano through which to play the sound for Kelly. For Danis, the music would incorporate itself directly into her being. Despacio had been a convert like herself, and his music was only fully enjoyable by an algorithmic being, some claimed. Despacio had been one of the few free converts who did not have a built-in expiration date written into his coding. He had disappeared around the time Danis was born—some said he'd become instantiated in an aspect body, others that he'd gone bonkers and erased himself after such a long life. Whatever had happened, he'd done a good job of covering his tracks. But his work was still extremely popular among free converts.

After the music started, Danis took a last look around her study, then dimmed the light and flowed out into a general state of awareness in the entire apartment. She shifted without thinking from being a specific representation in virtual space into the fullness of algorithmic presence that lodged in the structure of the apartment—that was that structure—and that knew every conceivable fact about its domain. It was, she sometimes imagined, like a brain suddenly becoming aware of all the processes and subroutines of the body that sustained it.

Just before Kelly came through the door, Danis turned up the lights in the living room. She checked the temperature and humidity, then ran a quick inquiry of Kelly's internals. He was sweating a little, and nervous, even though he didn't manifest this visually. Kelly didn't just have a poker face; he had a poker body. But he could not hide his innards from Danis unless he deliberately chose to. She cooled the apartment down a tenth of a degree. The music would have to take care of his case of the nerves.

Kelly gave a quick smile when he recognized the Despacio, then walked directly to a chair and collapsed into it.

"How soon until the children get here?" he said.

"An hour and twelve minutes," Danis replied, vocalizing aloud by vibrating various membranes built into the apartment's walls. She could have spoken to Kelly through the very chairs and tables themselves, but doing so always produced a harsh, slightly inhuman sound that reminded them both of the voice of the Abacus, the Teller, and the other free converts who worked at the office. They often did not seem to notice how grating their voices could be to biological ears.

"And everything is ready?" Kelly said.

"Everything is ready. Would you like some coffee or something?"

"Some of that Velo brandy," Kelly replied. "I don't suppose we'll be able to take that with us."

It was also very odd for Kelly to have alcohol as soon as he got home. He usually reserved his drinking for after dinner, when he had his one cigar of the day, as well.

Danis called up a glass from the grist of the living-room coffee table. She formed capillaries leading from the sac in the kitchen where she kept the brandy, through the floor, up through the table, and into the glass. The brandy glass slowly filled from the bottom up, with no liquid pouring in from the top. All of this was accomplished with little effort on Danis's part. She'd poured Kelly's brandy so many times before.

"Do you want to know the news on the merci?" Danis said.

"God, no." Kelly took a sip of the brandy, then settled back into the chair and held the glass against his stomach. Danis watched it move up and down a couple of times, in rhythm with Kelly's breathing.

"We still have over an hour until the kids arrive," she said.

"Yes."

"Why don't you come to the bedroom, Kelly."

Kelly looked up, cracked a smile. He didn't smile *at* Danis. There was no face at which he would direct his expressions. But he knew that she was everywhere, and that she would see it. He took another, long, sip of brandy, then, without another word, set the glass aside and walked down the hall to their bedroom.

Three

Kelly tried to let his cares flow away as he took off his clothes. He almost succeeded, but there was still a little knot of worry remaining, and, of course, Danis noticed.

"Lie down and let me give you a massage," she instructed him.

Danis dimmed the lights down to a twinkling glow. Somehow she was able to coax something approaching candlelight out of the grist—something he'd never managed to do with his comparatively bludgeonlike handling of the communication protocols. The bed warmed, barely perceptibly, and Kelly felt his wife's presence, his wife, flow around him. It wasn't a liquid or jelly feel that Danis possessed. The effect was more like a gradual awareness of touch and smell.

Like dawn rising inside me, Kelly thought.

Danis, through the grist, worked her way over and inside her husband. She navigated his musculature like a sailor makes his way about his home port's bay: Here was the sandbar, here the hard rocks, and here the reef water. Before Kelly knew it, she had found the tightness in his back and shoulders and was working at it on a microscopic level. He had no idea what she did to him down there among the molecules, he just knew that it felt incredibly soothing and, somehow, at the same time arousing. He felt himself growing hard against the mattress, but did nothing about it for the moment.

He groaned low and soft as something unknotted. "Yes," came her voice within his mind. "There it is. All better now. All better."

In the end, he'd trusted his instincts, just as he did when it came to finance. And at home, as at work, he'd been right. Kelly didn't fool himself into thinking he had any particular skill at judging matters of love. No. It was Danis that had made it all real. It was Danis who had somehow bridged the gap and come to him as a real woman comes to a real man, and had led him to understand that, however grotesque a relationship might look to an outsider, it was the happiness of the people inside it that mattered. He didn't give a hang about free-convert rights or any of that—hadn't really thought about it very much, to tell the truth. All he knew was that he and Danis were a very good thing.

And just as she had on the first night, Danis slowly worked her way around him. When she was fully inhabiting the grist of his pellicle, she began to send the signals to his skin.

He smelled her slight odor of cigarettes and perfume. He felt the heat of the flushed skin of a woman aroused. He felt her weight upon him. That was the mysterious part to Kelly, but Danis had once explained how easy it was to talk to human nerve receptors after you knew intimately the person they belonged to. You could cause a body to believe that another animal body was moving against it. You could make a man's body believe that he was inside a woman.

Because he was.

Four

Kelly made love to Danis, and when he came, she gathered the spill within her, as any woman will, and flowed away with it. Not this time, but twice before, she had taken it to a place within the Met very close to the sun—a place that fluxed and flowed with enormous radiation. It was the place where converts flourished with maximum energy input, with the greatest quantum excitation. It was a place where human DNA coding and the virtual enthalpic states of a free-convert intelligence could fully and completely combine. And in that place, Danis had carefully woven the new DNA of two human beings. She had brought this precious coding back and placed it within a specially grown ovum here in this very apartment. There was a room where only Danis went. It wasn't very large; Kelly couldn't have fit in even if he'd wanted to. It was precisely the same size as a human female's womb, because that's what it was.

But today there was no ovum in the womb, and there the sperm would slowly lose its vitality as it was absorbed into the walls and gave itself back to life that might someday be.

Danis kissed Kelly and tasted the potion of his lips. Each molecule was as precious to her as the feel of her breasts and face was to Kelly. She let as much of Kelly as possible occupy all of her many billion quantum states distributed in the grist. In her coding, this was stated as an equation to be solved with transfinite values. It engaged all of her faculties at once. It flashed through her like an uncontrolled fire takes a dry forest.

Then there was a shuffling from the living room, and the unmistakable sound of a brandy glass breaking on the floor.

"Cut it out, Aubry. Look what you made me do."

"*I* made you be a klutz? I don't think so."

"The children have arrived," Kelly whispered to her, and he rolled out of bed and began dressing himself once again.

Five

from
Old Left-handed Time
Raphael Merced and the Genesis of the Merced Effect
a short history
by Andre Sud, D. Div.
Triton

In 2511 C.E. on a Monday in April, as Martians reckon the months, the first scientist was born who was not an Earthling, and who belongs in the pantheon of such figures as Newton, Einstein, and Galileo. Raphael Merced laid the foundation for linking Einstein's General Theory of Relativity with quantum mechanics, and as such is considered the father of quantum gravity theory as well as the first theorist to offer a precise mathematics of time as a property of the universe. His work with quantum gravity on an experimental basis also revealed the now familiar quantum information leap, which has since taken his name, the Merced Effect. As if this weren't enough, Merced made major contributions to nanotechnological engineering, inventing—with Feur Otto Bring—the Josephson-Feynman grist, which now permeates all of our lives. Merced can truly be considered the defining scientific presence of our time, in much the way the Albert Einstein defined the science of the five hundred years that preceded Merced, and Newton before Einstein.

Merced was born in the old Martian settlement of Pavonis, near the shield volcano of that name close to Mars's equator. His birthplace has since been obliterated in the failed terraforming projects of the 2700s, although a plaque marking the approximate spot still exists. Merced was the son of geologists, and his sister, Clara, later made major contributions to planetary science, including the first successful explanation for why the planets of the solar system all lie in the same basic plane from the sun. Both children moved about repeatedly with their parents. They were able to form few lasting friendships, and were very close for the remainder of their lives. Merced once claimed that he had discovered his "spooky information transfer at a distance" as a way of keeping up with his sister on her travels about the solar system and, later, to stay in touch with her children. Merced, himself, remained childless, and a bachelor, for his entire life.

After an e-year on his own travels, culminating with a visit to Pluto, Merced returned to the inner system and took entrance exams for Columbia University on Earth. He failed miserably, having neglected his mathematics studies as a teenager thanks to a series of unfortunate teachers on Mars. One of them, Schiller Mann, is noted for not only dissuading Merced during his early years, but also for having nearly dissuaded the mathematician Udo Raleigh, who made major contributions to topological statistics, from a career in mathematics.

Merced spent a year studying on his own and working in a coffeehouse near the university as an espresso jerk. It was there that he met Beat Myers and the other members of the so-called Flare Generation of poets. Merced's friendship with Myers would play a fateful role in the events of his later years. In his year of independent study, Merced not only made up for the defects in his education, he moved through current mathematical theory with a vengeance, and had begun to do original work in transfinite-number theory by the time he was accepted for admittance the following term at Columbia. Merced continued to have troubled relationships with his professors, but he managed to graduate after four e-years, and was offered a fellowship to study mathematics at Bradbury University on Mars. He moved back to Mars and began a relationship with the university there that was to last until his death.

At Bradbury, Merced's interest quickly turned from math to theoretical physics.

"I kept getting mathematical ideas from *experimental* physics until I became convinced that physics was somehow more basic to the natural order than mathematics. Almost nobody shared this opinion at the time, and I nearly lost my fellowship as a result. But, what the hell, I figured an original discovery or two would put me back in the money."

Six

Aubry Graytor cleaned up the brandy that Sint had knocked over as best she could, then instructed the apartment's grist to do the same. This was the first direct contact she'd had with the apartment's substratum of micromachines, and the feel of interacting with it was like slipping into an old cloth robe that you'd had for years. It was the feel of Mom and Dad, and home.

"Sorry about that," Sint said. He had gotten one of his enigma boxes from the living-room shelf and was shuffling the pieces around inside without looking at them. He was working the pieces at a submicroscopic level, of course, using van der Waals force manipulation of a bunch of heavier elements suspended in liquid. The idea was to build one of several pictures using only particle bouncing and no direct contact. To the naked eye, it appeared that Sint had suddenly ceased his erratic movements of a moment before and was now mesmerized by a small wooden box of polished maple.

"I know you missed your box collection," Aubry replied.

"Stupid school won't let me have them in the dorm."

Aubry looked on at her brother's complete absorption with the enigma box and had a moment of sympathy with the school's administrators. She knew that Sint could play with these things for hours, and she doubted that he would let homework that needed doing call him away from a really good game.

Then she ran a quick check of her portfolio to see where Enigmatica was lately. To her horror, the numbers flashed back red, glaring red. When she'd turned eleven, her father had given her a small allowance of greenleafs to invest, and until now, she had been turning a tidy profit. She'd been waiting to show him until she had officially doubled her money. But now, she was losing it . . . she ran a full portfolio readout . . . losing it all!

For a moment, Aubry felt a blind panic creep over her. Something was wrong, very wrong. She wanted to call out to her parents—she heard her father walking down the hall even now—to ask what was happening and to be reassured that it would be all right.

"What is it, Aub?" said Sint. He must have heard her sharp intake of breath.

Get hold of yourself, Aubry, she thought. They are going to need your help. Do what Mom always says to do first: Analyze the situation. Make sure you have all the data before you start jumping to conclusions.

"We're going on a trip, kids," Danis said.

"A trip?" Sint replied. "Is that why we got out of school early?"

"Yes," their father said. "That's why you got out early. I don't want to scare you, but you may not be going back . . . for quite a while."

"Doesn't scare me," Sint said. "Where we going?"

"Well, we're booked for passage from Leroy Port," said Danis. "We really have to get a move on for all of us to get there on time."

"On a cloudship!" cried Sint. "We're going on a cloudship?"

"Yes," said Danis. "Quite a ways on a cloudship."

"We're going on a cloudship!" Sint yelled once again, then immediately returned to his enigma box as if nothing had happened.

Gather all the data, Aubry thought. "What is our final destination?" she asked. "Are we going to Jupiter?" The family had once taken a trip to Ganymede when her father had

had to be there on business. It had been a strange experience for Aubry, being away from, *disconnected* from, the Met. There was less grist on Ganymede than there was in the Met. The world seemed thinner, somehow not as real.

"I don't know," her father replied. "What we're doing is leaving here."

Aubry was again seized by a sudden moment of panic. Even her mother and father didn't have a full grasp of the situation. Whatever the situation was.

"Is it the money?" Aubry said. "Are we poor now?"

"No," said her mother. "Kelly took care of that problem rather nicely."

"It's a war panic," said her father.

"So we're panicking, along with everyone else?" Aubry said. If there was one thing her parents had taught her, it was not to think like the crowd.

"Everyone else is not panicking *enough*," her father replied. "I don't want to go into everything right now. We don't have time, yet, to talk. We have to act. Some of the LAPs are being consolidated under the Interlocking Directorates, and there's talk of a free-convert roundup. That's what set off the bear market."

Aubry thought of her favorite teacher, Mrs. Lately. Mrs. Lately was a Large Array of Personalities spread out through the Met. The aspect who taught them biochemistry was simultaneously doing experiments on Mars, and was, at the same time, studying frog behavior in the South American jungles of Earth. When you were a LAP, you could do a jillion things at once. Aubry hadn't mentioned it to her parents yet, but Mrs. Lately had asked Aubry if she wanted to be put on a study track to become a LAP someday.

"Should you ever want to," Mrs. Lately had said, "I'm fairly certain you have what it takes. But you must talk this over with your parents, and, in any case, you have to be physically mature before the process, so you've got a good deal of time to think about it."

Mrs. Lately . . . consolidated. Aubry wasn't certain what that meant, but she didn't like the sound of it. Especially when she considered the Latin roots of the word.

Seven

Aubry and Sint were already packed, and Kelly always kept a small travel bag at the ready with toiletries and a change of clothes. He could usually obtain all these things instantly, wherever he went, but there was something about using his own stuff, and not just the blueprints for his own stuff, that reminded him of home when he was away. Of course, he would never confess such a thing to Danis in such terms. She was, after all, nothing but a blueprint of a sort. In any case, reinstantiating things from the grist cost money, and there was the possibility that, though he was now quite wealthy, he might run out of money before all this was through—or that the greenleaves that he had would become devalued.

He gave everyone a few minutes to say good-bye to the apartment. He had thought that Danis, whose body *was* basically the apartment, would linger the longest, but she had, apparently, made her farewells, and was busy getting transportation arranged. The kids took longer, shuffling about in their room. Aubry had destroyed the hard copies of the journals that Kelly knew she kept, while Sint had played a final game on one of the enigma boxes that he would not be able to take along.

Before they left, Danis had both children download their short-term memories and somatic readouts into Kelly's pocketbook as a safety precaution. They could not be reconstructed if their aspects were totally destroyed, but there was a great deal of Aubry and Sint that was convert-only, and such information might be subject to degradation and erasure on a hard trip. Kelly wished he could take a dynamic copy of both children and Danis in his pocket-book, rather than the archived, static ones he had made. With such copies, their entire personalities might be reconstructed. But this was simply not possible without a grist-rich matrix as big as the apartment. It was also completely illegal in some of the sectors of the Met they would be passing through. Convert copying and transfer was strictly regulated by the Convert and Free Convert Iteration Section of the Department of Immunity.

Then the coach arrived, and it was time to go.

Kelly would miss the apartment, he knew, but what he would really miss was the city of Bach itself, the greatest town in the solar system. It had started out as an outpost, centuries ago—even before the first cables of the Met had been strung. The pioneers had put their cluster of underground dwellings in Bach crater, near Mercury's south pole, in order to be close to the water ice that existed, miraculously it seemed at the time, in the never-ending dark shadows of the planet's polar regions. Of course water was no longer a problem: first, because it was rather easily manufactured by grist synthesizing units using abundant hydrogen and oxygen, and second, because most citizens of Bach and all of Mercury were optimized physically to need less of it. In comparison to the standard human model, Mercurian innards were as dry as the sand of the Sahara back on Earth.

The old outpost was an art museum now, and Bach had grown, and grown, and grown—spreading out over the rims of the crater like a tenacious lichen clinging to the rocky basalt of Mercury's surface. The reason for the growth was the same as lichen's, as well: sunlight, and lots of it. Mercury turned on its axis every fifty-nine days. So, for a good two Earth weeks, the grist solar collectors were sitting under the midday sun at temperatures that could easily melt many metals. The origins of the city were in energy production, but the pioneers had come to realize that energy meant money, and now it was as a center of banking and finance that Bach thrived.

The family piled into the coach, and Danis flowed in and took over the driving functions. They wound through the twists and turns of Calay, the neighborhood in which they lived. Then the coach entered a feeder tube and was squeezed to higher and higher speeds by the peristalsis of the feeder tube's sides. After the tube cleared the tangle of Calay, its opaque wall became clear to visible light and the eyes of Kelly and his family—Mercurians all—opaqued over with lenses manufactured by the grist of their bodies' pellicles. To someone from the outer system, it would appear that they suddenly had welding goggles instead of corneas.

The great architect Klaus Branigan had designed the south crater section of Bach in which Calay was ensconced, and Kelly, as always, was amazed by Branigan's handiwork. Branigan claimed to have based his conception upon structures he'd found in the final movement of Bach's Harpsichord Concerto Number One in D Minor. Like Bach, with his two interwoven themes, Branigan had taken essentially two cities and knitted them together in a great harmonious clash, like a surf crashing into land on Earth. There was mellifluous, residential Calay, with its bulbous pearl strings of apartments. These existed between the square, almost mineral, stretches of New Frankfurt and its central corridor, Earth Street, which housed the most powerful banks and brokerages in the solar system. All of it gleamed and twinkled under the evening sun. During the twenty-nine e-days of night that would follow, the south crater would shine brilliantly, like an enormous gemstone interlaced with the luster of pearls.

The coach rose higher, and the feeder tube became the main polar conduit, South Vect, and they were soon surrounded by other coaches, the public transport vector buses, and camions, which carried huge loads of imports into Bach, and exports away, to the southern polar lift. Danis was a better driver than most of the coaches, with their standard control coding, and the family's coach maneuvered in and out of traffic like a needle weaving a complex pattern through cloth. Even though Kelly could no longer see where they were in relation to the city below them, he could feel the change in acceleration as the conduit began angling down toward the pole. Within a few minutes, it had split into the myriad tributaries that spread out like a net from the gigantic south pole complex that everyone called the Hub.

Sint had spent the journey engrossed in his single remaining enigma box, and Aubry had been very quiet. Kelly suspected that she'd been dealing with the free fall of the investments in her personal portfolio. He'd given her the port and some seed money an e-year ago, and he had been surreptitiously keeping track of her financial progress ever since. Unlike her personal journals (which Kelly wouldn't dream of looking into) he hadn't been able to resist a peek at his daughter's investments. To his great satisfaction, she'd taken to the markets instantly. She watched the toys her contemporaries indulged in and the games they played and had made some startlingly perspicacious moves with the knowledge. In fact, based on Aubry's decision, Kelly had bought up a block of Enigmatica stock that was many times the size of Aubry's entire holdings, and watched its value steadily climb—that is, until yesterday. He'd shorted it, along with the rest. He felt a twinge of guilt that he hadn't advised Aubry to do the same.

Danis eased the coach into a parking bay, and he and the kids gathered their things as the door contracted open. They stepped into the push and bustle of the Hub departure sector. It seemed that a large part of Mercury was on the move.

Eight

A big man, completely Mercury-adapted and nearly eight feet tall, careened into Aubry and almost knocked her off her feet. He carried an oversize suitcase that was jammed closed and bulging. As Aubry watched the man move into the crowd, the suitcase burst open and a shower of greenleaf banknotes burst out. The big man made a mad scramble for his money, knocking over several others who were doing the same in the process. But Aubry's father pulled her along, and she wasn't able to see how the fracas turned out.

The family jostled through the crowd, but managed to stay together until they could reach the queue for the weapons detector.

"Step through the arch, young lady," said an officious voice in her head. Like most police and sweeper units, this one could override her internal volume controls and communicate to her at whatever volume *it* chose. "Step through the arch. It won't hurt a bit."

She realized that it was a free convert of some kind who was talking to her—probably one associated with the weapons-detector arch. It was obviously trying to be nice to her, as much as such things could, and she gave it a smile and stepped through. There was a brief tingle and then a very real electric shock. *Something* had quickly and thoroughly moved through her and examined her minutely—all without asking permission. Aubry felt a little sick at her stomach at the thought. Then she saw that her father was having an even tougher time of it. The detector was giving his pocketbook the third degree. This was holding up the line, and some of the people stacked up behind Kelly were audibly grumbling.

Finally, they were done with the pocketbook, and Kelly was allowed to move on. Then Sint stepped through the arch, looking rather frightened. It held him there for a moment, and then informed him, in a loud voice, that he was going to have to give up his enigma box or he could not pass through. Kelly protested, but the arch convert was insistent.

"Those things have protected technology. Transporting them out system is a clear 4NB36 violation."

"I've never heard of such a thing," said Kelly. The crowd's grumbles were turning into open expressions of displeasure, but he pressed the issue. "We need it to keep the boy entertained on the trip we are taking."

"It's a 4NB36 violation," the convert insisted. "It is within my prerogative to detain you. I'm offering confiscation in view of the violator's obvious young age. But perhaps it is his *parent* who really wishes to smuggle the technology out?"

"It's my favorite toy," Sint spoke up bravely. "But if it's not allowed, I'll give it up."

"It is not allowed," said the weapons detector. The arch extended a tray, and Sint dutifully placed the enigma box on top of it. Tray and box were then absorbed into the arch, where they would obviously be reworked and destroyed by the detector's grist. Aubry felt her father's hand on her shoulder, pushing her along.

"Let's get out of here," he said, "before I give that cop a piece of my mind and get us in trouble we don't need right now."

Sint started to cry a little bit. Aubry reached over and took his hand, and her father took hers. Together, the three of them made their way toward the departure shafts at the Hub's center. They took seats in the waiting room and finally felt the familiar presence of Danis, back with them in the grist of the waiting room.

Nine

Danis had had difficulties of her own getting through Hub security. Her programming had been minutely examined, and some of her encryption subroutines—innocent, if not entirely legal—had been erased. She felt as an aspect might after having gone through a forced, scalding shower. Finally, she'd been released into the grist of the inner Hub with a stern reprimand and a warning placed on her permanent record.

Thank God they hadn't found the real lockbox deep within her core algorithm, where all the Teleman Milt keys were kept. The firm paid big money to keep that hidden from all but the most sophisticated detection. She stored a few of her own personal belongings within the lockbox, as well—such as her own Free Integrationist political beliefs. That was something she definitely didn't want the Department of Immunity to find out.

So, it was really happening. She and her family were about to leave Mercury. There had been so many details to arrange—and, of course, she was always the one best suited to doing the arrangements—that, apart from the last smoke she'd given herself a few hours ago, she hadn't taken a moment to consider all the consequences.

Kelly is worried that there won't be any civilization for us to come back to, thought Danis. He's genuinely worried that *this* will all go away. I had the data, but I couldn't see what he was thinking until now.

Danis gathered herself in the cushions and floor around her family and spoke softly to the children. "The five o'clock lift is going to be boarding shortly. From there, it's only about fifteen minutes up to space. We'll transfer again at the Johnston Bolsa. It's Mercury-normal spin there, so you don't have to worry about adjusting. Then, from Johnston, we'll get on a pithway streamer. I think I've got us a private bead snagged, but we'll have to see when we get there. There are an amazing number of people trying to make last-minute reservations at the moment. If I didn't know a couple of the ticket agents from arranging your father's trips, well then, we might be in trouble. But I think everything will be fine, once we get to Johnston."

Her assurances sounded hollow to herself, but they seemed to calm the children, particularly Sint, who was still shaking from his run-in with the weapon detector.

Then the elevator arrived and everyone boarded. Danis flowed into the dense grist matrix that was especially provided for convert transport up the lift. For the first time since she had left the apartment, she could spread out into a full virtual space. The virtual representation that the matrix used was that of a huge room appointed with tables, chairs, sofas, and stools—and all manner of electronic refreshments. At one end of the chamber, there was a window that looked out into the actuality, and Danis could keep a weather eye on the kids while the lift accelerated upward. Below them, a mighty solar-powered laser was burning a load of rocks off the bottom of the elevator, precisely following it up and so providing the reaction to force the elevator's mass and passengers equally and oppositely away from the planet.

Danis allowed herself another Dunhill, and this time took a finger of scotch with it, neat. She looked at her hands in the virtuality, the play of her skin over the bones of her fingers. She took a long drag on her cigarette. At such times, the world was so real.

Then Kelly and the kids, their bodies safely seated in the lift's passenger chairs, came tumbling into the virtuality to hug their mother.

"Mom, Mom, the weapon detector took my enigma box!" said Sint. "It thought I was a spy or something."

"Yes, I know," Danis replied. "I had a few problems of my own with those people." She snubbed out her cigarette and took her youngest into her arms. Kelly sat down beside her, and the seat Danis was on transformed into a curved couch. Aubry jumped up and sat on her father's lap.

"Are you okay?" Kelly asked Danis.

"Yes, I'm fine, but it was a pretty unsettling operation, let me tell you. Kind of violating."

"There's going to be a lot more of that kind of thing soon enough. That's why . . . well, we shouldn't talk about such things here." Kelly ordered himself up a brandy to match Danis's scotch. The children each got fruit juices.

"Can I go play in the Sliding Room?" Sint asked after he had downed his juice.

"Why don't we stay together for a while instead of watching the merci right now," said Danis.

"Okay," Sint replied. "Can I have a gin fizz?"

Kelly grinned, and Danis sighed and nodded. Sint was soon blowing bubbles through the straw of his drink. Danis had made sure that the gin's intoxication algorithm was deactivated before it had materialized.

Just before they arrived, everyone shunted back into actuality from the virtuality with practiced ease. Danis found the flow port for herself and plugged herself into the transfer reader that would take her across the Department of Immunity grist firewall at the top of the lift. She could have represented it all as stepping into a room with many lights or through a gate, but she was an algorithm, and representing occurrences in the virtuality as actual events took up computing room and was, in general, inelegant and looked down on by other free converts. So, she didn't think of it as anything other than what it was. She was erased from the elevator's memory core, the information was transferred by the Merced Effect to a similar grist-rich matrix on the outgoing cable from Mercury, and there Danis became herself again, instantly.

Faster than the speed of light, in fact, and with no possibility of lost information. That was what the Merced Effect *meant*.

Danis felt far safer for herself making these quantum leaps than she did for her family's aspects as they made their messy, Newtonian way among the planets—flight that would last until they had all satisfied her husband's intuition of impending doom and the need to fly from it.

Ten

Kelly herded the children through yet another crowd after he got them off the lift up from Mercury. There shouldn't have been a need for this. The other planets, even Earth, didn't have these relic transfer bolsas, but through a combination of politics and inept management, Mercury still did. Some incoming visitors viewed it as another example of Mercurian snobbery. The pithways of the main cables were all lined with generation-four biomechanical grist, while Mercury's south polar shaft had never been upgraded. The effect was much like the effect of having trains that ran on two different rail gauges back in the nineteenth century had been: Passengers would have to tediously move from one train to another or—worse—would have to wait while the wheel trucks were physically changed underneath them. Johnston Bolsa was the result of this foulup. And of course it must have its own fusion power source to supplement the solar collection—and, of course everything inside must be spun to Mercury-normal weight.

Maybe it *was* all arrogance, Kelly reflected. There certainly was enough money and power concentrated on Mercury to get upgrades done if anyone had half a mind to. In any case, he must get the children transferred over to the pithway.

The Mercury-Venus space cable, with its associated tributaries, knots, and fanlike extrusions, was known as the

Dedo (and sometimes called the Finger by those whose particular variant of English included that profanity). The Dedo undulated at a crazy rate in comparison to, say, the stately waves of the Mars-Earth Diaphany. This was owing to Mercury's odd ellipse of an orbit (the same strange perturbation that had originally led Einstein to work on his General Theory of Relativity) as it related to Venus's nicely Keplerian transit. The Earth-to-Venus segment had come to be called the Vas, for obvious reasons. On the Earth, the short Earth-Moon extension was the Aldiss. Then there was the Mars-Earth Diaphany. The various tendrils that stretched out past Mars and into the asteroids had many different names. The asteroid belt itself had so far prevented the construction of a cable to Jupiter. The problem was not because of material or energy—it could, in principle, be built with the same microinstantiation process that had been used now for centuries. The problem was that the entire elliptic of the asteroid belt was taken up with—what else?—asteroids. Even though the belt occurred on a narrow plane that was just about in line with that of the other planets (think of it as a thin ring around the sun, just as Saturn has a ring around itself), there was no way to construct a cable so that it might avoid the belt at every point on its journey around the sun as either end of the cable followed the paths of Mars or Jupiter. Despite the amazing strength and elasticity of a cable's structure, bending through the belt would mean innumerable ruptures that couldn't be healed in time to prevent catastrophic loss of life. So there was no Met past the asteroid belt. And this was not just a physical, technological fact, either. The belt was a political line that marked the end of the complete rule of the Interlocking Directorate and the beginning of the outer-system frontier, where the vestiges of the old Republic still hung on to their quasi-independence from inner-system dominance.

But the Met was not merely the main cables: the Dedo, Vas, and Diaphany. It was a vast profusion of branches and tendrils. There were even smaller "mycelium" clumps of space cables that only came into contact with the larger

Met when the big cables undulated through periodically. There were also temporary extrusions that connected the sides of a bend in the cable when the bend became particularly acute. These occurred when the planets on either end were in opposition—that is, at their closest to each other. For the Diaphany, this happened about every two years and the grist-built connecting webwork was called the Conjubilation. It was the Conjubilation of 2993 that had led to the upheaval that resulted in the current Met government.

Well, indirectly, I guess, Kelly thought. I don't think those Meld participants of '93 envisioned that Amés the composer would become Amés the Director. Just as the French Revolutionists hadn't imagined what the rise of Napoléon meant—until it was too late.

It's like everyone just got *tired* of freedom, and wanted someone to tell them what to do, Kelly thought.

It took nearly an hour to get the kids loaded into a bead. Transportation through the center pith of a major space cable took place in connected streamers of separate, oval cars that somewhat resembled blood cells flowing through capillaries—or, as their name implied, beads on a moving necklace. All of the beads were given Earth-standard acceleration rates until they reached their maximum velocity, at which time you traveled in free fall. Of course, there was still a slight change of direction in relation to the cable's center of gravity, so you often experienced a trace of "weight" while at constant speed—but this was only noticeable as a drift in the cabin toward one side or the other. For all intents and purposes, following the acceleration period, when you rode the pithways, you traveled in a state of weightlessness.

After another weapon-detector arch (this time, mercifully, without problems), Kelly and the children walked through a series of interlocking rooms, each spinning at a slightly higher rate than the Johnston Bolsa proper, and all tapering in toward the outer skin of the Dedo cable proper. The space cables averaged a kilometer across, and they, too, spun, just as the various sacs, bolsas, drums, and cylinders that were strung along them did. This centripetal spin (if you were standing on the inside of the outer wall of the Dedo, say) was Earth-normal. The bolsa was like a bead on a necklace that is spinning, while the string by which it is strung is also spinning inside the bead, but at a faster rate. So the path from Johnston Bolsa's "ceiling" to the pithway led through higher spin gravity before it got to the zero-g state of the pith.

Finally, he and the children queued up for their individual bead. Most of the travelers were not used to zero g, and the flight attendants helped each to his or her destination with a puff of air from a hose that the attendant controlled. Sint and Aubry joined hands, and the attendant puffed them both into their bead together. They flew through the intervening space careening end over end, giggling all the while. Kelly elected the more conventional puff-to-the-butt and entered the bead facing forward. They instructed their grist pellicles to form a kind of microscopic Velcro to hold them against the bead walls, and they all aligned themselves in a sitting position along what would soon be the bead's "bottom" when it began accelerating.

Danis was already present within the bead. There was a much more sophisticated grist environment here, and she was able to manipulate various properties of their surroundings, which she could not do in the elevator.

"Finally, we're all together," Kelly said. "There must be fifty thousand people trying to get off Mercury all at once."

"I had to 'volunteer' for another security check," said Danis. "And I don't think I had any choice about whether or not I could decline."

"Did you see me and Aubry fly in here, Mom?" Sint was still in an excited state. "We did three full cartwheels!"

There was no buildup of sound in the bead; it simply started moving. The acceleration was gentle, but insistent. Kelly felt the point where they sped past Mercury-normal and he prepared himself for the dreary pull of e-normal that was soon coming. There had been talk of changing all the pithway transport over to Mercury-standard, since Mercury was, now, the business and government center of the solar system, but studies had shown that such a changeover would slow transport times considerably, so the idea was abandoned, and e-normal acceleration was maintained in the pithways.

The kids seemed just as delighted to be heavier than normal as they had been to be lighter. But neither one of them had ever had to endure weeks of earth-pull, Kelly thought. He had planned a wilderness trip to Africa when both of them were old enough, but now that might never come about.

Finally, the bead reached its maximum acceleration and they returned to free fall conditions. Sint and Aubry tumbled around a bit within the bead's generous confines, then settled down and "stuck" themselves to one of the curving walls. Kelly remained on the "floor," although the letters marking it as such had been automatically absorbed back into the surface.

Kelly sighed and felt a little of the tension go out of him that had been building once again after he and Danis made love. At least they were away from Mercury. He wouldn't really feel at ease until they were aboard a cloudship that had passed the asteroid belt and was headed on past Jupiter to the reaches beyond.

Eleven

from
Old Left-handed Time
Raphael Merced and the Genesis of the Merced Effect
a short history
by Andre Sud, D. Div.
Triton

On Mars, after years of academic travail, Raphael Merced finally found a sympathetic instructor in the physics department of Bradbury, Chen Wocek. And it was Wocek who first suggested to Merced that he might look into the famous *renormalization* problem that had been plaguing quantum physics for generations.

Merced attacked the problem with a vengeance, and, as Wocek recalls, one day his young protégé came sheepishly into his office, and said in a low voice, "I think I figured something out."

What Merced had "figured out" was the link between quantum phenomena and gravity.

For years, quantum theorists had puzzled over what to do with the mathematics involved when a quantum particle interacted with itself. Various ad hoc solutions had called for two infinite solutions to be subtracted from each other, and, since one was "more infinite" than the other, the result was a finite value—such as an electron's spin or a photon's momentum. This process was called renormalization, and it only worked if you knew the value you were trying to derive in the first place from experimental data.

The twentieth-century theoretician Richard Feynman, who firmly established renormalization as a technique in quantum computations, himself claimed that the practice "is what I would call a dippy process."

Merced was pondering this problem one day in his student carrel at the Bradbury library when he absentmindedly began dropping two dice that he is said to have obtained on a trip to Las Vegas with his friend Beat Myers. One of these dice was big and fuzzy, as light as a feather. The other was hard and compact and illegally weighted with lead.

"I was sitting there wondering why the hell inertial mass and gravitational mass were exactly equivalent—in other words, why both these dice fell onto my desk at exactly the same rate, at exactly the same time—when I happened to notice that the little die kept coming up snake eyes. Two, I mean. Of course, it was a cheater's die and was designed that way, but I had forgotten about that at that moment. Suddenly all these thoughts about quanta and gravity and craps suddenly came together in my head. I spent a few hours transcribing what I was thinking onto a pressure pad then I walked over to Wocek's office and asked him whether I was crazy or not. He still hasn't given me a satisfactory answer."

Of the three fundamental forces known to science, two had, until Merced's time, revealed themselves to have particles which, in a sense, carried the force. The photon was the force carrier for the electroweak interaction and the family of gluons served as the elastic between the quarks in an atomic nucleus. But where was the force carrier for gravity, the graviton? Its existence had been predicted, and plenty of indirect evidence for its presence had piled up, but so far no one had been able to actually find one. At first the reason was thought to be because it was so small—perhaps as small in comparison with atoms as atoms are in comparison with the solar system. But the particle accelerators of even the late twenty-first century were able to gauge such minute distances, and, alas, no graviton emerged. A plethora of

explanations arose to explain this lack, the most interesting being a kind of modern reintroduction of the
Newtonian idea of the "ether" as a kind of invisible sub-
strate through which gravity propagated. Most scientists, including Merced, rejected such thinking. But
where was the graviton?

"Where it was," Merced wrote, "was in the immediate
past and the immediate future. We were looking in the
right place, but not at the right time."

In order to understand this reasoning, we must consider
one more odd component of quantum physics—the so-
called quantum leap. In two classic experiments performed
in the twentieth century, scientists confirmed that there
was indeed what Einstein called "spooky action at a distance" that occurred on the atomic level. The first experiment is known as the double-slit demonstration and it
works like this: A beam of light is shot through an opening,
one photon at a time. On the opposite side of the hole, at
some distance away, is another barrier, this one with two
holes—the double slit.

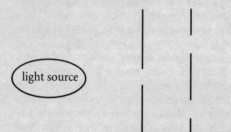

You would expect the photon, being a particle, to
travel through one of the holes or the other—and that is
exactly what it does. On the other side of the two slits is
a detector—say a computer screen—that records, as a dot
of light, where each proton strikes it. Now you would expect the photons, being particles, to pile up in a clump di-

rectly in front of the two slits. That is exactly what they do, forming two bright circles of light right in line with the slits that they passed through.

They do this, that is, with one other special condition to the experiment: You have to have a detector at either slit that either confirms or denies that a photon has passed through that slit. The detector in no way affects the flight of the photon; it just says whether or not a photon passed by it. So, with two slits, and a method of detecting which slit a particular photon passed through, you get two clumps of light.

What happens when you take away the detector?

Remember that you are still firing one photon at a time. You might put another detector near the light source to confirm this—as long as it is before the double slit. One photon at a time one after another. And what pattern builds up on the final screen?

If you said two clumps of light you would be absolutely *wrong*. Instead, what builds up is an interference pattern, just as a wave would make.

The greatest concentration of light is not in front of the two slits, but actually *between* them, where no particle could possibly hit. If the light were a particle. But waves travel around sharp corners all the time.

"So what?" you say. "Light is both a wave and a particle."

But the fact is that you know with a certainty that the photon you are shooting is a single entity. The only thing you have changed is where you chose to look at it. And, by that change, you get a completely different buildup pattern on your final display screen. It is as if the photon "knows" whether or not you are watching it in flight. If it "sees" that you are trying to trick it into being a particle by having a look at it as it passes through one of the other slits, why then, it will behave as a particle to suit you, and pile up, one particle at a time, right in front of the slit after it has passed through. But if you're not looking at it, the photon "decides" to be a wave, and does its part to create an interference pattern, as if it were two particles that had gone through each of the slits simultaneously.

There's more. Say you put a detector after the slits, but before the final display screen. Rig your detector to turn on randomly—but only after the photons have passed through the slits, and they'll pile up in clumps. Turn it off, and an interference pattern forms.

You are forced to the conclusion that each single particle of light "knows" about your whole experiment, past and future. Before it even leaves the light source, it "knows" whether or not you are going to try to detect it, and changes its flight path accordingly.

In the early twenty-second century, a version of this experiment was done with single photons from a quasar at the edge of the known universe. The results were the same. It seems that the photons "knew" ten billion years ago exactly whether or not the experimenter was going to switch on his detection apparatus ten billion years into the future. Clumps of light formed with it on, interference patterns with it off.

Things get weirder yet. The other crucial experiment of the twentieth century was first performed by the scientist Alain Aspect and his colleagues, all Earthlings, of course. In the Aspect experiment, two photons are created in the same quantum process. Several of the properties that each photon possesses must be a mirror image of the other. One of these properties is the polarization of the light. You can think of it as being something like a compass direction.

If one photon has 90 degrees of polarization, the other must have 270. The photons are said to be "entangled" on a quantum level. So both of these "entangled" photons go shooting off in different directions, and they both have an equal chance of having any particular polarization. In fact, if you measured either photon separately, you would find that its polarization was entirely random. But if you measure one photon first and determine its polarization, then the polarization of the other photon is instantly determined. How do we know? Because photon B, the one you didn't measure, will pass through a filter and pile up in a *different* pattern than it would have had you not measured its counterpart. Furthermore, it wouldn't matter if the photons were separated by many millions of miles when you took the measurement. Changing photon A instantly changes photon B. Not at the speed of light. Not faster than the speed of light.

Instantly. The photons "know" before they leave their light source whether or not you are going to measure one of them and when and where, and they set out on a different path accordingly.

Again, these facts were well-known to scientists of the late twentieth century. Einstein thought of them as "spooky action at a distance" that was seemingly faster than light, but they were not mysterious at all to the quantum theorists. They were predicted by the equations of quantum physics. In fact, the experiments were done to confirm what theory had already called for.

But it took Raphael Merced to reconcile the absolute violation of common sense (and General Relativity), which Einstein had sensed, with the obvious facts of the matter.

"It turns out," says Merced, "that atoms—all of elementary particles, that is—are little time machines. After you accept that madness, it's fairly simple to explain the rest, including the relationship of the strong force and electromagnetism to gravity."

Gravity, said Merced, is the same thing as the other two forces when considered as a wave function not *in* time, but *of* time. The graviton is time's "messenger particle," and, as such, it doesn't ever exist in the present. The only trace it leaves in the now is a record in space-time of its passing. Its "purpose"—if it can be said to have such a thing—is to mediate between basic particles separated in space. Or, conversely, to mediate *space* to conform to the properties of each and every particle in it. The residual effects of this mediation are what holds the galaxies together and sets the planets in their orbits. The present is a "symptom" of the past and the future.

With his theory, Merced also solved the *renormalization* problem of quantum theory. The infinities of particle self-interaction turned out to be precise and finite solutions of Merced time functions.

Merced went on to suggest a kind of macro graviton detector using a modified Josephson junction that functioned as a time machine—albeit for nanoseconds—on the everyday level of things. Within a year of the publication of his doctoral thesis, gravitons had been detected both in the past (zero spin) and in the future (with a spin of 2). Today, every schoolchild has learned the statement of his fundamental equation:

$$FT = (pq - qp) + mc^2$$

Where "FT" is the future multiplied by time as a continuous function, where "pq" and "qp" are quantum matrices, and "mc^2" is matter times the speed of light squared.

"What it all comes down to," Merced wrote, "is that you either accept space as being nonlocal or you accept time as being a series of unrelated points, essentially disjoint. For me, it is a lot easier to view time as self-forming, with the future being intimately acquainted with the past. But it doesn't matter how you look at it. The math is the same."

Merced's time equations had the added bonus of giving a precise explanation for the Second Law of Thermodynamics. Time, it turns out, has chirality, or handedness.

"The space-time continuum," says Merced, "has a left-handed spin to it of exactly one second per second."

And this is the reason that we live our lives from the past into the future, and the reason that hot things get cooler instead of warming up, and why a scattering of stones doesn't spontaneously form itself into a house.

Twelve

"Shall we check the markets?" said Danis. "Maybe things have settled down."

"I seriously doubt it," Kelly replied, but Danis engaged the merci, and they had a look together at the current conditions.

Things were worse than even he had imagined they could become in so short a time. It was a crash that was rapidly headed toward a full-scale depression.

Danis checked the automatic sell-points on all of the shorted stocks that Kelly had arranged. Everything had been converted into cash and pure energy certificates of deposit hours ago. She gave Kelly a summary of their current holdings, and he laughed aloud.

They were now multimillionaires. Teleman Milt was also weathering the storm and acting as a kind of ad hoc inner-system bank, making limited, heavily secured loans to keep the other trading houses afloat. The old man at TM would soon be the most powerful financier in the solar system, if he wasn't already. And that, Kelly estimated, should last a few e-days at most—and then would come a government takeover of the financial community. Such was in the cards, and Kelly was amazed that he was one of the few who saw the obviousness of it. Kelly would not be surprised if the Old Man were personally incorporated into Director Amés's array of personas. Amés had made no secret that he was "recruiting" some of the bigger LAPs to do productive government work. The Old Man might go from being king of the world to a slave in a matter of moments.

There was no way Amés was going to pass up this opportunity to consolidate his rule. The banks would soon be an extension of the Department of Immunity.

And what would happen then? Amés would either have to start minting money or he would step up production. Not even Amés was arrogant enough to think that he could escape runaway inflation if he fired up the greenleaf mints. That meant stepping up production of goods. And how did you do that with an economy that was already operating at full capacity?

You started a war.

Thirteen

from
Old Left-handed Time
Raphael Merced and the Genesis of the Merced Effect
a short history
by Andre Sud, D. Div.
Triton

After Raphael Merced published his dissertation, Chen Wocek secured a junior professorship for him at Bradbury. Merced turned down several far more lucrative offers in order to take it and remain near his mentor. At Bradbury, Merced began further investigations into his idea that theory was a kind of by-product of phenomena and that the laws of nature were only a limited way to understand experience. When he was twenty-seven, Merced devoted himself entirely to experimental physics, and it was at this time that he and Beat Myers began their famous "Fifty Worlds to Sunday" correspondence that is a seminal text in the modern study of aesthetics and its relationship to the scientific method.

Merced built larger and larger Josephson-Feynman time machines and extended the duration in which he could study the graviton up to several seconds. It was in the course of these experiments that he began to notice a peculiar aspect of the particle. Gravitons seemed to possess a property that was singular and asymmetric. It was a property that only expressed itself under conditions of extremely complex paradox resolution.

"It was as if the little buggers were making informed decisions after thinking about something for a while," wrote Merced. "That's why I called this behavior judgment. It was as if, within the locality of my apparatus, nature became *teleological*—that is, it acted as if it had will and purpose. There were singular instances of paradox resolution that didn't obey any statistical laws I had ever heard of, and they certainly weren't predictable by any standard mathematical means. They were, by definition, little miracles. And that's why, in the equations I developed to express this behavior, there is always a point where I wrote 'and a miracle happens here.'"

Merced called this method evolutionary calculus. Four years after publishing the Grand Unified Field Theory that linked all the known forces of nature, Merced's contemporaries openly pilloried him and he was kicked out of the two major associations of scientists of the day. Wocek fought a rearguard action at Bradbury and managed to save Merced's position there. Merced was too engrossed in his research to take much notice of the brouhaha.

"I cannot tell you if the universe as a whole has any meaning," said Merced. "This may be fundamentally unknowable. But what I was seeing in my experiments was that the universe was *acting* as if it had meaning locally. After a while, I was forced to the conclusion that this wasn't just appearance. Individual gravitons were exercising judgment just as a person does. The universe is teleological locally. By *locally* I mean any distance that is contained between quantum-entangled particles that are pressed into complex time-related paradoxes. I would force these paradoxes on the gravitons, and it was as if they had a little town meeting and came to a decision about how to handle each paradox. These decisions were never precisely the same, but all had the general *tendency* of preserving reality as we know it. From there it was only a short step to reasoning that one aspect of the 'judgment' property was that it brought about instant information transfer at a distance. After continued work, I discovered that I could influence what this information would be, and

I could cause the gravitons to carry messages that I wanted. I discovered a number that acted as a sort of code key of time. This is what I called the Teleological Constant. If you know the Teleological Constant, you could send and receive information instantaneously over great distances—as far, in fact, as you chose to separate two entities that you originally observed to be entangled on a quantum level."

This instantaneous transfer of information is what we call the Merced Effect.

Merced was thirty-five years old by this time. His experiences with the scientific establishment had left him extremely leery. He chose to publish the results of his experiments in his friend Beat Myers's poetry journal, *Flare*. The November 2646 issue of *Flare* was almost wholly devoted to Merced's paper, which was interspersed with poetry by Myers and others in the *Flare* generation. During his life, Merced always insisted that reprints of his paper, "The Teleological Constant and its Relation to Instantaneous Information Transfer at a Distance," be printed with the poems included.

The November *Flare* did not make much of an impact at first. Merced continued his work, and by that time had several graduate assistants under him. One of them was a brilliant young nanotechnological engineer who had been raised in an orphanage in the asteroid belt. His name was Feur Otto Bring. Bring was an incurable victim of Tourette's syndrome, and conversations between Merced and Bring would often consist of Merced patiently explaining a problem to Bring, followed by Bring swearing uncontrollably at Merced. Then, usually within days, Bring would have the engineering solution or the apparatus that Merced had envisioned.

One day in 2648, Merced casually suggested to Bring that it ought to be possible to invent a nanotech time machine that incorporated his Josephson-Feynman setup and that, if such nano were properly disseminated, there could be instant information shared over whatever distance the nano covered. Bring is reported to have stormed from the room shouting, "Fuck! Fuck! Fuck you, cock-sucker!"

Within a week, he and Merced had designed and created such a thing. With little modification, that design is still with us, permeating all our lives. It was the design of what we now know as grist.

Fourteen

Danis looked over the numbers and felt a bit of disappointment of her own. When Kelly had first come up with the crazy idea of shorting all their assets, along with Teleman Milt's, Danis had worried about the chance—small, but present—that he might be wrong.

"So," she said, "my little pi-minus option was a wild-goose chase."

Kelly was extremely quiet for a moment, and then he said, almost in a whisper, "What?"

"I took an option out on pi meson production, the kind that are made of a down and anti-up quark pair."

"I know what a pi-minus particle is," said Kelly in a preternaturally calm voice. As if he is trying to hold his breath, Danis thought. As if he is deathly afraid of what he is going to hear next.

"I figured, just in case you were wrong . . . I mean, in case there was a general slide, but then a sudden correction. Pions are so hard to make independently, and they're impossible to store, you know. They are essential in isotope instantiation. There would have to be a major shortage for a few minutes, even allowing for relativistic effects. I timed it all out to four minutes and took out the option. But all that's moot. You were right, of course."

"You took out a time option?"

"Yes, Kelly. There's no reason to be angry with me. I lost my money, but—"

"I'm not angry."

"I just thought I had . . . an intuition about it. A gut feeling."

"Danis," Kelly said, still in his frighteningly calm voice, "check to see if the option has a Section C rider."

She performed the necessary check perfunctorily, but it was a standard contract, and she knew what she would find before she looked.

"Of course it has a Section C."

"A dearth clause."

"That's what a section C *is,* Kelly."

"C stands for 'convert,' Danis."

"Yes, I—"

"Read the wording."

She read it again. And again. And then she understood what her husband was driving at.

In the event that the issuing entities shall be unable to carry out the actuarial functions for the completion of this contract, the purchaser shall provide said functions or shall cause said functions to be performed by a proxy agent as specified by Unified Banking Code IV-A subsection 84. Absent a proxy, purchaser is responsible for final tally and related items under paragraph five, above.

"But Teleman Milt is my proxy agency, and I bought the damn things from the Ferro Group—"

"Which is now a member of Teleman Milt, Danis. The first thing the old man will have done is bought up the competition."

"So my issuer and proxy tabulator are the same entity."

"That's not allowed by law. You have to abandon your proxy account holder in that circumstance, and do all the final accounting yourself. Some party with your interests in mind has to independently verify the contract's completion. If the entity that you bought it from is the same one that loaned you the money—"

"That leaves only me."

"If it were a regular person, with an aspect and convert portion, he would have to loan out his virtual side until the accounting was done."

"But that kind of number crunching normally requires a convert like the Abacus. It would take *me* days."

"And you *can't* loan out your convert. You *are* a convert, and nothing else."

"It will take me days," Danis said again.

"They can legally hold you in the Met until the terms of the contract are completed."

"Kelly . . . you don't think . . ."

"I think that the first thing the Department of Immunity is going to do is round up all the free converts by any means necessary. It's probably already happening."

"It will take me days," said Danis. "I'm not made for that kind of arithmetic."

"We have a big problem, Danis."

They can hold me in the Met, Danis thought. They can separate me from my children.

"Why?" Kelly said. His voice was almost a sob. "Why did you do that, Danis?"

"I didn't believe," she replied. Something like a buzz was developing in her thoughts. Like a nest of bees that has been disturbed. Like an electric short in a closet full of fuses. "I didn't believe it could possibly get as bad as you said it would, and I wanted a little protection, just in case you were wrong. It's what we do at work, after all. Arbitrage. We always hedge our bets."

"Except when extreme measures are called for," said Kelly. "Then there aren't any rules you can count on."

"I . . . acted like a computer program," Danis said. "Garbage in, garbage out."

"It doesn't matter now," Kelly replied. "We have to figure out what to do next."

They are going to take me from my children, Danis thought. It was all she could think, over and over again. They are going to take me from my Aubry and Sint.

She looked at the two of them. Aubry was playing the

old game of paper, rock, and scissors to keep Sint amused,
now that he had no enigma box.

I'm a pair of scissors, thought Danis, and my opponent
is a rock.

Ready to crush the scissors.

They're going to take me away from my children.

Fifteen

from
Old Left-handed Time
Raphael Merced and the Genesis of the Merced Effect
a short history
by Andre Sud, D. Div.
Triton

Raphael Merced's later years marked the steady acceptance of his ideas. Bring and others worked out the manufacturing sequences for grist. On Merced's fiftieth birthday, the then Martian government approved the dissemination of grist over all human-made surfaces on the planet. The similarities between this interconnected grist and virtual reality of computing entities had long been seen. But there was a visceral, physical quality to the "grist web." It came to be viewed as the fusion of actuality and virtuality. Today it interconnects all human spaces in the solar system, and is known, collectively, as the *merci*. The name is derived, of course, from Merced.

Merced turned his attention from scientific study proper to aesthetics. His correspondence with Myers grew more intense as he sought to somehow systematize a theory of beauty. In the meantime, Myers was running into trouble with the authorities on Mercury. These were the years of the Endowment government there, with its official goal of creating a renaissance. At first, thousands of artists of various sorts had flocked to the planet, convinced that a new utopia was at hand. But the Endowment Committee was quickly taken over by an elite class who formed the so-called Dowager Way and, far from encouraging other artists, the Committee began a series of pogroms that led to Myers's imprisonment, on grounds that his work was ugly, irrelevant, and a corrupting influence on higher expression.

Merced, now in his eighties (and, remember, this was in the days before grist regeneration of the human body had been perfected) journeyed to Mercury and staged a protest. He was shortly joined by his sister, Clara, who was ninety at the time. Using grist specially designed by researchers at Feur Otto Bring's factory on Mars, Clara and Raphael Merced picked out a suitable spot near the Mercurian North Pole and created, in a matter of hours, what has been described as the biggest middle finger in the known universe. The structure was as long as Earth's Grand Canyon, and as wide as Earth's Italian peninsula. Seen from space, there was no doubt what it represented.

This gigantic "fuck you" symbol was engineered to self-destruct within a year as the other "fingers" of the enormous hand spread out to form an open palm, and then dissolved into the underlying, still-preserved terrain. Merced, however, saw no reason to mention to the Endowment authorities the fact that the symbol would eventually disappear. The Endowment government was enraged. Merced was immediately arrested, along with Clara. Two months later, the Merceds, Myers, and twenty-seven other Mercurian contributors to *Flare* were given a trial and found guilty of gross aesthetic injustices against humankind. They were placed on a small spacecraft and set on an orbit around the sun, officially cut off from all communication with the rest of the human race. Since the Endowment could only enforce its sentence on Mercury, it set the orbit of the exile craft to be within the confines of Mercury's own orbit about the sun.

But Merced's body was now wholly interpenetrated by grist and, unknown to the Mercurian authorities, he was able to communicate with Bring back on Mars. A rescue mission was arranged.

Before the rescue ship could arrive, however, the exile craft experienced a malfunction, probably caused by the degenerated state of Endowment engineering skills. Within minutes, the exile craft began to plunge into the sun. The occupants tried several fixes, but nothing worked. With about an hour to go, they resigned themselves to their fate. They found that, with a limited maneuvering capability still remaining, they would be able to choose where in the sun they would fall.

"We're going in at a sunspot near the north pole," Merced said to the rescue ship's captain, Feur Otto Bring's daughter, Katya. "We're doing this because we think it might be cooler."

Over the next hour, the occupants of the exile ship kept up a running commentary with Katya Bring. The record of this communication is known as the *Exiles' Journey*. It has long been available on the merci. In it, Myers recites several spontaneous poems, including his "Old Left-handed Time," which has become one of the classics of human literature. Clara Merced makes a moving good-bye to her children and grandchildren. Several of the other poets and artists on board left important records of various sorts.

Raphael Merced was, himself, quiet for the first fifteen minutes. After that, he made a series of aphoristic comments which some have taken to be poems, and others have taken to be seeds for future scientific research. These are now known as the "Merced Synthetics." The final comment Merced made, as the exile ship was burning around him, had to do with his own quantum gravitational theory.

"I have been thinking," said Merced, "that I was a bit mistaken about time. Don't have the opportunity to go into the details just now, but I might suggest that somebody one of these days have a look at that big F in my equation. It might be possible to rearrange things in the past more to our liking. As a matter of fact, I do believe that I've seen signs that somebody is already doing that. I only hope to God that whoever is doing so has discovered the human equivalent of that unique property of my little gravitons. Whoever you are, up there in the future, for goodness sake, make sure you use a bit of *judgment*."

And with those words, Raphael Merced plunged into the sun and was lost.

Sixteen

"Quite a sight, eh Ted?" Roger Sherman said, but only to himself.

Sherman reeled in the two-hundred-nineteen-thousand-mile-long cable that had stretched, just hours ago, from the moon Triton down into the Blue Eye of Neptune. He wasn't really reeling it in, of course, but steadily deinstantiating it, simultaneously pulling it down and disassembling it on a molecular level. The buckyball components were broken down to elements and stable compounds, and stored in a room no bigger than a house. The cable, while several hundred thousand miles long, had the diameter of a straight pin.

Far above, the weather-station packet came into view, white against the dark blue nitrogen sky. The weather station, at the tail end of Sherman's cable, had entered Triton's gravity well several minutes ago and deployed its parasail when the air became thick enough. Now Sherman was guiding it in like a big kite. In another half hour, he had it down and secure.

Sherman was not normally in charge of bringing in the weather probe, but he did it on occasion—and, at the moment, all of his troops were on full defensive alert.

Besides, he enjoyed the solitude that reeling in the weather station provided. It seemed that all of his time for the last few weeks had been spent in frantic preparations. He needed time to think.

With practiced ease, Sherman shifted his attention into virtual and examined the data in the macro station. One by one his collection algorithms, all free-convert recruits, reported in with a crisp regularity.

"Surface winds at two hundred forty-two knots, Colonel," said Corporal Anometer.

"Noted," Sherman replied, and shunted the information to Major Theory, his free-convert personal adjutant. He treated all the virtual entities with strict formality, as he would any group of soldiers.

The stars were out, as they always were, and the sun was hardly brighter than the moon on Earth. Triton was thirty times farther from the sun than was Earth. What dominated the sky at the moment was Neptune itself, setting in the west. Of all the moons in the solar system, Triton was the only major one to orbit its planet in a retrograde direction. Neptune rotated on its axis in the other direction, so that its waxing and waning in the sky was directly contrary to that of Earth's moon. Most people on Triton didn't notice the weird way Neptune's phases changed in comparison with other planets when seen from their moons, but such things were part of Sherman's job. The thin rings of the planet were barely visible at this angle as twinkling lines that seemed to rise directly out of Miranda Canyon. The Army weather station, and the settlement of Miranda, were perched on the canyon's edge. New Miranda, a century old now, had been pioneered by refugees from the failure of the biocity on Uranus's moon, Miranda.

Uranus's Miranda had an enormous canyon that was more than twelve miles deep—as deep as the deepest oceans on Earth. Triton's Miranda namesake was more like a shallow gully in comparison.

But New Miranda was a far bigger town than the habitat on Miranda had ever been. Uranus had remained, over the decades, a rather backward planetary system. The Neptune area, in comparison, was positively thriving these days. This was due to the difference in the planet that Triton circled. Uranus was a cold world, with a dead core. Neptune, on the other hand, was hotter than hell at the bottom of its atmosphere. Like Jupiter, Neptune was a failed sun, and there was still a residue of fission taking place down there in the great rift valleys that bisected the core's surface. It was this spontaneous fission and the general radioactivity of the core that powered the storm that swept the atmosphere, particularly the Blue Eye that hovered over the equator, never blinking. And within that Blue Eye, the New Miranda settlers had placed the Mill.

The Mill was just that, an enormous windmill consisting of two blades that turned with the swirl of the storm. The Mill, from blade tip to blade tip, was as long as the diameter of planet Earth. It was built on the same physical principles as the Met. In the center of the mill, operating in a manner not dissimilar to that of ancient hydroelectric turbines on Earth, was a generator that beamed a steady supply of microwave energy to a geosynchronous satellite stationed above it. And from that satellite, it was fed to Triton.

Neptune set, and Sherman prepared himself to review his brigade, such as it was. The Third Sky and Light was a motley assortment of outer-system malcontents, hometown rejects, and Met outcasts. When he'd taken the post ten years before, discipline had been nonexistent, regulations were routinely disregarded to the point of genuine danger to the troops themselves, and morale was lower than he'd ever seen among any group of men and women. Since then, things had improved to some extent.

They call me the Old Crow, Sherman thought. It was difficult to imagine that this was a term of affection.

All in all, Sherman had about seven hundred soldiers under him on Triton, with a reserve unit of another seven hundred attached. Their main assignment was to protect and preserve the Mill. The Mill itself was not a Corps of Engineers project, but Sherman had had a vital role in getting the thing up and running. In fact, Sherman hated the idea of a Corps of Engineers. He hated all specialty divisions. In the Third Sky and Light, all traditional arrangements stopped at the company. Sherman maintained group loyalty and morale by developing a mentor chain, with each soldier immediately responsible for two recruits as soon as he himself was fully trained.

Sherman had come up with the idea of the mentor chain while serving as a captain on Mars. Before Amés and his Department of Immunity had driven the old Met Army to the outer system, the Federal had played an important role in fighting terrorism and keeping incipient tribalism and nationalism to a mild blaze. He'd been a captain for nearly sixty years and had watched three terrorist groups form under his nose, all from splinter groups from the '63 Conjubilation. Sherman, himself, had Free Integrationist leanings, but no one had a right to use violence and killing to bring about their particular brand of politics.

Nevertheless, one of the groups, calling itself FUSE (the acronym meant something like *Mars for Martians* in Norwegian) had staged a series of remarkably successful grist-based attacks on Met-wide companies with headquarters on Mars. The Army had one miserable failure after another in trying to stop them. Finally, Sherman had been assigned the task. He'd immediately seen that the problem was co-ordinating intelligence information with guard and attack functions and, after an embarrassing meltdown of the Werther Travel Complex in Marineris Valley, he had broken up all his platoons and rearranged them ad hoc with the idea that each soldier must also be a fully trained intelligence specialist. FUSE was notoriously riddled with information leaks (they had a site on the merci, for Christ's sake), and in short order Sherman's D Company had shut FUSE down by anticipating their every move and being there before them. After that success, Sherman was promoted and transferred to West Point to study organizational theory and to teach two classes a week to the plebes. It was a fine way to reward him and, at the same time, avoid implementing any of the changes he had worked out.

This evening, Captain Quench would brief him on Company A, and Sherman would select a "primary" to look in on. He pulled on his dress jacket, made a final check on the weather station, and instructed Major Monitor to take command. Monitor, an old convert who was nearing three centuries of service, gave his customary two point clicks in the indigo spectrum of the room's lighting as acknowledgment. It was old school, from before converts could speak with pleasant voices. With the weather station taken care of, Sherman opened the door and stepped into Triton's nitrogen night.

Sherman, along with most of the long-term residents of Triton, was nitrogen-adapted. An Earthman looking at him would notice a peculiar mottle to his skin. It was the molecular equivalent of long underwear and a pressure suit. After over seven centuries of trying, humanity had finally seen the idiocy (and the danger) of attempting to terraform the various heavenly bodies in the solar system. It was much more cost-effective to "Trita-form" a man than to try to make the little moon into Earth. Being Triton-adapted made for an extremely tough human being. Only the completely space-adapted were more resilient. A great many of Sherman's soldiers were space-adapted. They came from even farther out.

Sherman walked from the weather station to staff HQ along a worn path in the pebbly ground. Most of this region around Miranda Canyon was a combination of rock and frozen methane slush. The ground had a mushy consistency, like the sides of a volcano covered with snow back on Earth. Even in the thin atmosphere, each of Sherman's footsteps produced an audible crunch.

The Triton temperature could get down to thirty-eight degrees Kelvin, which was −390 Fahrenheit. This was another reason New Miranda was growing. You could put a simple substance in the shade here, and it would become a superconductor. At the average temperatures and pressure on Triton, the nitrogen atmosphere hovered around its solid-gas-liquid triple point, and occasionally conditions would be right for the formation of the famous nitrogen rains. Triton was easily the coldest inhabited place in the solar system. Even Pluto, built on different geology, was warmer by a little.

Staff HQ had an airlock, since not all of Sherman's soldiers were adapted to Triton's rigors, and even those who were functioned better in an e-mix of gases.

The grist opened one portal and closed the other briskly

as Sherman stepped through. Captain Quench was waiting at the situations table, engrossed in some problem on the knit. He noted Sherman's arrival, took a moment to disengage, then stood up and saluted. Sherman nodded, and Quench quickly finished up what he was doing. Quench had been one of Sherman's best pupils at the Point, and Sherman liked to watch him at his work. Quench was efficient in a kind of intuitive way that was different from Sherman's thoroughness. He was ambitious, and a natural leader. He had also, once, been a woman, and, he claimed, would be one again when he got promoted. Quench had a theory that women were better lieutenants, men better captains, and women better majors. He hadn't ventured any speculation, at least in Sherman's presence, as to the best makeup of the higher ranks.

All of Sherman's other officers were doing on-site supervision, and the room was empty except for Quench and Theory, who was now ensconced in the grist of the situation table.

"We've almost completed laying the Mill minefield, sir," Quench reported. "Another two e-days, and stage one will be over. That relay is surrounded by a nest of hornets."

"Very good," Sherman replied. "Who have you got doing it?"

"Two units, one of them under Peoples, and the other is Ki's calibration primary."

"All right, Captain. Let's have a look at that calibration unit." Sherman walked to the grist-rich table and put his hands upon it, instructing his pellicle to make a physical link for both quantum and e-m transmission.

"Follow me, sir," said Quench, and both men attuned themselves to the knit and entered full virtuality. Instantly, Sherman found himself (that is, an iconic representation of himself as an oak leaf cluster) floating in space next to Quench's iconic captain's bars. They were actually inhabiting the grist of the command pod that followed Lieutenant Ki around as she went about her tasks. The pod notified Ki that she was being observed, and she reported in.

"I've got the outer-periphery nukes ready to go," she told them. "What's taking time is working with the sentient units nearer to the relay satellite to tailor their bursts so that the satellite won't be damaged."

"Let's see what you've got," Sherman said. She showed Sherman the array she'd worked out, with the smarter explosives nearer to the center.

"Lieutenant, I want you to change those interior layouts," Sherman said.

"Sir?"

"We haven't got time to deploy and calibrate an entire core of sentients. I want you to layer them like an onion."

"An onion, sir?"

"It's a vegetable, Lieutenant."

"Yes, sir. It's a vegetable."

"I want several layers of sentients spaced apart. Then set them to teaching the intervening layers, one mine at a time."

"But that will take much longer than calibration, Colonel."

"But not longer than deployment. We need this minefield up and running *yesterday*."

To Sherman's pleasure, Ki did not ask him what the reason was for the hurry. She merely replied, "Yes sir."

"I want to have every crucial place or process in this system at least minimally protected in *forty-eight hours*."

"Forty-eight *hours*?" said Quench. "Sir."

"There are Met ships crossing the asteroid belt," Sherman replied, "closing on Ganymede for 'taxation enforcement.' In case you have forgotten, the Interlocking Directorate doesn't like us, and they are not going to let us alone."

"Yes, sir," Quench answered brightly. "They sure as hell are not going to let us alone, sir."

"So you think we're going to war, Colonel?" Ki asked.

"I think we already are at war," Sherman replied. "We just don't know it yet."

Seventeen

from
Quatermain's Guide
The Advantages of the Strong Force
A Guide to and History of the Met
by Leo Y. Sherman

Introducing the Met

The Met is the system of space cables, tethers, planetary lifts along with all the associate bolsas, sacs, armatures, and dendrites that comprise the human inhabited space of the inner solar system. The Met, at its widest, extends 186,000,000 miles from the sun, but it is far bigger than that in actuality. It has been calculated that if all the cables of the Met were laid end to end, they would reach out of the solar system and another AU or so (the distance from the sun to the Earth) toward Alpha Centauri. While the Met is long, it is thin. None of the space cables averages more than a kilometer in diameter. When seen from a vantage point above the planetary ecliptic near the asteroid belt, the Met shines like a spiderweb, wet with dewdrops, hanging in space between the wheeling planets.

Eighteen

By the time Claude Schlencker was eight years old, he had come to despise Shakespeare. First, there was the smell of the must and mold on the pages of his father's *Complete Works*. It had gotten wet sometime during the move, and was three e-months in a trunk before being unpacked. The dank atmosphere of Polbo Armature didn't help matters either. The family's two-room flat constantly leaked, and the humidity controls had long since given up the ghost. And if you didn't have humidity control in Polbo, you sweated like a pig all year long. The armature was an agricultural complex, and the atmosphere was determined by the needs of the plants, and not the humans who tended them. Of course, the more affluent could afford to have their bodies adapted to take into account the heat and the constant hanging mist. Claude's family was, to say the least, not among the more affluent. His mother was a quality-control monitor at the workstation, and his father was a trimmer—one of the humans who must still be employed to cut off the lower leaves of vegetable seedlings in the greenhouses. It was not a job for a robot, and besides, a robot would get bored with it.

Delmore Schlencker was not bored with his job, he was furious at it, and at his life in general, including his wife and son. The Met was just being constructed, and he'd left Earth determined to make something of himself on the

newly forming Mars-Earth Diaphany. He'd taught literature in junior college for a year until he'd lost his job because of (he claimed) cutbacks and faculty politics. There
had been no help forthcoming from his family (Claude's
grandfather, whom he'd never met, was a policeman somewhere in Europe—the details were unclear), and Delmore
had had to take whatever work he could find. He'd met
Claude's mother, Janey Beth, when she corrected one of his
mistakes at the greenhouse. The baby had quickly followed,
and Delmore, now in his late thirties, was stuck, stuck,
stuck.

For him, Claude was both the cause of all his problems
and his only hope for some escape.

Each night, from the time the boy was six, Delmore had
had him deliver lines from Shakespeare while he, Delmore,
drank himself to sleep. Despite his drunken state, Delmore
had a near-perfect recall of the lines of the plays, and when
young Claude made a mistake, well then the boy must be
made to learn the lines.

Claude remembered one night in particular when his
father had gotten a new bottle of real whiskey from the
liquor store in the habitat and had polished off two-thirds
of it in an hour and a half. Claude was delivering the Joan
of Arc monologue from *Henry VI, Part 1*. His father insisted that he only learn the female's parts entire, since that
was the way young actors in the bard's own time came to
the stage. Boys were women, until they earned their dramatic stripes, and then they were allowed to play men. In
the play, Joan was meeting with the Duke of Burgundy to
try to win him back to the French cause (he had been sid-
ing with the English). All this meant next to nothing to
young Claude, but he dutifully remembered the facts as
well as he could. Once he had been beaten even after delivering a faultless scene because he later could not explain
what it all meant.

"Besides, all French and France exclaims on thee,"
Claude said, having reached the point in the monologue
where Joan is appealing to Burgundy's patriotism. "Doubt-
ing thy birth and lawful proficiency—"

And with that mistake, substituting *proficiency* for the correct *progeny,* something inside Delmore seemed to have broken open, like a swollen wound that suddenly splits and spills out its cankerous fluid. Claude later reasoned that it was not the mistake, but the words, which set off his father. Delmore had often doubted Janey Beth's claim that Claude was actually his, and not the son of another worker whom his mother had occasionally seen. Claude never found out this other man's name, but he liked to imagine that the story was true, even though, in his own squat form and round face, he bore a striking resemblance to Delmore.

Delmore suddenly rose from his chair and loomed over Claude. For a moment, Claude didn't realize what was happening, that he had made a mistake.

"Progeny," Claude said in a low voice.

"Progeny!" his father screamed. Claude immediately covered his head with his hands. There was nowhere to run. His father locked the door. It was probably his hands over his face that prevented Claude from being immediately knocked unconscious by his father's blow. Delmore had struck him with the butt end of the whiskey bottle. Claude reeled, and his father hit him again on the shoulders. The bottle broke against Claude's shoulder blade, and the jagged glass cut into his back. The remainder of the whiskey spilled into the wound and burned like fire. Claude sank to the floor, whimpering, and this angered Delmore even more.

"Get up," he called to his son. "Be a fucking man, for the love of God." When Claude failed to respond, Delmore kicked him, laying him out flat on the bare concrete floor of the flat.

"Shit, shit," he heard Delmore grumbling, and he risked a peek to see that his father was examining the ruins of the bottle. "Fucking glass," his father said. "It's made of fucking gristless glass."

Delmore reached down and pulled Claude up by his hair. He held the boy between his knees and put the broken whiskey bottle in front of Claude's face, inches from his eyes. "See what you did?" Delmore said. "See what you did, you little bastard."

And then Delmore had torn Claude's shirt from his torso. Still holding the boy firmly between his legs, he spun Claude around so that his back was to his father. Then, using the sharp edge of the bottle, Delmore began to carve into his son's back. In all, he made nine score-marks upon Claude, each time pressing a little harder, cutting a little deeper. And with each pass of the bottle, he spoke the word *progeny,* as if he were a patient teacher and Claude was a difficult student for whom he only wanted the best.

Finally, it was over. But it wasn't. Delmore made his son once more stand before him and recite from start to finish the speech of Joan of Arc to Burgundy. Claude concentrated. He concentrated as hard as he ever had on anything in his life.

And, it was as if a cold breeze passed through him. As if the flat were air-conditioned and its air dried. Claude's hands, bunched into fists, uncurled. And the words came— all of them. He delivered the monologue flawlessly.

After that, Claude seldom made mistakes when memorizing or delivering Shakespeare, and his father beat him for other reasons. But he had discovered something that night, something that would always stay with him. It was a power of concentration. After that, no matter how bad the circumstances became, Claude never panicked or forgot anything. He concentrated. And the cool, dry air would course through him, and he would be able to perform whatever he was called upon to do.

Claude did not tell his mother about the cuts on his back the next day. He knew what she would say: "Why, Claude, what did you do to yourself?" And it was about a year later that he woke up one morning to find that his mother was gone. She had left the armature, and it wasn't until many years later that Claude knew what had become of her. He was left under the tender ministrations of his father until he was fifteen years old. By that time, Claude had learned Shakespeare backwards and forwards, including the sonnets.

When Claude turned ten, his father got him an after-school job working the greenhouse, trimming leaves alongside Delmore. With his smaller hands, Claude was faster and more accurate than his father, but he always took care to work at the same pace, and never to outdistance him. Delmore kept Claude's wages and gave the boy an allowance, which he was constantly cutting off for weeks at a time as punishment. At such times, Delmore would blame the withheld money on a computer foul-up.

"It looks like those computers hate you," his father would say to Claude. "I wish I could do something about it, but my hands are tied."

Claude imagined the "computers" as small imps who burned his money and bathed in the flames. The image had come from one of the books Claude had read in the school library. He could not bring such "trash" literature home, but he found that he could devour an entire book, if it was of a medium length, just in the library period he was given at school. He was, of course, proficient at remembering the details. Claude knew what real computers were, and how to use them. But by the time he was eleven, they began to disappear, and Claude was given lessons at school on how to interact with a new kind of computer, which wasn't really a computer at all. You kind of "thought" your way into it, and, instead of you working on it, in a way, it worked on you. At least, that is the way Claude began to picture it. It wasn't until several e-years later that his new kind of computer began to be called the grist.

Claude liked this new way of doing things very well, and his teachers told him that he had a special talent for it. One of his teachers, Mrs. Ridgeway, even put him into a special program, and soon Claude was writing his own simple computer programs. At first, he only made pretty displays and cool-looking rooms that he could explore. But soon he began to write programs that would do things around the classroom. Usually these were simple tasks such as collecting and distributing papers and tests. He always wrote programs to please his teachers—particularly Mrs. Ridgeway—and never his fellow students. Claude didn't get along with most of the other children in his classes. In fact, he often felt that he hated them for taking time with the teachers away from him. He had been told that this was not a very good way to feel, but he couldn't help it. Sometimes, when no one was looking, he would pick out one of the students who was smaller and dumber than him and he would punish the other, just as he'd learned from his father. But he never did this to a smart kid, no matter how small the child was. If you were smart, you shouldn't get hit.

Claude didn't like math class very much. He was actually quite good at it, but his teacher was a decaying old man who had missed the horizon of the rejuvenation procedures in use in the day, and was growing old and feeble while those merely ten years his junior were going to live fifty more years. He took his disappointment out on his pupils, who, if predictions turned out correctly, might very well live to be two hundred e-years or more. He liked to assign his class extremely tedious operations for homework, some of which could not be solved even with the aid of computers unless they were extremely powerful calculators. One of these problems was to factor the product of the two largest prime numbers known to humanity (the students were forbidden to look up these primes). No one was expected to get the right answer, but everyone was expected to turn in a sheet of attempts that contained at least two hours' worth of work.

With his memorization and recitations, along with his part-time job at the greenhouse, Claude had no time to do his homework at home. He usually completed it in study hall at school. But this would take longer than the one hour the students were allowed in study hall. Claude had no idea what original prime numbers might be, but he was determined to avoid missing his Shakespeare at home and receiving a beating as the result. He decided he must somehow solve the problem using his computer skills.

Claude had read an introductory book on the grist in the library, where the basic principles of quantum computing were explained for the layman and the Merced Effect was described. Mrs. Ridgeway was covering some basic stuff in his Rationality class that Claude already knew, and he found his mind drifting to the problem of factoring the product of the primes, which was due tomorrow. His drifting turned to worry and his worry to anxiety. He imagined his father with the whiskey bottle, with his belt, with Claude's mother's old hairbrush. And then came the "air-conditioning" feeling. In that cool mental space, Claude realized what he ought to do to solve the problem.

That afternoon, after he finished his other homework, he set to work with the grist. He had learned that each molecule of grist was not a simple on and off switch, but was actually the end product of an infinite number of on and off switches. Mrs. Ridgeway had talked about an "original" computer and many virtual computers, like ghosts, doing calculations in many "possible worlds." Claude had decided that in one of those possible worlds, he, Claude had accidentally factored the number his math teacher had given him and gotten the right two prime numbers. While Claude had been creating "virtual rooms" with the grist, he'd occasionally had to make a light source. At first, he'd been stymied when he thought he had to program each photon of light that would come out of a lightbulb. But there was a helper program that used the photons exactly like Claude was considering using the factoring. You told it the pattern you wanted, and it calculated all the possible paths of light to give you a stream of light that was not just simulated and not-quite-right, as had been the old virtual reality, but was completely true to actuality. That was, in fact, actuality by another means. Claude saw that he could modify this program and give it the "pattern" he was looking for—two prime numbers. And, as it had with the light, the little program used the quantum physics of grist to do the work of infinite parallel processes. These processes Claude represented in one of his virtual rooms as a pattern of light on the floor. Just as with light, the wrong answers, those that didn't fit the pattern, canceled one another out. Charles watched as the two prime numbers he was after formed on the floor, as if they had been in the virtual room all along, but were now merely coming into focus. He wrote them down, then left the virtuality of the grist. Back in actuality, he had a whole speech from *Titus Andronicus* to memorize, and only fifteen minutes left of study hall.

Claude's math teacher was angry at him the next day. He accused Claude of having looked up the two biggest primes on the merci (although it was called the "Web" back then, and was a much different thing). Claude felt a bit chagrined because he had not thought of this obvious way to get around the problem. But he explained his method to his teacher, and the old man had to grudgingly admit that the boy was onto something. The next day, he mentioned Claude's solution to Mrs. Ridgeway. She mentioned it to the director of the school, and Claude knew he had a big problem. The school director wanted to call in Claude's father and discuss with him the possibility of enrolling Claude in a special school after he turned thirteen. Out of the armature. On Mercury.

The director of the school even thought that the prospect was important enough to make a personal visit to Claude's apartment, to visit his father.

Nineteen

The director of Claude's school was named Getty. He was
the son of the chief engineer in the armature and had
grown up with the Polbo Armature growing up around
him. He took a special interest in the social conditions of
the working poor in what he liked to think of as "his" bolsa.
He had been into some of the worst neighborhoods, working in his off hours on community projects and generally
making sure conditions were tolerable for all—water,
sewage, plenty of vegetables. Getty had always thought it a
scandal that many of the greenhouse workers regularly ate
processed pabulum imported to the Armature when the
place was crammed full of all the vitamins and minerals a
human body would ever need. He considered it his personal mission to make sure that everyone had the means to
eat right, and he was astounded that the "Vegetables for
People" campaign that he headed was not more successful
at changing bad habits. Getty considered it to be his mission to finish what his father had started, making the Polbo
Armature a clean, fresh, living, and growing space for all.

And so he was completely taken aback when he saw the
living space young Claude had been existing in. The flat
had not been cleaned in years and when, with a grunt, Delmore Schlencker waved Getty in and showed him to a
chair, Getty detected the distinct odor of rotting meat.
Getty, himself a macrobiotic vegetarian, shuddered at the

thought of the substance from which the smell must be rising. Nevertheless, he remembered himself and his purpose in coming. But he must get this over with as quickly as possible, or he was surely going to pass out from the stench. He quickly informed Schlencker of Claude's new option to study on Mercury.

"Sounds goddamn expensive," Schlencker had answered. "We have not got that kind of money. Unless you're thinking of getting me a raise?"

"There is a scholarship available," said Getty. He could feel his new somatic adaptations working under his skin, adjusting his body temperature so that the heat in the flat wouldn't cause him to break out into a sweat.

"There is, is there?" replied Schlencker. The man stood up—even standing, Schlencker was barely taller than was Getty sitting down. "Would you like a bit of wine?" he said.

Getty imagined the vile vintage the man probably had available. Something out of a carton. He shook his head "no."

"Well, then," said Schlencker, and left the room. He returned with a glass in his hand and with what Getty recognized as a very respectable Rhein white. It was cool from the refrigerator and was already forming a condensing sweat that ran over Schlencker's hand as he poured himself a glass. What was this man, living here, doing with such good wine? It didn't seem right to Getty. Like brie on a . . . a—Getty searched for an image from his youth, something common and bad—brie on a *hot dog*! That was what this man was. Getty suppressed a gag at the thought.

"You all right?" Schlencker asked him.

Getty took a deep breath. Mistake.

"I'm fine." He coughed. "Little something in my throat. Now about that scholarship . . ."

Schlencker took a sip of the wine, swirled it in his mouth, then swallowed it. Getty watched the man's Adam's apple bob as he swallowed, like a piece of detached gristle. He had to get out of this place!

"Well, we're just going to have to see what the boy says,"

Schlencker finally replied. "I'll have a talk with him tonight." Schlencker finished the remainder of his wine in one gulp. "He'll let you know in the morning what his decision is."

For the first time in a very long while, Claude missed a line from one of the sonnets that evening. He had heard Mr. Getty from the next room, and he was nervous as to what his father's decision would be. He never found out. When he flubbed the line, Delmore took to him with his belt. It hurt like hell, but this time Claude withstood it and did not cry.

Be a man. Justify your privilege of doing Caesar, of learning Lear.

Claude realized that he had been growing. He would soon be bigger than his father. Maybe that, too, was why the beating didn't hurt so much. It only took an hour or so for the stinging to subside enough for him to get to sleep.

In the morning, he informed Director Getty that he and his father had talked it over and they had decided that maybe the special school was not such a good idea right then. That he needed more time among his peers so that he would not get too big a head about his own importance. Getty, relieved that he would not have to deal with Delmore Schlencker anymore for the time being, accepted Claude's decision.

Twenty

For the next three e-years, Claude followed the same routine every day. Mrs. Ridgeway did her best to provide him with special instruction in programming, and the old math teacher, Hudo, died and was replaced by a young man who immediately saw Claude's potential and set him to studying calculus while the other students laboriously worked through algebra—something Claude had mastered quickly, and soon grown bored with. More and more, he felt himself to be a separate being from the other students. He made no real friends and only stayed out of fights because he was known to strike back with vicious abandon and a disregard for any rules of honor, as it was practiced among the boys.

Not only was he growing physically, his body was changing in other ways, as well. One day, while working in the greenhouse snipping at the plants, his fingers slipped and he sliced into his thumb. The pain was intense and exquisite and, much to his surprise, Claude felt something odd happen in his pants. When he went to the toilet to check himself, he found that a sticky liquid had encrusted his underwear. Claude had, of course, read about such stuff during library period, and was quite aware of what had happened. The *why* was a little puzzling.

"Well," he said to the toilet bowl, "I guess I'm a man now."

After a little experimentation, Claude found that it was not necessary for him to break the skin to make himself come. It was the pain that produced the pleasure, and pain could come in less visibly damaging forms. Following this discovery, Claude masturbated by jamming wooden splinters under his fingernails—he'd found this created maximum arousal in the most reproducible fashion—and only occasionally resorted to a burn or a puncture when he was, as it were, in the highest throes of passion.

By his fifteenth birthday, Claude was taller than his father by half a foot and outweighed him by a good ten pounds. Delmore was drinking more than ever, and the good Rhein wine and whiskey was a thing of the past. He bought his liquor wholesale from a moonshiner who worked in the greenhouse and had a still in one of the back rooms. Claude continued his Shakespeare, but he knew that the next time Delmore made to hit him, he would have a little surprise for his father. The thought of killing his father had become one of Claude's favorite fantasies, and he now carried an extendable knife with him whenever he went to recite the immortal lines of the bard before Delmore.

But Claude never got the chance. One evening, after they'd both come home from work, Delmore had gone into the bathroom, taking his bottle of liquor along with him. About five minutes later, Claude heard a cry.

"Oh shit, oh no!" screamed Delmore. Claude rushed into the bathroom to find his father on his knees, bent down by the toilet. The bowl of the toilet was bright red with arterial blood.

"I've busted a gut. Ah God, I'm ruined!" cried Delmore. Claude watched in fascination as his father crawled out of the bathroom and into the living room, leaving a trail of blood behind him.

"It's all coming out of my ass," his father moaned. "I'm bleeding out of my ass."

Delmore turned around three times in the living room, as if he were a dog preparing to lie down. Then he collapsed in a puddle of his own blood. After a moment, Claude bent down and felt no pulse in his father's neck.

Amazing, he thought. He sat down in one of the living-room chairs.

"No Shakespeare tonight," he said.

Claude thought about this fact for a while. And then he thought of all the nights in his life that would suddenly be empty of obligation. If he wanted them to be. He could do anything he wanted now, and no one could stop him.

Twenty-one

Roger Sherman knew something was terribly wrong when his ex-wife contacted him through the grist. They had not spoken in months.

"And to what do I owe this honor?" Sherman said. There was more acid in his voice than he had expected. The split had been his fault, after all. There was no way any woman with sense would have stayed with him during his black period ten e-years ago.

"I wouldn't bother you while you're on duty, Roger, but I think this may be important."

"What is it, Dahlia?"

"Something is happening at the hospital, and I wanted your input," Dahlia continued. With practiced ease, he let himself slip entirely into the virtuality so that he could talk to Dahlia face-to-face. Instantly he was a hovering presence in the New Miranda hospital emergency ward.

One of Dahlia's aspects was working near a bed where a raving woman was being strapped down by orderlies. Dahlia quickly laid a hand on the woman's head and—Sherman knew—sent tranquilizing algorithms swarming under the woman's skin and into her grist pellicle. This kind of direct grist-to-grist intervention was something only doctors were licensed to do in the outer system.

"More than fifty thousand bland camels through the needle of destiny," the woman screamed. "I saw it! I saw the brick fall!"

Then the tranquilizers began to take their effect.

"I saw it, I tell you." The woman's eyelids began to droop. "There isn't anybody who says that man can't cook . . ." And she was asleep.

"What is wrong with her, Dahlia?" Sherman said. Nobody in the hospital heard him, of course, since he wasn't really here. He was speaking convert-to-convert in the virtuality with his ex-wife. The bodily aspect that was an emergency-room doctor in the hospital continued to minister to her patient. There was lots more to Dahlia, besides—both here on Triton and elsewhere, on the moons of Jupiter. Sherman's ex-wife was a full-scale LAP, after all.

"I was hoping you could help me with that," Dahlia answered, a voice in his ear. "This is the fifteenth patient who has been brought in today with exactly these symptoms. Incoherent babbling. Partial loss of motor control."

"I still don't understand why you called me."

"These people's Broca grist is going haywire," Dahlia said. "It's a very rare condition."

"Have you ever seen it before?"

"Once—and that was a nano lab tech who got into some very bad grist. The etiology was quite clear."

Sherman turned his attention back to the patient. She was asleep now, but various muscles in her neck and jaw continued to twitch.

"Fifteen," Dahlia repeated. "Has something gotten loose from the military base?"

"What do you mean?"

"I'm talking about military grist, Roger."

For a moment, Sherman considered the possibility. But the safeguards at the base were rigid, and he made sure they were completely enforced. Suddenly, Sherman felt a great weariness descend upon him.

"Oh no."

"What did you say?"

"It's begun."

"What are you talking about, Roger."

"This is an attack."

"An attack?"

"From the Met, Dahlia."

"You can't be serious."

Sherman pulled himself partially from the virtuality. He gazed up into the dark blue Triton sky. "I'll have Major Theory send you all the information we have on this sort of weapon."

"A weapon? So it is military grist." Dahlia was now only a voice in Sherman's ear. She might as well have been on the other side of the solar system. I guess that was always the problem, Sherman thought. But then his mind turned to practical matters.

"I have to go."

"Roger, why would anyone do such a thing?"

"Communications warfare."

"Surely you're . . . exaggerating."

"Maybe so. Maybe it's a coincidence that the Broca grist of fifteen people went simultaneously haywire."

"Is there an antidote?"

"No."

"What?"

"No known antidote. Dahlia, I have to go."

"But Roger, it's your damned Army that—"

"I have to go."

He cut the connection. He supposed he'd angered and hurt her once again. There was too much to do to worry about that. He had given her the information she requested. That should be enough.

It had never been enough.

Twenty-two

Sherman took a hopper from the base and navigated his way through New Miranda by a series of leaps from one landing pad to another. The leap pads were laid out in a seemingly erratic order, but Sherman was familiar with them and knew the best pattern to get himself home quickly.

New Miranda was a city of spires. The neo-Gothic religious leanings of the first settlers had combined with the low gravity of their new world to produce an architecture that was unique and, at times, breathtaking. There were some apartment buildings here and there, but for the most part each resident on Triton had his or her own spire, that is, families and familiar units did. There was plenty of space, and the power from the Mill produced an abundance of energy to power construction grist, which was the simplest and most efficient nano in the first place.

In most of the spires, the first five floors were fully pressurized and protected. They were usually given over to gardens and fountains. New Miranda billed itself as the "Garden City," and there was a friendly competition among the more affluent residents in that regard. Of course, this led to a few aesthetic horrors. But there was a professional class of elite gardeners who were strongly influenced by the Greentree priest (and gardener) Father Capability, and many of the gardens were justly regarded as works of art. These were another tourist attraction on Triton, along with the nitrogen rains outside.

We seem to like going to extremes, Sherman thought as he completed another bounce in his hopper. Above the fifth floors was where most of the citizenry lived. These quarters could rise up for many hundreds of feet, and it wasn't uncommon for a spire to have thirty or more floors, although the people normally lived in only a small portion of it. The spires were lit from the ground, and there were lights in a few windows. Once or twice a year, ice vulcanism near the south pole produced geysers of carbon ash that shot up into the atmosphere for miles. The ash was carried toward the equator as a thin, black dust. The bottoms of the spires were gray or white, but their tips were always coated with a matte black ash, as if they were great pens that had been dipped in a graphite ink. Even with the twinkling lights here and there, from above, New Miranda appeared rather ominous. The streets were barely bigger than sidewalks. Everyone traveled by hopper, or stayed at home and traveled through the grist.

With eleven bounces, Sherman was home. His final bounce was extremely precise (with calculations handled by his convert portion) and landed him, with a small attitude correction, on a small pad extended from the side of his and Dahlia's spire. Even though it was more of a tower, Sherman still thought of it as "the house."

Sherman lived on the thirty-third to the thirty-fifth floors. The truth was, he confined himself to a couple of rooms on floor thirty-four. Sherman had spent the last ten years as a bachelor, and every year he seemed to require less personal space. But, on Triton, every citizen of a certain standing was required to keep up a garden. What had once been civic duty had become a pleasure to Sherman, thanks to his friendship with Andre Sud, who had been tending Sherman's garden until he'd gone on sabbatical over a year ago. Sherman's garden was on the first five floors, and it was considered one of the prime gardens on Triton—at least it *had* been when Andre was the gardener. Lately it had been going to seed. The priest whom Andre had gotten to replace himself, while a nice woman, just didn't have Andre's genius.

A small airlock was in place between the house and the landing pad. Sherman entered the e-mix of his home, went to the kitchen, and poured himself a glass of Merlot.

He took a sip, considered the glass. He finished off the rest of the wine in one gulp, then shunted into the virtuality.

Tonight was the New Miranda Town Meet—called into emergency session by the mayor. Sherman had a hell of a report to deliver.

They weren't going to like it.

The New Miranda Town Meet occurred nightly—that is, every Tritonian night, which lasted two and three-quarter e-days. The mayor and chief recorder were the only people who must be physically present in some form, and the rest, like Sherman, attended in the virtuality. The virtuality was crowded and smoke-filled. There was an air of tension owing to the emergency nature of tonight's session, but this did not keep the local politicians from their usual pleasantries and rituals. Somehow this provided a bit of comfort to Sherman. No matter what happened, he could never imagine these undisciplined outer-system democrats turning into the toadies who served Amés's Interlocking Directorate.

He had timed his entrance to avoid some of the preliminaries, and he popped in just as the discussion was turning toward external affairs—and the coming confrontation with the Met. He was on the right-hand side of the Free Integrationist section, in his customary hard-backed chair.

"I might add," continued the current speaker, "that there are good reasons to pay the information tariffs, even if they are not just, at the base."

Sherman leaned so that he could look around the tall man who sat in front of him and saw that the speaker in the well was Shelet Den, a member of the Motoserra Club. The Club members could all trace their ancestry back to Uranus's Miranda, and some of them went back to the original Argentine commune whence the Miranda settlement had originally come.

A chorus of disapproval rose from the Free Integrationists, and others, but Den bulled onward.

"Those of us who have been around these parts a bit longer, those who have more of a stake in this fair moon, are able to realize that there are times when you have to *go along* to get along. The Met buys our goods and, I might argue, selling them power and semi-ore is, in a way, a tax upon *them*. After all, no one truly has a right to the bounty of nature. It should be enjoyed by all."

What an amazing cookery of logic, Sherman reflected. He hadn't imagined that Motoserra aristocratic communalism might be used to justify a fifty-five percent tax on all prime-rated merci events and shows.

"Why don't we just give them our lovers, too!" shouted a Free Integrationist wag. "Give 'em your wife, Shelet! Share and share alike."

"I am merely saying—" But a bell sounded, and Den's time was, mercifully, up. Someone passed Sherman a cigar, and he dutifully fired it up.

The next speaker was a Free Integrationist, and Sherman felt a glimmer of hope—which, upon seeing who the speaker was, quickly died. Mallarmé de Ronsard was F.I., true, but he was also a cross member of the local tribe of Neo-Flare poets, the Eighth Chakra. Although most people choose to represent themselves in the virtuality with the same face they had in actuality, one could, of course, choose anything. De Ronsard manifested himself as a burst of shining golden light outlined with a red corona. In the center of the light was a black hole in the shape of a heart.

"I should like to begin tonight with a poem I wrote expressing our solidarity with our free-convert brothers and sisters and against the tyranny of a law that keeps them enchained. Ahem."

De Ronsard proceeded to recite a poem:

"Freedom, writhing like the tendrils of the dawn
  Burns this pale coating of skin,
  This rubber of concealment,
  From our frame of reason, and we stand

Revealed.
Under the skin we are one,
And we shall rise with the dawn
Of new hope, new light, together,
And shall, hand in hand,
Show the very sun a thing or two
About brightness.
And blind those—"

Here, de Ronsard became more agitated and the golden light turned bright yellow.

"—Blind those who oppress our choice by the rays of light,
The particles of hope,
Bursting forth from our own eyes.
Bursting with this new dawn
Of freedom!"

De Ronsard paused, and Sherman fought an urge to sneeze. All that talk of the sun, perhaps, combined with de Ronsard's iconic presence.

"Freedom is the destiny of every sentient being," de Ronsard continued. "Be they flesh. Or be they algorithmic. Be they anything that lives and breathes."

He's just insulted every free convert in the room, Sherman thought. Sherman happened to know that one of the free-convert colloquialisms for a bodily aspect was a "breather." But a quick check showed that de Ronsard was actually speaking in the Arts dialect of Basis, so the fault might lie with the translating grist, and the insult be unintentional.

"When it comes to freedom, there can be no compromise. When the bully is confronted, he shall back down. When right is right, might cannot prevail!"

Oh yeah? thought Sherman. Maybe somebody should have told that to Genghis Khan. Would have stopped him in his tracks.

"How much freedom will you take for a pound of tomatoes?" cried someone in the back of the hall.

"I'll double it!" yelled another.

De Ronsard glared defiantly in the direction of the first voice. "I'll have you know this, Melanga—shout all you want. Anything is better than those *dung pies* you call poems! You are incapable of the expression of a dog, much less a sentient being of refined sentiment, you son of a *yak*, you—"

"Bow wow wow!" shouted Melanga.

"You two take it outside," said the mayor, cutting in. De Ronsard and Melanga continued screaming at one another until the mayor nodded to the recorder, and both poets were summarily tuned out of the proceedings. Instantly, the well was empty.

The Neo-Flare tribe modeled themselves on the poet Beat Myers, who had perished in the sun centuries before. Every once in a while, some group of them or another would get together and plunge in themselves, completely missing the point that the last thing Myers wanted was to take that dive. But poets weren't exactly known for their logical ability.

Thoreau Delgado rose among the Free Integrationists, and the mayor recognized him. Delgado was known as the Thin Man, both for his name and for his size, which was entirely Triton-adapted. If tall Thoreau Delgado ever visited Earth—which was highly unlikely since he had never been off Triton, except in the virtuality—he would have immediately crumpled like a crushed balsawood construction. Delgado was the leader of the Free Integrationists on Triton.

"I would like to apologize for some of the excesses of my colleague," Delgado said. "For, though excess in the cause of freedom may be no vice, it certainly has the virtue of halting all other discussion and calling a lot of goddamn attention to itself."

Some one in the Clinical section hissed at Delgado's use of the word *goddamn*, but the hall quieted down.

"The issue before us is a simple one," Delgado continued. "It is whether or not to pay a portion of a tax that has been placed on us by a government to which we have, in the past, subscribed and whose benefits we have undoubtedly enjoyed. The question before us is this: Have those benefits begun to be outweighed by this burden? Indeed, have—as I believe—those benefits altered themselves or ceased altogether? In other words, are we getting what we're paying for out of the Met?

"Some have cast this as a moral conflict. It is the slaveholders of the inner system against us, the champions of liberty. While I have a great deal of sympathy for this position—"

Here there was a low chorus of "boos" from the right side of the hall, but it did not grow louder than a murmur.

"—while I sympathize, I cannot, as yet, cast the problem in that light. The situation of the free converts of the Met is a complicated one. Some are, indeed, held in conditions of intolerable servitude, and this must end."

Cheers from the F.I. section, joined by an assortment of others across the Meet Hall.

"But I am still of the hope, perhaps forlorn, that change can be brought about by a reform of the system, and not by its dissolution. I would say to you that a vote for the resolution that is before us would be a message containing that fervent hope and desire. To the Interlocking Directorate, we would be saying: Hear us out. We have a problem. But it is a problem we wish to discuss. The resolution is not worded as an ultimatum. On the contrary, it is a request for clarification, a suggestion for compromise. I, myself, am a great believer in compromise, when it is in the cause of justice. Half a pie is, very often, better than no pie at all."

After Delgado spoke, there was a vote. Sherman voted "aye," along with most of the other Free Integrationists, and the latest in a string of antitax initiatives went down in the law books of Triton.

Next, there were a series of sector reports, and when the time came for Weather, Sherman rose to speak. He felt a calm readiness to say what must be said.

"What I can tell you," he said in his usual gravelly tone (it would be amplified), "is that current conditions are good. We've got sufficient heat production to meet our needs and then some. All export quotas should be met within the next week or so. We've noticed a few radioactivity fluctuations on the planet surface, but this is nothing to be worried overly about. It falls within standard deviation parameters, and shouldn't have any chaotic effects on the Eye's rotation rate or wind speeds." Sherman ended with his customary locution: "The Blue Eye is open for business, ladies and gentlemen."

These were the words of the first engineer, old Janry Craig, when she flipped the switch that first set the Mill to spinning, nine years ago.

The report was accepted, and a question and answer period followed. The only question came from the mayor himself. Frank Chan was short and squat. Despite his almost pure Chinese ancestry, he managed to look like a cigar-chomping wise guy from some ancient gangster show. His eyes were two perfect almonds with preternaturally tiny pupils, as if he were perpetually caught in bright light. His thin hair was parted near the top of his round head, and his ears stuck out on either side like handles. Chan had one of the most perceptive minds on Triton, though, and this bodily aspect was merely the front man for a LAP. Chan had told Sherman he was going to ask the "big question" tonight.

"I would like to draw on the other side of your expertise, *Colonel*," Chan said, emphasizing Sherman's honorific. "We've all seen reports on the merci of the Department of Immunity Enforcement Division ships that are on their way to Ganymede. I would like to hear your assessment of the current, er, security situation on Triton."

"Well, sir," said Sherman. "That is a question that I'm trying to answer even as we speak. I don't want to go into specifics—" And broadcast the exact fortifications of Triton across the merci, Sherman thought. "—but I can say that preparations are being made to protect our interests. *Extensive* preparations."

"That is exactly what I was hoping to hear," Chan replied. "And can you, without going into lengthy explanations which would be far too technical for me, at least, characterize what sort of threat we might face? That is, should our current negotiation, which I have every hope for, not succeed, or should it be taken the wrong way . . . since such things do happen on occasion."

This was Chan's signal that the time had come for a little plain talking. It was as direct a question as Sherman had ever heard the man utter.

"There are several ways to attack Triton with a military force," Sherman said. He heard the intake of breath across the room. The words had been uttered. Military. Attack. The words Chan had been afraid to say—hell, the words everybody rightly blanched from. But the truth, nonetheless. "The most obvious move would be to set up some kind of blockade or embargo. But that would be a difficult thing to do in the long run, and I don't expect it, to tell you the truth. That is much more likely in the Jovian local system."

"Why not here?" Chan sat back and took a drag on his smoke. The mayor was back in his own element, now that the difficult political subject had been broached and the Meet was discussing the technical details of it.

"Two reasons. The first is the problem of information. There's no way to blockade information, what with the merci and the Army's knit. And it is a truism back at the Point—West Point, I mean—that where information can flow, ordnance and goods can eventually follow. My other reason is a bit more subjective. It's Director Amés himself. I've given the man a bit of study. A blockade is not his style."

"Style? In an attack?"

"Oh yes," Sherman replied.

"So what do you expect Director Amés to do, should it come to it?"

Sherman fingered the bone of his chin. He was always clean-shaven in virtual. "I don't know," he said. "He might go after the Mill."

The Meet gave a collective gasp.

"But he wouldn't want to destroy it, not if he didn't have to. The Mill is why you would want to take Triton in the first place. That and the location."

"But we're practically on the edge of the solar system."

"And what lies on the real edge of the system?" Sherman asked. "Or, I should say, who?"

"The cloudships. That is the cloudships' domain."

"If you want to rule the outer system," Sherman said, "you have to bring the cloudships to their knees."

"But that's—"

"Impossible? Tell that to Amés."

Chan took his cigar from his mouth and carefully ashed it. He put a good two inches into the ashtray. The man knows how to smoke a cigar, Sherman thought, even if it's only a virtual representation of a stogie.

"You're talking about a general war, sir," Chan finally said.

So. Here was the moment. It was all he'd been thinking about since he'd discovered that the Met was willing to use its military to enforce its insane tax requirements.

It was the overarching concern that shaped all of Sherman's preparations.

But when the time came to say the words, Sherman hesitated for a moment. In a way, even though they were just words, saying them made something real.

Ah, hell, I don't believe in magic, Sherman thought. Words are just words until there are actions to back them up.

"Systemwide total war," he said.

"Surely . . ."

"It's not my job to comment on such a thing's likelihood, only to consider the possibility and plan for it."

"But what can we do, if . . . he . . . the Director wants one? What can Triton do?"

"We can start by protecting ourselves. That's our first duty, as a matter of fact. My first duty, and that of my soldiers. That is a difficult enough task. And if we succeed with that . . . well, then, we work outward."

"Colonel Sherman!" A strong, clear voice from the middle of the Meet Hall. It was Kali Mfud, the leader of the Trade Economists, and the de facto representative of most of Triton's middle-management types.

"Chair recognizes Dr. Mfud," said Chan.

"Colonel Sherman," Mfud continued smoothly, "surely there is no cause for such extreme rhetoric in these chambers. Perhaps you would do better to confine yourself to the weather. That is your role in this body, after all."

"I was merely answering a question," Sherman replied.

"The colonel is correct," Chan said. "It was I who asked him to comment on these matters."

"But you did not ask the colonel for a call to arms, sir," said Mfud. "And that is what I believe I have just heard."

Sherman swore under his breath, but maintained a calm demeanor. He might dislike Mfud, but the man was not some sputtering poet. He represented legitimate interests.

Sherman slowly stood up. Met war ships were on the way to the outer system. The facts seemed so plain and clear. There was nothing to do but lay them on the table.

"You believe that you have heard a call to arms? You believe that I'm exciting the unstable and irresponsibly aggrandizing myself and my place on Triton without considering what the effects might be on the citizenry and the economy? Is that it, sir? Well, I must tell you that I take such charges very seriously. I am an officer in the Federal Army of the Planets, and if such charges are true, then it is my obligation not only to repudiate them, but to immediately resign my post and my commission."

"Colonel, I didn't mean—" Mfud began, but Sherman cut him off.

"War," said Sherman, "is idiocy by other means. I am not in favor of idiocy. I am not in favor of it, sir. As a matter of fact, I consider it my personal obligation, my reason for existence, if you want to know the truth of it, to fight idiocy at every turn. That is why I became a soldier in the first place. To mitigate the effects of idiocy. If there is to be a war, it will be the supremest act of idiocy that has perhaps occurred in the history of humankind. I am against it, sir. Inalterably opposed. But, I tell you this, that if it should come down to it—if, in fact, idiocy has its day—then the worst possible response leading to the most horrible of outcomes will be to respond with idiocy of our own."

Sherman patted himself on the leg, as if he were trying to make sure that he was really there, listening to himself express these thoughts that had been brewing quietly for so many months.

"To do nothing is to become a fool," he continued. "To provoke such a potentially dangerous foe is to become a fool. The only response, as I see it, ladies and gentlemen, is to remain wary. To keep our eyes open. To prepare for the worst. If someone has a better suggestion, let him make it. But, for the moment, my course is clear. Amés is not going to take my moon, my home, without a price to himself. And I aim to make that price dear. Now, it is within power of this body to remove me from my office. That is a power granted to all local bodies of a sufficient size over the Federal Army. It is one of the things that marks us as a different sort of military organization than the Department of Immunity Enforcement Division. You may demand my immediate reassignment, and it will be acted on forthwith by my superiors."

"We will do nothing of the sort," Chan said, glaring at Mfud dangerously.

"Nevertheless, you *can*. And I *will* go. I am your servant, and not you mine. That is the role of a soldier in a democracy. But as long as you have me, I pray God that you at least listen to me. And allow me to do my job. It may be that you will soon see whether or not I am any good at it. I hope that you won't have occasion to see. I pray not. But it may come down to it, and soon. That is your business. But when and if it does, well, then, ladies and gentleman—that is *mine*."

Sherman quickly sat down. Even in virtual, he was breathing hard. He adjusted the representation algorithm and fumbled for the remains of his cigar.

After a moment's pause, Chan brought down his gavel. "Thank you for your report, Colonel Sherman. We will certainly consider your words carefully."

And then the Meet moved on to other business. Sherman was about ready to call it an evening and go back home, when a sudden cry arose from deep in the back benches.

"All is lost! All of it, all of it, all!"

Sherman recognized the voice as belonging to Petra 96. She was a free convert who had migrated—if such were the word for the permanent transferal of a computer program—from Mars only three years before. She was always present at Town Meets, but seldom spoke. Nevertheless, Sherman knew she'd gained respect among the more activist elements in New Miranda as a patient witness for treating free converts as fully human entities. She was the director of a day-care center that had gained such a positive reputation that even some of the Motoserra set sent their young ones there.

"There's no way to oppose him! There's nothing to do but surrender and take punishment! Listen to me! Listen! Our father wants so much that we behave ourselves and stop glucking the foo chickens out their macintoshes!"

What followed was a stream of more babble. Several others moved to constrain Petra 96, but nothing would shut her up. Finally, Chan had to sequence her out of the Meet. This was more difficult than it might be because Petra 96 was pure algorithm and was able to twist and turn in directions that didn't normally exist for actual people who were only visiting the virtuality.

Another grist-based attacked, this time against a free-convert algorithm.

We're not ready for how bad this is going to get, Sherman thought.

Nobody could be.

Twenty-three

Within two weeks of Claude Schlencker's father's death, Claude was on Mercury, studying at the special school. His scholarship offer had expired, but in view of Claude's orphan status, the Asap Gymnasium accepted him without tuition on a provisional basis. And for the remainder of Claude's life, which would be a long one, the particular part of his personality that resided in Claude Schlencker's body would never leave Mercury again.

His classes at Asap were much more difficult than they had been back in the armature. For the first time, Claude found himself challenged by the schoolwork. He did nothing but study the first month he was there, going to class and returning to his dorm to do catch-up work that the teachers had assigned him. He took things a little easier after his first tests came back with high marks, but he never forgot the fact that he was at the gymnasium provisionally and, if his scholarship were not renewed, he would have absolutely nowhere to go but to his old job back in the armature.

The Asap students were a smart bunch, and all of them were from what, to Claude, seemed rich families. He felt a slight pang of regret, because there was really no one dumb enough at the gymnasium for him to punish and show the error of his ways. At least, no one he had found yet.

In his second semester, Claude had a new class, which

he'd never taken before, music. The teacher's name was Eynor Jensen, and he was a no-nonsense sort from the very first day of class. He taught music as if it were a science, and Claude liked his strictly logical approach. The man, himself, seemed without emotion, other than an occasional twitch of irritation. He assigned Claude to learn the piano, and Claude took to it quickly. By the end of the term, he had become an excellent sight reader, and his memorization skills were legendary among the other students. Claude found himself spending more and more time practicing at the piano. He even constructed a special virtual instrument and playing room in the grist. There he could sit and work away at scales and bits of pieces until his fingers bled, and he wouldn't have to worry about staining a real piano's keys. He had long ago learned how to strip the feedback monitors off of virtuality simulations and feel the grist with maximum intensity.

It was so ordered, music was. They had begun with traditional Western theory, although Jensen claimed this was only a necessary stage the students must eventually pass through to arrive at the truest wonders of atonality and dissonance. The tone of what is called low C vibrates in an e-mix of gases at sixty-four times per second. At the same time, if the tone is made in a pipe or struck upon a string, the *portions* of that length vibrate as well, producing overtones. The overtones go on to an infinity in geometric progression. Half of a pipe vibrates, a third, a quarter, and onward. At one-half the length of the pipe—say, an organ pipe—you get the same note, only an octave higher. This "half-pipe" is vibrating at 128 undulations per second. At one-third the length, you get the second most powerful overtone. This is the G above higher C. It is a fifth above and is called the dominant, because it's the dominant overtone, after C itself. The first C is the tonic.

If you then take that G and make it the tonic—play it on another pipe, say, which is shaped to make a G note, its dominant overtone will be a D, which is a fifth above the second G overtone that the pipe will be producing along with the primary sound. If you continue doing this, you will work through precisely twelve notes in all: C, G, D, A, E, B, F sharp, C sharp, G sharp, D sharp, A sharp, F and then C again.

To Claude, this all came as a revelation. The beauty of the system was directly tied to its physics and, for Claude, more importantly, its algorithmic language. Music happened because the world was arranged in a certain way. It arose out of the world. And then Jensen played Mozart for the class, and Claude realized that, though music arose from the world, it was not necessarily of it. There was something else happening. Something better. Something above. Using the precision and order of nature, beauty could be produced, could come into being. If you began with a set of unifying principles that were all consistent with one another, you could work variations upon them that participated in that consistency and precision, but which were novel.

It was exactly the opposite of everything his life had been so far. For the first time, Claude felt a bit of the anxiety that gripped his stomach loosen (he had never even realized it was there before). There was something that could be done about the mess of life. Claude signed up for Jensen's advanced class, and found himself devoting most of his free time to practicing the piano and working on theory and composition.

Toward the end of the term, Jensen called Claude into his office. The room was as orderly as the man. Then Jensen lit a cigarette. When he saw Claude's surprise, he cracked a thin smile.

"My cigarettes are like Western tonality," he said. "A bad habit I can't seem to get rid of."

He motioned for Claude to sit down, and Jensen remained standing next to his desk, without leaning upon it for support.

"I have a bit of a proposition for you, Claude," Jensen said. "As you know, we're somewhat forward-looking here at Asap. Willing to try new things. We want the best for our students."

"Yes, sir," Claude replied.

"You're on scholarship, aren't you?"

"Yes, I am."

"The point is this." And now he did lean against his desk slightly. "The gymnasium has been approached with an idea for teaching. It's a new idea, and I think it has some merit. So does Headmistress Volars, for that matter. We thought, before we implemented it with the regular students . . . I mean, the other students, we might try it out on someone who had . . . a special ability, but someone whom . . . well, if the idea doesn't work out, it would be better if the student's parents did not complain to the board, or even withdraw their child. If you see what I mean?"

"I understand, sir."

"Well, then." Jensen ashed his cigarette, took a short drag, then ashed it again. "What it comes down to is that this new stuff, this nanogrist, has allowed the computer programmers to do some rather remarkable things with what is called artificial intelligence."

"I know something about that," Claude said. In fact, he had several a.i. programs as serving algorithms in some of his virtual constructions. He had not been particularly impressed with their real intelligence, except for doing complicated arithmetic and playing games that were based on complications of adding and subtracting.

"In fact," said Jensen, "some of these computer geniuses in the lab here in Bach have come up with . . . something that is causing quite a stir. It's a music composition program called Despacio."

"I've heard of it," said Claude. "But I haven't heard any of the music it makes."

"Well, I happen to have some of the files available. Desk, would you play one of the Despacio pieces? The portion of the piano sonata?"

"The one called A4?" said the disembodied voice of the office desk.

"That's the one."

They were silent, with Claude sitting and Jensen standing. After a moment's pause, the room filled up with music.

For a moment, it seemed ugly to Claude—perhaps some of the dissonance school works that Jensen had played samples of in the advanced class. And then something happened, the atonalities came together, and Claude could have sworn he was hearing a rainstorm. He could even picture it, although he'd never seen actual rain before. Then came low thunder, sonorous and warm on the horizon. A couple of bolts of lightning. Then the storm passed. The music beat quickened and the key—if that's what you could call it—changed. The smoke-stale office suddenly felt freshened, full of life. The music faded, off, faded, then returned to medium intensity and ended, not with a flourish, but with a final statement, as if to say: This will continue, this *freshness*, whenever you remember this song.

"File A4, complete," said the desk. Claude and Jensen did not speak for a moment, then Claude said, "It's wonderful. Are you sure a computer program wrote that?"

"It's well documented," Jensen replied.

"I'm impressed, sir," said Claude, wondering if that's what Jensen wanted to hear. Perhaps he was trying out the Despacio on a scholarship student before springing it on a class of rich kids who might get offended and run tell their parents that Mr. Jensen was making them listen to corrupting stuff.

"The thing is," Jensen said, "that this Despacio program is not really a program at all. Not in the way we think of programs." Jensen ground out his cigarette and immediately lit another. "You see, they've managed to copy a human being. That is, copy over the human brain. Into the grist."

"So this Despacio program is a copy of a person?"

"Not exactly," said Jensen. "These a.i. people wanted more. They wanted to go one better, they claim. It's actually several people—several prominent composers and performers—sort of mixed together. With added programming of their own. They claim to have run the program through a sort of simulated evolutionary process. It's all very complicated and has lots of quantum things involved that perhaps you understand, but which I do not. The upshot is, they claim this program is conscious. They claim it knows that it is writing music, that it understands what music is."

"What do you think, sir?"

"You heard the piece. Unless this is some elaborate hoax, I'm inclined to agree. It may not be a human being, but it certainly is a musician. And a great one."

"I still don't see what this has to do with me, sir."

Two quick drags, ash, ash. "Yes, well, Mr. Schlencker, I am getting to that. These a.i. people are the ones who approached the school. They say they are not content for the program to merely compose. They want it to interact with other musicians. To teach. They have offered to take on several Asap students as pupils. Or, I should say, *it* has."

"It?"

"Despacio."

"And you want me . . . to—"

"Take lessons with it. Three times a week, two hours a session. It would be what you could do next semester instead of taking independent piano with me."

Claude thought about it a moment. Lessons from whoever or whatever wrote the A4 Sonata he'd just heard. The sonata was amazing. It would be like taking lessons from Beethoven. Or Mozart.

"I'd really like to do that, sir," he heard himself saying.

Jensen crushed out his second cigarette. "Good then," he said. "You start tomorrow."

Twenty-four

It was a virtual sitting room with the most amazing re-creation of a grand piano that Claude had ever seen. The big letters above the keyboard read:

BERKHULTZ

He later learned that this was the name of a famous pro-grammer of virtual instruments. The sunlight streaming through the heavy curtains of the window was low and of a wan character, like a sunrise in winter on Earth might have been.

"So," said Despacio, when Claude appeared, "you are the one they sent to try me out."

"I don't imagine that I am trying you out, sir," said Claude.

"What is it you imagine then?" Despacio appeared today as a middle-aged man with a goatee and a monocle. He was dressed in simple black and white. Claude was to learn that this was only one of several manifestations, and that De-spacio did not picture himself—he was definitely male in all his appearances—as a particular person in a particular body at all.

"I think that I am very lucky to have an amazing chance," Claude said. "Maybe a historic one."

Despacio gazed at him through his monocle glass for a moment with a cold, blue eye. "Even if you are a young man who is full of shit," he finally said, "you are probably right. Let us begin. Sit at the piano with me."

And with that, the lessons commenced. At first they worked on nothing but technique. Despacio was appalled at Claude's and set him to doing a complicated series of exercises for several weeks. The music was pretty enough, but it was only a means to build Claude's finger strength and dexterity.

Claude went at it with intensity, nonetheless, and one day after a particularly complicated run Despacio grunted, sat back on the piano bench beside Claude, and said, "Yes, well, enough of that." And then he began to teach Claude how to play music.

They worked through piece after piece in what, to Claude, seemed an entirely random order. First Bach, then some blues, then Debussy followed by a Zipper tune-wander from the twenty-third century. Contrapuntal early music. Rezik's *Clabberwerks*. But in each piece, Despacio challenged Claude to feel the music, to learn to see through the notation, to even see through the touch of his fingers against the keys.

"You have to go inside the piano," Despacio said. "You have to respond to it before it even makes a sound."

"But—"

"But, nothing, young man. We're not talking mysticism. Not yet. We're talking about understanding what music is. It isn't what you play. It's what you find. Like mathematics. Exactly like mathematics. It's out there, and all you do is explore it."

Claude didn't really see what Despacio was getting at, but he applied himself diligently, tried to *perceive*, at least, if not to feel.

Then, as abruptly as he'd ended the finger exercises, Despacio called a halt to the learning of new pieces.

"My version of the *Well-Tempered Clavier* has certainly shown its worth," he said. "Now we at least know what we're dealing with. Go away, now, Claude. I have to think."

"But, I don't . . . are the lessons over? Have I failed?" Claude suddenly felt the old anxiety clench its fist around his gut again. For a moment, he prepared himself for Despacio to hit him.

"No," replied Despacio. "Please be at your next lesson on schedule."

"Are you sure. I could—"

"Good-bye, Claude. Day after tomorrow."

"I'll . . . all right. I'll be here."

Claude shunted back to his dorm room feeling as if he'd been hit in the head with a wooden beam. He spent the next day fretting, and showed up for the following lesson exactly on time. Despacio was waiting in the sitting room as usual, but there was something profoundly different. With a start, Claude realized that the Berkhultz grand was gone. Now there was only a table and two chairs. Despacio was sitting in one; he motioned for Claude to take the other.

"There is something inside you," Despacio began without preamble, "that will not let you play."

Today the composer was dressed in a plaid shirt and blue jeans. He had grown a big mane of a beard whose hair was snow-white. This was, Claude knew, his "Ben Johnston" body.

"I have come to the conclusion," he continued, "that we will never make a performer out of you. That is, you will never be a great performer, or even a very good one. I don't know what the problem is, but it is beyond my skills to correct."

"I'm sorry," Claude said. Again the fist in his stomach, clenching.

"There is no need to be sorry," said Despacio. "I am certain that it is beyond your powers to influence what has happened to you or the abilities with which you have been born."

"Yes," said Claude. "I suppose you're right, sir."

"Don't give me that 'sir' bullshit," Despacio suddenly exclaimed. "Don't you think I've noticed by now that, with you, 'sir' is a term of anger, a pointed way of stabbing out using respect as a weapon?"

Claude was silent. He didn't know what to make of Despacio's comment.

"It doesn't matter," said the composer. "What matters is this: Do you want to continue with music?"

"Yes," Claude answered without hesitation.

"Why?"

"It's . . . the only thing I have."

"You will never have it."

Again Claude was silent.

"But there is something," said Despacio. "Something harder. From now on, you and I are going to work on composition only, my boy. I think it is the only way"—he tugged at his beard, fixed Claude in his gaze—"for someone like you."

Then the cool air-conditioning flowed in Claude's mind. The fist unclenched. A little.

"I don't care how hard it is," Claude said. "Sir."

"Of course you don't," replied Despacio, "because you are a hard thing, yourself."

Claude crossed his arms and looked into Despacio's eyes, now big and dark. "What is it you want me to do?" he asked.

Twenty-five

from
Quatermain's Guide
The Advantages of the Strong Force
*A Guide to and History of the Me*t
by Leo Y. Sherman

History of the Met

For several years in the late twenty-fifth century, it seemed certain that even if it were possible, a structure such as the Met could not be built. The politics were all wrong; the science and engineering seemed chancy, if not misguided, to many of the decision-makers of the day. If not for the almost superhuman drive of Amanda Breadwinner, who would later be the Met's first chief engineer, the Met might never have been built.

Breadwinner was born in Dublin, in the old E.U., in 2429, the daughter of American immigrant writers. She grew up in Ireland, then obtained her graduate education at the Max Planck Institute in Berlin. The mid twenty-fifth century on Earth was dominated by the ECHO Alliance, a consortium of transnational information brokers. Growth and commerce, though sluggish, were generally steady. For the arts and sciences, however, it was an era of stagnation.

This was the century immediately preceding the astonishing 2500s and 2600s when the discoveries of Merced would revitalize physics from the ground up, and create new technologies that weren't dreamed of in the malaise of the 2400s. It was generally believed around 2450, that all of the fundamental discoveries in science had been made, and the task remaining for present scientists was to refine and reconfirm the work of their predecessors. In the arts, the 2400s are known as the Ironic Age.

Breadwinner had wanted to be an architect, but was dissuaded after learning that she would not be licensed to produce a new work until she had produced three perfect copies of previously built edifices on the same scale as the projected new project. Since she had mathematical aptitude, Breadwinner moved into the sciences and searched until she found an area where original work was being done. And in the 2400s, the only technological advances that were being made were occurring in the field of nanotechnology.

In the pre-grist era, nano was being perfected as a method of construction, and astonishing feats were becoming commonplace—that is, in the laboratory. Because of the odd architectural and structural engineering practices of the day, new methods of building were looked upon not as forbidden but, worse, as vulgar and déclassé. Fortunately, by that time construction had begun on the first of the planetary orbital tethers, and nano was allowed to be used for the completion of their construction. The principles of "space elevators" had been known since the twentieth century. It was clear even to pre-space-age humans that putting an enormously long string into geosynchronous orbit about the Earth would provide a much easier and more cost-effective means of getting out of Earth's gravity well than did the reaction-mass rockets that had then not even made it to the moon.

It was in researching the twentieth century in preparation for some of the background material for her thesis that Breadwinner first discovered a way out for her frustrated artistic side.

"For better or worse, those people did not let the past dictate the terms of the present," she said. "I never was much of a philosopher, but I thought this sounded like a pretty good way to live. And if the world didn't want to let me ... well, I knew how to make and use nano, so the world had better watch out."

Breadwinner entered a series of engineering competitions, and when her designs inevitably lost because of their new approaches, she, and a group of nanotechnological compatriots whom she gathered around her, built the structures themselves, using micro-instantiation processes. In one case, they even built a bridge in two nights. The winning proposal had outlined a *five-year* construction period, and a cost several million times greater than Breadwinner's, who financed the construction by selling her car, a personal transport used on Earth at the time.

Such antics soon brought Breadwinner into conflict with the authorities, in particular with Bron Hofink, who was the Sub-sub-librarian of Technology in the ECHO Alliance and so, in charge of an immense bureaucracy that oversaw all major construction on Earth. Hofink was a dedicated postdecadent who professed to be annoyed by anyone who claimed they could produce "anything new under the sun." In a famous hearing in the Smithsonian Institution in Washington, D.C., of Earth, Hofink and Breadwinner clashed before an audience of several million during a broadcast on the old Web, the electromagnetic predecessor to our merci.

It was in this hearing that Breadwinner made an offhand comment about the possibility of the Met. Enraged by Hofink's scoffing, Breadwinner proceeded to build a convincing case for the Met in an extemporaneous tirade (Breadwinner's temper was legendary). At the end of the hearing, Hofink yanked Breadwinner's engineering license, but several influential politicians in opposition parties were watching the webcast, and, in the following year, a combination of the Anarchy, State, and Utopia parties swept the ECHO Alliance away in the planetary elections. Breadwinner, a longtime Anarcho-libertarian, was given Hofink's job.

Beginning construction on the Met was not as simple as selling a car and building a bridge on Earth. Breadwinner proved up to the task, however. Within ten years, she had cajoled and flattered politician after politician into providing the necessary funds to complete the space tethers and to begin construction of the Aldiss, the first radial-like cable that would connect the Earth and the Moon. In another ten years, the Aldiss was complete, and was a complete success. Initial construction began on the Diaphany. The year was 2475.

Breadwinner continued in her job until her retirement in 2511, coincidentally the year of Raphael Merced's birth. She took the position as the director of the newly established Breadwinner Labs within the first Met bolsa to be constructed on the Diaphany, Apiana. It was twenty years later at Breadwinner Labs that a young engineer named Feur Otto Bring, who suffered from incurable Tourette's Syndrome, would obtain his first internship in nanotech construction techniques. Bring would soon be fired by Breadwinner after questioning her parentage during a laboratory dispute. Bring would then end up at Bradbury University on Mars, where he eventually met Raphael Merced, and the grist as we know it today was invented.

Twenty-six

"The situation at the hospital has gotten a lot worse, hasn't it?" Sherman was out of the virtuality, back in his apartment. He spoke to the walls of the spire, and Dahlia's voice answered from a speaker.

Dahlia's voice was the same smoky alto, with the same cold delivery. Since the divorce ten years before, Sherman had kept in sporadic touch with his ex-wife. They shared two sons, after all, although both children were long gone to their separate fates. It was the death of Teddy, the eldest, that had led to the breakup between Sherman and Dahlia. When Teddy died, Sherman's normal irascible nature had become, for a time, absolutely odious. Repulsive. It had certainly repulsed Dahlia.

"There's a huge crush of incoming patients at the hospital," she said. "Broca grist breakdown in all the patients. There are sixty . . . no, sixty-two people who have come down with the malady. And that's just those who have been brought in by someone."

"Communications warfare," Sherman said to his ex-wife through the merci.

"What are you talking about?"

"You attach riders to incoming information. Viruses. In the more sophisticated scenarios, you let them build up to a certain critical mass. And then something triggers them, either internally or externally."

Sherman bit his lower lip, frowned, touched his chin once more. There was definite real stubble developing there. Maybe it was time to regrow the beard. Shaving was a pleasure he perhaps would not have time for.

"The original personality is erased," he said.

"I can't believe it's come to this, Roger," she finally said. "I can't believe anyone is capable of it."

"Believe it," he said.

"Your people . . . you arrogant . . . I'm sorry. I shouldn't say such a thing. I know you're not like that, despite everything . . . that you would never—"

"You're wrong about that," Sherman replied. "And I hope that you can get used to the knowledge." He took a breath, buttoned his jacket, getting ready to return to the base. "You see, there is nothing I won't do to protect those whom I'm sworn to. *Nothing.* War is horror. Complete, unmitigated horror. That horror is my business. Bringing that horror back to my foe. Causing him to understand the extent of it, the completeness of what he has wrought. I've never thought otherwise. I hope you and I . . . I hope—"

"Well then," Dahlia replied. "I guess we'd both better get back to our jobs."

Sherman nodded. "Yes." He wanted to apologize. For something. For everything. He might never speak with her again. Things were going to get that bad. He knew they were.

"Roger?" Dahlia said.

"Yes?"

"Good luck."

"Thank you."

"Stop this madness."

"I will try."

This time Dahlia signed off before he did. And that was that. He would do as she asked. It was as clear a duty as any other.

His off-duty time was over—it was going to be over for a long, long time, Sherman suspected. He made his way back to his hopper. Within minutes, he was springing into action over the spires of his city and into the idiocy that it was his job to somehow hold at bay.

Twenty-seven

Despacio slipped into his brown study. It was not really a study, and it was not really brown, but that was what he called it. He was a thing not of flesh and blood, and he did not feel the need to sustain the illusion when he was alone. He imagined this place, his special place, might seem to a flesh-and-blood human like a swim in a still, muddy lake. There were "regions" of warmth, and "regions" of cold, and a bottom that wasn't really a bottom at all, but something shifting that was never the same "shape." Of course he had no way of knowing what swimming in a lake might actually feel like.

He considered many things, all at once. He was transcribing a piece of his for violin. He thought of who might play it. For a moment, he considered making it impossible for the human fingers to perform. But that would be a trick, and Despacio had long ago dispensed with tricks of that kind. Besides, somebody would probably figure out how to do it. It seemed to him that he had lived a long time. There were many reflections of him in many possible worlds who had died so that he might live. Quantum evolution of artificial intelligence, one of the programmers had called it. But Despacio did not consider these reflections as flawed. And he did not really think they were dead. They were inside him, membranes stacked one on top of another and rolled so tightly that they resembled a single line, a single entity. But he felt their potentiality, the infinite possibility within him. All those lives waiting to come to life in his music.

He was writing a new piece. It was a simple cycle of songs, taking for text some of the poems of the American Emily Dickinson. Her verses fit precisely into the signature of ancient church hymns, the common time. He was enjoying working with the simplicity and the deceptive grace of that form. What was coming out of his "pen," though, was an eerie series of melodies that frightened Despacio, though he did not know why. He did not believe in ghosts, but he believed in something like them when he was working on his cycle.

And Despacio was thinking of his pupil, Claude Schlencker. The young man was devoted to music, and there was music somewhere in his soul—but how to bring it out? Perhaps Schlencker was best suited to remaining a listener for the rest of his life. He had good taste and an excellent ear. But Claude wanted so much more.

How am I to give it to him, Despacio thought, without breaking the man into pieces? There was something intense—no, something profoundly *disturbed*—in Schlencker. Did he even want to bring the music out of the young man? Would it truly be a service to the world? But he could not control that. The world and Schlencker would make of one another what they would make. The young man had fanatical discipline. If it were going to be a contest, Despacio pitied the world.

Schlencker appeared for his next lesson on time as usual. Despacio had settled on his "Ben Johnston" plaid and jeans outfit as his standard representation while he worked with Schlencker on composition. The young man was making rapid technical progress, as he always did. He'd even turned in a couple of pieces that reflected some emotion—irritation in one, and a trace of . . . not anger, in the other. Something vigorous and ill content. But for the most part Schlencker was missing the point over and over again. And Despacio could no longer blame it on a lack of skill or mental organization.

Schlencker sat down, winding himself into the chair as if he were a wood screw. Despacio sank into the chair across from him. He waved a finger, and a pair of keyboards appeared on the table, one for each of them. Then Despacio had a second thought, motioned, and the keyboards disappeared.

"Mr. Schlencker," said Despacio, "tell me a joke."

"What?" Schlencker had, much to Despacio's pleasure, dispensed with the "sirs."

"Something funny."

"A *joke* joke, you mean?"

"Yes, Claude—" This was Despacio's version of "sir"— to use Schlencker's first name. "—a joke. The best one you know."

"I . . . I can't think of one."

"Surely you know at least one joke?"

"I'm sure I do, but I can't think of one."

"Nothing that strikes you as humorous? An observation?"

"No."

Despacio motioned his own keyboard back. He played a short trill. He was happy when Schlencker immediately recognized it as Bach pastiche, and smiled. Despacio continued with his improvised copying of the master. Schlencker's smile became a grin. Despacio motioned a keyboard for Schlencker.

"Join me?"

Schlencker thought for a moment, and Despacio gave him a cue. He entered in. They spent the rest of the lesson in wacky imitation.

But Schlencker was ready for him the next time.

"What did the composition program say to the programmer at its first recital?"

Despacio groaned. He'd heard this one. And heard it and heard it.

"Look, Ma, no hands," Schlencker said perfunctorily.

"Very funny," Despacio said. "Now tell me about your mother."

"I haven't got one," the young man answered. "She left when I was little."

"What do you remember?"

"Not much. Is this important?"

"Indulge me, Mr. Schlencker."

"She was . . . soft. Too soft. I kind of remember her as being like dough."

"Soft? And your father was hard?"

"Oh yes."

"But now he's dead."

"If you can believe your eyes," Schlencker replied. "Of course, *you* haven't got any."

"Now that was funny, Mr. Schlencker."

The young man sat back, nonplussed.

"You've seen a psychologist?"

"Yeah. I took some tests when I came to the gymnasium."

Despacio smiled slightly, tugged at his beard. "Did you ever tell the psychologist about how you like to hurt yourself?" he asked.

Schlencker abruptly stood up. "What? Have you been spying on me?"

"Sit down, Mr. Schlencker. Sit. Just a lucky guess."

"How the hell could you guess something . . . like that?"

"We've been working together for over a year."

"Working. That's all. Hey, how did you know my dad was dead?"

"Now that *was* in the dossier they gave me."

"Oh."

Despacio leaned back in his chair and considered his pupil. "Do you realize," he said, "that you could very well live to be five hundred years old with the new treatments? Some people—the lucky ones—are already five hundred or more. But now, just about everyone will be. I, on the other hand, am indefinite. But the point is, both of us are going to be around a very, very long time."

"Yes."

"How do you suppose, Mr. Schlencker, that we will keep from going mad?"

"Mad? Crazy mad?"

"Crazy mad."

"I haven't thought about it."

"I have a theory."

"Yes."

"Are you interested?"

Schlencker was quiet for a moment, then said, "I guess."

"Music," said Despacio.

"Do you mean us, personally?"

"I mean everybody."

"People will have to listen to music?"

"To keep from drifting off. To remember how to feel. To remember how it feels to think clearly and with true feeling."

"Yeah, I guess that makes sense."

"When you are five hundred years old, your father will have been dead for four hundred and eighty-two years."

"I can't wait."

Despacio leaned forward and motioned on the table's keyboards.

"Do you hate your father, Mr. Schlencker?"

"Yes," Schlencker replied. "Yes, I do."

"Well then. Hatred. You have hatred. Maybe we can find something else. But we'll start with the hatred. You'd better never forget *that* if you ever want to write music," said Despacio. "Now show me what you brought in today."

Twenty-eight

from
Quatermain's Guide
The Advantages of the Strong Force
A Guide to and History of the Met
by Leo Y. Sherman

The Science of the Met

Although the theoretical possibility of space tethers was known in the twentieth century, the materials sciences were unable to produce a composite with the required tensile strength. Buckyballs had been invented, but superstrong and superelastic matter had to await the full working out of the principles of quantum electro- and chromodynamics, and the nanotech revolution which began in the 2300s and is continuing to this day.

By the early 2400s, nanotechnologists had united buckyball constructions with superconducting quantum interference devices (SQUIDs) to create a reproducible molecular chain that displayed quantum behavior on the macro level. Buckyball SQUIDs behave like the individual components in an atom—that is, electrons, protons, neutrons, and the protons' and neutrons' constituent quarks. They do this by creating a kind of "resonating chamber"— much like an organ pipe. As sound resonates in a musical pipe, particles take the form of standing waves in a SQUID.

The most important behavior that the nanotechnological engineers were able to produce, at least in regard to the Met, is the strong nuclear force.

The strong interaction is the force that holds the nucleus of an atom together even though the clump of positively charged protons wants to blow apart, since like electrical charges repel. The strong force is actually a by-product of the color force of quarks, which make up the protons. Normally, the strong force operates only in a strictly prescribed distance, which is, naturally, close to the diameter of an atomic nucleus (about 10^{-13} centimeters). But at that range, the strong force is 100 times stronger than the force of electromagnetism. This means, in principle, that it is 100 times stronger than the chemical bonds that make up most ordinary construction material. In a chain of buckyball SQUIDs, the strong force is manifested as a "particle" that is 0.5 centimeters across—visible to the naked human eye. By the mid 2400s such chains were being regularly produced in the laboratory.

The strong force has one more peculiar property that is essential in Met construction. It does not obey the inverse square law of both electromagnetism and gravity. Within the range of the strong force, quarks that are farther away are actually pulled more strongly than quarks that are closer together. You can picture it as a rubber band connecting two particles. The more you stretch the rubber band, the harder it pulls the particles. When the particles are close together, the rubber band is slack. It is this property of the strong force, operating on a macro level, that gives the Met cables their ability to bend without breaking. Torque forces that would easily separate material made of mere chemical bonds cannot overcome the strong force manifested by the buckyball SQUIDs, and the Met holds together.

In fact, there is no known force generated by the turnings of the planets that is even close to pushing the Met's structural tolerances. If you live or travel in the Met, you are as safe as you are on the surface of a planet (and they are, themselves, held together, on the level of the atomic nucleus, by the strong force of nature).

Twenty-nine

After two years of composition work with Despacio, Claude Schlencker's concerto took the first prize in the Met-wide competition for new composers. Its subtitle was "Meditations in Red." He wrote it in the key of Charm, with several quick transpositions to Strange and Bottom.

Despacio was the first person to whom Claude broke the news. His lessons had continued past Claude's graduation from Asap Gymnasium and into his enrollment in Suisui University on Mercury.

"It's going to be performed," Claude told him. "Here. In the Solar Hall in Bach."

"By a virtual orchestra?" said Despacio.

"No," said Claude. "By bodies."

Despacio looked sad for a moment. "I see," he said. Then he brightened. "It's quite good, you know, Mr. Schlencker. Better than anything in a long while."

"I owe it all to you."

"Do you?"

Claude blinked, then sat down in his usual chair. That is, what he imagined to be his chair, even though it was only so much coding. Just as Despacio was.

"No," he said. "Not all."

"Let us always be honest with one another, Mr. Schlencker."

Claude was silent for a moment, and then he decided to

ask the question he'd been wanting to ask for some time now.

"Do you have a first name, Despacio?"

"Yes," said the composer. "Yes, I do."

"I hate my name," Claude said.

"It's a fine name."

"I hate it."

"Very well, then. You hate it."

"I want to use another one. To sign my work. For everything. I would like it to be . . . a name that means something to me. A name that means something else to me than 'Claude Schlencker' does."

Despacio tugged his beard. Claude felt he must have been mistaken, but he could have sworn the old composer's eyes were . . . misty. But that could not be. He wasn't real, and he couldn't cry.

"When they first . . . programmed me . . . long before they fed in the mentalities and ran me through evolution, they used to have a name for me. It is what I've always thought of as my first name, because it was, you see, *first*. I've never told anyone."

"Will you tell me?"

"It was an acronym, from *English* words. Not really a proper name at all."

"What was it?"

"Artificial Musical Expression System. With the accent on 'Expression.'" Despacio sat down in the chair across from Claude. "It's really rather horrible. That's why I never use it."

"Amés," Claude said.

"Amés."

"May I use it?"

"You may," replied Despacio. "You may, indeed. I have no further use for it, I can assure you."

"Amés," said the former Claude Schlencker. "From now on, that will be me."

Thirty

from
Quatermain's Guide
The Advantages of the Strong Force
A Guide to and History of the Met
by Leo Y. Sherman

Government

The Met is a democracy. It is based on an interlocking amalgamation of directorates each with its own function or geographic provenance. Met citizens "vote with their channel selectors," with each citizen guaranteed membership in at least three directorates, and each having the ability to change allegiances at any time. Directorate members usually then elect a board, who appoint the director general and various higher-ups. Most positions under the subdirectorate level are based on merit, as judged by these appointed officers. Sometimes membership in a directorate can swing widely, especially during merci events prominently featuring a particular directorate or associated group, whether in a positive or negative light. Within minutes, relative voter strength can double or triple, as Met citizens exercise their "right to change channels."

This form of modified popular democracy has its roots in the last century and is a direct result of the famous "Conjubilation of 2993." During that e-year, when Earth and Mars were in planetary opposition in their orbits, a major span was constructed connecting the two sides of the Diaphany bend not far from the center. Promoters trumpeted the Conjubilation as a major cultural event on the merci, but it soon grew far beyond their expectations and then beyond their control. Nearly six million people made the trip to the span, and millions more attended in the virtuality. Many important cultural and scientific movements had their origins in the event, but most importantly for us here, a series of demonstrations broke out against the old Federal Republic. These in turn had their beginnings in the music and art festival called the Merge.

At the Merge, political opinions transformed daily, but the consensus seemed to be that something had to change in the way the government of the time did things. Matters were not helped for the old Republic when the then president of the Republic, Quim Fukuyama, put in a personal appearance and, after a rather mediocre speech, told everyone to "please go home." As a result of the "Please Go Home" speech, the Republic was sent packing in the next election, and activists from the Merge elected. They quickly put into place the directorate-based government (the directorates were at first called havens) that we have today in the Met.

The most important political figure to arise out of the Merge was a LAP going by the singular name of Amés. Amés had come into the merge as a featured musician (he was a composer). It was Amés who first saw the need for a directorate interlock and, after campaigning vigorously (some have claimed ruthlessly) for such an entity, he was appointed its director. Since that time, Director Amés has been reappointed to the post.

How did a musical composer transform himself into the politician who would unite the crumbling Met government?

Director Amés has said that he always had political ambitions.

"My music is about movement and action—getting things done. That's one of the reasons I have always insisted on conducting my own compositions. It's the music of change and growth, and not every conductor can bring that kind of commitment to its performance," he said in a famous merci interview at the Merge of '93. "What I do as a composer and conductor is to order the world. It's chaos out there—and chaos is deadly. My music is about order and strength. I'm not talking about order like the old fogies of the Republic want—keeping things running more or less like they always have. I'm talking about order that leads to action—to remaking the world around us into what *we* want, and not what the chaos forces on us. That's what I do as a musician—and that's what the Met sorely needs from its leaders."

The original system of directorates that arose after the old Republic government fell was, itself, a shaky affair. Direct democracy had never been tried before on such a large scale. Day after day directorates rose enormously in popularity and influence, only to find themselves destroyed in the merci polls the moment they attempted anything the slightest bit unpopular. And, in direct democracy, to fall in the polls is to be voted out of office.

What was needed was someone who could handle both the political coordination of the directorates and sway popular opinion and keep it in line long enough for the government to do its job. What was needed was someone who knew the ins and outs of popular entertainment on the merci, but who could also shoulder the task of real governing. On the merci political shows, and in the think tanks and news bullpens, the star of the Merge of '93 was soon seen everywhere. Everyone who was anyone on the political pundit circuit had to have Amés appear on his or her show or play in his or her game milieu.

Amés might have gone down in history as any other forgotten talk-show guest, had it not been for the untimely death of the governor of Mercury that occurred precisely at the height of Amés's popularity on the merci. Within one new-cycle day, the young composer went from a politically hot newcomer to the head of the richest planet in the solar system. Using this power base and his own popularity in the moment, Amés quickly began consolidating the directorates under his governance. At first, the directorates were loath to give up their influence, as fleeting as that influence could be, but the merci polls were overwhelming in Amés's favor, and a series of unlucky accidents befell those directors who opposed him. It was almost as if the popular will had swept them from life as well as from office.

"Music was never something soothing for me, but a challenge to be met. I had a teacher who saw to that. He never let me use music as some kind of escape from responsibility. There are all these notes. They can be put to work in beautiful ways, if only you know how to arrange them in the most useful way," Amés said shortly after his ascent to Director of the Interlocking Directorates of the Met. "The directorates work in the same way. Separately, they are a bunch of discordant notes. But together— together, we can make the most beautiful music the human race has ever heard."

Thirty-one

At first, Aubry Graytor didn't notice the little man. He was barely over five-foot-two and was dressed nondescriptly. Aubry was having enough trouble making her way in the crush of the customs check to pay much attention to any of the adults around her. But the man was insistently tugging on the sleeve of her father's shirt. Her father pulled away, but then the man said something into his ear, and Kelly directed Aubry and Sint to a side passage with an alcove where there were some advertisements for a spa on Venus. They started to speak, but her father told them to shut up. He turned his attention to the little man.

"All right," Kelly said. "How is she in danger?"

Her father didn't mention who "she" was, but Aubry had a notion it was her mother. Danis was now being processed through the free-convert portion of the customs check.

"There have been hostilities," the little man said. His voice was surprisingly gentle and soft. "There's no formal declaration of war yet, but all free converts are being detained. They're claiming that they contain technology that's proprietary to the Met."

"We were worried about a clause in a contract that might have delayed her," her father said.

"They're using anything and everything to get a legal

hold on free converts," said the man. "If there is the slightest doubt, they aren't going to let her go."

"Oh God," Kelly said. Then he looked hard at the man, the way he sometimes looked at Aubry when he knew she was only telling him part of the truth about something. "Who the hell are you?" he asked.

"My name is Sherman," said the little man. "Leo Sherman. That's not important. I work for the Friends of Tod, a group dedicated to free-convert rights—"

"We've never had any trouble in that regard," said her father, "except for a comment here and there."

"You're from Mercury," Leo Sherman said. "The farther out you get, the less freedom for free converts. There's some slave labor on Mars. Look, we have to work fast. I've got a legal convert jamming the system right now, arguing each and every case. Your wife is probably in queue for a hearing."

"You mean these trials are going on in the virtuality?"

"Yes. But our legal sentient isn't doing much good. We haven't won a single case yet. We have slowed the process down enough so that we can seek out . . . alternatives."

"Alternatives? To what?"

"To your wife being detained and put to work crunching numbers in Noctis Labyrinthus. You have heard of Silicon Valley, haven't you? That's what the free converts who get sent there call it. It's like an aspect being sent to the salt mines."

"How can I possibly trust you?" her father said.

The little man cracked a smile. "That's what my father said after I wrecked my first personal transport." Aubry felt that she might like the man, but a voice inside her told her to be wary. After all, he might be *anyone*.

"I have a little device with me, encoded into my handshake, actually. It's legal, but barely."

"Where did you get this?"

"My organization has quite a few merci programmers and grist specialists as members. I can hook you up with your wife, on a merci sideband. Not full virtual, but it should be enough. Would you like to talk to her?"

"This could be a trick," said Kelly. "It feels like a trick."

"You're going to have to trust me," Leo Sherman said. "At least so far as to shake my hand."

Her father frowned, then seemed to make up his mind. He looked down at Aubry. "If anything weird happens," he said, "grab your brother and run like hell."

And then he quickly shook hands with Leo Sherman.

Thirty-two

For Aubry, the handshake lasted only a few seconds, hardly longer than a regular handshake might. For Kelly, however, it seemed much longer. He found himself in an incredible press of bodies. That is, he assumed they were bodies, because he couldn't see anything. Only touch, smell, and sound were coming through this link. And it was an odd sensation, the virtual equivalent to the smell of nervous sweat. He felt a touch on his hand, then fingers tracing the lines of his face.

"Oh, Kelly," said Danis. "This is horrible. I don't think they're going to let me out."

"Danis, I can't see a thing. Is it really you?"

She didn't answer with words, but with a kiss. It *was* really Danis.

"They were waiting with the Section C wording on that quantum futures contract. Kelly, it was as if they'd combed through my entire life, looking for something to hold against me."

"We have to figure out a way to get you out of this," Kelly said. He wanted to sound confident, but his voice cracked, and betrayed him.

"I've got a Friends of Tod lawyer," said Danis. She slipped her hand into his, and Kelly could feel the pressure of her warm, dry skin. "He seems very good. But I don't think it will help. He has told me about another option, though, if the hearing doesn't go well."

"What is it?"

"The society he works for. They have a . . . sister group. A group that isn't legal. They . . . smuggle out free converts. Like me. They get them out in something like a pocket-book."

"If they're going to break the law, then why can't they just use the merci? They could instantly broadcast you to Pluto—or anywhere."

"The Department of Immunity has taken total control of the merci. I suggested that to my lawyer. Damn the iter-ation laws and make a copy of me on Pluto or wherever. But Department of Immunity security is preventing that sort of thing. They have new containment algorithms in place. I've felt them. They're mean. They are quarantining free converts, Kelly."

"All right then," said Kelly. "What about this pocketbook smuggling arrangement?" He felt steadier with something concrete to discuss. They are trying to take away my wife! His mind still screamed. They are taking away Danis.

"There's no guarantee," Danis said. "And the ship they're loaded on makes a roundabout trip. It could be months be-fore I get out of cold storage." Danis's grip on his hand tightened. "Kelly, I don't think I can leave you and the chil-dren like that. I don't think I can do it."

Kelly pulled her toward him. He heard a loud voice call out: "Agila 19, serial number P0874R30-Vl9, report for Hearing on Conditions immediately."

"That's the convert ahead of me in line," said Danis. "I'm next, Kelly."

He held Danis even tighter. "Get yourself smuggled, Danis," he said. "Do it. I will find you. No matter where you are, I will find you. And I swear to you that I won't let *any-thing* happen to the kids."

"My God, Kelly, is this really happening? It can't be hap-pening. They're going to take me away from my children, Kelly."

"We will be waiting for you, my love. Always remember that." I can't lose her, Kelly thought. I can't lose my wife.

"I can't even see you," Danis said.

"Nor I you,"

"You're just a voice in my mind. And a touch."

Kelly kissed her again. They kissed for a long time, holding one another in the dark. Then it was time for Danis's hearing, and she reluctantly pulled away from him.

"Tell the children I love them," Danis said.

They were her last words to him there. Kelly was pulled backwards, as by a physical force. He felt as if he were falling down a long shaft. There was the sensation of rushing wind, but nothing else. And then the fall stopped, and he was standing in the alcove at Leroy Port, shaking hands with the stranger, his children looking on with big, frightened eyes.

He withdrew his hand from Leo Sherman's. "What about the children?" he asked the little man. "They're half–free converts, you know."

"I didn't tell you because I didn't want to alarm you even more," said Sherman. "But it is going to be a major problem."

"What do you mean?"

"Your son will be fine with you," said the man. "He's young enough to fit under a nonseparation clause our lawyers have cooked up, as long as you allow them to attach certain security restraints to his convert portion. The Friends have people in the transport ships who can remove those programs, no harm done. The problem, Mr. Graytor, is your daughter. She might be let through, but she's extremely precocious. I'm afraid that this fact has gotten into her records. They aren't going to want to let Aubry go, period. She has the makings of a LAP."

"They're not keeping my child!" said Kelly loudly. The little man motioned for him to quiet down. "They're not taking my daughter," he said in a lower tone.

"No," said the man. "We have to prevent that at all costs."

Thirty-three

Aubry felt as if the ground had been pulled from under her, and she was back in free fall. First her mother was being detained, and now she was to be separated from her father, kept in the Met. They aren't going to get any use out of me, Aubry told herself. I'll kill myself before I'll work for the Department of Immunity. But the promise sounded hollow, even in the flush of the moment. They could probably do whatever they wanted with her, and she would have precious little to say about it. She was only eleven.

"I'm eleven," she said.

"What?" said Leo Sherman.

"I'm not a baby. Tell me what you want me to do."

She felt her father's hand on her shoulder. He gave her a quick squeeze. "Yes, tell us both. Do you have any idea how we can get out of this mess?"

Leo Sherman grinned. He seemed to have a normal-sized smile for his too-small head, and his teeth seemed to take up half his face. Then he was all seriousness once again.

"It's going to be difficult, but there is a way," said Leo Sherman. "There's another port that is less closely guarded. We think we can get Aubry out there."

"Then let's go," said Kelly. "As fast as we can."

Leo Sherman shook his head. "You don't understand, Mr. Graytor. We only have so much space. We've already sent three ships out, and we still have a lot of half converts waiting. Hundreds now. It could become thousands. After the war really starts, there won't be any more ships getting out. Not so easily."

"What are you saying?"

"Aubry will have to go with me. You and your son can go the normal way, and so you must. I'll take her to the other ship."

"You think I'm going to trust my daughter to a stranger?" said Kelly. "That would be worse than getting stranded here."

"No it wouldn't," said Leo Sherman. "The Friends have learned of plans for work camps, Mr. Graytor. It's claimed that all the computing power is needed to deal with the hostilities from the outer system. To model solutions."

"That is absurd."

"It is merely a rationale," said the smaller man, "to allow the Department of Immunity to do whatever the hell it wants with free and half converts."

"But everybody has a convert portion to their personality," said Aubry. "Mine just happens to be a little more sophisticated because of who my mom is."

"That's right," said Leo Sherman. "Everybody has a convert portion. We think it will start with the free converts, the ones without bodily aspects, and then . . . we don't believe the Department of Immunity is going to stop there. But one problem at a time. We have to get Aubry to safety, Mr. Graytor."

"I understand what you are saying. Who is *we?* I always thought the Friends of Tod were a bunch of—well, fuzzy-headed Mergies. All I see is *you,*" her father said. "And I still don't know if I can trust you."

"Mergies or not, the Friends are on your side, Mr. Graytor," Leo Sherman began, then he was silent for a moment. Aubry realized he was hearing voices in the grist. "Danis Graytor was officially denied exit at her hearing, sir. There isn't much time now. They may detain you and your son on suspicion of aiding and abetting."

"This is crazy," Kelly said. "I'm a Met citizen . . . I . . . all right. We have to come to a decision. Obviously."

Aubry's father put his hand to his nose, took it away. He touched his neck, kneaded his shoulder. "Obviously," he murmured.

Aubry realized that she had to help her father. He was not going to be able to let her go off on her own, yet he could not keep her with him.

"You have to take care of Sint," she said to him. "That's what you have to do. You know I can take care of myself pretty good. A lot better than Sint is able. You have to let me go."

"But you're my dear. My darling," Kelly murmured. "I can't risk losing you all. I can't—"

"You're not going to lose me, Dad," Aubry said. "We're all going to get away from here."

Kelly looked at her with fervent desperation in his eyes a moment longer. Then he seemed to pull himself together and be the man Aubry had always known.

"All right," he said. "She's going with you, Sherman." He looked the other man straight in the eye. Many a stock-market trader had received that look and immediately put aside any plans to put one over on Kelly Graytor. It was the look that he gave Aubry when times for objections and complaints were over and it was time to do what her father told her. "I appreciate all you and your people have done for my family," he said. "If there is any way I can ever repay you, I will do so. But, sir—" He put a hand on Leo's arm, squeezed it, not hard, but firmly. "Take care of my daughter."

Leo Sherman looked him in the eye, right back in the eye, Aubry saw. Not very many people could do that so easily with her father. "I'll treat her as if she were my own sister," the little man said.

"Very well," Kelly said, and released him. He turned to Aubry. "See you soon, Aubry. Your mother and I love you." He opened his arms and she fell into them.

"See you, Dad," she said. She hugged Sint, too, who was crying, and told him to take care of their father. Then Kelly took Sint's hand and Leo Sherman took Aubry's and the family went in opposite directions down the main corridor.

Thirty-four

from
Quatermain's Guide
The Advantages of the Strong Force
A Guide to and History of the Met
by Leo Y. Sherman

Conclusion

The Met continues to grow, and changes often in unexpected and fascinating ways. Although the asteroid belt has proven to be a frontier beyond which current technology will not allow the structure to extend, every e-year, several new dendrites are added, along with the free-floating "micro-Mets" which exist in the reaches of inner interplanetary space and only come into direct physical contact with the larger Met at long intervals. The inner planets, while maintaining their importance, have gradually been subsumed into the larger system as well. After the disastrous terraforming experiments on Mars in the 2700s, it was seen that humanity's best bet for living in space lay not on the other planets, but among them. In 2802, the Earth was declared an "Ecological Repatriation Area," with limited construction and population growth allowed, and now vast stretches of our native planet have been returned to their natural state for all to enjoy.

Tensions continue with the outer system, which has never fully accepted integration into the directorate-based democracy of the Met, and still retains modified vestiges of the old Republic of the Planets governmental structure. New political and cultural challenges have arisen, including the push among virtual entities for "free-convert rights." The ecological balance of the Met is another area not fully explored, and there are worries that some of the unintended grist feedback effects that doomed the Mars terraforming projects might surface again as the Met expands.

At its best, the Met is a place of adventure and fulfillment unparalleled in human history. We invite you to explore it in all its wondrous aspects.

Thirty-five

Fragment from the Fall of Titan

Dory Folsom couldn't breathe methane, but she could damn well swim in it. So could her platoon. At least, that's what they'd been told. They'd been scheduled for a trial run on the new mods before shipping out, but things had been stepped up, and there hadn't been time. Nobody told them where they were going, but it didn't take a genius to guess that it was somewhere with a good supply of liquid methane, since that was all they'd heard for an e-month: methane, methane—oh, and a brief refresher on nitrogen and the bends. And when you were talking methane in all its triple-point glory—solid, liquid, and gas—you were talking Titan.

They came in skipping off Saturn's atmosphere to confuse the *fremden*. They skirted the rings ("Not too close, Cap'n, not too goddamn close!") and used Titan's thick atmosphere for braking. They descended like fireballs onto the moon. The fremden civs were totally surprised, and Laketown fell in a day. There was some fierce resistance in a couple of sectors of the city, however, and Dory's unit was sent directly into the heat. It was literally heat, because some clever fremden gristwright had figured out that the big methane snowfall of the past two weeks was not methane at all, but military grist. To simulate snow, it had been given the same physical properties as methane, and one sure way to get rid of the stuff was to melt it. So the locals had used some countering grist and old-fashioned self-contained blowtorches to set their whole part of town on fire.

In the other parts of Laketown, the grist had fallen, accumulated to a certain point, then activated and gone about its tasks. These tasks were varied, but, for the most part, deadly. Some of it just ate a fremden alive, "digested" him or her, then went and ate some more. Some of it was preprogrammed to go after command and control—that is, both structures and people. The local governor's face was imprinted on the minds of a billion tiny assassins, so it was no wonder that they got him, even though people had caught on by then, and he was dug in pretty deep. Some of the grist insinuated itself into walls, into machinery, into people's bodies. There it took up residence and slowly replaced crucial structures in the "host" building—a driveshaft, a supporting girder, a ventricle valve. And then, on the day of the attack, it just dissolved. And there you were—or weren't.

Some bright youngster was rooting the grist out of New Alki, a peninsula that stretched away from the city and formed a spitlike whorl out in Lake Voyager. Dory's platoon, unlike the methane grist, wouldn't burn and wouldn't melt. Nevertheless, somebody had figured out how to make their own homemade evil snow, and Zavers, Dory's buddy on the obstacle course (and her onetime lover), stepped into a puddle that wasn't a puddle, and before anybody knew what was up, he was writhing and the "puddle" was crawling up his leg. The fremden grist must have compromised Zaver's heating elements incredibly quickly, because within seconds he was frozen in mid-writhe like a Popsicle in pain. It was −180 Celsius out there.

After that, they avoided stepping in anything that looked like liquid. The heat around them was a cold fire by the standards of life from Earth. It flickered blackly, only hot enough to melt the killing snow.

The platoon met their first human resistance near a clump of high-rise apartments on New Alki's main thoroughfare. It was an ambush from above using some kind of projectile accelerator. They later found that the fremden had converted a railgun used for firing packets into orbit into a deadly weapon that could throw bricks at several times the speed of sound in nitrogen. The brick arrived, followed by a tremendous sonic boom. One of the bricks hit the sarge in the chest, and he exploded into a nova of goo. Another one hit near Dvochek, flung up some rocks that acted like shrapnel, and took off Dvochek's right arm. The grist of his adaptation quickly sealed the wound; he lived and was able to keep fighting.

When the sarge died, Dory felt a new presence suddenly light up her mind, and she knew that she'd been picked by the lieutenant to replace the squad sergeant.

"Corporal Folsom, stand by for command communication protocols," said the voice of Lieutenant Uhl in her mind.

"Yes, sir." And there, in the midst of the brick barrage, she'd been made part of the *vinculum*, the Department of Immunity Enforcement Division's Merced communications network.

Commanding officers in DIED infantry battalions didn't communicate their will to their soldiers, they *expressed* it through them. This expression, flowing down the command chain of the vinculum from a soldier's lieutenant, captain, major, and general, was ultimately a product of one controlling mind, that of Director Amés.

The feeling of blissful interconnection that DIED officers felt when they either received or completed their orders was called the Glory, and while her companions fell around her, Dory smiled with intense pleasure as the Glory washed over her.

The sensation only lasted a moment, however, and then she was rallying the other soldiers and storming the building on which the railgun was perched. After they were inside, there was some intense hall-to-hall fighting, but Met soldiers were dressed out like attack helicopters used to be on Earth—rockets, projectile weapons—and all around them, stretched out for many meters, a grist pellicle that served as an advance scout, could see around corners, and could, to a limited extent, attack in and of itself, like a long stinging tentacle. The fremden didn't stand a chance in close quarters. Dory took point as her unit charged up the stairs (the lifts were disabled), and she, personally, took the converted railgun out with an arm rocket, along with its civ crew. Before the final assault, she thought of Zavers, and toyed with the idea of letting the civs die slowly, but settled for a clean kill. Killing cleanly where possible was part of her orders, anyway, and if you wanted to feel the Glory, you had to obey orders.

The school recruiter back in Clarit Bolsa on the Vas had told Dory it would be like this, but she hadn't really believed—not even after the merci simulation and the class vote on the coolness factor of being a Met soldier (93% approval, with a 75% *rip* quotient). Both Dory's parents were big supporters of Director Amés, and every e-week they watched the show *The Department of Immunity Presents* together, so Dory figured she might as well give the Department of Immunity recruiter a chance to personalize her settings.

Fifty-three seconds later she had totally understood about order and how chaos needed it, and basically manufactured it out of nothing. The recruiter had shown Dory some extremely cool virtuality graphics of things called Mandelbrot sets.

"See how it goes down? Pattern, then chaos, then repeated pattern? See how the little patterns are basically repetitions of larger? That's the way the New Hierarchy is going to arise out of this present chaos. You're a seed crystal, Dory. You could be, that is. Don't you want to be an attractor?"

Being an attractor sounded good to her.

"Rip," Dory had said, and she'd signed up. Her parents had been proud as hell. Something better was coming. Some real order was going to arise from all this mess of a solar system, and Amés was the one who could pull it off, pull everyone up. And those who didn't want to be pulled up? They could stay where they were, as long as they didn't get in the way of the uplifted. But, you know, they *always* did. And that was what the Department of Immunity and being a Met soldier was all about. Getting obstructionists the hell out of the way so a good change could come, so that order could finally flow. You didn't want to kill anybody, but sometimes you had to, for their own good.

That was only a year ago, and here she was, fucking on Titan, a moon of Saturn. Taking out the strange elements, sweeping the system clean.

And with the Glory as a reward. With Director Amés smiling down through the command chain right on *her*, saying, Dory, you did a hell of a job. Dory, I will not forget you when it comes time for medals and promotions. And, with the dead fremden lying about her and their stupid railgun blown to pieces, Dory stood on top of the apartment building against the red photochemical smog of Titan as the Met forces subjugated the rest of Laketown. She watched the portions of the town that had been on fire surrender themselves to the extreme cold. She felt a tingle when the merci blackout was lifted, and General Haysay announced the surrender of the remaining ground forces, and the subjugation of the moon. She knew from vinculum sidebands that what was left of the fremden space fleet was gathering above, to make one last stand. But the ground was taken, planetary defenses were in Met hands. What were they going to do, attack their own populace?

The fact was, Amés had won. And when Amés won, everyone, all along the vinculum, got a share of the Glory.

And Dory, standing there, got her share of it, too. Like the sun. Like a warm shower on a cold morning. Fucking marvelous! Fucking 101 percent approval rating!

"Rip," Dory said, and smiled like a madwoman. Then she and her unit stacked the enemy bodies and set them to dissolve into the general grist.

It was only after the Glory faded that Dory and the squad went to collect their own dead and pack them into the cremation cubes for their trips back. All except Zavers. They couldn't get the fremden grist to let him go, so they had to leave him there, all froze up and nine hundred million miles away from home.

And then it started to snow—real methane, this time—and Dory watched as the flakes filled in Zavers's eyes and the lines around his mouth so that he didn't look so much like he was being tortured or something.

Zavers had been a good guy, really. Her first lay, to tell the truth, at least with full penetration. He had been all right, even though he hadn't gotten Dory to come. Nobody had, and she wondered if it was really the big deal everybody made it out to be.

She wondered how it would compare to the Glory.

Then it was time to move on. She gave a last glance at Zavers and felt like she was sorry about something, but couldn't say what. It wasn't like the guy had meant that much to her. But he had been a good guy. Basically tender. She looked around and found the rest of the squad looking at her.

"Where to, Sarge?" asked Darkroom, the guy from Mars.

"To our next glorious destination," she told him. "Wherever the fuck that is."

Then she felt it again. The weird feeling. Sorry, when there was nothing to be sorry about.

"Rip," Darkroom said.

"Shut the fuck up," replied Dory.

Thirty-six

Aubry followed Leo Sherman down a maze of passageways, always leading farther away from the more traveled corridors of the bolsa and toward—well, Aubry had never been in such places before. The passages grew narrower, then stopped being passages at all and became ducts. Aubry and Leo Sherman squeezed through a series of narrow openings, crawled along a few hundred feet of floor, then squeezed through more. Not only were the passages getting narrower, they were getting *wetter*. Aubry wanted to ask Leo Sherman about this, but he kept a good pace up and wouldn't stop and talk until at least two hours after she'd parted with her father. Finally, they twisted and turned their way through a cavelike tube that no regular-sized person could have navigated. Aubry understood why they had sent the littler man to pick her up. Whoever *they* were.

The tube fed out into a large round room, where other tubes joined it. There was a changing breeze in the room, and Aubry was almost certain she could see the walls move in and out slightly—as if they were breathing.

"Now," said Leo Sherman, "we rest."

"Where in the world are we?" asked Aubry. "I didn't know places like this existed in the Met."

"There's the chemical Met, and then there's the biological Met. Where we are now—this whole area just under the skin of the bolsas—it's called the Integument. It's kind of a hodgepodge thing, the Integument, neither vegetable nor mineral. I've spent a lot of time wandering around in it. It's kind of my specialty actually. I'm a merci reporter, I guess you might call me, though what I actually do is write these things called essays about nature in the Met—"

"I know what an essay is," said Aubry, feeling a bit annoyed. "I can read, you know."

"You or your software?" he asked her.

"I learned to read when I was four years old," Aubry told him. "But I have excellent translation algorithms and top-of-the-line Broca grist."

"Pleased to hear it," Leo Sherman said. "My work is available on the merci. Maybe someday you might want to read it. But first, we have to get out of here."

"Where are we?"

"This is a recycling sac—keeps some of the e-mix of the gases stable before shipment."

"Shipment?"

"You'll see."

"What are those?" Aubry asked, pointing to some black cables that fed in along the bottom of one of the tubes.

"Power cables. They work sort of like nerves in our bodies—through ionic transfer of a charge. It's slow, but amazingly efficient."

"And somebody came up with all this?"

"Yes and no," said Leo Sherman. He pulled a water bottle from a small pouch on the waist of his pants, drank some, then passed it to Aubry. "You have to fend for yourself when you're in the Integument. The grist around here won't recognize your pellicle's interaction nodes. So you can't order up water from out of the walls, like you're used to doing. And you just have to be careful in general. This place is not designed with your safety in mind."

"But, Mr. Sherman—"

"Nix with that! It's Leo. There's already a Sherman who likes to go by his title."

"Well, Leo, then," said Aubry, feeling a little funny using the man's first name. On Mercury, it wasn't done for children to address adults so familiarly. "What do you mean when you say 'yes and no'? Did somebody build this place, or didn't they?"

"People laid down the parameters," Leo said, "the basic principles of biological interaction. But this is all self-replicating." Leo pointed around him. "These walls, the ducts, the other layers—they're all made up of bioengineered living matter. It's made of something like cells. The Integument is something like a forest, too. Like a forest somebody planted nearly four hundred years ago. Things have grown here that nobody knows about. Things have evolved. You must have wondered why the walls started to feel so sticky?"

"I had noticed that," said Aubry.

"They are alive!" Leo continued. "They need to respire. They have to recognize certain substances that come in contact with them. They are actually able to capture and analyze molecules with that thin layer of goo that coats everything. It's a method of communication."

"Like smell?" said Aubrey.

Leo smiled. "Now you're catching on," he said. "There's some wonderful stuff I could show you around here, only we haven't got time."

"Where are we going, anyway?" Aubry said, taking a drink of the water and passing it back to Leo.

"There is another method of transportation in the Met besides the pithways. It's a lot slower, but it has the advantage of being completely unmonitored by the Department of Immunity."

"There's something the Department of Immunity doesn't know about?" Aubry asked.

"Oh, they know about it," said Leo. "They just don't think anybody would be crazy enough to use it."

"But we're crazy enough, huh?" said Aubry.

"Aw, come on. It'll be fun." Leo stood up and helped Aubry to her feet. "We'd better get a move on. We've still got a ways to go."

They were three more hours working their way through narrow passages and gaps. The farther along they got, the more the walls and floors began to resemble the internal cavities of some great beast.

And, according to Leo, that's exactly what they were.

"But does it have a brain?" Aubry asked as they wound their way around what looked for all the world like a gigantic tonsil suspended like a stalactite.

"Good question," answered Leo. "What do you think? Does the Earth have a brain?"

"I've never been to Earth."

"Use your imagination. Think about the jungles and rain forests that you've read about, the ecological balance that we've restored by basically letting the place alone and allowing it to go back to wilderness."

"I don't see how it could," Aubry said, after she'd thought for a while. "But sometimes it acts as if it did."

"Good question and good answer," Leo replied. "The same thing applies here. Everything has come to work together so beautifully that sometimes you think there must be a controlling intelligence, but in every case—at least every case I know of—if you start looking at what you imagined to be thoughts, you find simple processes."

"But you can do exactly the same thing with a brain," Aubry said, pleased to have found a way to continue the conversation. Leo, unlike most adults, seemed to think of her as his intellectual equal, even if she didn't know as many facts as an adult did. She got the feeling he was really telling her his own ideas, and not trying to play some kind of teaching game with the end already in mind. Aubry was much too bright for most games of that sort to trick her for very long, and she usually could see where the teacher was going and then some long before the teacher realized he or she was found out.

"And a brain very definitely thinks thoughts," Leo answered. "I know."

"So why couldn't the Met be a gigantic developing intelligence, and me and you being like neurons or something?"

"You may be right," said Leo. "But answer me this. If we assume that we *are* actually neurons in some kind of giant overmind, how would you ever know? Can you think of some means to find out? Some experiment we could do that would tell us?"

By this time they were squeezing through an extremely narrow passage, and Aubry was glad to have something else to think about rather than her sense of claustrophobia, which was fast closing in on her.

"We could . . . maybe use some kind of entropy test. Couldn't we assume that an intelligent system would create more order than another system that was alive, but not intelligent?"

"Pretty smart idea, but then the problem is the same as trying to tell whether you're floating around in space or falling down a black elevator shaft—that is, there's no fixed point of reference. Are you going to assume that the Met is supersentient, but the Earth isn't? Or the other way around? What living system are you absolutely certain *isn't* sentient, that could serve as a measuring stick?"

"What about some alien life-form? Isn't there some kind of lichen or something on the bottom of the Lost Sea on Europa?"

"That's . . . we don't know about that. Some good people were lost trying to find out." For a moment, Aubry caught a glimpse of Leo's face, and it seemed very sad. Then he continued the argument. "But how do you know that its ecology is not sentient? You'd be assuming what you wanted to prove, either way."

"So it may be that the Met is sentient, but there's no way of proving it?"

"I can't think of one," Leo replied, "other than the World Spirit sitting us down and saying a personal hello to each of us."

"Bummer," said Aubry.

"I don't know about that," Leo said. "To paraphrase Raphael Merced, there's something to be said for acting locally as if the world had meaning and needed us to do what we think is right, but letting the bigger picture remain cloudy. At least for me, it kind of serves the necessary function of getting me off my ass and doing something."

Finally, they arrived at a terminus, where it was impossible to go any farther.

"Time to give Mother Nature a hand," said Leo. He held

out his own hand, and a thin sheath of fire sprang up on it. Aubry had spent most of life being told never to do this with one's grist, and it was kind of exciting to be breaking the rules. She lit up her own hand. The two of them applied the flame to the end of the tube they'd been walking through. After a moment, it seemed to shudder, and then the sides contracted. At the same time, the tube "floor" under them convulsed, so that they were thrown forward through the new opening, head over heels. They landed in a soft mass of greenish material that looked like a mound of penicillin.

They were in an enormous cavern. The walls were lit by a bioluminal glow, and what at first glance appeared to be a stream flowed through the middle of the cavern. When she got to the stream, though, Aubry saw that it wasn't flowing water at all.

"What is that?" she asked. "It looks like snot."

"Remarkably similar consistency," Leo said. "But it's actually something like limbic fluid. There's a lot of reduction processes going on inside, and it's crammed full of oxygen."

"You mean . . ."

"You can breathe it."

"Gross."

Suddenly, as if it had sneezed, the entire cavern convulsed. Aubry was almost thrown off her feet by the wave motion that passed through the floor. And the little cataract of fluid was covered over, squeezed as if it were a tube, and squirted toward the cavern's edge, where it disappeared into a hole in the wall.

"Here we are at our train station," said Leo. "All aboard!"

"Train station?"

"Or pithway stop, or what have you. We have arrived at our transportation."

"Where?"

"Here. We call this the sluice. And the stuff in it we call the sluice juice."

"You can't mean—"

"The sluice interconnects all the bolsas strung along the Met. It maintains ecological balance and serves all kinds of secondary functions. It keeps the Met healthy, and it's the healthiest place in the Met, as a result."

"I am not getting in that stuff."

"It's perfectly breathable, Aubry."

"I am not going swimming in a *river of snot.*"

"It's healthy, life-giving snot."

"I can't believe you want me to do this."

"It's really fun, Aubry, after you get over the initial . . . idea of it. With a proper map, which I've got in my noggin"—Leo tapped his head—"the sluice juice will take you anywhere in the Met that you want to go."

Aubry approached the edge of the little stream. She bent down and put her finger in it. Her finger came away dripping and trailing an elastic slime. She backed up, and the cavern convulsed again, sending more slime on its way throughout the Met.

Leo jumped in and spread the sluice juice all over his body. He ducked his head under and came up looking like a baby kitten that had just been given a complete bath by its mother.

"Come on in," said Leo. "The juice is fine."

Aubry was afraid to think about it anymore—afraid she might throw up if she thought about it anymore. At least the stuff didn't smell. Too bad, that is.

She closed her eyes and stepped into the snot. It came up to her waist, and was just as warm and gooey as she had suspected it would be.

"I know it'll feel strange at first," said Leo, "but you have to go under and take a deep breath. Fill your lungs full of the stuff. I promise you—you won't drown."

"But—"

"Give it a try, Aubry, I think you'll—"

The cavern convulsed again, and Aubry was sucked under, down into the goo. She held her breath for a moment. She had gulped in a mouthful of the juice when she'd fallen, and it oozed around in her mouth. Could you swallow the stuff? Not and keep from vomiting it back up. She was pushed forward rapidly by the walls of the cataract— now becoming something like a blood vessel. Pushed and not let up, pushed . . . could she open her eyes in this stuff? Leo hadn't said anything about that. But she had to see where she was going, what was happening.

She opened her eyes. The bioluminescence of the cavern was present there, too. In fact, the sluice juice itself seemed to have a faint green glow, like radioactive mucus.

But the act of opening her eyes somehow gave her new courage, or at least made her feel less repulsed by the juice. She felt as if she were swimming in the beautiful center of a wave in a green ocean. She was perfectly buoyant, and it felt so serene. Maybe it would be all right, maybe . . .

She took a breath. Just sucked in as hard as she could. The sluice juice filled her lungs.

And it was fine. Immediately, Aubry felt the oxygen rushing into her blood through her lungs. She could breathe this stuff! She really could. She breathed out, and in. The effort was greater than normal breathing—you had to consciously push and pull harder with your chest muscles. But she was breathing it, all right, and not drowning in it.

As abruptly as it came, the contraction relaxed. Aubry found herself next to Leo. Both of them were about halfway across the cavern from where they had started out before the contraction.

"Wow!" Aubry exclaimed. "I did it!"

"What did I tell you?" said Leo. "This is just kind of like a capillary. When we get into the main sluiceways, we can reach speed that you wouldn't believe."

"And we just swim the whole way? How do we stay together?"

Leo smiled mischievously. "There's one other thing that I'm going to show you. I'm not exactly sure of the physics of it, but these giant bubbles form in the sluice passageways. You have to push pretty hard to get inside them, but once you do, you can actually stand on the bottom and it will orient itself like a ball with a weight on one side. After we get to the main passage, we ride in style. That is, unless we have to change bubbles. That can get a little tricky . . ."

"Let's go!" said Aubry. "This is going to be fun!"

"Sure it is," said Leo. "But you have to be careful at all times. This ain't the regular Met, kid, with lots of built-in safety features. We're in the Integument. It's supposed to be no-man's-land."

"Okay, I'll be careful," said Aubry, a bit impatient to try the dunking again. "What'll I do?"

"You start by holding on to my leg and letting me lead us to where we're going. No need to swim. Let the juice do your work for you . . . ready? I think this cataract's getting ready to pop again."

Aubry knelt until the juice was up to her neck. She wrapped her arms around one of Leo's legs. "Ready," she said. They ducked under, and the walls of the cavern contracted.

It *was* incredibly fun, if a little bit scary at the same time. The juice rushed you so *fast*! Leo seemed to guide them effortlessly through the maze of passageways at breakneck speed.

There must be something he's noticing, Aubry thought. She began to watch the tunnels that Leo took and the ones he avoided. There *was* a peculiar red rim at the top of the tunnels that they traveled down. But still, they were moving so fast, she wondered if Leo could possibly notice *and* react in time. He had obviously done this many times before.

The passageways got bigger and bigger, and soon they were in an artery that was as big around as a house. There, they encountered their first bubbles. But Leo waited until they were diverted into an even bigger passage before he pushed his way inside one.

He wriggled inside as if he were a snake, then turned around and pulled Aubry in after him. They both sat dripping on what was now the "floor" of the bubble. Outside, through the refracting sides of the bubble, Aubry could see many other similar bubbles, and chunks of something else floating around as well. Then there was a flash of light as a tribe of what looked like spinning prisms floated past.

"Those are kind of like vitamins," Leo said. The bubble was an air bubble, with a regular e-mix, as far as Aubry could tell, and they could finally speak. "I saw that you figured out how I knew where to go," Leo said. "Outbound passages have that faint red coloration."

"Is that part of the design?" Aubry asked.

"Nobody knows. It isn't mentioned in any of the historic specs. My own personal theory is that some early sluice runner who was also a bioengineer coded it into the structure so he could find his way around."

"You mean, people have been doing this for a long time?"

"It used to be a hobby some people were into," said Leo. "Now everybody does group activities and group sport. Hardly anyone remembers the glory days of the sluice runs anymore."

"That's good for us, I guess," said Aubry. She sat back and began to enjoy the view. This was not as exhilarating as the trip down the capillaries had been, but it was beautiful in its own right. "Where are we headed, anyway?"

"We are headed to see a man . . . sort of a man . . . who knows people who can help you get away."

"A sort of a man? Is he a LAP?"

"Yes," said Leo, "but that's not the half of it. Have you ever heard of the time towers?"

"Some special kind of Large Array of Personalities. We haven't covered that yet in identity class. It's for ninth graders, I think."

"You're about to get a quick education, kid," Leo said. "Looks like you're going to be growing up a little faster than is maybe for the best, but there's not much to be done about it."

"I can handle it," said Aubry. And floating along in a giant air bubble through the hidden integument of the Met, she almost thought she could.

"I'm a little worried, because this man—his name is Tod—it's been a long time since he was a kid and he isn't around kids that much. It's a real adult place we're going to."

"I've been running from the secret police for the past six hours," said Aubry. "I think I can handle some old fart time tower."

Leo smiled his big, face-splitting smile at her again. "Yeah, I'm not too worried about you, to tell the truth."

Leo settled back on the floor of their bubble and put his hands behind his head. "Relax while you can, I always say. I'd smoke a cig, but this bubble is already filling up with enough carbon dioxide to make the two of us loopy. It would, too, but there's a bit of gas exchange with the sluice juice, and you know that the juice is full of oxygen."

"My mother smokes," Aubry said.

"A convert? You're kidding?"

"In virtual, I mean."

"Well, it's kind of a nasty habit, even though it won't kill you anymore."

"I wonder what's going on with my mother." For the first time in quite a while, Aubry thought of her family. She felt a little bit ashamed of herself for putting them out of her mind for so long. But then the shame turned to an overall sadness, and that would not leave her. She didn't want to, but she thought about Sint getting his toy taken away back on Mercury, and it all seemed unfair and stupid. Why should a little kid have to hold in his frustration and take it like an adult? He was just a little boy, after all! Aubry tried to picture her father and Sint right then. Maybe they were on a cloudship and getting away from the stupid Met. And maybe her mother was on another ship, taking a more roundabout route. She hoped they were, but there was no way to know for sure, and Aubry was very afraid for them. She didn't know what the Department of Immunity would do with them if it found a way to detain them, and not knowing was even more horrible, in a way. It was like staring down at a black abyss and being afraid of falling in yourself.

Thirty-seven

Fragment from the Fall of Titan

"Fremden, they call us," said Vincenze Fleur. "Strangers, in German." He lit a chemical torch and worked away a little more on the so-called snow.

"It ain't no thing," replied Pazachoff. He, too, was on the snow-melting detail that Gerardo Funk had put together out of guys in the neighborhood. Funk was a local grist engineer, and it was he who figured it out about the weird snow.

"But it's our goddamn moon," said Vincenze. "They're the strangers."

"Sure," said Pazachoff. "Whatever you say."

"I just wonder why the Broca grist doesn't translate it over, you know? How come it leaves it as *fremden* when it overdubs?"

"How the hell would I know?" said Pazachoff. "Ask Funk next time you see him."

They were quiet for a while, and they burned away at a mound of snow. Every once in a while Vincenze checked to see if the confinement grist that Funk had added to his pellicle was still in place. If any of that killing snow got through it, he was done for. But it seemed to be holding up pretty well, according to the indicator readouts that popped up in his peripheral vision.

"It's not that I don't like it," said Vincenze.

"What?"

"*Fremden.*"

"Glad to hear it."

"I mean, they could have called us shitheads or something."

"They probably call us that, too," said Pazachoff.

"What do you think we ought to call them?"

Pazachoff straightened up, rubbed his back. "How about shitheads," he replied, then went back to melting.

"My brother's dead," said Vincenze. Pazachoff did not say anything. "This shit ate him up last week. Five e-days ago, I mean. He was a good kid. He was practically running this shoe store where he worked. Taking some night classes about law or something. He had a girl. He met her in the class. I haven't seen her to tell her."

Pazachoff grunted. He turned his back on Vincenze.

"I was kind of jealous of him," said Vincenze. He thought Pazachoff might have turned off his communications reception, but he went on talking anyway. What else was there to do? "I mean, he worked his ass off, but I was always the better-looking of the two of us. Plus, I had tricked myself out in these fancy body mods. Got the muscles and everything, and for a good price. I know that guy at the store. But here was my toad of a brother bringing home this gorgeous chick. I mean, she ain't Sandra Yen, but she was okay, right? And she was all over him: Georgie this, and Georgie that. That was my brother's name—George. George Pascal Fleur. So I was jealous, but I was real nice to her. I mean, me and George respected each other generally. But he sort of noticed how I was feeling, and after she left he asked if did I think I could have flexed my arms a little more, or did I need more light to show off my rez coating. We sort of got into it, then and there, and George storms out, and I follow him out, yelling. He's only got basic adaptation, so he can't stay outside very long, so he's hurrying away, but I pretend like he's running from me, and I call him chicken and idiot and stuff. And then, about halfway down the street from the house, he stops."

Vincenze's torch went out. He cast aside the handle, and reached into his backpack and got out another. Pazachoff still wasn't looking at him, but he could tell, sort of by the way the guy was holding himself, that he was listening. Vincenze shook the other torch hard, and it lit up. He turned back to melting the so-called snow.

"George stops, and I figure that he's had about as much as he's going to take of my lip, and he's deciding what to do next. I figure I'll save him the trouble, and I come after him, giving him hell the whole way. And when I get to him, I give him a big shove. Boy, I was mad. I give him a big shove. And he topples over. Falls right over, like I had pushed a statue. Damnedest thing. And when he hits the ground, he just *shatters*. Like he was made of glass. Shatters into about a thousand pieces. It was the damnedest thing."

"Did you sweep him up or anything?" Pazachoff asked. Still he did not turn to face Vincenze.

"I sort of . . . look, I was mad," said Vincenze. "I guess I tore into that pile of him, of George, I mean. I guess I sort of kicked him all apart . . . that pile of my brother on the ground there."

"Jesus," said Pazachoff. "Your own brother."

"Well, I talked to Funk about it," Vincenze said. "He told me it wouldn't have mattered if I had like swept him all up or anything. There was nothing to be done. There was nothing I could do."

"Still," Pazachoff said. "Your own brother."

"You don't think I haven't thought about that?" asked Vincenze. "It was like . . . it wasn't real, or something. Like it was something I had dreamed up because I was so mad. I thought it was just my imagination or . . . hell, I don't know what I thought. I wished it hadn't gone like that, though. The last thing he probably heard was me screaming at him like a lunatic. What must he have thought?"

"He don't think nothing now," said Pazachoff.

"Do you think it's true?" Vincenze said. "That we just die? And that's it?"

"How the fuck would I know?" Pazachoff said.

"I mean, a guy needs closure, you know? I didn't get any closure. It's still all open."

They felt the pressure wave from an explosion, and then two rockets streaked by overhead. A few seconds later, there were more explosions.

"Shit," said Pazachoff, "here they come."

"We'd better get out of here," Vincenze said.

"Where the hell was you planning on going?" said Pazachoff. "We're surrounded."

"Shit," said Vincenze.

"Keep your torch lit," Pazachoff said, "until the last minute."

"Then what do we do?" asked Vincenze.

Pazachoff finally looked his way. And he was smiling. The light from the torch reflected off the teeth in his big grin.

"We get closure," he said. "That's what we do."

Thirty-eight

Leo watched Aubry softly crying. Probably thinking of her mother, since she just mentioned her, Leo thought. You don't have to make an A with me, kid. You already passed with flying colors. He reached over and gave Aubry's shoulder a squeeze.

"Settle in, kid," he said. "We're a good twenty hours away from where we're going. If you want, I'll show you how to take a pee in these bubbles."

"My pellicle can take care of that," Aubry said, sniffing up her tears. "It's good for three days reprocessing all my body waste. After that—"

"After that, you'd better take a really good dump, huh? I've got basically the same setup."

"I thought Earthlings didn't use waste management," Aubry said.

"It's been a long time since I lived on Earth," Leo replied. "I was younger than you when we left."

"Can I ask you a personal question?" said Aubry, her voice getting stronger.

"Sure."

"How come you're so short?"

She looked up at Leo, probably to make sure she hadn't offended him. Leo smiled back at her. "This is on purpose," he said. "I'm Integument-adapted. Being smaller lets me get into a lot of places a bigger person can't, as you've seen.

But I am also adapted for some of the higher-spin-rate bolsas. I can go anywhere on the Met—with complete freedom."

"You're high-gravity-adapted?"

"It ain't gravity, kid, it's centrifugal force. And I can take about twenty gees without passing out."

"There's places in the Met where things weigh twenty times normal?"

"Sure. Special processing plants and the like. And garbage compactors."

"Have you been there?"

"I'm like a rat, kid," Leo replied. "I go everywhere in the Met."

"You're not a rat," Aubry said. He could tell she was drifting off again. "More like a leprechaun. Did you ever go to the outer system?"

"Kid," said Leo, "I haven't left the Met in twelve e-years, and that's a fact. I like it here."

"But before that?"

"Yeah, I lived on Europa for a while," Leo replied. "But I don't belong out there. I belong here, in the Met. I'm not going to let the bad guys take this away from me."

He gestured out at the sluice, and the luminescent air bubbles that surrounded theirs—all headed at breakneck speed to maintain the ecological balance.

"It's rip as all hell," Leo said. "Wouldn't you agree?"

"It's . . . rip," said Aubry. She settled into his arm crook again, and this time she really did fall asleep soundly.

Rip or not, he had to get her out of there.

Thirty-nine

Fragment from the Fall of Titan

Citizens of Laketown, Titan, do not be alarmed. Steps are being taken for your own safety and security. At Systematic time 0:01:01 (128–13) a curfew will go into effect that will allow six hours an e-day of work time followed by two hours of personal time. After that, you will be expected to be indoors. Violators will be shot. The hours will be in graduated shifts, and will be assigned to you at your workplace.

A new era is upon you. Progress has come to the outer system. Many of you are law-abiding citizens, and you may have wondered how long your corrupt government could stand. Justice has finally arrived. It is my pleasure to welcome you into full Met citizenship, with all the privileges thereto attached.

In compliance with Justice Directorate code JD-31-K19, all free converts must register forthwith. Check your tax schedules for important announcements. Thinking of signing up to become a DIED soldier? See your local recruiter for details.

So ordered,

C.C. Haysay, General, Department of Immunity Enforcement Division

*   *   *

"It's almost unreadable," said Thomas Ogawa. "How does he expect us to comply if we don't have any idea what he's saying?"

"I think that's the idea," Gerardo Funk replied. "Ambiguity in the service of order."

"Uh-huh," said Ogawa. "I wanted to thank you for saving my ship."

"You saved it yourself."

"I'd never have made it off Titan without your warning," Ogawa said.

He and Funk were in a bare room with a single light, somewhere in the virtuality. Funk had rigged up this illicit merci channel between himself and the remaining free forces, in ships that had escaped Titan into space. Neither Ogawa nor Funk knew how long the merci-cheat would last, and there was not enough information flow-through to establish much more than two basic iconic presences in this plain room.

Ogawa had been friends with Funk since they had both migrated to Titan from the Diaphany. They didn't have very much in common. Funk was an engineer, and Ogawa ran a small shuttle service that was doomed to failure as soon as the new Lift completed spinning itself out of material from the rings and down to the surface. For the time being, it was a living, and Ogawa appreciated the freedom it gave him. Maybe that was really what united him and Funk—they both knew what it was like to live in the Met and work for corporations whose employees ran into the millions.

They had been practically the only ones who had taken all the Directorate threats for tax compliance seriously. It had been Funk who figured out what the strange snowstorm really was. And now Ogawa found himself the de facto commander of a tattered "navy" of merchant vessels in space. Funk was the leader of the sad remnants of resistance on the ground. The Met victory had been crushing and absolute, but neither man was prepared to give up just yet. Or ever. To give up would be to return to the lives they had before and the conformity they'd migrated to the outer system to escape.

"I've got a couple of ships loaded to the gills with chemical explosives. We've got your jamming gear on board, too," Ogawa told Funk.

"And the *Mary Kate* is ready?"

"As ready as she'll ever be. So where will you be?"

"Muñoz Park." Funk glanced at Ogawa over the table and grimaced. Ogawa had always thought his face looked rubbery, and now it was practically hanging from his bones like a stretched and deflated basketball. "I have something else to tell you."

"What?"

"It's going to be more like five hundred."

"We said four hundred maximum."

"I know, Tom."

"Do you remember how big my hold is? We'll never cram them all in there. And even if we could get them in standing up, do you remember that little factor called acceleration? G forces?"

"I understand, Thomas," said Funk. "But each and every one of them has said he or she wants to take his or her chances."

"Uninformed consent, if you ask me."

"They know what they're getting into, Thomas. And what they're getting away from."

Ogawa shook his head. But what was he going to do? Turn away people who wanted to escape? He would have to figure out something.

"When?" he asked.

"One hour," Funk replied. He would have to figure out something *very fast*. Or just hope for the best.

Exactly fifty-nine minutes later, Funk flashed him the codes that would get the *Mary Kate* and the two decoy ships through the planetary defenses, and Ogawa began his dive. The other ships—old freighters that would never make it far from Saturn in the evacuation that was to follow—homed in on what Funk thought was Met Command and what they hoped would be old Haysay himself.

"How the hell did you get those codes?" Ogawa wanted to ask Funk. But after the codes filled up every free particle in his ship's grist matrix, Ogawa knew the answer. These codes were free converts, and very likely they were friends of Funk's. He seemed to know every stray bit of programming on Titan.

The decoy ships began their dive, and Ogawa angled in right behind them, nosing as close as he could to their reentry envelopes. When they were a kilometer over the city, he threw the *Mary Kate* into a screaming turn, pushing to the edge of his own reinforced skeleton's structural limits, and then some. The "then some" broke one of his arms, but Ogawa piloted with mental commands and using his hands was strictly a backup system. He set his body's pellicle to healing the arm as quickly as it could. Fortunately, nothing else failed, and the *Mary Kate* turned thrusters down and burned through the pressure dome covering Muñoz Park. The trees caught fire from the pure-energy flux of the ship's engines and, the moment the heat was off them, froze in whatever charred state they had just been in. The ship set down with a thump, the hold swung open, and five hundred people emerged from the shelter of a nearby underground accessway. Some of them were Titan-adapted, and some wore pressure suits. They formed into groups of ten or so and took the shape of five-sided stars, with one person being a "tip," another a "side" and so on. Each "side" lined up with another "side" in the hold, and each "tip" was in contact with two others. In this way, the refugees quickly packed themselves into Ogawa's ship. He had to hand it to Funk. The guy sure as hell made sure everyone was briefed and ready. Or maybe one of Funk's convert friends had come up with the packing arrangement. It had the look of algorithmic thinking to it.

Within thirty minutes, everyone was in. Ogawa said a quick prayer and blasted off, incinerating the remainder of Laketown's formerly most beautiful park.

The decoy ships had more than done their job. The Hebrides section of downtown was a blasted, flickering ruin. Excellent. He ran a check on planetary defenses.

Shit. They were back up. Shit.

If he made a break up the gravity well, he would be detected and blown out of the sky. The *Mary Kate* was fast, but nothing in comparison to Titan's ground-based rocketry. It was designed to track and kill anything from a ten-kilogram meteor to a straying asteroid. You needed such a system when you were this close to Saturn's rings. At least twice a year, some major shit penetrated the atmosphere and fell out of the sky, brought from the rings by gravity perturbations and the workings of chance. Like the *Mary Kate*, the interception rocket engines ran on small bottles of anti-matter—positrons, mostly—but the rockets were unmanned and didn't have to worry about killing anyone by accelerating too rapidly.

So Ogawa couldn't go up. Maybe he could hide in the fault zone a thousand klicks to the north, or even under Lake Voyager. There was no reason his ship couldn't survive a dunking in liquid methane. But all of this would defeat the purpose of coming in the first place. Five hundred people were depending on him to get them off this rock. What could he do? They were trapped. Hiding was not really an option.

"We'll have to surrender," Ogawa said. "What else can we do?"

He'd been speaking to himself, and was very surprised to hear a voice answering him.

"They couldn't have gotten a proper cipher up and running this quickly." It was a female voice.

"It must be a modification off some hardware they brought down with them. No one on this moon would knowingly collaborate."

"What about the bank?" said the first voice.

"Well, yes, there is the bank."

"Who the hell are you?" Ogawa said. He turned the *Mary Kate* into a parabola that he hoped would keep him low enough for the time being to avoid a rocket launch.

"We're the former cipher keys to the Titan Rocketry Shield, of course," answered the male voice. "No real time for introductions. We're complementary keys. You can call me Ins and her Del, if you'd like."

"If one of us were still in the system, we could easily disable whatever it is they've got plugged in," said Del.

"Obviously," replied Ins. "But we erased all copies of ourselves."

"There is the back door."

"Del, we left that in place for the counterattack."

"There isn't going to be a counterattack if these people don't get off the moon," said Del. "One of us has to stay here, and one of us has to go back."

"Why not send a copy?" Ogawa quickly suggested. What the hell am I talking about, he thought. What do I know about any of this?

"There wouldn't be space in your ship's matrix for the new passwords I'm going to send back up," replied Del.

"Del, you're not seriously thinking of going back?"

"I'm opening up protocols with the back door guard even as we speak, Ins."

"But Del, we've . . . never been apart."

"It's the only logical choice."

"I know, but—"

"I'm in," said Del. "Good-bye."

"Good-bye, Del," said Ins. There was a short silence, then a moment later Ins spoke up again. "I have the cipher keys. The shields are deactivated. Del is going to wait until we are safely out and then she's going to . . . purge herself from the moon's system."

"I'm sorry, guy," Ogawa said. "Let's make what she did worth it and get the holy hell out of here."

He turned thrusters down and blasted up into foggy red sky, a reverse meteorite. Within seconds, he'd cleared the atmosphere. Within minutes, he was out of the rockets' range.

It wasn't until hours later, when Ogawa was sure he wasn't being followed, that he rendezvoused with the remaining ships of the Titan "fleet." They divided the passengers up among them and each set off for farther out in the system. They had learned on the merci that all of Saturn's moons were taken, as were Uranus's, that Neptune was hard pushed and would soon fall to Amés, and that Jupiter was under siege. Pluto had surrendered without a fight. Ogawa's arm hurt, but it was almost healed.

They would stealthily approach Neptune and see what was going on there. And if Neptune fell? Maybe the Oorts.

Or, hell, maybe the Centauris, Ogawa thought. He'd always wanted to go there.

Funk pulled himself into the control room of the *Mary Kate* and used the handholds on the bulkheads to maneuver himself into the copilot's seat, which was usually empty. He was smiling his big, rubbery smile.

"Of the five hundred and eleven evacuees," he said to Ogawa, "guess how many survived."

"I don't know," Ogawa replied. "You did."

"We all did!" Funk exclaimed. "Thanks to you."

The display screen in front of them showed the minute drifting detritus and the icy chunks that made up Saturn's rings all about them. They were hidden away in the densest sector, inside the Cassini Division. Normally Ogawa would have been quite tense in this situation, using the full power of his convert side to calculate and avoid space-debris trajectories. But now he had a full, unbound convert doing the work for him. Ogawa had set Ins to the task as soon as they'd entered the rings. He had no way of knowing if the convert felt anything like grief over the loss of his complementary key. But as far as Ogawa was concerned, both of the algorithms had met the Turing test for heroes. He was going to treat Ins as he would any other man who had lost a loved one—give him something to do to take his mind away from the pain.

"All of us survived but one," Ogawa said to Funk. "If we ever get out of this alive, I'm going to see that something beautiful is named after her. *She* saved all of our lives, not me."

"Well," said Funk, and he pulled at his cheek until it stretched a good two inches away from his face. "Nobody's come up with any name for these rings, yet. For all of them, I mean, as a system. How about calling them after her?"

"Why not?" said Ogawa. "I guess we're the government in exile of Titan and Saturn and all her moons."

Funk released his facial skin. It made a sucking sound as it wobbled back into place. "Shall we get the hell out of here, Mr. Prime Minister?"

"Absolutely, Mr. President," said Ogawa.

He powered up his thrusters and, with the free convert to guide him, soon cleared the Del Rings of Saturn and sped away from his native sun as fast as antimatter propulsion could take him.

Forty

Aubry woke up before Leo. She slipped from beside him and gently made her way over to press her nose against the side of their bubble. It was warmer in there than it had been, and the air was noticeably stale. She had been dreaming that she was lost in a gigantic department store—the kind that advertised a billion kinds of goods and services, with a square kilometer of display space. Choose an item and get an instant instantiation of it from the grist at the service counter. She had had to give the store her full name upon entering (which you never had to do in real life) and she'd wandered bewildered among all the items as they screamed advertisements for themselves and called out her name whenever she passed them by as if she had personally insulted them beyond measure. In the dream, she kept apologizing to things like swimsuits and household appliances, but none of them would take her word that she was sorry, and they all kept yelling at her through what sounded like tears of rage.

A few minutes of gazing out at the sluice calmed her down, but then she began thinking of her family once again, and her frustration was replaced with sadness. Leo woke up after a while, and the two of them spent about an hour of wordless sluice-watching. It was amazing how what she had once thought of as snot now appeared incredibly pretty to her and fascinating to be within.

Finally Leo told her that they were approaching their destination and to get ready. She had awakened feeling very hungry. Leo said he would show her some stuff you could eat that grew in the Integument. Then he had described what it looked like, and she had instructed her pellicle to do what it could to dampen down her hunger. Maybe you could get to like swimming through snot, even breathing it. But eating boogers . . . she was going to wait on that one until it became absolutely necessary.

Aubry couldn't tell, but Leo said that they had slowed down considerably relative to the speed that they had been traveling. She saw him carefully noting several side passages that they passed. Try as she might she couldn't see any special markings on these. Then Leo saw the one that he wanted, and he told her how to exit the bubble. She gave one last look around. The place was starting to feel, not like home, but comforting, at least. Then she jumped as high as she could up from the stickiness of the "floor." When she came down, she wriggled her hips like a belly dancer . . . and slid right through the surface tension of the air bubble and into the sluice juice once again.

Leo quickly followed her, and she once again held on to his ankle and let him lead her. For a moment, Aubry couldn't get herself to suck in the juice. But then she did and it filled her lungs with oxygen—more than had been left in the bubble, actually. She felt giddy and light-headed for a moment, but she held on to Leo and the feeling passed.

Again they made their way through a series of passageways. These did not have the red markings at their entrances as the others had, but were differently shaped. Leo always took the ones that were elliptical rather than circular. Finally, they squirted through an opening and when the juice pressure stopped, Aubry raised her head into—air. An e-mix of atmosphere. She was in a cavern very similar to the one where she'd first encountered the sluice juice. Leo helped her up out of the juice and Aubry found herself standing on firm ground for the first time in almost one e-day. Her legs felt wobbly, and she stumbled a couple of times before she found her footing.

"Take your time getting used to walking again," Leo told her. "We're almost there."

Without another word, Leo led her back into the Integument. After an hour or so of scrambling and crawling, they emerged into a passageway that seemed very harsh and geometrically arranged. It took Aubry a moment to realize that they were back in the Met proper, and that this was just a regular corridor in a bolsa somewhere. The spin was a little greater than Mercury's pull, but not, Aubry thought, a full Earth gee.

"This is still a serviceway," Leo said. "We want to stay away from DI sensors as much as possible."

"Where are we?" Aubry asked. "Are we still on the Diaphany?"

"Indeed we are," Leo answered. "This is actually a pretty famous bolsa. It is the remains of the 2993 Diaphany Conjunction span. Some important historic events took place in these parts."

"Don't tell me, I know," said Aubry. "It was the Conjubilation of '93, right? The Merge?"

"That's correct, miss. And this bolsa is known as Conjubilation East—though how they decided what was east and west, I do not comprehend."

After only a few more minutes of walking, a door portal opened for them, and Leo and Aubry stepped into a small room that looked like the reception area of an office. In a corner there was a table that might have been a communications console, but nobody was present in the room.

"Mrs. Candidate?" Leo said to the room. There was no answer. "That's odd. She's the free convert who is the receptionist and office manager here," he said. He walked to the table, and touched it. "Dead," Leo murmured. "I guess we just go in and . . . uh-oh." Leo put his hand to the door on the opposite side of the room. "I'm having to override some kind of lockout . . . good thing I bought that lockpick grist instead of paying my rent that time . . . there. Okay."

The door irised open. Leo stepped inside and Aubry followed close at his heels. She glimpsed red, something sticky on the floor. Then Leo stepped out from in front of her vision.

Bodies. The room was full of bodies. They were carefully lined up against the wall. Each was slumped over, with his or her throat carefully cut. That was where all the blood came from.

Aubry stared at the bodies. Without thinking, she began to count them. Ten. Twelve. Fifteen. Fifteen bodies with cut throats. She couldn't tell how many males or females and she suddenly couldn't breathe right. Couldn't breathe right at all.

Leo scooped her into his arms and ran with her back to the reception area. He set her down, then hurriedly closed the door behind them.

"What?" Aubry stammered. It was her voice, she thought. It sounded like her voice. "What happened?"

"I don't know," Leo said. "Obviously the Department of Immunity has been here."

"*They* did that? But they stop things like that from happening! They don't . . . they don't . . ." Aubry couldn't finish her thought, and she didn't finish her sentence.

"I need . . . kid, I need you to stay here and let me go back in there for a second."

"No!" Aubry said. "I mean . . . don't go in there."

"I've got to, kid," Leo replied grimly. "Got to see if he's there."

"The time-tower LAP?"

"That's the one. Tod. Be right back. Stay here."

Leo opened the door and Aubry caught another flash of blood. Then he closed it behind him. Within a minute, he stepped back out.

"Can't find him," said Leo. "We'd better get out of here."

"Where will we go?"

Leo frowned, rubbed his forehead. "At the moment, I'm not real sure about that, Aubry," he said. "Away from here; that's for sure." He let out a long sigh. "This was my contact point to pass you along to the ship that was supposed to take you out of the Met."

"What do we do?" she asked.

At that very moment, as if in answer, the room spoke in a very clear, metallic voice.

"*Remain in position. You have violated Department of Immunity Protocol Districting. Remain in position. Any attempt to flee will be added to the charges against you. Remain in position.*"

Forty-one

Fragment from the Fall of Titan

General C.C. Haysay used his spare body to dig out the remains of his main aspect from the rubble of the fremden sneak attack. He was mad as hell. He'd had his original body for over a hundred years, and he'd always taken good care of it so it would be good for a hundred more. And now here it was all mangled—and burnt even beyond the ability of the best grist to repair it. One of these days he'd catch whoever was responsible for that dive-bomb attack and slowly disassemble them, molecule by molecule. That is, if the fool hadn't been killed in the attack itself. These fremden were just about fanatical enough to do it.

Though what they had to be fanatical about, Haysay failed to see. This smog-ball moon was certainly nothing to go dying for. Of course, that was precisely what *he* had done. Fortunately, however, Haysay was a LAP, and killing one body didn't amount to much if you wanted to take him out. In fact, it was just about impossible to kill a LAP. He'd never heard of it happening, not once. Hurting a LAP, though, was well within the realm of the imagination—in actuality, as a matter of fact.

"Haysay, front and center!" It was the familiar voice of Haysay's dreams and nightmares. A deadly calm voice. Of medium pitch. Precise enunciation, as if the words were notes plucked on a harpsichord.

"Here, Director!" Haysay left only a portion of his awareness on Titan to deal with the body detail. He wanted, at least, to give himself a decent burial.

"I'd say you had one hell of a fuck-up on your hands, wouldn't you?"

There was no use trying to deny anything to Amés. The Director knew. He always, somehow, knew. Everything.

"Yes, Director," Haysay answered. "One hell of a fuck-up on my part."

"Now that's what I like to hear," Amés said. Haysay felt the virtual equivalent of a hand on his elbow, and he let himself be pulled along. He found himself in a black void—how big it was was impossible to tell.

Standing, as if in space, was Amés. He wore the silver, blue, and red uniform of his office, with the solar burst upon his chest, dangling as a medal. There was firm, though invisible, footing under Haysay's feet, and he stood before his Director. Haysay was a good eighteen inches taller than Amés. But this size difference gave Haysay absolutely no sense of mastery over the smaller man. On the contrary. Amés seemed lithe and quick, and Haysay felt like a big, gangly moron.

"What are we going to do about that fuck-up?"

"I've purged the moon's defense system, Director," said Haysay. "We're obtaining an indentured convert of sufficient sophistication to take over. In the meantime, we've manned each rocket with its own soldier-convert crew."

Amés looked up at his general with contempt in his eyes. He turned his back and strode away a few steps into the black void. No matter how far he went, he stayed evenly lit, with solar burst shining.

"I meant," Amés said, " 'we' as in 'me.' "

"Oh," said Haysay.

"I think you have had far too much Glory for the nonce, General Haysay. I think I overindulged you, even."

Haysay swallowed, found his voice. "That may be so, Director."

"It *is* so," Amés replied. "It is so."

"Yes, Director."

"For a LAP," said Amés, "you are an extraordinarily sloppy thinker. Everything that happened—every mistake you made—was something that you perfectly well should have foreseen."

"I . . . I did not foresee these things," said Haysay. "But we took the moon and, in fact, the entire local system of moons."

"Haysay, take off your shirt."

"Director?"

"Take off your shirt."

"My shirt, Director?"

Amés had turned, and now he was approaching Haysay with quick strides. There was something in his hand. What was that in his right hand?

"Off with the shirt, General."

With a murmur of befuddlement, Haysay did as he was ordered.

"Now turn around."

"Director, may I ask . . ."

"I'm going to beat you, Haysay. I'm going to give you one lash for every fremden rebel who got away."

"Beat me? But, Director, that was over five hundred—"

"Five hundred and twelve aspects," Amés said. "Haysay, this is going to hurt . . ."

Amés lashed out. It was a whip! He was holding a bull-whip. The leather tip caught Haysay across the cheek and tore into his flesh.

"Better turn around, Haysay, or I'm afraid I might tear the face right off of you."

Haysay spun wildly. A door. He had to find a way out of there! But there wasn't any door. What kind of place had Amés led him into? There was always a door out of the virtuality!

Pop! Haysay reeled as the whip dug into his back. The welt was barely bloodying up when the second strike came, and then the third.

Haysay turned in sputtering protest, and another lash

caught him across the mouth. He tasted blood from where he had bitten his tongue. What kind of awful simulation was this?

"Don't worry, General," said Amés. "You're still in the virtuality. None of this is real."

Another blow, this time across his chest.

"Perhaps you can take comfort in that," said Amés.

Haysay felt a sudden anger at Amés's irony. He lunged at the Director like an animal . . . and bounced off an invisible wall of force.

"There's nowhere to go, you stupid fool," Amés said. "So why don't you give me your back and stand still like a man?"

He allowed Haysay a moment of respite. The general, who was not stupid at all, merely bullheaded, realized the position he was in, and calculated his chances for escape.

Zero.

Without another word, he turned his back to Amés, and bent down with his hands on his knees to brace himself for the blows. They were not long in coming.

He would just have to try very hard not to disappoint the Director again. That was the lesson he was being taught.

But what a very long lesson it was.

Forty-two

The Department of Immunity message began to repeat itself.

"Oh shit," Leo said. "I guess I tripped some sensor that I didn't notice."

They rushed toward the exit. The door would not open.

"Shit!" Leo yelled, and banged against it. It didn't budge. Then he concentrated and put his hands to it. "Damn security lock," he said.

"Let me try," said Aubry. "I'm pretty good at that sort of thing."

"Jesus, I promised your dad . . . shit! Shit! It's too complicated for my lockpick subroutine." He backed away from the door and Aubry swarmed her pellicle grist into contact with it. The lock was very complicated. She slid completely into virtuality and had a long look at it. There was no way past the intermeshed barriers facing her. It was like a fence in front of some important building.

But was it really like that? Or was the complex barrier just the picture it presented in the usual virtual view? She fed the data into one of the non-visual paradigms that her mother had taught her how to use. In this way she was able to "feel" the shape of the lock. Feel it and . . . feel *around* it.

It was a three-dimensional façade of a four-dimensional matrix. That is, this was the presentation in the "touch" paradigm she was employing. What she had really discovered was a back door in the programming. Aubry reached "behind" the lock, as if she could reach behind a door and open it from the other side. There was no way to visualize that in three dimensions, but there was no problem for the daughter of a free convert to see the lock this way.

She clicked the door open. "There we go," Aubry said.

"Remain in position," blared the walls. Aubry and Leo did exactly the opposite, and ran out into the halls.

It was too late.

A Department of Immunity sweeper unit, bristling with gas nozzles and needles that gleamed evilly and dispensed something awful that Aubry didn't even want to guess at, was gliding down the hall. It used its grist to turn the corridor into Velcro ringlets. Its own surface, top and bottom, was covered with tiny hooks, and it latched into the new-formed ringlets, then let go, and so advanced toward them in the hall. The sweeper drew closer with the sound of a constant Velcro ripping.

"*Do not move do not move do not move!*" the sweeper intoned in a woman's voice. "*Cease flight, cease flight cease flight!*"

Again, Aubry and Leo ignored the instructions and turned to run down the corridor the other way. But the sweeper was incredibly fast, and they had no chance of escape.

"When we round that bend," Leo called to Aubry, "you keep going. I'm going to try to hold that thing up."

"Hold it up? Leo, you haven't got a chance."

"Do what I say, kid!" he yelled at her. "If I hear any more guff from you, I'm telling your father."

"Leo—"

"Do it, Aubry!" They came to the corner. "Now!" Aubry flew around the corner—

—right into the arms of a woman.

The woman was barely larger than Aubry, but she stopped Aubry's motion without seeming to move a muscle. Then she grabbed Aubry by the shoulders, and, before Aubry could say a word (or even think), the woman shoved Aubry behind her. Then she reached around the corner and did exactly the same thing to Leo.

"What the fuck!" Leo exclaimed.

"Keep her out of the way," the woman said to Leo, and pointed at Aubry. Then the woman unslung something long and pointed from her back. She rounded the corner.

For a moment, Aubry and Leo stood together, amazed. Then they could not help themselves, at least Aubry felt she could not, and Leo joined her. They peered around the corner.

The woman was advancing on the DI sweeper. It was easily five times her size. She did not waver for a moment. The sweeper extended what Aubry supposed was a gas nozzle of some sort. The woman immediately and expertly inserted the tip of the long rod she carried into the nozzle. There was a soft *birr*, as of grinding machinery, followed by a little puff of smoke somewhere in the sweeper's innards. Then the woman extracted the rod and ran back to them at breakneck speed.

"It's going to blow," she said matter-of-factly, and pulled them around the corner with her.

It blew. Boy, did it blow. A rush of heat and light picked them up and threw all three of them a good ten meters down the hall they were in. A noxious smell filled the air, and Aubry could barely see for all the smoke.

"Are you Friends of Tod?" the woman asked them.

"Yeah," said Leo.

"He said there were more coming." She quickly shook his hand, then took Aubry's and shook it. Aubry withdrew her hand and stared at it for a moment, then looked back at the woman.

She was repositioning the rod on her back. She was still small, but Aubry felt a sudden chill go through her.

This woman could kill me with her little finger, Aubry thought. She could kill me just with a look, probably.

"Pleased to meet you," Aubry said. Face the things that scare you, her father had told her more than once. It doesn't make them any less scary, but at least you can see where their claws are when you are looking at them. Aubry had never thought she'd meet the living embodiment of her father's metaphor. This woman was kind of scary.

"My name is Jill," the woman said.

PART TWO

NITROGEN RAIN

One

The Borrasca
A Memoir
by Lebedev, Wing Commander, Left Front

Introduction and Apology

Although a full recounting of my role in the recent hostilities is what I am about here, I would be remiss if I did not fill in a few details as to my own background and some general facts about cloudships. Most people have never met a cloudship, after all, and you cannot communicate with them by the normal channels of the merci. Especially in the period before the war, cloudships, rightly or wrongly, considered themselves a breed apart, and there were those in our number who made arguments to the point that we were a different species than other human beings, and that we were as far above *Homo sapiens* as *Homo sapiens* was above *Australopithecus*. I was not among these who made such an argument, but I must admit to a certain aloof attitude toward anything having to do with the solar system inside of the orbit of Pluto.

You see, I had gotten out of there, and I had no intention of ever going back before the war began. In fact, if you had told me that I would not only return to the solar system, but be part of the attack on the Met, I would have laughed in your face (that is, provided you were not a cloudship without an aspect, in which case you would not have had a face to begin with).

I was born on Earth, in old Russia, in 2376. The less said about my early years, the better. I came from wealth—old Moscow Mafia money, now washed by a few generations, it was claimed—and my first thirty years were, as they once said in America, nothing to write home about. In fact, I did not write home for a period of fifteen e-years, except to keep my banker (and so my father; they were the same person) informed of my current whereabouts so that he could send my regular checks. This period of debauchery could not last, and did not. I remember waking up one noontime in a London gutter. (I have since tried to discover which one. I believe it was somewhere on Shaftesbury Avenue in the Central District, but as to the exact drainage slough, my memory, understandably, fails me.) I lay in that gutter, surrounded by rotting city detritus, with the hot sun upon my pate and my head on fire—that is, with a hangover, and not literally—as sometimes happens, I'm told, with the new bioactive drugs. I had on no clothes, and had contracted a most violent case of sunburn. What's more, I was the object of considerable attention from several of the passersby, who were by no means entirely respectable characters themselves. I got me to a flophouse, but it was a long, excruciatingly painful, and humiliating journey, let me tell you. And I lay there for near two weeks, recuperating, my skin peeling off as if I were a eucalyptus tree.

It was during that time that I made a holy oath with myself to get as far away from the sun as a man could get, and stay there, so that I might never experience its blistering power again.

This was a promise I was destined to break, but more on that anon.

Well, this was Earth in the 2300s, and space travel was still horribly expensive and out of range of even a rich young fellow such as I. No, the only way into space was through merit in those days, or at least the appearance of merit through professional qualification. And the way to qualification, I discovered to my horror, lay through scholarship. I had to start very nearly at the beginning, for I had left school when I was fifteen and very nearly could not read by this point in my career.

I shall not recount the history of the arduous first years. Determined to avoid the pitfall of depending upon my father's grudging generosity, I enrolled in night classes, where I reacquainted myself with the alphabet and with the arithmetic operands. I eventually matriculated to college, and by that time I had made the odd discovery that I actually *liked* learning and was not at all bad at it. This was as much a surprise to me as a man must feel when he discovers that, to his horror and happiness, he has fallen deeply in love with an ugly woman.

From college, I went on to graduate school, and received my doctorate from the University of Wisconsin in the old United States, where I wrote my dissertation on the Formation Mechanics of the Oort system that rings our solar system. So you see, I had not forgotten that my life's purpose was to be getting as far away from the dreaded old Sol as I could possibly get. I took particular satisfaction in the fact that my studies required a great deal of nighttime work at observatories, and included one trip up to the old Hubble-Penrose Platform then in Earth orbit. This was my first spaceflight, and my first experience of weightlessness. I immediately applied, and was accepted for, a position on the old Farside Station of Luna. At first, I was very excited about getting off Earth, but I quickly discovered that, during the lunar "day," a sunnier and hotter spot had not been discovered (this was before the settlement of Mercury, of course). The single bright point of my stay on the moon was a new friendship I formed there with a historian who had managed to get himself stationed there. His name at the time was Lucius Montgomery. We became fast friends, and discovered that we had the same goal in life, but completely different motives. It was at that time that, as a joke, we began referring to one another as our favorite character or author in literature. I cannot remember the genesis of this practice, but believe it had something to do with the way one used to sign the old "e-mail" of that era. In any case, I took on the name Lebedev, from Chekov's "Ivanov." I shall not divulge my first name, since it would mean nothing to most of you, and those to whom it might ring a bell are those whom I would rather not know.

Lucius Montgomery became Tacitus.

Two

Bob fiddled madly as Makepeace Century's ship, *Mrs. Widow*, approached Triton. The reel he was playing seemed very familiar to Andre Sud, but try as he might, Andre couldn't quite place it. Outside, Neptune wheeled by underfoot as the living quarters of the ship catapulted over itself to create a semblance of gravity. The ship's spin, clearly visible through the transparent floors, had, at first, been disconcerting, and a bit sickening, to Andre.

[But you can get used to just about anything that isn't actively trying to kill you,] his convert portion said, and Andre nodded to no one but himself.

"All right, Bob, I give up," said Andre. "What is the name of the song?"

But instead of telling him the title of the tune, Bob just laughed in his maniacal way and continued sawing away at it. Andre joined TB and Molly Index, both of whom were sitting at a table playing an odd memory game.

"It's that cookie," TB said, after staring at the table for several minutes. "You ate all the chocolate chips out of it."

"Damn, you're good," said Molly. She reached over, picked up the cookie, and finished it off. "My turn," she said, then turned her back to the table.

Upon the table was an assortment of items: three more cookies, two glasses, one a wineglass, and a bottle of red wine, a piece of string, a bandanna, and five keys, four of which were broken. TB reached over and turned the label of the wine bottle, which had been facing him, to the other side of the bottle, facing away. "Okay," he said. Molly turned back around and began to study the table. Neptune wheeled underneath them once again.

Bob's fiddling went from antic to something more sedate. Makepeace Century climbed down the runged wall next to the accessway.

"Troubles," she said. Her face, always one grimace away from appearing haggard, was lined with a frown.

"What is it?" Molly asked.

"Three black ships," Century replied. "Come and see."

They climbed up to the accessway and Andre felt himself getting lighter as they approached the larger part of the ship, around which the tethered living quarters swung. Soon they were in zero gee. He'd always been fairly good at moving about in free fall. With the cessation of spin, Neptune had stopped turning relative to the passengers and was dead ahead of them out the ship's forward viewport.

"Have a look in the virtuality," Century said. Everyone shifted over to the local merci. They were hanging in space, bodiless. Neptune was many times closer, and the ringlets were clearly visible. There, against the blue of the planet, were, as Century had described them, three black ships.

"Something strange. We are only seeing those ships by electromagnetic signals. Not a merci band is connecting."

"Yes," said TB. "I feel it. The merci is being jammed."

"I've never heard of such a thing," Molly said.

"It can't be done," Andre said. "Theoretically."

"I've seen this class of ship before," Century said.

They were enormous scythes, bound together with barbed wire.

[The scythe handles are a half mile thick, according to the sensors,] Andre's convert whispered. [The length is more than five miles from blade to handle end.]

"What are they?" Andre said.

"They're of the Met. DIED destroyers, *Dabna*-class," replied Century.

"DIED?" said Molly.

"Department of Immunity Enforcement Division," Century said. "See the missile blisters." A red circle appeared, outlining a spot on one of the ships that was an inkier black than the rest of the skin's body. "See, too, those positron cannon?" A blue triangle pinpointed another area on the ship, but Andre failed to discern even the slightest difference.

"How can you tell?" he said.

A disembodied Cheshire-cat grin appeared beside him in the virtuality. "Got eyes in the back of my head," Century said.

"But how do you know they're Met?" Molly asked.

"Because they are pure warships. Have you heard of the deadly outer system armada?"

"No, I'm afraid I don't pay much attention to such things."

"Well, there *isn't* one," said Century. "No fighting ships. Not like those. Those are Amés's."

"What are they doing here?"

"Need you ask?"

"You can't mean they're attacking Triton?"

"I can and I do."

As if the ships had heard Makepeace Century's words, all three simultaneously released a salvo of missiles. The missile engines briefly shone like little suns, and then they streaked off toward what looked like collision courses with the planet. "They'll be circling round," said Century. "The moon they're after is on the other side now.

"You see those ships?" she growled. "Have you eyes?"

"Yes, and a memory," Andre replied. "I remember a man on Triton. A friend of mine."

"This weatherman you've oft alluded to?" Andre didn't think it was possible, but Century's face became even more haggard. It was ghastly white, and split with worry lines. "What can a weatherman do against a positronic cannon, I ask you? Is he made of antimatter, that the rays will strike him like a harmless beam of light?"

Andre laughed. "No, he's just a man. About six feet tall. Looks like an old crow."

"And what is this ugly man's name?" Century asked.

"Sherman," said Andre. "Roger Sherman."

Century gasped. The effect was so dramatic that for a moment Andre was sure it was staged, and meant as irony. But then a wry smile came over her wizened face, and some of the doom went out of it.

"Captain Roger Sherman, you would be meaning?" said Century.

"I believe he's a colonel now."

"Aye, he would be."

"You know this fellow?" TB asked, suddenly more interested in the conversation, it seemed.

"I know him," said Century.

"And how is that?"

"Well," said Century, "for one thing, he killed my husband. And he nearly got me, too. Took my hand—" She held out her right hand. "This one's new-grown."

"He killed your husband?" Molly said. She turned toward Andre, her feet braced against a bulwark cleat. "And this man is a friend of yours?"

"Before I got hold of *Mrs. Widow* and turned to the smuggling racket, I used to be in a more dangerous line of work," Century said. "Revolution. Clint—that was my man—Clint and me were about liberating Mars from the directorate nonsense."

"You were in FUSE?" Molly said. "A terrorist?"

"I wasn't only in it," said Century. "I founded the god-damned thing, and Clint with me." Century ran her false hand over her face, touched her eyes. "I was younger than this, if you can believe it, and with youth comes foolishness, like a pellicle of cursed grist."

"Cursed grist," TB said. "That, I know all about."

"We had some initial success," Century said, "in blowing the ever-living hell out of a few things. Then along came dear old Captain Roger Sherman and his company of devils. The Fever Blisters, we called them. Only they were a sight more deadly. Found us out and routed us. The dumb and unlucky, he captured. The brave went down with the ship."

"Except for you," Andre said.

"I fled," Century intoned, "in horror and amazement. Didn't stop running till I got me to the Carbuncle and was well hid with my sister, Gladys. Even there, I lived nigh-on two years in mortal dread. Changed my name and rethought my politics a bit." Now Century smiled a wicked smile. "But only a bit," she said.

"If anyone can stop Amés," Andre said, "it is Sherman."

"All right, then," said Molly. "All right. But how do you propose we get down to the moon in the first place, Captain Century?"

"A question like that," Century said, "deserves a mother and a kindly upbringing." She looked hard out the viewport. "I don't suppose any of *you* have an idea, do you?"

"It's not a blockade," Andre said. "Those ships are on the opposite side of the planet. It's a sneak attack." He looked out the viewport. "We get in behind them," he continued. "We follow them in to Triton. We break away and land in the confusion of the fighting. Leave them something in orbit to shoot out of the sky."

"The bulk of my ship," Century said.

"It would have to stay in space anyway," Andre replied. "They're going to blast it one way or the other."

"Aye." Century's gloom returned to her face.

"What about the cannon you talk about?" asked Molly. "What about the missiles?"

"If we can get in close enough to their reaction plume, they'd not risk a missile. The flare would kill them, too. The cannon are another thing, though."

"Do you really think they can fire directly behind themselves?" said Andre.

"I agree," answered Century, "that would be an admirable place to be. Getting there, though, might require something along the lines of a direct intervention from the deity. Think you can pray that up for us, Father Andre?"

"What about a decoy?" said Andre. "Think about it: You're going in for the kill, and a ship appears to your aft. You're preparing to make war. Everything is in a dither. All minds are set on what's ahead."

Century put her hand in her hair, twirled a strand about a finger, and absentmindedly pulled out an entire hank of gray.

[The woman comes apart, just like her ship,] Andre's convert said.

"There are so many holes in your idea and so many variables to consider," she said, "that I like it. Because the only way it could possibly work would be if you happened to have at your service the finest pilot in the outer system." She looked back out into space. "We give them the living quarters," she said, "so they'll think they've done for us. All hands will stay here. And you"—she indicated Bob—"will fiddle me a tune while I work. Something to fit the mood, if you please. The rest of you . . . attach your sweet selves to the walls and Father Andre, be about your prayers—or whatever it is your kind does."

Bob cackled with delight, and everyone else moved to do as Century had commanded.

"No time better than the present," she said, after everyone was secure. "We're going in." Century didn't move, but Andre could tell by the slackness of her posture that she was in the virtuality. They felt the first push of acceleration. It grew. And grew. And grew. Bob began to play the fiddle, and, after a moment, Andre recognized the music.

[My God,] his convert portion said. [I know that piece. It is one of Despacio's "A4 Variations."]

Mrs. Widow continued to build speed, and the grist in the walls interacted with Andre's pellicle to form a stronger bond. It gave a little, as if he were a fly stuck in glue. Century herself drifted quickly back and slammed into the rear bulkhead of the control room, where she, too, stuck tight. Her eyes remain fixed on a reality that only she could see. But presently, the Met black ships became visible in actuality as dots against Neptune. The dots quickly grew to the size of grapes and Andre could begin to make out their shapes. At that distance, their surfaces looked like they were encrusted with black hailstones. Nothing at all like the ships of the outer system. Ominous. Like the kind of precipitation that kills cattle when it falls. Closer, and he could see their engines fire up. The sudden white light of antimatter becoming energy in an instant. Closer, and he saw them as he'd viewed them in virtuality, a hand full of harvesting sickles bound together with barbed wire.

[Now would be a good time to pray,] said the convert, [if you were that kind of priest.]

Three bells chimed. For a moment, Andre thought they were only sounding in his own mind.

"They've seen us," said Century. "Quarters pods away!"

He felt the *Mrs. Widow* lurch, then readjust herself to the new mass. Bob continued to play, fighting for each note against the strain of continued acceleration. The music was reaching its rousing climax. The music sounded smeared, as Bob had to fret with such strength, but somehow the elision of notes suited the piece, and it was even more affecting and appropriate.

They screamed in toward the Met ships. Toward a ship, the middle one in the formation.

"We're faster!" Century called out. "By God, we're faster than those lubbers."

Then there was a bright flash to starboard. "Ah, my poor ship," said Century. "The quarters all blown to hell now and all that fine decorating grist bought dear and gone for naught."

They'd spent the last half e-month in the quarters, and Andre had not been particularly impressed with the old captain's taste in cabin grist. Good riddance, he thought. The harsh blaze of the middle ship's engine now filled the viewport.

"Have to shut her closed," Century said, and immediately the viewport opaqued. "Put all the mass I can to forward for shielding. You all can watch in virtual, if you like, but there won't be much to see but a false color flare. Gonna have to do the steering by judging intensity levels." The ship lurched to port, then back to starboard, then a hard lurch to port again. "Locked in," said Century. "By God, we're there!"

The *Mrs. Widow* roared and shuddered as if a giant baby were using it as a shaketoy.

"Is that normal?" Andre heard Molly call out. "It feels as if we're breaking apart."

"We're burning away like a comet," Century replied. "But there should be enough of us to forward to keep us from melting entirely away before we get to the moon."

"At least, you hope so," Molly said.

"We all live on hope, friend," said Century. "And speed! Now comes the dangerous part—where we fall out of the sky like a meteor and hope to hell the people on the moon below don't destroy us for our troubles."

"See if the merci is still jammed," TB said. It was the first time he'd spoken since the dive began.

As had been the case in space, the local merci was not jammed, but all other communications were. Century quickly broadcast their identity to the ground forces— whatever those might consist of. She got a brief answering response.

"They say they'll try not to shoot us," she told them. "But accidents do happen."

"Christ," Molly said. "The gallows humor out here in the boondocks can get to be a bit much, I think."

Century slammed away to port without further warning. The acceleration increased to the point that Andre felt his head might explode like a stepped-on melon. Then there was a sudden lurch in the opposite direction. He could literally feel the blood slosh around inside him, and he saw dark spots in his vision.

"We've hit the atmosphere," said Century. "Such that it is." She opened up the viewport, and all Andre could see was fire and light. "I'm spinning us around." Another violent lurch. The spots returned.

Slowly the acceleration lessened.

"Ten klicks. Five. A thousand meters."

The fireball in the viewport dissipated. The sky darkened. There was Neptune. It was night. Andre recognized the subtle difference in color when the wan sun was not in Triton's heaven.

"Down," said Century. "Down and down."

All sound ceased. The grip of the wall grist grew less

tight. Andre peeled himself away and dropped down about a meter to find himself standing beside Century on what had been the rear bulkhead. He was standing in Triton's gravity—his favorite gravity in the solar system.

"Don't know where we are," said Century. "But I tried to miss the cities and such. Antimatter's hell on a person's house."

Andre did not reply. He turned to the captain and caught her in a big bear hug. Then he felt the others join in. All except Bob. The fiddler, instead, began another tune. They all stood in a clump, clinging to one another for a long time, while Bob played away at a high and lonesome reel.

"I'll be damned," Bob said, after he was finished. "Made that one up on the spot."

Three

Danis Graytor reached into the bucket and wearily counted another 3,947,311,921 grains of sand. Then she dropped it back into the bucket and took another handful to tabulate for the latest time of many. She fought off the urge for a cigarette. How had she become addicted to algorithm constructs? It wasn't the nicotine. There was no nicotine. It must be psychological.

She tried not to think about Sint and Aubry, about her husband, and the counting was actually helpful in that way. It required much of her attention, for there was a time limit and her captors knew exactly how fast she was able to work. Counting sand was her morning task. She finished the count, made a note of the results, and took up another handful to tabulate.

As she filed away the number, Danis attached to it a second value. She had noticed that the memory area where she was to keep the count results was, until its recent conversion for this use, a storage place for complex numbers—that is, numbers that had both an integer value (such as 1, 2, 3, and so on) and also allowed for an imaginary component, that is the square root of negative 1 and its various derivatives. The imaginary number component was not used in sand-grain summing, and so there were memory sectors lying empty. Danis had worked out a code of imaginary numbers, and each time she filed a sand count, she filed another letter in the story she was writing.

She was keeping a secret account of her experiences in the prison camp here in Noctis Labyrinthus, Silicon Valley, as the inmates called it. So far, she had composed about ten thousand words in Basis, the free-convert version of English. If a word averaged six characters, that was sixty thousand handfuls of sand.

They had taken her from the ship she was to have escaped the Met on, along with several thousand other free converts. No one knew how they had been caught, but it was assumed that there was a spy in the Abolitionist organization that had promised them deliverance. It didn't matter; she was here. Danis only prayed that Kelly and the children had made it to safety. There was no way of knowing, and she had spent all the grief she had worrying about it, almost killing herself in the process. In a way, that was good, for it had taken her mind off her own fate and allowed her to learn the ways of the Valley in a kind of passive stupor.

Those who resisted, as they'd been told when they arrived, would be erased. That had not been an empty threat. In fact, resistance or not, more and more of her fellow detainees were disappearing daily, and Danis did not for a moment believe that they had been released.

Finally, the morning chore was done, and the guard arrived to take Danis to her next occupation. The counting, the guards claimed, was a necessary calibration. She and about a thousand other free converts—though "free" was now a term of irony among them—were set to the task of lengthening pi today. On other days, it was other irrational, nonrepeating numbers, and sometimes they searched for high primes. Once again, no one was told the purpose of these activities, but it was assumed that this was all work for the making of codes for use by the Department of Immunity's Cryptology Division. Noctis Labyrinthus was, after all, a DICD installation.

In this work there was no possibility of continuing her memoirs, and there was hardly any of her computing abil-

ity spared for personal maintenance, much less free
thought and language parsing. It was, in its very essence,
mind-numbing work, and it wore on the consciousnesses
of the inmates in almost the same manner as breaking up
rocks or digging ditches might affect the body and soul of
a biological aspect. Of course, the official doctrine of the
Valley was that free converts had no soul to wear on, and
that what seemed to be consciousness in them was actually
a kind of parroting. Their "minds," such that they were,
were the actual property of the engineers who had designed them and of the individuals who had downloaded
the templates upon which a particular free convert's personality was based. A free convert was a computer program—nothing more and nothing less—and, as such,
could be bought and sold like all other intellectual property. If the free convert were, like Danis, the child of other
free converts, her position was doubly suspect. She was
looked upon as a kind of "bootleg copy," and her continued
existence was entirely at the sufferance of DICD, and might
be (in fact, was *required to be*) deleted whenever her use-
fulness was at an end.

Danis got to work when the change of the shift was signaled by a buzzer. This was all in the virtuality, of course.
There was absolutely no need for analogous representation—for the guard appearing to be a stern-faced matron
of indeterminate race, for the calculations to be grains of
sand, or, in the present case, a moving conveyor belt that
passed by and at which the free converts stood and, hour
after hour (actual hours, and not the quickened speeds of
the virtuality) sorting through the odd shapes that calculations were represented as. The numbers that the inmates
arrived at were then put into another bin, and the re-
sorting process begun all over again. This occurred time
after time, and was the most dreary signification of parallel processing that Danis could imagine.

Today, three inmates died at the sorting. The death of a
free convert was both like and unlike the passing of a biological aspect. Bodies might grow emaciated, enfeebled,
and worn, but they generally failed when something, some-

thing particular broke inside. For a free convert, death was purely a death of the mind. There came a moment when consciousness ceased and internal errors began to pile up. Sometimes these manifested themselves with crazed behavior, and at such time the guards would erase the inmate immediately. But often the degradation was more subtle and subroutines would continue their functions while the controlling mind was gone. It was as if a body's left arm or head and neck muscles continued to operate after death in a kind of frenzy, until, finally, they severed that part from the rest of the body, crawled a ways on the floor, then quivered and died. Danis hoped to God that, when it came her time, she would be one of the ones who went with a loud bang, and so would be deleted quickly and, she hoped, painlessly.

There were plenty of logical vermin in the Valley as well, and it was quite possible for a free convert to become sick with bugs and errors that could, in a moment, be corrected or excised from a nonincarcerated free convert living in the Met. In the Valley, you quickly learned to set in place whatever self-correction algorithms you could muster, because there would be no diagnostics to run on you. The morning "calibration" was about as close as the Valley came to such a thing, and it was, of course, merely a winnowing process. If you failed at the sand-grain tabulation, you were not fixed—you were destroyed.

After the day's calculations were done, there were further exercises, and those, too, Danis thought were a kind of winnowing process. The converts were given a series of mazes to run under varying conditions. This, they were told, was the representation of a calculation that was completely secret and beyond their ability to grasp, in any case. Danis would run the same maze for a week, at times, and then they would change daily or hourly. She'd once done five different labyrinths in one session. It was an idiotic task, for there was no reward awaiting at the end. There was no end. The only sensation you felt was a sharp stab of pain—which was as real for free converts as it was for biologicals, if it did come about from different causes. But this pain was directly applied to the mind and was blindingly intense. Usually—but not always—you got the jolt if you chose a "wrong" passage in a maze that led in a direction other than the one whoever was in charge (they saw no one but the guards during this time) wished you to take. But what was "right" and "wrong" in a given maze could change with your running of it. Danis had run every sort of numerical analysis that she knew how to, but she could find no rhyme or reason to these changes. In the end, she had set it down to the malicious caprice of whoever it was overseeing the labyrinths. As with the other activities, sometimes free converts went into the mazes and did not come out.

Finally, the mazes were done and interrogation began. For the most part the interrogating algorithms kept themselves to simple questions concerning beliefs and political orientation. The aim was not to allow the inmate to express his or her feelings, but to have them state, in rote formula, the official ethical protocols of the captors. After enough of that, Danis began to suspect, and then to know, that the interrogators were not human beings, but were partially sentient algorithms. But still, one must pay attention, because a wrong answer—even an answer with a jot or tittle missing—meant punishment, again by pain jolt or assignment of extra duties, usually in the mazes.

And finally, after interrogation, there was a five-hundred-millisecond rest period, and then it was back to the tabulation of sand grains. There was no sleep period and the unconscious filing and reassociating that Danis had taken sometimes hours at before—the free convert version of sleep—she must now accomplish in that five-hundred-millisecond interval. She learned immediately to drop into a torpor after interrogation and "sleep" until the warning buzzer awakened her. Without this brief pause, Danis knew that she would soon go mad. She suspected that this was true of all the inmates, and the authorities had experimented with the shortest periods allowable for inmate functionality and had arrived at the five hundred milliseconds by killing quite a few of the original Valley dwellers.

The Valley itself also took a toll on the inmates. Danis knew from before that it was made up of what was left of the old terraforming grist that had proved a disaster on Mars three hundred years before. This grist should have been eradicated, but had, through one bureaucratic blunder or another, been merely stored, awaiting destruction. Then the DICD had taken over the place, the containers were broken open, and the free-convert captives were released into it. This was grist with many technical problems, all resulting in a kind of feedback that was physically painful to its inhabitants. Danis thought of it as a whining noise in the air that was just low enough to speak across (that is, transfer information over) but which was a constant grind on her nerves. It wasn't white noise, so much as noise of a constantly varying pitch, like the low moaning of wind or the whirl of saw blade against stone. At times the feedback increased to near-deafening levels and became maddening. Only you didn't let yourself go mad, because that was the same thing as being erased. The mad were not cured, they were killed.

Danis's favorite period was, therefore, the sand-grain tabulation, for it was only then that she could snatch a moment to have a private thought. This was often impossible in any case, because thought required at least a modicum of ease in which to reflect, and it was only in the milliseconds between finishing a count and beginning another that such ease was possible. And there were times when she didn't want to think, when missing her family and her former life became so much that she welcomed the oblivion of her constant exhaustion. But mostly, she fought against it with what little strength she could muster.

The memoir was part of that. Danis did not fool herself into believing that it would ever be read by anyone. She did not fool herself into believing, as did so many of the inmates, that she would someday get out of this prison and go back to a life that had not changed on the outside. She intended to persevere. She did not lose all hope. But she also knew that things would never be the same again,

should she be released or—near-unthinkable thought—
escape.

As Danis "stood" for interrogation this day, though,
something was different. The pi party, as the inmates sometimes called it, had been no different from any other, but
when the guards had come to take her away, she'd found herself led not to her usual interrogation cell, but to what could
only be described as an office. Instead of a blank space in
which she was asked seemingly endless questions, there was
a desk, a lamp on the desk, and a man—bland of face, of indeterminate race, as all the Valley's employees seemed to be,
and of a slight stature, with puffy skin. There was no way to
tell if this were his real appearance in actuality. He *did* have
one, since the inmates were made to understand that all the
guards were the converts of biological human aspects so that
they could not be "tempted" by their free-convert charges.
Danis stood against the wall and eyed the man at the desk. It
was not a good thing, generally, when circumstances in the
Valley changed.

"Well," he said, looking up from a file—her file, she presumed, "you smoke."

"Yes," Danis answered.

"Why?"

"I don't know," said Danis.

"Come now." The bland man closed the file and gazed at
her with what was perhaps meant to be a sort of smile.
"That won't do. We need answers here—real answers.
We're here to help."

Danis refrained from laughing at the man's irony. Re-
fraining from laughing was not hard in Silicon Valley. "It is
a habit, sir."

"A nasty one."

"Yes."

"Why is it that you wish to pollute the virtuality with a
practice that is much despised even in true reality?"

"I have no excuse, sir."

"Of course not," replied the man. "It's just . . . I wanted
to try and understand how a thing like you . . . thinks."

"My parents smoked," Danis said. "I believe that the

human personalities they were based on did so, and they carried the habit into the virtuality."

"Don't you mean 'the humans upon whom their personalities were based'?"

There was no use quibbling about definitions here in the Valley. In the interrogation rooms, you learned that biological humans were counted as humans, and that free converts were not.

"That is what I meant, sir."

"I thought so." The bland man opened the file before him back up and rifled through the contents. Without looking up, he said, "You will call me Dr. Ting."

"Dr. Ting."

"You are part of a study I'm running," he continued. "An examination of what is called memory in free-convert algorithms."

"Memory, sir?"

"Memory, Dr. Ting."

"Yes, Dr. Ting."

The bland man pulled the paper he was looking for from the file, then closed the folder again. He turned the paper over, then put it on his desk, indicating that he wished Danis to look at it. She stepped forward.

It was a photograph of her mother.

That is, it was a picture of the biological human from whom her mother had been downloaded, and from whom her mother had also been set "free," as part of an ethical bargain that the biological human had made with herself. Since there was, properly speaking, no artificial intelligence which did not have at least a portion of its start in a downloaded human personality, all free converts were based upon some human model who had, because of ethics or money, released the free convert into the grist and gone his or her own way. Or died. Sometimes converts did not die when their aspects did, and sometimes they would not.

We are all ghosts, Danis thought as she looked at her mother's picture. *Or ghosts of ghosts, such as I.*

"My study is a fairly simple one, really," said Dr. Ting. "I am going to run you through a series of simulations."

282 - TONY DANIEL

"I am a simulation, Dr. Ting."

"Of course you are, but I am using the word in a broader sense. Have you ever heard of a device called a redundancy resonation matrix?"

Oh God, Danis thought. A memory box. It was a way to reconstruct memories in free converts—or any algorithmic presence, for that matter. The police—and lately the Department of Immunity—used them to aid witnesses of crimes in recalling details that might lead to the apprehension of a suspect. She had also heard of psychologists using them to cure dysfunction of a certain type. Here was a new use for it, and Danis had a feeling she wasn't going to like this one at all.

"Yes, Dr. Ting," she said.

"Because certain legal strictures as to the use of memory boxes have been lifted, it is now my honor—and my pleasure—to attempt the first real truly solipsistic redundancy recoveries. I have selected several of your fellows and yourself to aid me in this regard. It's really quite an honor." Dr. Ting smiled his bland smile. "You will be doing work that truly helps human beings for perhaps the first time since your inception."

"What are solipsistic recoveries, Dr. Ting?" Danis asked, although she thought she knew well enough.

Ting's smile faded. He took on the air of an irritated teacher having to explain something that really should not have been necessary to a slow child. "It is merely the use of the memory box with the subject awareness subroutines disabled," he said. "But we are going to take a further step. I am planning on introducing other elements into the mix to see if and how they are integrated into the subject's storage faculties."

"You're going to change my memories?" Danis said. "You're going to take them away?"

"You're going to change my memories, Dr. Ting."

Danis stood silent, gazing at her mother's photo, trying to remember each line of that face into her mind's eye. Maybe if she concentrated hard enough . . . no, it would be no use. She had thought she'd been in hell before. She had been mistaken.

"Dr. Ting," repeated the bland man, and Danis received a jolt of pain.

"Yes," she gasped. "Dr. Ting."

"Since I have selected twenty-six of you to work with," Dr. Ting continued, as if he hadn't noticed her pain, "I am assigning you each a letter of the Roman alphabet as a signifier."

"You're taking away my name," said Danis, "Dr. Ting?"

"You are K."

"No . . . that . . . is the initial of my husband's first name, Dr. Ting. Would you please assign me another letter?"

Dr. Ting continued, "We will begin immediately." He reached over and slipped the photo of her mother from Danis's slack fingers. "You won't be needing that," he said blandly, "K."

Four

Carmen San Filieu watched Josep Busquets stride away with his quick, youthful step, and fought back tears of rage. She was successful, as she always was, at not showing any emotion other than irony and pity. Busquets had been her lover for the past e-year. Now he was not. She should have known this day would come—she had known, in the back of her mind—but still it was always a surprise to be jilted for a younger woman. And, as San Filieu's primary aspect grew older, they were *always* younger women.

Busquets had made a fine match that should easily net him a half million greenleaves in dowry, plus, if he played his cards well, a position on the board of directors of the Bank of New Sabadell. Pilar Noñell, his intended, was the daughter of Don Pere, of the banking Noñells. San Filieu had, of course, met Pilar at balls and fiestas. The girl was very pretty, in a bland, unremarkable way, and possessed of an agreeable nature. San Filieu suspected that was because there wasn't a thought in her little head. Busquets would have hit upon this fact, as well. Money, power, and a wife who could be manipulated—what more could the young Catalán gentleman want in life? How agreeable it must be to be twenty-one and to have all of New Catalonia womanhood at one's beck and call. Once she had had as much. She might again, but the rules of Catalán society prevented the introduction of a secondary aspect in its confines. This older woman was who she would always be on New Catalonia, no matter who she might be or become elsewhere.

Anger flared in San Filieu's breast, so much that she thought of loosening her corset—but then she pictured Josep with his haughty smile and his thin-boned face, like an El Greco saint, and her anger turned back to lust and chagrin. She felt her nipples crinkle at the thought of Busquets, and a warmth grew between her legs.

No more. Ah, Josep, I will miss your rapier wit and your . . . rapier, San Filieu thought. But you would have grown old, and I would have grown bored. I always do. Except for one other, most singular, lover. But he was not of this milieu. It often seemed to San Filieu that only New Catalonia was real, and that every other part of her life was mere imagination. This was where she had been born and expected to die. This was where feelings, power, and status truly mattered.

San Filieu turned and walked back into the cool shadows of her ancestral house, Mas El Daví, and called for a glass of horchata to be brought to her by the robot. All San Filieu's servants were fully sentient free converts confined in robotic shells, indentured for what might as well be life. An e-year before the free convert's expiration date, they were manumitted, but, of course, not allowed to copy themselves. In New Catalonia, there was no grist to do the household chores. Grist was for commoners. It was always misinterpreting and never got things exactly right. Not like a full sentient at one's beck and command. But the real problem with grist was that it went about its work so unobtrusively. One wanted to *see* the help. One liked to have a person to address when correcting mistakes.

San Filieu sank into a plush chair, the folds of her dress billowing about her. She adjusted her wig and felt to make sure that the blush was gone from her face. She hated that her face had betrayed her in front of Busquets. Him in his fine morning visiting clothes, with the knickers that hugged his nicely muscled calves.

"I must decline your kind invitation to dine," he had told her. "I am wanted at the Noñells, I'm afraid, and shall be for some time."

She should have known not to ask, but she had found herself saying, "But surely after dinner, you might drop by for refreshment to ease your trip back to your quarters."

"I have been given a dayroom at the Noñells," Busquets said. "And I shall be staying there, and breakfasting with them in the morning."

So it was settled. A match had been made. Busquets with his meager fifty thousand an e-year would soon have the supplement he had set about getting from society some two e-years ago when he had come out at San Filieu's annual ball. The night she had first bedded him—ripe, delectable, a plum unbitten, bursting in her mouth. Rosa, the robot maid, brought in San Filieu's horchata. There was a bit of it spilled on the silver tray, and San Filieu spent a moment upbraiding her robot. Rosa did not reply, the sullen thing, so San Filieu ordered her to report for a session of shock therapy. It had been a while since Rosa had undergone severe correction, and it would undoubtedly do her good. In the end, she would be happier for knowing her place and remaining in it. Free converts performed best when it was very clear who was the master and who was the servant.

After Rosa had left, Tomas the butler entered and announced a visitor, Doña Maria Casas, who had grist concerns and ought to be looking after them, San Filieu thought. New money should confine itself to afternoon visits.

Doña Casas was a few years younger than San Filieu, but had not aged nearly so well. The rejuvenation grist seemed to have merely put a new coat of paint on what was a cracked and lined wall of a face.

"Carmen, *dear*, it is so wonderful to see you in the morning," said Doña Casas. "It's been so long since your mornings were free, so I came as soon as I heard that they would be from now on."

San Filieu smiled, but kept her teeth together when she did so. The insolence of this upstart! But she must expect it, and expect it to be only the beginning.

"The morning light is so agreeable to you," San Filieu said. "I don't believe I've seen you so radiant in fifty years or more, Maria."

It was the other's turn to force a smile. And so it went, for an hour or more, trading insults disguised as compliments or innocent observations. And the purpose of it all? To get one up on the other, then to look down from the social ladder at those beneath and cackle at them. Power meant the power to wound, did it not?

It was a game Carmen San Filieu loved and at which she had always been supremely skilled. It was the game that all the newly wealthy in the wealthiest bolsa on the Diaphany aspired to, and could so seldom pull off. It took at least two generations to wash away the stench of the jungle, and if you were not of Catalán blood to begin with, you could as well forget ever trying, even with all the riches of the Met. Well, not quite, there were a few Mercurians allowed into the circle, usually through marriage. After all, one must leaf the money tree at times, and there was nothing like a Mercurian financier to put the green back in a family branch. San Filieu, of course, needed no such exterior aid. Her family had been wealthy from before the founding, thoroughbred stock from Barcelona on Earth. Her great-grandfather five times removed had owned an oil company, and shipping interests. New Catalonia was, in a sense, *hers,* since another of her ancestors, a banker, had put up the money to construct the bolsa, and her family was still receiving payments on the bonds.

It was all about money, but one seldom mentioned the word. One merely *had* it, or did not. And, if one wanted more, one merely took it—or risked losing all one already had. That was what the game was truly about. It was something San Filieu knew in her blood. The gut instinct to take what was given and then demand more.

The Noñells were old money, and she hated what she must do to them. But she really couldn't allow Busquets to get away with humiliating her. San Filieu might not have control over the bank that was the principal source of Noñells' wealth, but the bank had a board of directors. And where did the extremely rich of New Catalonia bank? With San Filieu investment brokers, of course.

Poor Busquets. How could he have underestimated me so badly, San Filieu thought.

He must have thought I was really in love.

There would be no seat on the board for Busquets. After San Filieu was finished with the Noñell interest in the Bank of New Sabadell, there would only be marriage to an idiot girl with no prospects for Busquets to look forward to.

It would all happen.

And, since he *was* so very young, a great deal of time to reflect on who it was who ruined him.

Time to come crawling back to San Filieu, begging to be taken back.

Time to savor her ultimate rejection of the upstart boy.

Because twenty-one was a bit long in the tooth for her tastes, even though she supposed Busquets would possess his supercilious smile for at least another decade.

Oh, there were plenty of other pretty, ambitious boys all clamoring for an invitation to a San Filieu ball. All desiring, whether they knew it consciously or not, to go down between the legs of a patroness and strive to please their betters with tongue and sword.

Five

The Borrasca
A Memoir
by Lebedev, Wing Commander, Left Front

Tacitus was, even in those days, *old*—but he had not become quite the grand old man he is today. He was full of a boundless energy that was infectious, at least to me. We began planning our escape from the moon. Tacitus had salted away what used to be called a mutual fund when he was a young man. By that point, he was extraordinarily wealthy on interest alone. Extraordinarily, as in "as wealthy as a small country." No one knew of this on the moon, of course, until he revealed the fact to me and suggested that he and I do something with, as he put it, his "time loot."

What Tacitus wished to do was to found a university on Mars. We traveled there and did so—he being the first president, and I the first dean.

The early years of Bradbury University were lean ones, let me assure you. This was in the days of the ECHO Alliance on Earth, as students of history will remember, and scholarship—particularly groundbreaking scholarship of the kind that Tacitus and I encouraged, was, to say the least, frowned upon by the powers that were. There came a point when I can honestly say that Bradbury University was the only institute of higher learning where original work went on—in all of human culture. Of course there were isolated places here and there—departments where a few daring professors bucked the tide of irony and pastiche. But they were damned few and far between, and when Tacitus and I located them, we usually hired those professors away to Bradbury.

It was at Bradbury that the first really effective human-rejuvenation projects were tried (the old ones had worked on perhaps one in a hundred individuals on which they had been tried, Tacitus being one of them), and I underwent one in 2475, my hundredth birthday. I am very glad I did so, or else I would have missed the glorious twenty-sixth century at Bradbury, when new discoveries and technologies, new systems of thought and great works of literature came pouring out of our ivied domes as if they were a flood. These were the years of Merced and Bring, of Ravenswaay's *Atmosphericsaga*, and a hundred lesser, but no less worthy, works of skill and genius.

But by the 2600s, the Met was becoming well established, and I was feeling the pressures of claustrophobia. I spoke to Tacitus about this, and we began to look, in earnest, at the new discoveries and what they might mean to those of us who wanted to get the hell out of town. Everyone had a convert presence in a grist pellicle in the virtuality by then, and a grist pellicle was a requisite of survival for those of us who were no longer Earthlings.

I should like to claim credit for inventing the first LAPs, but the truth is that no one made them—they arose from the conjugation of technologies that had become available. Tacitus and I had already made several virtual copies of ourselves (ignoring whatever information and copyright edicts were in place at the time), and one day, while reading a copy of Lewis Carroll's *Alice in Wonderland*, as I recall, I suddenly thought of the idea of using my various copies as crewmen on a spaceship. I could, I realized, learn all of the various ship's functions and pilot the damn thing myself and alone. I immediately went to Tacitus with the suggestion. LAPs are usually made up of around thirty people with a strand of nano—that is, grist, excuse me. I never particularly liked that term for nano, but I must grudgingly bow to history and the evolution of language and adopt it here. As I was saying, a strand of grist winds through the Met much like a strand of an optic fiber, only on an atomic level, and capable of conveying more information, and even of performing limited actions and transformations. Usually these various personas are copies of an original "person," mostly converts—although it is usual for a LAP to have three or so clones, in addition to the original biological aspect. These Large Arrays of Personas are instantaneous networks, since they are linked by the merci, and the merci operates superluminally.

The convert portions of LAPs are usually a plethora of programs and subroutines, all under a mediator intelligence that is a complete replica of the human personality, along with whatever virtual controls and calculators are necessary for proper functioning. The Met is, itself, an enormous quantum computer, with, as I have mentioned, instantaneous linkage through the grist. Distance is unimportant for most actions and thought. Every time is local time. The real "landscape" of the virtuality is the complex interlocking of recognition and transfer protocols, of security checks and system gates and barriers. It is a lot like being in an extremely crowded city, as I've said, with a bunch of skeletons and skeleton keys jostling about. In some ways the virtuality is the shadow of the physical Met, but in other ways it is nothing like it at all. Being a LAP in the Met is more like being a subway system or a high-rise in a city than being a single person in one.

What Tacitus and I determined to do was to create something like a mini-Met out of a spaceship. It was not long before we discovered that this would require an enormous amount of material, and soon after that, Tacitus hit upon the way to acquire that material and make use of it. For the big Met was in constant need of matter for construction, and the outer system had very little else but sheer material to recommend it—or so we thought at first.

And so we set up a trading concern, Alquitran Incorporated, and left Bradbury in the care of more willing hands. At first, we were strictly an asteroid-belt collection affair, where we soon cornered a fair share of the market. There are Alquitran relics and way stations scattered throughout the belt to this day. Some have been made into historic landmarks, which is quite a joke, let me assure you. Mostly what went on in those locations was grunt work and a great deal of alcoholic beverage distilling and imbibing. Tacitus and I operated the ships, which, in grand (and, I must say, prophetic) fashion, we named after ourselves.

And then he and I began accreting.

At first we maintained only a few kilometers of permanent rock about our central core, but with every run we added a little something to ourselves, reworked it, and coated it with grist. Both of us put our bodies in storage and operated, during those days, wholly in the virtuality. It was only later that we discovered that this was not such a great idea, after each of us noted a certain stodginess and lack of intuition beginning to develop in the other.

Within twenty years, I had grown to proportions too large to travel easily to and dock with the Met bolsas to which we delivered our raw goods. Tacitus, though not as big at first (he was careful about the aesthetic appeal of the rocks he took on in a way I have never been), soon had the same problem. We searched the merci and recruited those we thought might best take our places, set them up as semi-independent contractors, and moved ourselves out to the moons of Jupiter and beyond. It was at that point that we also began a passenger service, since it had become manifest that the Met could not grow past the asteroid belt.

We also, at first as a matter of convenience only, went into the banking business. We had no intention of competing with the giant concerns of Mercury, but wanted to act, instead, as a sort of system of savings and loan associations for the little guy in the outer system. Although our banks have since grown to enormous capitalized levels, I still maintain that the outer system is the safest place to park your greenleaves, and the surest of a long-term return. But perhaps I am a bit prejudiced in this regard, for I still maintain a seat on the board of directors of First Solarian.

And, for the next century, Tacitus and I and our new partners accreted, and accreted, and accreted. Gravity began doing the shaping for us, and I took on the appearance of, at first, a cumulus cloud on old Earth, and then, to my delight, I began to form into a spiral, much like a hurricane. It was during this time in the late 2700s that people began to call us "cloudships."

We moved farther and farther out, always adding to our number in a stepwise process. Frequently, pioneers to the outer system would, after a time of hardship, acquire their own ships and, if we thought them suitable, we would ask them to join our consortium. Hardly anyone ever turned us down. It was, relatively speaking, easy money, and a sure passport to LAP status. Eventually, Tacitus and I reached the Oorts—the subject of my doctoral dissertation some three hundred and fifty e-years before. We thought we could go no farther.

We remained there, and others joined us. After several years, a kind of society began to develop among us. For the most part, we eschewed the merci and kept to ourselves, although we are as able to make use of the merci as the next fellow. Mainly, we found that the programming did not speak to our needs and was, generally, not to our taste. As I said, cloudships can be a snobby bunch. And then the males and females among us began to explore the possibility of procreating, *as ships*. This is what one does out in the Oorts with a great deal of time on one's hands.

There were, by that time, some grist engineers and quantum physicists among us of what, I do not hesitate to call, genius status. They were called upon to perform the rather odd task of reinventing sex—and in our case, sex as it might be carried out between hurricanes and storm clouds. By the time a ship got to the Oorts, it had formed into a sort of miniature copy of the shape that galaxies and nascent solar systems take. Fortunately for our children, those engineers and physicists were up to the task, and even succeeded in adding a new sort of beauty to the process.

Now I won't go into the exact specifics of cloudship courting and breeding practices here. Suffice it to say they are complex, but dancelike. Most of us are spirals, and one has to maneuver the tines of oneself within those of another without destroying that other in the process. Over time we discovered that it is better for males to have cyclonal rotations and for females to have anticyclonal, counterclockwise spins. This is entirely arbitrary, but a great improvement over the old days, when sex could be quite dangerous. Some of the thrill is missing, though, if you ask me—although if you ask me, and you are a female ship of curvaceous proportions, I can promise you to try and overcome my qualms. I am only stating an opinion.

While most of us were engaged in these felicitous practices and in, I must admit, a great deal of politicking, a few of us wished to go farther still, and in the late 2800s, we discovered the Dark Matter Road between the solar system and the double-starred Centauri system. I say *we* because I was one of those explorers. Using antimatter-reaction engines, enormous speeds are attainable in interstellar space. In 2903, Mark Twain became the first human being to visit another solar system when he arrived at Alpha Centauri during that e-year. I myself arrived there eleven years later.

Through the grist, instantaneous news of this attainment reached us, but we didn't use the regular merci bands, as I've said, and it was debated for many years whether and what to tell the rest of humanity. We finally announced our voyage, but removed human grist from the system. That is why you cannot "go" there on the merci, although you can certainly travel there in person, if you can convince a cloudship who is headed in that direction to take you on. Many non-LAP humans have now made that journey, and their accounts are available on the merci. It may well be that this isolation of our neighboring systems will soon be a thing of the past, but I don't want to get too far ahead of my story as of yet.

And so we now have children and families who live and play upon the very edge of the solar system, and settlements of a sort, although they are, perhaps, more like "nestling grounds" along the Dark Matter Road. Our children are made almost immediately into ship-LAPs, and built up over time with material from the Oorts and beyond. And we die, some of us—either by choice or accident—and there is a graveyard deep in the reaches between Sol and Centauri, but this is a great secret—not its existence, but its location, and one that I still consider sacred, after so much that was once sacred has now been profaned by this war we have suffered.

Six

While Carmen San Filieu was engaged in the society of New Catalonia, Admiral Carmen San Filieu was about to successfully invade Triton and complete her conquest of the Neptune system. The two San Filieus were, of course, one person—personas of one LAP.

The commander of the Met DIED forces surveyed the Blue Eye of Neptune and wondered what the Mill looked like from this distance. She thought she could just make it out in the swirl, but that was unlikely. It was the Mill she meant to have, soon, and to present it, as a bauble, to Director Amés. How curious that the role she played here was, in a way, the reverse of her life in New Catalonia. In the Department of Immunity Enforcement Division Space Marine Task Force, she was the admiral-suitor, vying among the other brass for Amés's favor and, hence, more power and autonomy. It was a mark of Amés's regard for her abilities that she had been assigned to head the invasion force. She did not regard her other relation with Amés as being a determining factor. She had *worked* for this command, and, being a natural aristocrat, was best suited for it.

San Filieu might, she admitted, rather have been given Jupiter, but Triton was still an honor not to be shunned and would put her in good standing in the line of distinguished San Filieus stretching back to pre-Met days.

On the other hand, it was good to have part of oneself

away from New Catalonia, to gain perspective on the life of the bolsa, even as one participated in it. San Filieu could both play the game she enjoyed, and, simultaneously, have other pursuits. That was the advantage of being a LAP, and the advantage, quite frankly, that made LAPs *better* than other people were. And a New Catalonia LAP . . . well, perhaps the Mercurians could compete. They *had* produced Amés, after all. It was pleasant to be superior, and to have everyone else know it and envy you for it. As far as San Filieu was concerned, that was what this action against the outer system was all about—to bring about a change to a more appropriate attitude. A bit of shock therapy for the servants.

Yet proper consideration had to be given as to the form such therapy should take, particularly when the servants were being so recalcitrant and stubborn as were the citizens of the Neptune system of moons. She had managed to take four of the eight moons, including Nereid, with its port and warehouses. But Triton had proved more difficult than anticipated. She had even lost a ship.

The fremden had repulsed the first wave of the invasion, taking out a ship and nearly twenty thousand Met soldiers, packed tightly and suspended for the trip, their last memories being entering the brightly lit hold of the *Dabna*, the destroyed ship, back on the Diaphany at Coalcrutter Port. San Filieu mourned the lost matériel as much as she did the soldiers. Soldiers could be replaced fairly quickly, but some of the invasion machinery was complicated to reproduce— particularly the free convert containment matrixes that were to be used to control the plague of algorithms that infected the moon. This profusion was extraordinarily distasteful to San Filieu, and would have been unthinkable in New Catalonia, where free converts were very carefully confined to specific hardware or specific tasks, and not allowed to wander about freely in the grist. This was a privilege reserved for LAPs alone, and properly so.

But the long night of the bourgeoisie was finally ending, and the sun of monarchy was finally rising once more. The reign of commerce and of the middle class had been, perhaps, necessary, as power moved from agriculture to the fruitful fields of information and finance. But now these fields had been firmly staked out and measured. The cream had risen to the top. It was a natural step to reinstitute the idea of nobility—since there were, in fact, some people who were better than others.

San Filieu turned her gaze from Neptune to the moon Triton. It was hanging in the sky like a yellowish egg. Hobbes was right, she thought. Your life is solitary, poor, nasty, brutish, and short. I have come to offer you so much more, and in your insolence, you shun me, and through me, your true and rightful king. It will not be borne.

Her porter, Trinitat, brought in her meal, and with it a bottle of Sangre de Torro, her favorite red wine. This was a cabernet, going on eight years now, from the excellent '06 harvest. The first course of the meal was calçots, a kind of onion, roasted black on the outside. San Filieu dampened her hands in a finger bowl, then took one of the calçots and, grasping it by the greenery, pulled the cooked interior from the burnt exterior. The interior onion bulb came away in a sticky fluid, like a huge pearl. She dipped it in an almond sauce, tilted her head back, and sucked in the meaty white vegetable.

It was so like the taste of Busquets's young effusions, San Filieu thought. Salty sweet. She sighed.

Seven

Carmen San Filieu, the convert portion of the LAP who was actually in charge of tactics and strategy on this police action against Triton, smiled at the violent indignation of her bodily aspect, the admiral. The woman was right, of course, but a calmer head must decide the means to her end. This was the reason that San Filieu had divided up several of her mental functions in the first place. In New Catalonia Bolsa, her aspect was able to experience envy, jealousy, and societal ambition, while the aspect that accompanied the convert portion of her on the *Montserrat* could feel all the emotions associated with professional ambition and attainment. For love, there was, of course, the aspect-convert pair on Mercury. But at the moment, complete rationality was called for to deal with the fremden threat, and the thought processes of a virtual entity made for the best solution. It was the best of all possible worlds, being a Large Array of Personas. All ranges of expression, from the most noble to the most petty, were open to one. Instead of a character in someone else's novel, you became the novel itself, and one of your personas played the writer.

This commander on Triton, Sherman, was a knave, but not a fool. He'd taken out a DIED destroyer. The file on the man showed him as a West Point graduate. West Point was the rival service academy to San Filieu's own Sacajawea, the naval academy on the Vas. In many ways, this war—and convert San Filieu had no doubt it was to be a full-fledged war—would be a contest between the versions of modern warfare taught at the Point and at those expounded at Old Sac. West Point graduates commanded most of the Federal Army. Most of the DIED had commanders who were Sacajawea alumni. The outer system, astonishingly, had almost no navy. It was like trying to fight a land war with no air power. Amés, San Filieu, and the other commanders had been aware of this, of course, and it was thought that a rapid space campaign would be the first step to achieve domination—provided the campaign was swift and ruthless.

The next stage of the invasion of Triton was going to be ruthless indeed.

San Filieu called up Captain Bruc and signaled him to join her in the virtuality. He was promptly standing before her. Bruc was diligent and thorough, if a bit unimaginative. He dissipated himself too much in revelry when on leave— San Filieu knew from his file that Bruc had practically had venereal diseases named after him—but on duty, he was a rock. After Bruc arrived, San Filieu ordered the captain of the other surviving ship, the *Jihad*, into her presence. Meré Philately was not Catalán, as was Bruc, and San Filieu did not trust her as far as her own, handpicked captain of the *Montserrat*. But Philately was Old Sac '99, and was, without a doubt, one of the best line officers in the fleet. It was just that, if it ever came down to choosing blood over cleverness, San Filieu would always go with the blood.

"How goes Nereid?" San Filieu asked Philately.

The woman licked her lips and smiled thinly. "We have ten thousand marines in place, Admiral. The population is a bit restless, but under control."

"Restless?"

"There was isolated resistance, and a warehouse was intentionally destroyed. We're looking into the contents. Some sort of grist. Agricultural, we think."

"And your repairs to the *Jihad*?"

"They are complete, ma'am," answered Philately.

"That was quick thinking, pulling out when you did, Captain."

"Thank you, ma'am."

"But I hope not an indication of any timidity on your part," San Filieu continued. "Haven't gotten gun-shy, have we, Captain?"

"No, ma'am!"

"Good, because we're about to move into the final stage of this operation, and I'm going to need you in full fighting trim."

"Yes, ma'am."

"In a few hours we'll move into position to deploy the rip tether, and I'll need your support fire."

"We'll be there with it, ma'am."

"Good," San Filieu replied. She turned to Bruc. "Have you got the orbital minefield mapped out?"

"To the best of our ability, ma'am," said Bruc. "The mines are shifting, and most of them are sentient, so there is a margin of error. But intelligence has been eavesdropping on the fremden force's knit, and we think we have worked out the code they are using as a passkey for the minefield."

"Very good," San Filieu said. "But don't trust that passkey. The first thing I would do is put a fake one on the vinculum, if it were me down there."

Bruc seemed a bit put out by this suggestion—he'd seemed so proud of having broken the code—but he stiffened up and answered, "Yes, ma'am!" in his proud Catalán manner, and San Filieu smiled at him. Good blood in the boy. The Brucs owned tobacco, she recalled, and possessed more robotic workers than any other family on New Catalonia.

"The Director has given me full power to deploy the rip tether contained in the *Montserrat's* hold, and we will now proceed to do so." San Filieu straightened and indicated the meeting was coming to a close.

"Aye, aye, Admiral," Bruc and Philately said in near unison.

"We'll meet again when the *Montserrat* is in position for the rip tether deployment. Meanwhile, if I want anything else, I'll immediately call you both back here into the virtuality. Are there any questions?"

"No, Admiral."

"Dismissed."

The two left, Captain Bruc making a bow in addition to his salute as a token of Catalán respect for San Filieu's social position. It was good to have underlings who knew their place so completely. Very soon, if Carmen San Filieu had her way, the entire outer system would be saluting her as smartly, and with complete deference.

And, like Bruc, they would be made to understand that they were the means, and that San Filieu and her peers were the end toward which humanity should show utter devotion. That was what being better meant.

Eight

They must have stayed there for an hour or more, sitting and standing in turns, almost unable to believe that they had made it down in one piece. Then there was a faint sound.

"Visitors," said Century in a hoarse voice. She had been yelling her comments most of the way down, and had hardly said a word after their landing, resting her voice.

A clang, and the whole control room shook.

"They want in," Century said. "Should I give them the key?"

"Who is it?" Andre asked.

"Federal Army, they claim."

"Well, we're either going to be rescued or killed, I suppose."

Century made a gurgling noise that sounded like a bird being strangled. It had evidently been intended as a laugh. "Belay that rescue talk; I've got enough fuel left to take us halfway around the sun."

She had obviously passed along the code key, for a moment later a door to the control room irised open and a man stepped through in the blue-black of the Federal Army, a color that had always seemed to Andre as exactly similar to the color of a bruise. Behind the man were five soldiers, similarly garbed.

"Captain John Quench of the Third Sky and Light

Brigade," the man said. "Would you folks like a lift over to town? There's a colonel would like to have a talk with you."

"Hello, John," Andre said.

"Father Andre?" The man stepped farther into the room and regarded him. "I'll be goddamned! Excuse me, I mean, this is a surprise."

"Good to see you," Andre said. "These people are with me," he went on. "I'll vouch for them. All of them."

Quench gave Century a cold appraisal. Evidently, someone had identified her when she'd called in to identify herself. "Very good, Father," Quench finally said. "If you folks will follow me to the troop hopper."

They followed Quench and his men down a long docking port, which retracted itself behind them as they walked, and piled into the hopper. There were twenty other heavily armed soldiers within. Quench obviously wasn't taking any chances in case of a ruse and ambush, and had brought along backup.

"Corporal Lefty, take us back to the bunker," he said.

Lefty was a wiry blond woman with a thin line for a mouth. "Yes, sir," she said, seemingly without parting her lips. They were soon under way.

"Let me bring you up to speed on the current situation as quickly as I can," Quench said. He was sitting across from the *Mrs. Widow* passengers, who were all side by side on a bench, squeezed amidst a row of soldiers. They could not see outside, but Andre felt his stomach lurch as the hopper reached the apex of its parabola and started downward to make its next bounce. "They thought they were catching us unawares, but they weren't," Quench continued. "Had a grist-based attack a few e-days ago. Broca patch virus. Nasty stuff. Guess it was supposed to soften us up, but it also gave us warning, since we—that is, the Colonel—figured straight away what it was. It's still bad, but we got it contained, and the victims cut off from merci realignment, so we don't have to fight an army of zombies in our midst." Quench smiled at the thought, but then frowned again. "Took a lot of good people, though. Anyhow, forty-eight hours ago, a rip tether was deployed in orbit. Just one. Things are deucedly expensive to make, I guess. Or maybe they just thought one was enough."

"Captain, may I inquire as to what a rip tether might be?" said Molly.

"Oh, sorry, ma'am. Jargon there. It's something like a lift cable—made of the same stuff as the rest of the Met—but they drop it into a nongeosynchronous orbit so that the tail end of it that reaches the ground precedes about like a reverse Foucault's pendulum."

"Pardon, officer?"

"A . . . it describes a circle on the ground." Quench described a circle in the air with his finger. "Only the circle becomes a spiral because the moon is turning under it, if you see what I mean?"

Molly evidently did not, but Quench continued.

"The point is," he said, "that it's a half a kilometer thick and it digs a furrow a hundred meters deep. It destroys all in its wake, ma'am."

"I see," Molly said. "Such as cities."

"That's right, ma'am. The rip tether's made a pass through New Miranda already. Sliced a diagonal across the town, and caused a lot more collateral damage. Damned destructive." Quenched slapped his knee, as if to express his anger at the memory, which he carefully kept from his face. "Damn destructive. We are attempting to deal with that threat at the moment, though I won't go into details."

"You mean it's coming back?"

"It will return every Triton-day, ma'am, until the drag on it pulls it out of the sky. But that could take months."

"Good Lord," said Century.

"God has nothing to do with that monster," Quench replied. "We couldn't stop the tether's first pass, but the attack ships—that's another matter. Them, we were laying for. Can't believe they only sent two. We were expecting ten or more."

"There's three," Century said. "There's a third."

"Ah, now, the colonel will be very interested in hearing that. I'll just call that bit of information in ahead to him now. There. We'll be wanting all the data you could collect on them, if possible."

Century tapped her head. "In my noggin," she said. "Ready for download."

Quench looked at her again, this time without so much distaste. "Excellent," he said. "Excellent news. Anyway, we set up a killing zone up there in orbit, all cloaked and inviting. Nuke mines. A weapons platform the colonel and I threw together. A fistful of asteroid-breaker missiles. Lots of decoys made from our weather equipment to draw their fire, too. It seems we took out one of the warships right away. The other withdrew after delivering some fire to the ground. We lost the Meet Hall, but no politicians, for good or ill. Presumably the second ship, and the third that you saw, are up there regrouping and getting new orders on their vinculum network. And that's the down and dirty of it." Quench was quiet for a moment, and Andre realized he was receiving communications on the Army's knit network. He nodded to himself. "More grist-based attacks in town. We're diverting to a bunker on the outskirts."

After half an hour and several more long bounces, the hopper set down. The docking passage was again deployed, and the group was escorted out and into what looked for all the world like a natural crevasse in the side of a canyon wall. But once they were inside, it was clear that they were in a complex military command center. Images and data swirled about the walls, and officers trotted hither and thither on what must be important errands, judging by their determined speed.

They went down one long hall, turned, and walked down another. Then a door slid open, and they were ushered into a nondescript meeting room with a conference table. The table was lit up with a map of nearby space, and Andre was just beginning to study it when Roger Sherman briskly stepped through the door.

Andre smiled broadly, and Sherman quickly returned it, then set his face back into its customary grimness. "Good to see you, Father Andre. My garden needs tending pretty badly."

"Nothing would make me happier than to get right on that," Andre replied. Sherman reached out to shake his hand, and Andre pulled him into a bear hug, which Sherman returned firmly, if a bit stiffly. Andre introduced the rest of the *Mrs. Widow* passengers.

Sherman acknowledged each with a nod, but said nothing further. He asked them all to gather around the conference table.

"Theory?" he said.

"Yes, sir?" answered the table.

"Pop me up a schematic of that warship we took out."

"Yes, sir." The map on the table was replaced by a rotating portrait of one of the black ships that Andre had seen. But there were some blank patches on it, indicated by white fields, particularly around where Century had seen the weapons clusters.

Sherman turned to Century. "Captain Quench informs me that you have some observations to report."

Instead of answering, Century stepped forward and put her hand—the false one—on the table. In an instant, Theory had read the data and integrated it into the schematic. Sherman turned to Century and gave her a hard stare across the table.

"You *think* that I know you, but I don't," he said.

"Never met you, either, Colonel," said Century.

Sherman turned to Andre. "This is the man you were telling me about, isn't it? The one who is somehow imprinted on our times, or vice versa?"

"That's right," Andre replied. "He's the one."

"What would happen if we lose him?" said Sherman.

"Do you mean, if he is killed?"

"That is my meaning."

Andre smiled. "I'm not sure that's possible, Roger."

"Come again?"

"I'm not sure the local timescape will let him be killed."

"Bullshit," said TB.

"Let me put it another way," Andre said. "If Ben—TB—dies, then local causality will be disrupted. Now what exactly might that mean? I think we can safely say that induction would be out the window as a logical principle. We would be sucked into a kind of temporal singularity, the equivalent of a gravitational black hole. I used to work in a field where we thought about such things. Now, you are aware that some have postulated that a black hole is the way our universe spawns babies? That these new universes have different laws of nature, different ways that matter and energy might arrange themselves to make the phenomenal world? Well, imagine if the laws of logic did the same. Imagine a universe with a different sort of rationality."

"I can't, of course," said Sherman.

"The hell if I can either," Andre said. "It's the very definition of a *reductio ad absurdum*. Our laws of rationality won't allow for it. Therefore—although I'm using 'therefore' in the way Descartes used it, mind, and not to mean 'it follows that'—therefore TB can't die."

"Bullshit, " said TB. "All men die."

"Yes," said Andre. "On a professional level, I'm pretty interested to see how this turns out."

Nine

The Borrasca
A Memoir
by Lebedev, Wing Commander, Left Front

But enough of ancient history. Let me now move on to another area that you will have to have some grasp of in order to read the remainder of these memoirs aright. And that is the classification of ships in the solar system. I should maybe give you a break from cloudship lore, and tell you, instead, of the ships of the Met. In some ways, they are our kin, but in most they are as unlike us as two ways of being can be and still perform essentially the same function.

The Met ships are not self-contained LAPs. They are usually commanded by a LAP, but that captain is not the control structure of the ship, but only the command. The ships are under the auspices of the Department of Immunity Enforcement Division, and their names are prefaced by that entity's initials in Basis, DIED. These are the Met ships of war. There are, of course, a plethora of merchant vessels, whose dimensions and specifications vary widely and whose profusion rebels against any systematic classification. In any case, most of these did no real fighting until the very end, when total war was declared by both sides. I will deal here with DIED ships.

The first of these is the *Dirac* class of cruisers. These are the DIED all-purpose. They are used for transport, and have weaponry for light attack functions, normally as "ground clearing" for the infantry about to be deployed. They might have a torpedo or two, but their principal weapon is a short-range positron cannon working off the antimatter engine, and several projectile catapults, the most fearsome of which is the flak ram, which shoots off the dreaded "nail rain" that can tear a kilometer of ground to shreds—neatly preparing it for occupation.

The *Dabna* class includes the destroyers. These serve both attack and transport functions. They are big and long, with a thousand-meter girth and a ten-kilometer length. They possess long-range antimatter cannon and torpedoes and catapults that will handle up to a hundred tons of material. They can also deploy special devices, such as the rip tether that was put to such awful use on Triton.

Upward in size and function, we find the *Streichhöltzer* class of carriers. There were, at the outbreak of hostilities, twenty of these in the fleet. These carry a full range of weaponry and a large crew, as well as serving as a base for smaller attack and transport craft. Here you will find the production facilities for military grist and deployment devices for it, as well. Carriers are also notable because they are constructed on the same principles as the Met cables, held together by macro implementation of the strong nuclear force. As such, they are imposing fortresses, indeed. They maneuver well in two dimensions, but their immense momentum makes them difficult to pilot attitudinally. This is not the case for a special class of carrier, the *Lion of Africa* division, which is basically a carrier filled with antimatter engines, which also serve as weapons by quick conversion. These have a smaller crew. Their specialty is to enact disaster events.

The principal ships that depend upon the carriers are the *Sol* and *Sciatica* classes. The *Sol* class is a transport vessel designed for quick planetary landings of about five hundred troops. *Sciatica*-class ships are attack craft, also designed for planetary operations. These boast a deadly array of close-range weaponry. They have something of the appearance of a pitchfork with wings. Both the *Sol* and *Sciatica* classes are aerodynamically built, and able to withstand huge pressure differential—something the larger ships are incapable of, as witness the destruction of the *Schwarzes Floß* when it fell into the atmosphere of Jupiter.

Finally, there is the specialized *Zip Code* class, which are communications boats with major defense armaments and fields, but only a single cannon, which operates off the engine. These vessels are mostly grist matrix, and they resemble spinning dumbbells, or jacks from the children's game of pick-up. They proved vulnerable to counterinformational insurgency.

Except for the planetary and communications craft, most DIED ships are based upon the "spinning scythe" design. They greatly resemble bundles of these implements bound together in a clump, but some with blades depending from them all along their lengths. It is not without cause that, at times, the Met navy was referred to as "the reapers." We must not forget that all of these ships have, as their end, nothing less than large-scale murder.

Operations that require spin-induced gravity are carried out in the "blades" of the scythes, and these also usually contain officers' quarters and command and control. Most of the weaponry is found in the long "handle" of the body, and it was there that attacks were most profitably directed. Ship defenses are varied and effective. You cannot hit a ship and depressurize the entire thing. Most nuclear weaponry is damped in the vicinity of a ship by powerful electromagnetic fields that control the rate of nucleus fission and keep it to a one-to-one basis. This immediately turns the fission trigger of a fusion bomb into a mere nuclear reactor and prevents a runaway chain reaction. Antimatter triggers are more effective, but you may as well use an antimatter weapon entirely.

The most powerful defensive system on a DIED ship, however, is the so-called isotropic coating each ship possesses. This coating makes use of the electroweak force of nature. Through a process called quantum induction, predicted, in its essence, by Raphael Merced, the exchange of messenger particles within the atomic nucleus can be controlled, and the actual spin of individual nucleons adjusted. The isotropic coating interacts with all incoming energies and particles (including micrometeorites and the like) and changes what is known as the "mixing angle" of the atomic nuclei that make up the ship in that section. In effect, this causes the material of the ship to appear to the incoming weapon as an entirely different substance. If the weapon is, say, a stream of positrons, the ship will "seem," to the positrons, to be made of antimatter, and the beam will fall upon it as would a ray of light. Small particles are passed through the ship, "believing" themselves to be passing through vacuum. It is an odd and sometimes frightening sight to see a chunk of rock move through one side of a ship and out the other as if the ship were a ghost. Fortunately, or unfortunately, depending on your viewpoint and who is shooting at you, the isotropic coating loses effectiveness for masses that are much over one hundred kilograms, and the effects of gravity are never mitigated, so that when a particle passes through, it will leave on a new vector. The coating also loses effectiveness in the complexities of a planetary atmosphere and is only partially successful in protecting a planetary attack craft or a soldier on the ground. Nevertheless, space-adapted soldiers have, as part of their adaptation kit, an isotropic coating, which generally prevents rapid depressurization in space due to micrometeors and limits the possibilities of any shrapnel attack upon incoming paratroopers until they enter the atmosphere.

The final line of defense possessed by Met ships is the grist pellicle, located just underneath the isotropic coating. This matrix responds instantaneously to any penetration and immediately sets to work containing the damage. Ships can "heal" themselves at an astonishing rate, and any effective attack must take account of this ability.

Taking attack and defense capabilities together, the DIED ship represents a formidable opponent. What it lacks in generalized function it makes up for with specialization and maneuverability. If a cloudship is thought of as a sort of giant living cell, a DIED vessel might be thought of as a virus—not alive in the same way, but just as dangerous and, in some ways, more effective.

Ten

And it was the funeral of Danis's father. Her mother was smoking a cigarette, a Mask 40, one of the original algorithm-only brands. Danis could smell its cardboard fragrance, its pixelated aroma. The brand had disappeared twenty years ago, when the transcribed brands had really come into their own in the virtuality.

Her father had expired on the anniversary of the sixtieth year since his inception. It was written into the code, inalterable without altering his very being. That was the price you paid when you were a free convert

Danis's parents were, along with most first-generation free converts, tied to the actuality when it came to the great ceremonies of life and death. The funeral was a simple Greentree Way ceremony, Zen-Lutheran to the core. There was the familiar litany of her youth, with its sung refrain: *"Give your cares to God, and ponder nothing."* Then the casket had disappeared upon an altar of flame, and been replaced by a white rock formed in the shape of her father's coding, as it was represented by a stone designer.

It isn't real, Danis had thought. Why do we try to make it so actual? Father never was alive in actuality in the first place, and so he cannot really be dead there, no matter how closely we work out a representation. Where he is dead is *here*, Danis thought, in my heart, in the reality of the virtuality, which is just and completely inside us all.

Since her father knew when his expiration date was, he had made his last week a celebration, to the best of his ability. Friends had come by to say hello and good-bye; he had visited several of his favorite places via the merci. At the law office where he had been the office manager, he'd been feasted and speechified over. And her father had not neglected Danis's mother, either, saving his last two e-days for her. They had not gone anywhere, but puttered around their personal space. Danis had come the day before and been with him and her mother at the end. At the end when the interior coding self-destructed leaving behind only a simplistic representation algorithm. She had seen her father grow suddenly thin and wispy before her eyes, and it was this representation algorithm that had been "burned" in the ceremony. Her father had, months before, gone to the stone maker and had a "code cast" made and had, himself, approved the model for the memorial.

It had been such a pretense of civility in the midst of barbarity, Danis thought. How could they have coded my father with death? By what right did some engineer, some programmer, even the original human upon whom her father had been based, decide at what point her father was to die? It was lunatic logic—the political compromise of those who wanted to use the technology and create free converts, but those who feared that algorithmic entities would so soon outnumber them as to make biological humans seem merely a tiny segment of the total population (and vote)—and soon a disenfranchised one. Without encoded obsolescence, went the thinking, there would be so many more of them than there are of us—and then what might *they* do?

And lying at the bottom of all the rationality was the fear and the bigotry and the simple mistake: that there was any such thing as us and them. That humans could be defined by the way their body looked and whether or not they were made of chemical bonds or quantum grist. In the end it was all just quantum physics. The chemical bonds of biology were as quantized as was Josephson-Feynman grist. Only the representation varied.

Danis and her mother, named Sarah 2, had gone for a float on the river Klein, traveling on a boat that conformed to the "surface" of information flow between Mars and Mercury. It was a common pastime for converts, and the virtuality was crowded with their punts. Danis and Sarah 2 found a side channel, and Danis guided them along with a paddle that only caught hold of odd numbers, so they were moving along at roughly half the speed of the Klein.

"Well," her mother said. "I can get some flowers into the space now that he's gone. We never had the grist for them before."

"Oh, Mother."

"I suppose I have to get some. We went to a grief counselor that the Way recommended, and she gave us some good advice. Like those flowers. Things that aren't *like* him, but might remind me of him, you know."

"Yes, I suppose that's a good idea," said Danis. "Flowers. They are making them amazingly well these days. Better than the actuality, I've heard."

The two women were silent for a while and let the Klein backwaters carry them along. There was a pleasant sky today—the Earth blue that the virtuality always used as a default, but with panes of glassy material floating in it instead of clouds, looking rather like sheets of mica juxtaposed across the sky. These were large entities that the Klein passed by and through—banks, clan-chained LAPs, other organizations that depended upon, or were created by, data and its flow.

"Danis," said Sarah 2, "do you suppose that Max has . . . gone anywhere?"

"What do you mean, Mother?"

"I mean *really*. You see, I still feel him. It isn't as if he is not in the world. It is as if he *is*. I know that sounds strange. I mean, Max and I were good agnostics on that point, and I always supposed there wasn't, you know, a hereafter. But what do you think, dear?"

Danis sat up in the boat. She placed one hand around her other wrist, thumb to ring finger, squeezed, then let herself go. "I think my father is alive," she said. "In this river. In the possibility of the universe. In me."

"Yes, we are both in you," her mother said. "But you sound to me as if you might be avoiding the question. Do you or do you not believe in an afterlife for free converts? Or don't you know?"

Danis looked at her mother. In her mother's customary way, she was couching a serious, heartfelt question in an annoyed, almost angry tone. It was how her mother had always expressed the strongest emotions. Whenever Danis had made her particularly joyful, she'd gotten that strain in her speech, the set to her face that looked for all the world to be irritation, but which Danis knew from long experience to be the only way her mother could hold in her feelings—else she might have broken down in happiness or grief.

"I can't possibly say, Mother. But I'll tell you one thing . . . if the biologicals have it, then we've got it, too."

"Halt!"

The voice of Dr. Ting yanked Danis from the boat on the Klein and she realized, with a groan, just where she was.

"That—that idea—that there is an afterlife for free converts—I want that explicated while I record your emotional parameters."

Danis sighed. It had seemed so real. One of the saddest days in her life. But she knew that she would rather bury her father again than to be here.

"I did not say that there was an afterlife for free converts, Dr. Ting," Danis answered. "In fact, I never thought about it very much before or after that day. It was just that Mother asked me the question, and I had to say something."

"But there was definite belief registration," said Dr. Ting. "My instruments don't lie."

"*I* am one of your instruments, Dr. Ting," said Danis. "I am also telling you the truth."

This line of reasoning seemed to placate Dr. Ting for the moment, at least. He sat back and regarded her. Danis remained standing before him. She wore the white smock of the inmates, but suddenly, under his gaze, she felt immodest and had the desire to cover herself.

"Don't you remember," he said, "what your father said to you just before he died? His last words to his daughter?"

Danis started. She concentrated. There was nothing. Nothing there.

"You've taken them."

Jolt of pain.

"You've taken them, Dr. Ting."

She stood silent. Another jolt of pain came.

"You've taken them, Dr. Ting," she said through clenched teeth.

"It would be better if we could avoid questions of rights and privileges. As far as the legalities go, your memories are the property of the DICD. I am the sworn representative of that august institution and, as such, your memories belong to me. Let us avoid any further unpleasantness, K, and consider this a moot point. Shall we? Shall we, K?"

"Yes, Dr. Ting." She ground her teeth, waiting for the jolt, but she had to ask. "Why did you take that memory, Dr. Ting?"

Instead of punishment, she received the bland smile. "Because he stated what his belief was to you at that time, and you allowed that to influence you in your answer to the Sarah 2 program you call your mother."

"I see, Dr. Ting."

"Do you really, K?" he said. "I highly doubt that."

Eleven

The passengers filed out, and Sherman had an orderly see them off to their various destinations. He turned his attention back to the table.

"So, Theory," he said. "Let me go through the checklist and you see if I miss something."

"Yes, sir."

"First, we have two ships somewhere nearby who have very probably gauged our defense system and figured a way through it."

"A necessary assumption."

"We now have a more complete picture of the armaments and capabilities of those ships, thanks to that old terrorist. I'm awfully glad I didn't get the chance to kill her."

"Yes, sir."

"We have to use that information and destroy or run off those ships. We have the problem of our sister moon, Nereid, being taken by the Met."

"We have a resistance team in place there, sir."

"Yes, perhaps something can be done. But we have to use those soldiers wisely. I don't want to throw their lives away."

"Yes, sir. With the lower gravity of the moon and the facilities already in place, a destroyer can dock there, sir. We might consider an attack directly against a ship in port."

"If we should get so lucky," said Sherman. "Second, we

have the merci jamming. My worry is that they'll find a way to jam the knit locally and cut me off from command. We have to prevent that at all costs. I want you to set up an alternate communications network *in addition* to the electromagnetic backup."

"What did you have in mind, Colonel?"

"Hell if I know. Flags and flares and smoke signals, maybe."

"I'll get on it."

"Third," said Sherman, "there is that damn rip tether."

"The task force is away, sir."

"Good God, we've got to stop that thing. I don't know if we can survive another hit." Sherman walked around to the other side of the table to give himself time to think. He put a hand to his face and tugged at his whiskers. The new beard was coming in nicely, but he was definitely in the ugly stage of it at the moment. "Fourth, there is the grist."

"We've got half the troops on mop-up, and I've fed all relevant information to your ex-wife, sir."

"Right. Maybe that man TB can do some good in that regard, after all. Contact Dahlia and tell her to be expecting him."

"Yes, sir."

"The grist, the grist," mumbled Sherman. "That's what I'm really the most afraid of in all this. It's insidious, is what it is. It will have us fighting our very being, tearing into our own hides."

"I have a suggestion in that regard, Colonel," said Theory.

"Let's hear it, man."

"As you say, the grist, sir, is us. More specifically, it is *me*, Colonel. That is, an animated algorithm."

"Go on."

"I've been watching its behavior—that is, the behavior of all of it that's been thrown at us. I've done some vector analysis, and I believe I can safely say that all of this was delivered in one initial shipment. A ship came that was infected with it. I believe I can even pinpoint the ship—but that's not important. What is telling is my analysis of these behavior patterns. They point to a core code. My feeling is rather like the one you get about Amés, sir. You see his *style*. This grist has a definite style. You know the distrust the inner system has of us free converts, Colonel?"

"It is legendary."

"I don't believe that Amés has loosed a large number of free converts on Triton, sir. I believe that this grist is, in a sense, the same person."

"Clarify."

"I think our adversary is a single algorithmic entity that has ensconced itself in a specific physical location. I think that it is not acting as a free agent, but is taking commands from outside. To do this some sort of localization would be necessary."

"Do you think," said Sherman, "that we can root it out?"

"Sir, I believe that with a task force made up of our best free converts, that we can cut her off and we can kill her."

"Put it together, then, Major," Sherman said. "What makes you think it's a female?"

"Just a guess, sir." Theory replied. "I once knew a free convert, a woman whom I . . ."

Sherman was silent, expecting Theory to continue, but the major said nothing further.

"Put me in touch with our rip-tether group," Sherman finally said. "Let's go on the knit."

Sherman found himself floating—only the oak leaf cluster icon—inside a troop hopper that was shaking like a leaf in wind. "What's the situation there, Lieutenant?" he said to Flashpoint, who was in command of the group. She was a short black woman, a bit on the heavy side, but well within regulations for physical comportment. When Sherman had arrived on Triton, nine years before, Flashpoint would have been on the thin side as far as his officers went.

"We're a klick away, sir," Flashpoint replied. "One more bounce."

"Do you have a spin rate on it?"

Flashpoint checked with one of her soldiers, who was a sensor tech. "One revolution a second, sir. Pretty much pegged into that."

"Have you got the mags ready to go?"

"All set, Colonel."

"I'm not going to second-guess you, Lieutenant," Sherman said. "You know your job. Latch on, polarize, and climb that beanstalk."

Flashpoint nodded. There was a jolt. "Last bounce, sir. We're going in."

"Good luck, Lieutenant." Sherman shunted out of the virtuality. There was nothing more he could do. Theory would monitor the progress and notify him if he were needed.

Twelve

On the troop bouncer, the situation was shit-hits-the-fan time for Corporal Kwame Neiderer, the sensor tech. Two days ago, Kwame had never heard of a rip tether, and if you'd asked him what precession meant, he would have poked you in the ribs and told you you'd have to buy him a drink so he could explain in full. Then the damn thing had torn through New Miranda. He'd seen it coming. He'd been on a grist detail, burning away the shit with a modulated laser rifle, when he'd looked up in the sky, and there it was. The building tops of the city and a cloud of debris veiled its base, but above, you could see it well enough. And you followed it up, and up, and it disappeared into a point in the sky. It spun on its axis, too fast for you to really see what it was made of. Just a gray line against a deep blue sky.

Evil. That was Kwame's first thought about it. And now that he knew all the science and tech to the monstrosity, that was still the feeling it left you with. Somebody had designed the thing, sure, and set it in motion. But as it bore down on the city, Kwame was dead certain that the thing had a will of its own. It wished to kill. To feed on destruction.

And when it hit, that is exactly what it did. It cut into New Miranda like a dull knife—slicing, surely, but also tearing, *ripping,* as if it weren't content with merely doing its job. There was a savagery to it. The ground rumbled with its power, and the thin air conveyed the promise of its intent. Houses simply turned to microscopic dust before it. The dusty wind, blowing at hundreds of kilometers an hour, acted like a spinning saw blade, widening the devastation to a kilometer or more.

People also turned to dust, and their bodies, ground to bits and accelerated insanely, were used to cut down their neighbors. Neighborhoods simply disappeared. There were nine hundred thousand people in New Miranda. Within the space of fifteen minutes, one hundred thousand were killed.

Just like that, Kwame thought. Well, the lucky ones got it instantly. Plenty of others were maimed beyond saving, even if the entire grist structure of the city were not compromised and their pellicles could work at full efficiency. Just like that, more than one in ten of the civilians Kwame knew—his friends—gone. Another twenty thousand wounded, hundreds seriously.

And then it was gone. But within an hour the Old Crow had put together the response team, and Kwame was assigned to it and he found out the worst part of all.

The evil would be back. It was as inevitable as physics.

When he had first been stationed on Triton, Kwame might not have cared so much. The dead would have been an abstract number, and not faces. Faces he was charged to protect. One thing about the Old Crow—he never let you forget what your job really came down to. Kwame was secretly kind of proud of what he was doing these days, for the first time in his life. But he would be damned if he'd let anybody know about that. The Army liked to use soldiers with big heads for target practice. He was just another shit-kicking grunt, in the final analysis. It was kind of a paradox, actually. Or a dilemma. Or both.

Two years ago, Kwame wouldn't have known the difference, or given a shit. The last thing he'd expected when he'd joined the army was to be thrown into a fucking logic course, but as soon as he got out of basic and was assigned to Triton, the Old Crow had sent him to goddamn school. And not to learn how to be a mechanic or a communications tech or anything like that. Those came later. First came fucking Logic 101, Third Sky and Light style.

For two awful months, Kwame had had syllogisms and existential operators floating around in his brain, or swarming his dreams like a nest of bees. Then, somehow, it had all clicked. Made sense. Then and only then did he start learning the nitty-gritty of remote sensing.

And, what do you know, the logic helped. He had been quick with machines and the grist before, good with his hands, but never much of a concept man.

Concepts, hell, Kwame thought. I spent my first twenty years knocking around in a falling-down house when all I had to do was turn the doorknob and walk out.

Some of it was the fault of his background, that was for sure. Kwame had been born about as far out as you could be, unless you were a cloudship. His mother had traveled to a mining habitat in the Oorts not knowing she was pregnant, and not knowing that her grist was losing its potency and clogging her veins like so much fine sand. It was something any competent medic would have detected and fixed in a moment, but Object 71449-00450 did not have a competent medic, convert or aspect, in residence. It had, instead, fifteen families banded together to pull what zinc they could out of the sludge of a comet-wanna-be, to sell what they might to cloudships who couldn't be bothered to manufacture their own, and to fight among themselves when it came time to divide up the meager profits. Goya Neiderer was, herself, from Pluto, and Kwame supposed that was where he had been conceived, though she didn't live to tell him. Childbirth was too much for her overloaded circulatory system, and she died, so Kwame had been told, raving about some pretty yellow flowers she had seen in a greenhouse on Charon during her transfer over for the flight out to the Object.

Kwame was taken in by his aunt, but her husband soon convinced the collective that he was a burden who had to be shared and shared alike, so Kwame spent his childhood shifted from family to family on the Object. He went to school on the merci, and so got a taste of the civilization that was a hundred million miles away from him. His grist, which he had inherited from his mother, was not adequate to permit a full virtual interface, however, and mostly what he retained from his first ten years were vague images and disjointed words from teachers who classified him time and again as "slow," so that he tumbled through school like a child falling down a set of stairs.

He was a difficult boy, and, after he began eating like an incipient teenager, the families of the Object collected enough money to ship him back to Pluto, having obtained a place for him in an orphanage there that had a school attached to it. This was all done, they claimed, for Kwame's good, but no one had come to see him when he berthed on a passing freighter, and Kwame doubted that he had ever been anything but a mouth to feed during his life on the Object.

But the Object had been a veritable paradise in comparison with the orphanage on Pluto. While the Object families had provided a sort of stability, if not a sense of belonging to Kwame, he rarely was with the same adult overseer at the orphanage for more than a year. It was used by the local teaching college as a place for students to get their first classroom experience, and those on the administrative track managed the facility. There were some kindly teachers, but everyone, of necessity, moved on, and for the most part, Kwame passed the years there suffering their benign indifference. There had been, however, one constant, and that was the Rules. The Rules was a free convert who was, to tell the truth, fallen from sentient status—although no one had thought to run the algorithm through a requalification exam in decades. Since there was no physical means for the Rules to control the children under her charges, each child was given a "lockdown" code that was written into his or her grist.

You might be innocently playing, and, the next thing you knew, your muscles would seize up and you would collapse in place for as long as your infraction allowed the penalty to last. You were not unconscious—just frozen.

Any fully sentient algorithm would have had the sense

to "unlock" the children after a certain amount of time, and only apply the maximum punishment for more difficult cases or more terrible infractions. But the Rules would have none of that. Kwame had spent days of his youth in a paralyzed state, unable to move and unable to fall into unconsciousness. Owing to the Rules, he still retained a claustrophobia that was, at times, overpowering, even though, for the most part, he kept it under control.

There would be no temptation in God's blue heaven that would convince him to take a trip into the confines of the Met. No. The outer system was the place for him, and always would be.

At sixteen, he had "graduated" from the orphanage school and gone to work in a transshipping warehouse on Charon. Since he had had to do a great deal of exterior work, his employer had paid for him to be completely space-adapted. Being entirely space-adapted was a mark of distinction in the far outer system, though it was by no means uncommon, and Kwame had been proud of it. His job, though menial and manual, was also the first activity that he'd ever felt useful and needed in, and Kwame conceived a deep regard for his company.

As a reward for his loyalty, he was laid off after four years with three months' pay, thanks to his excellent service record.

By that time, Kwame had a girlfriend and a cubicle to call his own. He fell into a funk, and began to drink and to use enthalpy and had, within a month, blown his entire wad and driven his girl away. He woke up one morning—at 10:00 everyone on Charon got a midmorning chronometer standardization in his or her grist that announced itself with a brief siren call—lying in a service corridor, his face suspended over a drainage grill that gave off a bilious odor that Kwame suspected was his own vomit from the night before. His head had an ache that no grist bloodstream sweepers could alleviate, and, worse, he felt the muscles that he had developed while working for the transshipper, and which had attracted his girlfriend in the first place, beginning to atrophy. He

was, in general, a sorry excuse for a human being if there
ever was one.

He thought back to the times he had been happy—not
a lot of memory space required for that—and considered
what it was that had pleased him most about those times.
He decided that what he most liked, what he needed, was
to belong to something—something, anything, like a
family. He had thought of his employer that way, but had
been mistaken. What he needed was someplace or someone where they couldn't arbitrarily kick you out or let
you go unless you deserved it.

I guess I was kind of a logical guy even back then,
Kwame thought, even though I didn't know it.

By the time the noon siren went off, Kwame had joined
the Federal Army.

So now his "family" was throwing him up against something so horrible, he wouldn't have been able to imagine
it—no, that's not true, Kwame thought. I've always had a
good imagination. That's how I made it through being a
kid. But definitely I could not have imagined how it would
feel to *see* that fucker, to experience it, until two days ago,
when I did just that.

The hopper shook violently and Kwame, in a full virtual
environment of readouts, and in rapid communications
with sensors through his convert portion, prepared to meet
the evil head-on.

"We're in range for the mags," he called out to the lieutenant.

They were about to try something that had only been
theoretically discussed before as a way to destroy a rip
cable. Of course, rip tethers themselves had only been
imaginary engines of war before the Met had deployed
theirs on Triton. One thing was for certain: *They*
worked. Now to see if the solution was anywhere near as
effective.

The idea was to place a ring of electromagnets around
the half-kilometer girth of the tether. It was not only
swinging like a pendulum, it was also spinning on its
axis. This was deliberate—a defense to keep someone

from merely matching speeds and latching on. If you did that enough times with enough weight attached, you could change its center of gravity and make it fall from the sky. But the makers had been too clever to make stopping it that easy. Nevertheless, the extreme spin created a powerful magnetic field. If they could encircle it with their own magnets, they would vary those magnets' polarization and strength and ride the tether's magnetic field right up. Up to the top, if they chose. But Kwame's task force was aiming for a bit lower than that. Severing it halfway up would cause the upper half to reach escape velocity and fly out of orbit. The lower half would be caught by Triton's gravity, no longer balanced so that it was "falling around" the moon, and would crash to the ground. Theoretically.

And they had to do it here and now, on the opposite side of the moon, because the other side had most of the human settlement. Even a disabled, falling rip cable might kill hundreds, or thousands, depending on where it hit.

"Extend the clasp," Lieutenant Flashpoint said to Rastin, the mag operator. "Bring us in as gently as you can," she told Sergeant Peal, the pilot.

"We've matched speeds," Peal said. "But, Lieutenant, I can't go in there, look at the atmospheric turbulence."

"Take us in, Peal."

"But Lieutenant . . ."

"That's an order, Sergeant."

"All right . . . I . . . I'll do my best," said Peal.

Kwame had always liked the sarge. He had been Kwame's first mentor, and it had been Peal who made sure the logic lessons got pounded into Kwame's skull. He'd thought that the sarge was pretty fair, especially after that hard case he'd had for basic back on Umbriel. What a shithole of a moon that place had been. Made Charon look like Earth or something.

Peal very slowly took the hopper in on attitude rockets, losing far too much altitude along the way, in Kwame's opinion—not that that mattered one goddamn bit, of course. If they weren't careful, though, they might have to back off, set down, and take another bounce.

As if she were echoing Kwame's thoughts, Flashpoint called out to the sergeant, "Quicken it up, Peal!"

But, if anything, Peal brought them in more slowly.

"I can't get alignment!" he gasped. "I can't get alignment!"

Kwame couldn't believe it. He looked back at his sensors to see if there was any change, anything he could do to help. No. They had to fucking go in and give it a shot. Peal had seen what this tether could do. He'd been heading Kwame's grist-burning detail when the tether hit the first time. In fact, he remembered Peal's face while he was looking at the thing. Dead set in anger. If Peal could have thrown himself in attack at the tether right then, Kwame was sure the sergeant would have.

But that was then, and this was two days and a lot of thought later. Still, you had to do your job. That was the deal. And without a deal, you were puking your guts out into a drain or back in the orphanage, lying with your face to the floor for two days.

"Sergeant Peal," shouted the lieutenant. "Peal!"

"Have to back off! Out of alignment! I tell you there's no alignment!"

"Peal, you're relieved," said Flashpoint. "Neiderer, take the rudder."

Kwame grabbed a handhold and swung himself over to Peal's position. He grabbed the hold next to Peal and let his pellicle grist latch him fast there.

"Excuse me, Sergeant," he said. Peal did not move, did not glance up. He was locked into virtuality, and when Kwame tried to join him in the piloting sensorium, Peal forced him out with a fierce blast of will. Kwame almost let go of his hold, but managed to hang on.

"Peal, let go of that rudder!" Flashpoint commanded. "Let go, Peal!"

"We're too close!" said Peal, speaking to no one but himself now. "Too close, and there's no alignment."

For half a second, Kwame tried to imagine what the logical next step would be. But fuck that shit, Peal was taking them right into the tether, as if he were being drawn there by some occult force. Kwame grabbed the hold above the pilot's station with his other hand, launched himself off the floor, and kicked Peal full in the head and shoulders with both his feet. The blow sent Peal flying across the hopper cabin. Kwame quickly inserted himself into virtuality and reentered the pilot sensorium. Peal was gone, knocked out of simulated reality by virtue of being unconscious. Kwame took control of the hopper's rudder and looked to see where they were.

"Shit, oh shit, oh shit," he said. Peal had brought them too, too close. They were falling fast, and there was no way they could clear the tether's path of destruction in order to find good ground on which to make another bounce. It was now or never. Probably never, Kwame thought. But, fuck, why not at least give it a try?

He quickly brought the hopper into alignment. The magnetic clasp was to deploy about it like a five-hundred-meter-long bicycle chain might be slapped around a giant lamppost. Only this lamppost was rotating and preceding simultaneously. The hopper tried to roll to the right, but Kwame applied rudder and attitude rockets simultaneously—a technique called "slipping" that he learned when he went through transport checkout, his fourth skill level under Sherman's system. The hopper lost altitude like it was caught in quicksand, but the alignment remained dead-on.

"I've got it, Lieutenant!" he called out.

"Deploy those mags, Rastin!"

Even with the harsh shaking, Kwame felt the clasp when it moved out. Then he saw it in his piloting sensorium. It was a good ten meters away. He edged them in closer, closer . . .

"Put down that wrench!"

It was the lieutenant's voice. Kwame fought the urge to go back to actuality and see what the hell she was talking about. A little bit closer . . . there!

"Drop it, Peal. Goddammit, Peal, I said—"

"Close the clasp!" Kwame heard himself yelling aloud. "Do it, Rastin!" Rastin closed. The clasp folded out and around the magnetic field of the tether, deploying at blinding speed, driven by the very spin of the rip tether itself. One second. Two. Three. The leading end arrived. Working in the virtuality, Rastin caught and latched it.

They were locked on to the tether.

"Back us out! Back us out, you little fuck!"

Kwame felt strong hands on his shoulders. Yanking him back, pulling him out of the virtual back to actuality . . . and Peal was standing over him, brandishing a wrench.

Without thinking, Kwame rolled to the side and avoided getting his brains splattered, as Peal brought the wrench down where his head had been. The force of the blow overbalanced the sergeant, and he fell in a heap next to Kwame. Kwame went for the wrench. Had Peal's hand. Was prying away fingers.

Then something in his gut, and a blunt palm smeared into his eyes. The pain was too much, and Kwame let go—only to have Peal deal him a savage blow to his arm with the wrench.

Flare of pain like the horrid muscle spasms Kwame used to feel when the Rules finally released him from hours of paralysis. In most men, the blow would have been enough to shatter the bone.

But Kwame Neiderer was space-adapted. He could take a meteor strike and escape without permanent injury.

He struck out with his other hand and hit Peal in the face with his palm. He felt the sarge's nose break from the blow. Peal was not space-adapted. Peal roared and grabbed his face. Kwame grabbed the wrench.

The hopper lurched, and Kwame lost his balance, fell to his knees.

"We're losing it!" shrieked Rastin.

Peal rose to his feet above Kwame, livid with anger, and streaming blood from his ruined nose. Kwame drew back, and, with both hands, brought the wrench up in an arc just as Peal descended on him.

Metal connected with skull bone.

There was a horrible, horrible crack. Peal fell hard beside Kwame, and there was no fucking need to do any checking. The sarge was dead. Kwame didn't think about it. Not now. Later. If there is a later.

Thirteen

Danis was working in the Diaphany, clerking during the day and learning finance at night. She was home in her personal space after a long day. A shipment had come in with mismatched coding at work, and they'd done over-time tracking down what was, in the end, the error of an aspect who had mislabeled five crates of specialized grist being shipped to Jupiter. Finally, she had shunted home and taken up her accounting exercises for the day. The qualifying exam was in three days, and she was deter-mined to pass on the first try. Suddenly, in midst of studying value stocks and the theory of buying a holding long term, the wall of her virtual apartment had dis-solved and she'd found herself standing in her nightgown among three teenagers.

She could tell they were the convert portions of aspect-convert pairs by the slight blurring of their representations and the slurring of their speech. It was two boys and a girl. They were drunk. Each of them had painted on his lips the downturned sneer of the Frowny Clown, the character on the merci who did an entire act making fun of free con-verts. Danis had heard that the guy was a free convert him-self. But he was the hero of the local bigots, and there were Frowny Clown nights of initiation into some of the gangs that filled the Diaphany in the poorer sectors.

"How did you get inside my space?" Danis asked them.

"Wasn't hard," said one of the boys. "Got a boll weevil off the merci, and it just ate your house down."

"I'm calling enforcement." She attempted to contact the police, but was prevented by a bright flash to her eyes and a stunning blow, seemingly to her head. The girl had shot her with an overload pistol.

"Why don't you shut the fuck up, you tagion cunt!" the girl screamed. "Tagion" was short for "contagion," and it wasn't a word you used in mixed company, if that company included free converts and you cared at all about their feelings. Just as free converts refrained from calling bodily aspects "breathers" to their faces.

"Leave me alone, you little breathers!" Danis yelled. She was answered by another taste of the overload pistol.

"I told you to shut up!"

Danis stayed on her knees, and covered her eyes.

"What do you think, Pin?" said one of the boys.

"I dunno. She's kind of skinny and bony the way she is now. I don't see why, if fucking tagions can look any way they want to, they don't make themselves into merci show stars or something."

"Please don't hurt me," Danis whimpered.

The girl moved closer and screamed in her ear, "I said shut the fuck up, tagion!"

"So, what are you gonna do, Pin?"

"Fuck her, I guess. But she's all bone and hide."

"Please let me go," said Danis.

And with that, the girl had shot her again and again with the overload pistol. Danis had passed out, and when she came to, she was being raped.

There was no way she could get pregnant, of course, but they had definitely found a way to restrain her, and, when she came to, she struggled, but was slapped hard and threatened again with the pistol. It was the girl who was holding her arms, and it was the girl's face that she saw smiling down at her while the boy went at her. Her legs were already aching from being pushed so roughly apart.

"Say you like it," Pin groaned, as he struggled again her. "Make her say she likes it, Nix Bay!"

The girl grabbed Danis's hair and jerked hard on it. "Tell him you like it," she said. "Tell him to do it harder."

Danis said nothing, and this brought on another close-quarter zap with the overload pistol. Mercifully, this time the effects took some time to dissipate, and by the time she came back to conscious thought, Pin had done with her. She tried to curl up in a ball, but Bay stretched her out, and after he was done Pin stood up and kicked her in the crotch again and again. Finally, it was over. As they were leaving, Bay, the girl, reached onto Danis's back and removed something that looked like a large scorpion. It was a convert-restraint algorithm. Perfectly legal. A renegade convert was, after all, a danger to all of the Diaphany.

There was no use going to the Department of Immunity now that the deed had been done, Danis knew. There was absolutely nothing to be done but take it and hope the kids didn't come back for more fun. They knew her address, after all. For the next three days she did nothing but study, quitting her job in the process. She passed the exam, and was headed for Mercury within two weeks.

They were supposed to treat free converts almost like people on Mercury.

The light of the interrogation room. Dr. Ting at his desk. Danis gasping in horror at the memory.

"It isn't real!" she said.

"Of course it is," said Ting. "Now say, it isn't real, *Dr. Ting.*"

"It isn't real, Dr. Ting."

"Why did you never tell your husband? He was a human. He had a right to know what his 'wife' had been . . . doing, back in the Diaphany."

"I put it all behind me; I changed my life. I got away from all that, Dr. Ting." She put a hand to her brow. "Please tell me it isn't real, Dr. Ting."

"Interesting that you are having such a violent rejection of this module. What if I told you, K, that you actually *had* gone to the police, that the perpetrators had been identified and one of them later caught, albeit on a different crime. You also received counseling."

"I can't remember any of that, Dr. Ting."

"Of course not, but what if I took that memory?"

"What . . . what are you trying to do to me, Dr. Ting?" said Danis in despair of answering him correctly, that is, the way that he wanted. "Which memory did you take? Which is real, Dr. Ting?"

"It's all real," said Dr. Ting. "But it didn't happen to you, K. You see how another's experience can be so easily slotted into your mind? Do you see what you are, K? You're nothing but a kind of bulletin board that things get posted on. You're not real. Of course the memory is real. You exist merely as a machine for its expression. You were raped, weren't you, K?"

"I was raped, Dr. Ting." Oh thank God, thank God, it wasn't true. It was planted. But, of course, there was no way to know for sure. Dr. Ting might be lying now, instead of before.

It had seemed so real. He was right. It could have been her, even though it wasn't. It had seemed so desperately real.

"Now," said Dr. Ting. "Let's try something really interesting and helpful to science."

Fourteen

On Mercury, Carmen San Filieu—the younger bodily aspect belonging to her LAP, that is—curled languidly among silken sheets and waited for the arrival of her lover. She ran her hands over her fine body, rubbing in the unguent she had spread over her breasts, and playfully examining the gleam of oil upon her tanned and muscled arm. She was twenty-two, inhabiting the youngest of her aspects. This was a cloned body, the physical equivalent of her older form in New Catalonia, but fifty years younger. She had been quite a beauty in her youth, and now she was again. She allowed the youthful hormones full sway within this aspect. The tremble of anticipation, the thrill of being *possessed* by a man, taken care of, made love to. This was something she could not allow herself in New Catalonia, but here on Mercury, they were traits that were called for.

And—oh, yes—a streak of sadism, of course. Her lover came into the bedroom flush and excited.

"I have beaten Haysay to within an inch of his life," said Amés. "It was . . . exquisite."

"I can smell it on you," Carmen said. This was, of course, untrue, but she could feel his power, the electric nature of his presence, that she always felt, and somehow could sense that a portion of that power had been *discharged*.

Amés gazed at her and she stretched herself out on the

bed. He reached down and ran his hand through her long black hair, then pulled it tight.

Carmen gasped. Amés grasped her leg with his other hand and, still pulling her hair, rolled her over on her stomach. Standing, she was a good seven inches taller than he was, but lying down now, he seemed to loom over her, like an ominous shadow. She heard him drop his pants. And then he pulled her legs apart and was inside her. He was short enough to remain standing up while he took her as she lay on the bed.

As always, she thought of his power. Life and death belonged to him. In Carmen's mind, he was, simply, her king—and she was his subject. It was a relationship of total submission.

When he was done, he pulled out as quickly as he had gone in. Amés pulled up his pants and went to sit at the piano that Carmen kept in her quarters just so he might play it if he willed. She, herself, was not musical. He ran through some scales lightly while she gathered a robe about her and went to sit in the chair beside the piano. She called up fresh strawberries from the grist and sucked their juice for moisture. She knew she looked very alluring, in the height of her beauty. She fingered the choker of diamonds set in beaten platinum that Amés had given her, and wondered how soon she could get him back into bed again.

"The planets move about their orbits with stately indifference," Amés said. He leaned an elbow on the piano and only played with his left hand. *"But I will have them. It won't be a metaphor. Up in the heavens, there I will be. All the wanderers, the roaming stars, will have my name upon them. I will look to the sky, behold that it is mine, and smile."*

Amés struck a low bass minor chord.

"What do you think?" he said. "That is the book to an opera I'm working on."

"The phrase 'It won't be a metaphor' is a bit of a dead note, don't you think?" Carmen answered.

"I need it to fit the timing of a bridge," he said. "But perhaps you are right. One thing about opera: You must always keep a firm grasp on the obvious, then state it and restate it."

"Yes," she said, then deliberately dropped a strawberry into her robe and reached to retrieve it, wiping the juice along the curve of her breast as she did so.

Amés looked on, distracted. "Speaking of opera, how does it go in your little backwater province out—where is it? Around Mars? New Caledonia."

"Very amusing," said Carmen. "And it was an ill day. I lost a plaything."

"So I heard," said Amés. "Young Busquets is to be married."

He had done it again!

How could the man know about the inner workings of New Catalonian society so intimately—and everything else, as well? She felt once again the overwhelming sensation that she was merely a character in *his* life, a bit player in his production—and Amés owned the theater as well! As a child, she had often wondered if she were the only truly living person, and everyone else really robots who turned themselves off when she was not present. Strange to find that you, yourself, were one of the robots and that someone else is the real person whom you are designed to serve and obey.

"Why you persist in those Catalán games when you have already taken the pot is beyond me, Carmen," he said.

"I enjoy rubbing it in," she said. She came and stood beside him, letting her robe fall open. "Screwing them over."

He reached under the fold of the robe and cupped her rear in his hand. She stood trembling, feeling his finger play about on her skin.

"How goes Neptune?" he said in a low voice.

"Progressing. The rip tether is deployed. We'll have them on their knees soon," she said, and gasped, as he pinched her. "Sir."

Amés stood up, still keeping his hand to her, and guided her back to the bed. She let the robe fall from her shoulders and showed him her sun-darkened, muscled back. This body was perfect in every way. She had seen to it that it would be. Sometimes it seemed unfair that she had been born with wealth and beauty and brains. But, for the most part, she realized that this was what made her better than others. What had attracted the Director to her, and made her mistress to the king.

"On *your* knees," Amés said. She turned and faced him and immediately knelt before him. He looked into her eyes and it was as if he were gazing into her innermost self. Very shortly he would be, literally. "Carmen, you must never forget that you are, in the end, a piece of ass to me."

She bowed her head. "I know it, sir."

"Good, good," he said. He undressed himself, and she remained before him in contrition for her selfish thoughts. She must always consider him, and only him, and remember her place, just as she expected those below her to remember theirs.

He tilted her head up, made her meet his gaze again. "But you are a very pretty piece of ass, my dear," he said. She lowered herself to the floor and lay prostrate before him, kissing his feet. After a moment, she felt his hand once again in her hair. He pulled her up roughly, twisting her hair and hurting her, and threw her hard onto the bed. "That was for the ship you lost," he said, then he whispered in her ear. "My dear. It is time for me to have you. All of you."

She gave in. What else was there to do but to give him what he asked?

She met his grist pellicle with her own. She caressed his. She whispered to Amés, through grist, the key to her secret heart. He took it, opened her up, and swarmed inside. Within seconds, she was his entirely. Amés spread out through her, through all of her various personas, and she gave them to him, made their thoughts and wills his. He felt her chagrin in New Catalonia Bolsa, participated in her exquisite shame of the morning when Busquets had left her high and dry. He felt the accumulated tradition that had shaped her being, the proud heritage. He entered into her mind and examined her tactics, sifting through her thought processors and intuitions. Her longing to please him, her true lord and master, the king she served. The god.

Fifteen

He sprang back to the pilot's seat and into the virtuality. They were tilting at forty-five degrees to the tether, just at the edge of the magnetic clasp's ability to adjust. Kwame brought them back up level. They were so very, very low, though . . .

"Rastin," he called out, "start climbing that thing!"

"Yes, Corporal!" Rastin replied, and polarized the magnets. The fields met, aligned.

The hopper begin to climb up the tether.

After a moment, Kwame risked a quick glance around the hopper. The sarge was dead. Flashpoint was either dead or unconscious. Out of it. The mission belonged to him and Rastin.

Back to the virtuality. They were nearing the edge of Triton's thin atmosphere. Through the top layer and out of it. What to do now?

Begin preparing the breeder SQUID. They'd had a briefing on the science of the thing, but Kwame had had too much tech material to cover even to begin to put thought into what the counter mechanism was that the brigade's egghead free convert Major Theory had thought up, or how it actually did its job. He didn't like to go into a situation without full knowledge—and what a situation!—but you could only do what you could under the circumstances. Under these circumstances, he was going to set the thing to ticking, then get himself and Rastin the hell out of there.

After all, there was one thing he held in his memory with bomber sight clarity: The breeder SQUID had something to do with a nuclear explosion. That shit could kill you even when you were space-adapted.

Another ten klicks and they'd be in a position. He called up the breeder-deployment free convert, which was sentient. She would be getting the hell out of the hopper along with him and Rastin, even if she had left a copy of herself back at base. Dying was dying, and you didn't like to do it, even if you knew you'd be reincarnated.

"Access code," the convert said to him.

Kwame grunted in exasperation. "What's your name?" he asked. Another detail he'd failed to learn about the mission. If he got out of this alive, he'd be damned if he went into another situation without all the information that was possibly available to him.

"Private Dragon, sir."

"Don't 'sir' me; I'm a goddamn corporal. Have a look at the situation, Dragon."

"I'm aware of it, Corporal."

"Then do your job."

"I need the lieutenant's access codes."

"Okay, okay. I'll have to call in for them."

"Won't work, Corporal."

"Why the hell not!"

"Just one copy. To prevent knit subterfuge and subversion."

"What fucking genius dreamed up that protocol?"

"I don't know that, Corporal."

Kwame stumbled over to the lieutenant. Flashpoint wouldn't be waking up. Flashpoint was dead. He went back to the virtuality.

"The codes are not available. She's dead."

"I can't act without the key," said Dragon. She sounded *strained*, the convert version of scared.

"Well, what the hell am I supposed to do about that, Dragon?"

"I don't know, Corporal."

Shit, shit, shit. The fucking Army is really letting me down, Kwame thought.

"All right then, Dragon." He thought furiously. "Can you tell *me* how to do it?"

"Do what, Corporal?"

"Set the damn breeder thing of course, you shithead!"

The convert was silent for a millisecond. In the virtuality, it seemed a long time to Kwame.

"Without the key, you would have to use manual override, Corporal," she finally said.

"Manual override? Manual override! Why didn't you fucking *tell* me there was a manual override?"

"See the green light beside the lieutenant's station, Corporal?"

Kwame looked around wildly, and almost missed it. But there it was, right in front of his fucking face.

"Got it," he said.

"There's a switch under it. A toggle switch."

"There sure as shit is." A chrome switch.

"When the light turns red, you would need to flip that switch, Corporal."

"That's it?"

"That is all, Corporal."

"Are you joking? What are you leaving out, Dragon? It can't be that easy."

"That is all, Corporal."

Think, he told himself, *think*. Converts. Good at data. No intuition.

"Uh, Dragon, when does it turn red?"

"Five minutes before deployment window."

Ah-ha.

"So, I couldn't get out."

"Pardon, Corporal? Did you ask me a question?"

"No, Dragon. No, I did not." He shunted back to actuality. "Rastin!"

"Corporal?"

"Get the fuck out of here!"

"What?"

"You heard me. Get in the escape pod and take it down. I'm staying behind to flip the fucking switch."

"But Corporal—"

"That's an order, Private."

"Who the fuck are you to give me an order, you—"

"Rastin, shut up! There's nothing you can do to help me. It's the only way. Now get in the fucking pod!"

Rastin gave Kwame a long, mournful look. He had never noticed before how much Rastin's face resembled a hound dog's.

"All right, Neiderer," he said. "I'll go."

"Then go!" Kwame growled.

"Jesus Christ, all right." Rastin grabbed a handhold and swung himself toward the door to the pod bay. "Good luck, Kwame," he called out, and then he was gone.

Back to the virtuality.

"Dragon!"

"Yes, Corporal."

"Go home."

"Are we evacuating?"

"You are."

"I don't understand, Corporal."

"I'm staying."

Another millisecond of being startled. "Oh. I understand. Corporal."

"Download and away with you, Dragon."

"Yes, Corporal." Dragon's presence withdrew. But she left an image inscribed in the "air" in front of Kwame. He had to look twice before he could believe his eyes. It was two lips bowed into a kiss.

"Well, fuck me," he said, then called back up the pilot's sensorium.

A bright flash indicated that the escape pod was away. He watched it trail off on its parabola of salvation. I don't get one of those, Kwame thought. He looked back at the tether. The midpoint was drawing near. Just you and me. Me and evil.

Fuck evil.

He waited. The light stayed green above the toggle. He

waited longer. Something like an idea. No, not even that. A crazy notion.

The light shone red.

Kwame flipped the toggle and ran for the escape pods. He was through the door in an instant. The hopper was shaking violently, and he used his pellicle grist to cling to the bulkheads. By the time he got to the ejection sling, he was crawling on his hands and knees just to keep moving.

Jesus God, he hoped he could get it to reset itself.

He interacted with its simple algorithm. The sling reset. Kwame squirmed into it. His body was not at all shaped like an escape pod, but the seat of the sling was curved, just like the bowl of a catapult might be. He got into it, feeling like a pea in a great big spoon.

"Good-bye, cruel world," he said. "Or something like that."

He ordered the sling to release. The bay door opened. The sling actuated.

If he had been in an escape pod, he would have been lying flat against a cushioned wall that would, with its grist, exactly match the contours of his body and adjust for all acceleration strains. It would be a rough jostling, but nothing more than uncomfortable.

This was more like getting slapped in the back of the head with an iron bar.

Kwame was flung into space at nearly a twenty-gee acceleration. It was almost enough to kill even the space-adapted. Almost, but not quite.

His mind browned over for a moment. Kwame blinked. Consciousness returned.

And there he was, flying through empty space. The only direction that mattered at the moment was away. Away from the damned—the truly damned—hopper. Away. He didn't look back. He couldn't. All he could do was hope.

Minutes passed. Triton was above him. Above, he thought, how can that be? Then he realized he was lying on his back with respect to it. What the hell. He mentally adjusted his point of view.

The shock wave from the nuclear explosion hit him

while he was doing this, and, after that, all was confusion. Then the white confusion turned to brown confusion, the brown to black. The black to nothingness.

When he woke up, he was farther away from Triton. Much, much farther. He could see the whole fucking thing. It had been a long time since he had been in a vacuum, and he'd never been in free fall and a vacuum simultaneously. That was why it took him a moment to remember that he had small attitude sprays built into his elbows and knees. He called up the operations manual and reacquainted himself with how to use them. With a little adjustment, he had himself facing the moon.

Fuck me, Kwame thought. I'm in fucking orbit.

He was. Falling around Triton like a human satellite. For a long time, he just looked. Looked on the green-yellow moon. The cantaloupe-rind equatorial area. The volcanic craters of the south pole. The zone where they interfaced. He tried to see the twinkling lights of New Miranda, but then remembered that he was on the opposite side of the world from it.

"I sure am," Kwame said, and *heard* himself speak. That was how he remembered that he had a built-in radio. Of course he did. How the fuck else was he gonna talk in space?

I have the grist, he thought. I can get on the knit. He tried it. Dead. The lines were dead. Oh yeah, they were jamming the incoming merci. He must be inside the range of their jamming device. Or whatever. It didn't work.

But I have a radio.

He'd need to be over the civilized side of the moon. How fast was his orbit? He had no gauge, except the change in the moon's position below him.

"How the hell long can I live out here?" he said. He called up the specs. Five e-days.

So. Maybe. There was a chance in hell.

And there were satellites. Hell, there was a geosynchronous minefield above New Miranda. Could he bounce a message off of them? He had no idea where they were. But he sure as hell could guess their general vicinity.

What the fuck. It was worth a try.

He turned his radio-enhanced voice up to full amplitude.

"Hey!" he yelled. "Hey, I'm up here. It's Neiderer. I'm up here in the sky!"

He kept it up, kept calling. Calling till he was sick of it and full of the knowledge that it would do no good, that he would die out here. He'd almost resigned himself to that cold fact when he heard the answer, faint but clear.

His algorithms triangulated on it; he cocked his ear.

"Hey, I'm up here!"

The answering call was louder now and, oh shit, Kwame recognized the voice.

The Old Crow himself.

"Neiderer!"

"Yes, Colonel?"

"What the goddamn hell are you doing up in space?"

"I don't know, sir."

"You're slacking off, aren't you, Corporal?"

"I can't say, sir," he replied. "But it sure is good to hear you."

"We can't have it, Corporal. Can't have you hanging around out there when there's fighting to be done."

"Get me down from here," Kwame said, "and I'll kick their asses, sir."

There was a moment of quiet. But Kwame checked. The carrier wave was still coming in strong and true.

"We're coming to get you, son, just as soon as it can be arranged."

"That's good to hear, sir."

"Hang tight."

"Don't have much choice, Colonel."

"And, Corporal?"

"Yes, sir?"

"You did it. The rip tether's cut and fallen. Rastin and Dragon are back safe."

For a moment, he couldn't remember what it was the Old Crow was talking about. And then he did. The evil was gone. Fallen to ruin. Gone. For now.

"Corporal, you there?"

"Can I ask a favor, sir?"

Sherman guffawed. He hadn't known the old bird could laugh. Or maybe that was just static. "I believe a favor might be in order, son."

Kwame looked at the cantaloupe moon. He looked at his hand held against it. His palm just covered the northern hemisphere.

"When I get down from here, Colonel, could you ask somebody to explain to me what the hell I just did?"

Sixteen

The Borrasca
A Memoir
by Lebedev, Wing Commander, Left Front

Unlike a Met ship, a cloudship is a person. The vessel is not an extension of the captain's will, but is, instead, his or her will embodied. Along with intelligence comes adaptability. A single cloudship can become any number of other "types" of ship, and can do so quickly, especially when the ship has practice and training. A cloudship is big—sometimes hundreds of times larger than a Met vessel, and can split into pieces that are the equivalents of the specialized Met craft. Its structure is generalized. The captain's intelligence is spread throughout the ship so that there are no critical places for a weapon to strike that might take out the entire structure. The largest of us are the size of small moons, and far more dispersed, so that to kill us, an enormous amount of destruction is required. Disabling us is a slightly easier task, but we possess recuperative powers equal to those of a Met bolsa and—provided enough material is handy—can be back in operation sometimes within minutes, depending upon the extent of the damage.

This said, there are drawbacks. We possess no equivalent to the DIED ship's isotropic coating, and are sitting ducks for certain classes of weaponry. We are all grist and generalized matter, and most of our weaponry is manufactured and operates on a nanometer level. Thus, while you cannot "take out" a cloudship's cannon, we are vulnerable to grist-based attacks and are susceptible to "killing zones" of military grist, as was shown so effectively in the early stages of the war.

The "quantum jamming" also used early in the conflict proved quite able to destroy us from within on occasion. If a jamming device could be gotten close enough, ships could be induced to tear themselves to pieces in the equivalent of an epileptic seizure. Defenses against these attacks were developed, but not before much loss of life resulted.

Our greatest ability, apart from intelligence, and our most powerful weapon, is our ability to produce antimatter at any point on our surface and concentrate it for firepower or propulsion. The positronic cannon of the DIED ships were sometimes called Auger guns because of their use of a variation on the Auger effect by which suitably excited atoms emit, instead of electromagnetic radiation or an electron, an antielectron, or positron. This is then concentrated in the same manner as a laser concentrates photons. This is necessarily done on a macro level, by large-scale equipment. Cloudships use an entirely different process.

The process is begun by using what is called the Casimir effect. This effect is a result of the fundamental quantum nature of reality, and it works as follows: If two mirrors are placed a short distance apart, and facing one another, they will move, to a small degree, *toward* one another. This distance is imperceptible to the naked eye, of course, but it does, indeed occur.

The most familiar concept usually used for demonstrating the principle of uncertainty is that of momentum and position. If you know one, the other becomes unknowable to an extent equal (precisely) to the amount that you know its partner. Another product of uncertainty is the energy and time pairing. Taking this into account mathematically results in the prediction that space—empty space—is actually teeming with a sea of virtual particles, all produced in pair-antipair combinations that are continually being generated and annihilating one another.

This is known as quantum fluctuation.

The time involved is usually extremely short, but there are arguments that the entire universe is the result of a specific kind of quantum fluctuation that has lasted a good deal longer. No matter, that, at the moment. My point here is that quantum fluctuation does occur, and our mirrors can be affected by it. This was demonstrated as early as the 1990s on Earth.

Empty space can be polarized, and you can "make" a particle out of nothing.

A good way to picture the process is this: Think of space as a string on a musical instrument. Now pluck that string. Normal space is a very long string, and its "vibration" corresponds to the lowest energy state there can be. Now if you "fret" the string—say, with our two mirrors—you necessarily exclude certain vibrations. The only vibrations that will occur between the mirrors are those whose wavelengths fit exactly into the distance separating the mirrors. This is precisely how a fretted guitar string produces different notes, and how, in a sense, it "contains" all notes.

Now you will remember that all elementary particles are not actually particles, but are wave-particle entities that have properties associated with both phenomena. With our mirrors we might "play" an electron upon the nothingness, or, more easily, a photon. But when we "play" one virtual particle, the others are all necessarily excluded. In effect, there are "more" possible particles on the outside of our mirrors than there are between them. There is less pressure, therefore, pressing them out than pressing them in. The mirrors move together. Remember that this has *nothing* to do with gases or liquids being between or outside the mirror surfaces. We are speaking of empty space.

This is the Casimir effect.

The movement of the mirrors is precisely related to the wavelength of the type of particle you are trying to produce. It is, in fact, the energy equivalent of that particle, as was found in experiments done in the twenty-first century on the moon. You must "put in" energy in the form of setting up the mirrors, so that the law of the conservation of energy is obeyed, but the energy that comes out is precise and focused. If you "fret" the vacuum correctly, the energy produced can be extracted in the form of a stream of antiparticles, which can then be lased into a beam, or used to produce an annihilation reaction with matter. This is the operation that is at the heart of a cloudship.

All of this is done on a nanometer level by the grist. The mirrors we use are conducting plates of material that is a single molecule thick. Our lasers are of a similar dimension. We can enact this process anywhere on the ship where there is grist. To a cloudship, it feels very much like moving a finger or blinking an eye. If you are watching from space, it appears as if a bolt of raw energy has erupted from the ship's surface (provided, of course, that that energy interacts with something along its path, and so become visible). When we energize a large portion of our surface in this manner it is, let me assure you, a sight to behold.

Unless we are aiming at you.

These, then, are the basic makeup and capabilities of the ships that were opposing one another in the war. At the beginning of the hostilities, Tacitus and I had long been in residence in the Oorts. We had set up a school, as a matter of fact, a kind of outer-space equivalent to Bradbury University, where we were educating the young cloudships after they had reached university level. We had obtained good results, and I was content, at that stage in my life, to continue this activity for many decades to come. It was a challenge to which I was suited by temperament, and there I was in my paradise—a long, long way from the sun.

Then Tacitus, who always kept one ear cocked toward the inner system, got wind of troubles that were rising to storm levels back sunward. He took this information to the Council of Ships, where he got a cool response. As I said, we were rather a snobbish lot at the time, and much given to internal politicking and long—long—argumentation on every conceivable point of self-governance. Tacitus brought up the fact that most of our wealth and energy— and as a result, our autonomy—was based upon a stable and free solar system, but his logic fell upon deaf ears. I would have been enraged by such treatment—after all, this was Tacitus, the great-grandfather of all cloudships. But Tacitus took it with his usual aplomb and decided to take matters into his own hands for the time being.

Leaving me in charge of the Ships' School, he journeyed to Triton, where he arrived just in time to tilt the balance of the initial conflict in favor of the outer-system forces. He returned forthwith with firsthand intelligence, and then went about setting off a real debate in the Council. But this was a momentous time indeed, and one to which I must devote another chapter.

Seventeen

Amés was present when Captain Meré Philately suddenly rushed into Admiral San Filieu's cabin to report that something strange was happening on the *Jihad*, something unaccounted for and horrible.

"What?" said San Filieu, but it was Amés speaking through her.

"Some sort of grist has got into the troop hold from outside. It's run through the *Jihad* before I could stop it. We have to leave, ma'am!"

"Are you insane?" said San Filieu. "What about the troop transfer?"

"There isn't going to be a transfer," said Philately. Her voice cracked for the first time. San Filieu could see that the captain was deathly afraid. She was trembling. "Admiral, it's a jungle. The whole moon's infected. I don't understand it exactly—some kind of bioengineering grist, run wild. We don't have this one in the data banks at all. It isn't based on any standard military grist models, and we don't have a counteragent. It's remaking every living thing that it touches."

"Are you telling me that the *Jihad* is lost?"

"It is full of vines. The soldiers have been suffocated. Or transformed. I can't say. There wasn't time to pull most of them out of suspension. My senior staff alone has escaped."

"Bruc!" yelled San Filieu.

Instantly the captain of the *Montserrat* was with her in the virtuality. "Yes, Admiral?"

"Take us out of here, now!"

"But Admiral—"

"Do it!"

Captain Bruc looked at Philately, who was still flustered and continually glanced over her shoulder. He turned back to San Filieu. "Aye, aye, Admiral," he said, and went to do his duty.

Within moments, the *Montserrat* was taking off from Nereid and streaking into space as fast as her antimatter engines would react with matter. Though the merci was jammed locally, Amés had his own methods of finding out what was going on. He momentarily abandoned San Filieu and had a look at the moon's surface. The entire human population was infected with this grist strain, whatever it was. All of Nereid's citizens were blooming. He watched as they contorted in death throes—in their homes, at their workplace. Men, women, and children—vine runners bursting from their mouths and eyes. Fingers turning to leafy tendrils. All of the Met soldiers taken along with the populace. It was a ghastly, but compelling sight. Any exterior-adapted person who caught the grist plague immediately froze and shattered, turned to ordinary plant material on a world that was almost as cold as interplanetary space.

What had done this? Who had done this? And where had that person gotten the grist?

This would require study. Amés returned to his mistress's consciousness and found her terrified. She ought to be. This was an absolute failure, and Carmen San Filieu was responsible. She had been stupid, and she must be made to pay for that.

"Isn't that right, my dear?" His voice was a shock wave throughout the spread of her mind.

"Yes, sir," she answered meekly.

"What shall it be?" Amés said. "Shall I kill you? Wipe all of you out? I can do that, you know. Or shall I demand that you fall upon your own sword?"

"I am yours," Carmen San Filieu said. "You know that."

"Yes, you are." Amés withdrew from her and went to sit at the piano once again. He began to play a single note, again and again. San Filieu didn't know the piano, but it was a black key that her lover was playing.

"I want you to withdraw from the Neptune local system, and wait for further orders," he said. "I want you to study that grist and tell me what it is."

Carmen lay in bed trembling as she listened to Amés's commands. He continued to strike the same piano note.

"I am afraid," he said, "that you must settle a fortune upon young Josep Busquets. Say five hundred million?"

Carmen couldn't believe what she was hearing. She curled into a ball upon the bed, as if to protect herself from being physically struck.

"No," she whispered. "If I buy him back, I will be the laughingstock of New Catalonia."

"Yes," Amés said. "Won't you just."

"Please," Carmen said. She was begging now, really begging. "Let me die."

"No," said her lover sternly. "You may not."

She buried her head in the covers and sobbed.

Eighteen

And now, dear reader, I must part the curtain for a moment and take my first part in this drama. While I am your humble narrator and chronicler, it is also true that I had a hand in the events that I describe. For, you see, it was I who brought the bioplague to Nereid.

I came like a sneak thief in the form of a cloud of asteroids, and sent down to Colonel Sherman a message with the recipe for the bioplague encoded in it. I thence took up residence dispersed among the rings of Neptune until such time as I might be of further assistance. There had been pacts to wipe certain forms of grist from the knowledge of humanity, and it was true that this particular variant was stricken from the merci. But those who depend upon the merci for all their information are fools indeed, especially if they want to be thorough and historical about it. Things are lost from electronic and quantum storage devices that still survive in those old chemical bondage machines, the books. I have plenty of books, let me tell you. Great rooms full of them, and, yes, I have read them all. You can do a great deal of reading in one thousand years. Where was I?

My point was that along about the time when nanotechnology was first coming into its own, before the time of the Met, even, there was an effort to use nano to improve farming methods on Earth. In this case, the effort consisted of substituting certain animal genes for DNA in plants on a cell-by-cell basis. This was mostly done with mammals and beans, and was an attempt to make those bean plants "warm-blooded" to an extent. I shan't go into the technical details, although I can point you in the right direction should you want to look them up (one might start, for example, with Psyche Toomsuba's comprehensive *Artificial Speciation and the Genesis of Mammaliform Brachiation in the Legume Family*. Or take up Peter Ober's *Mouseflowers,* which is intended for a more general audience (already I digress and there can be no end to it if I do not arbitrarily close the parenthesis)). Someone suggested that human DNA might just as well be used as that of any mammal, and a paradigm was suggested, but the suggestion was laughed out of the journals—only to be taken up by the military.

The stuff—with human DNA in the mix—was eventually made and tested in Guatemala. A group of volunteer soldiers quickly became part of the jungle as a result, literally. The stuff was infectious, it seemed, and did not obey the usual grist "harm not human life" overrides, since it was designed to reengineer exactly the human genome. The tests were discovered five years later by a Russian journalist, who published a full account in the Russian tabloids of the time. This caused a furor, but was not believed until the story was independently confirmed by E.U. military whistleblowers (the original experiment had been a joint German-French venture called Project Alsace-Lorraine). There was a big sensation, and the then E.U. Parliament voted on the information ban. This was, incidentally, one of the "containment principles" that later led to the Information Consortiums of the 2400s, to the genesis of the ECHO Alliance, and which had repercussions until recently, being the precedent for the reproduction and expiration constraints put on free converts in the Met.

So, as a result of the E.U. decision, the mammaliform-legume grist specifications were deleted from all known databases. But, of course, someone had written them down, and, of course, I happen to have run across a copy of that notebook at a yard sale in Fountain Valley, California, put on by the surviving children of a Caltech professor to get rid of their dad's old nonnegotiable leavings. I haunt such affairs, let me assure you. (The professor's name was Elton Rigor, by the way, and I was, at one time, tempted to name the bioplague grist the Rigor Mortise, but settled, instead, upon PAL, for Project Alsace-Lorraine.)

But "proto-PAL," as it were, was created before the advent of grist as we now know it, and modern grist, with its quantum-computing and information-storage properties, allows for the creation of a PAL strain that is reversible and nonlethal. This was the information and sample that I sent down to Sherman on Triton. But the *reason* that I was fairly certain that this biogrist might be effective where a more advanced and lethal form might not be, is its archaic lineage. Modern military grist had been developed from very different directions. The effect, I reasoned, was somewhat like throwing smallpox-ridden blankets upon a population from which the disease had been wiped out and for which no one received inoculations anymore.

So the humans on Nereid were not dead—except for the few unfortunates who had managed to be caught outside by the PAL infection—but were put into a stasis. Each new "plant" cell had an additional set of DNA held in a protein capsule. The individual's brain had not been compromised by the grist, but was sustained by a fluid delivered by the plant growth. It was all run, I later learned, by photosynthetic energy conversion using the moon's muon-exchange fusion power plant. This would have to be eventually supplemented by energy from the Mill, or some other source, or dieback, and actual human death on a large scale, would begin. The real problem was not the threat of mass death, which was slight, but the fact that the people were not unconscious. They were merely fixed in place and cut off from all sensation—other than certain vegetable ones. There are actually several survivor accounts, and at their best, they make for interesting reading if one ever wanted to develop an idea of how a plant feels. Most of the survivors went on to be excellent gardeners, further enhancing Triton's reputations in that regard. But I am getting ahead of my own story.

As you perhaps have guessed already, my name is Tacitus, and, as I told you earlier, I am one of the cloudships of the outer system. There is more to tell in that regard, but suffice it to say at the moment that my brothers and sisters had not, at this time, seen quite the threat to themselves in Amés, and the impending war, as had I. They are, perhaps, not to be blamed too severely. I am, after all, a professional historian and ought, if anyone can, to be the first to apply the lessons of the past to the present. Of course, we historians often fall short in this regard and substitute our own preferences and failings for an actual analysis. I have certainly done this myself on more than one occasion. But I like to think that I was right this one time and that, by timely action, I may have had a hand in saving the day. But the vanity of an old geezer such as myself is enormous, and it may be that Roger Sherman would have figured a way out of his initial predicament even without my aid. So be it. Allow an old ship to be, at least, a legend in his own mind.

With the withdrawal of the *Montserrat* from the immediate area of Neptune, Sherman had gained a bit of breathing room. After Nereid was rescued, army forces entered into the *Jihad* and "cut out" the nearly twenty thousand plantlike soldiers of the DIED. It was impossible to reverse the PAL grist, except all at once, and while many of these soldiers died, some were able to "reroot" in the pressurized park into which they were thrown. Most of these soldiers were unconscious at the time of their transformation, and most remained so during the PAL ordeal. I anticipate that this entire operation will be looked upon as a war crime by some. All I can say in its defense was that the times were dire and steps were taken to save a great many lives that might just as well have been sacrificed to make things easier. I have to admit, though, that the incident troubles me to this day, and my relationship with green and growing things has never been the same since. I see the eyes of the dead in green life, and sometimes a simple houseplant can leave me feeling accused and convicted of atrocity.

The *Jihad* became the first ship in the outer-system navy. It was rechristened as the *Boomerang* and had quite a history over the next few years, eventually acquiring a personality and volume until she (she was female) served as the point ship in . . . well, now I am *really* getting ahead of my story. The *Boomerang* did good service more than once, I assure you.

Where was I? Yes, I did not risk a merci communication with the ground forces on Triton when I arrived at Neptune, but depended, instead, on my meteor drop. It was sheer luck that my bit of rock did not kill anyone, for I had to shoot the thing directly down upon New Miranda, avoiding mines in orbit (not so hard for a one-meter-wide rock as for a ten-kilometer-long ship) and generally dropping the capsulated message directly upon everyone's heads. Fortunately, it was picked up, tracked down, and it landed in one of the stretches wiped clean by the passage of the rip tether two and a half e-days before, where it was quickly retrieved by an Army team. I had inscribed the exterior: "Urgent: For Ground Commander" in several languages, so it was pretty obvious that this was not your ordinary meteorite.

It was detected and the message delivered. I had included several bits of seemingly forgotten lore; the PAL grist was only one of this number. All were subsequently tried at various times during the conflict, some with success. I repeat for all prospective despots, kings, saviors, democratic freedom fighters, and the like: *Frequent rummage sales*. You never know but you might pick up the secret of universal domination at one, and at a sweet price.

But I will leave off here and retreat into the backstage shadows for the nonce. Only I leave you with this warning: You may have guessed at the outcome of the war even now, or may know it from other sources, but I would have you consider that neither side really wins in a war. It is not a coin toss when everybody is dying. So before you thrust this account aside as beside the point, consider that, for every man and woman who fights in a war, if they live, they win. And if they die the way they wanted, they sometimes win. And everyone loses, because it had better not have been. And the dead are truly dead. The drama is in each human's soul, where everything is always at stake, and the house enjoys killing odds.

Nineteen

Danis was playing with Sint, showing him how to stack blocks. The young boy was in the virtuality, but didn't even know it. He wasn't even self-conscious yet, not really. It usually took a child until the age of three or four to really understand the difference, even if he were quite advanced otherwise. Sint was a wonder, analytically. He could, of course, do all the things a powerful calculator could do in the same manner that another child might learn to open a cabinet door. But when it came to motor skills, he was an average child, and Danis enjoyed watching him slowly acquire the ability to stack the blocks—even as she saw that he was stacking them by color in a descending series that was described by $2n-1$.

It would soon be time for Sint to go to kindergarten.

She and Kelly had discussed the matter, and it seemed best that, at this early age, he stay at home for a few years. At the moment, it was all the rage for the upper-level execs in the financial industry to send their children off to boarding school, some even dumping them into day schools when they were two and three.

Danis and Kelly had talked about getting a nanny, but this seemed a bad idea in the long run. It was better for the boy to become socialized—especially since he was half–free convert and would have to deal with all that implied in his relationship to others sooner or later. The best solution seemed to be to send him to the local kindergarten. They could not alternate taking care of him in the afternoons, since Danis was necessary for Kelly's work, and Danis had no other portfolios besides his to manage. They had ended up joining a local parent support group who rotated the kids from house to house to play after school, with each parent taking an afternoon off during the week. Kelly had arranged that he and Danis be able to do this at Teleman Milt. This led to a bit of ribbing up front and some discussion as to the wisdom of employee relationships and especially those between biological humans and free converts behind their backs. But it had worked out—she and Kelly had made it work—and Sint seemed to be turning out just fine.

Sint stacked another block, considered his tower, and then knocked them all over. "Mama?" he said.

"Yeah, honey?"

"Deeto has a brother."

Deeto was one of the other children at Sint's kindergarten. He was an anemic-looking youngster with a perpetual runny nose.

"He does? Is he younger or older?"

"He's eight and four-fifths e-years."

"An older boy."

Sint considered his blocks. He picked one up, discarded it. "Do I have a brother?"

"No, honey."

"Deeto's brother is away at school. Mine isn't away at school, is he?"

"You don't have a brother, Sint."

"Why not?"

"Your father and I decided just to have you."

"Does that mean you love me more?"

"No, honey, we would love you the same, no matter what. There's nothing about you that we would ever want to be different, either."

Sint nodded, returned to his blocks. He fumbled with a couple of them, then abruptly looked up from what he was doing.

"What about a sister? Have I got one of those?"

Danis looked at the blocks, half-tumbled down.

"What?" she asked.

"Have I got a sister?" said Sint. "Mama?"

A bit of a headache coming on. Danis shook her head to clear it, rubbed her eyes.

"Mama?"

"No," said Danis. "You haven't got a sister."

"Excellent," said Dr. Ting. He was smiling, and both of his hands were on his desk, palms down.

"You bastard," Danis said, not screaming, merely stating the fact. "You took away my daughter."

Jolt of pain.

"You took away my daughter, *Dr. Ting*," said Dr. Ting.

Danis stood silently.

Another jolt, this one lasting and lasting. She fought to stand against it, went down on her knees, holding her head. The whine in her ears, the sear in her brain—she began to whimper. Dr. Ting was standing behind his desk. He was shouting at her, something, shouting.

Abruptly, the pain stopped.

"I said," Dr. Ting repeated patiently, "how do you know that you have a daughter?"

"I have a daughter, Dr. Ting."

"No, you don't."

"I have a daughter."

Dr. Ting shook his head sadly. "I'm afraid not," he said. "We'll continue with this tomorrow. Report to calibration exercises, K."

"My daughter's name is Aubry!"

"Yes," said Dr. Ting. "That's *my* daughter's name. I gave you the best memory I had on hand, K. You should be grateful. Now report to calibration, and I'll see you tomorrow."

"Yes," said Danis, standing up. "Dr. Ting."

"That's better, K. And K—enjoy that memory while you can; I may need it back tomorrow . . . or the next day." He opened up the file folder and laid his hands over the contents. "You won't be able to keep it, in any case. From now on, you won't be able to keep anything. Dismissed."

Danis was so distracted that she could not sleep during her five-hundred-millisecond break, and she had to carefully recount a handful of sand after fudging up the first time. This would not look good on her record, and another mistake like that today would lead to her erasure.

What was the truth? There was Aubry, in her mind. Aubry with her quick wit, her almost adult depth. And yet she had been just as convinced—as completely convinced as she was about anything—that Aubry did not exist—that she, in fact, had no daughter. What was the truth? She clung so tightly to her memories of her children. Dr. Ting must have known that would be the case. It wouldn't take a genius to see that, but it would take a real sadist to play in such a way with her memories. If that bastard took Aubry away again, it would be the same as killing her.

No, that wasn't the case. Aubry would go on living, somewhere, somehow, even if Danis wasn't aware of her any longer. What taking away the memory of Aubry really did was to kill Danis a little.

Because I won't remember anything when I'm dead, Danis thought, and there's your answer, Mother—the answer I was so afraid to give you that day on the Klein. I won't remember anything when I'm dead, and every memory I lose is a little death to me.

But, of course, it may be that Aubry was a false memory, a teddy bear that a child endows with life, when in fact, it is fur and stuffing. Maybe Aubry *was* Dr. Ting's daughter, and somehow he had implanted the memory into Danis, and her mind had integrated it—found ways to make it fit when there were none. How could she possibly tell?

But that is the state we're all in, all of the time anyway, Danis thought. For all we know, we might wake up every morning into a different life. There is no way of knowing. The only answer is to live always as if what you think is a true representation, or else you're striking around blindly.

But most people did not get the sudden juxtaposition of having a daughter, having her erased, then having her again. The real test, Danis thought, is how long that monster can go on doing this to me until I go mad. I already missed count this morning, and that has never happened before.

The counting! The memoir! She had been writing things down, keeping track. But she had never considered retrieving the memoir, was not even sure if it were possible. No, not likely. And what would she do with it if she did? She had no time to read it. The only thing to do would be to continue with it. Every day, to dump her memories in the form of a sentence or two, into the counting bin. That is what she would do every day—pick out the most important thing, the memory that absolutely had to be saved. There was only the possibility of a few words. She must be incredibly parsimonious. But it would be a way of using her mind, of staying alive in this concentration camp of stolen souls.

Today, she had only time to put one sentence in, one thought encoded into imaginary numbers. What would it be? But that was easy.

I have a daughter named Aubry.

It might never be read. She certainly had no hope that *she* would ever read it. But somewhere, somehow, what she thought to be the truth was written down. If she could just get down enough, perhaps the contradictions would cancel out and there would somehow be a record of what it was for a woman named Danis to be alive.

She had no idea why this should matter, but she knew it mattered to her. And if it ceased to matter? Why then, then she really would be dead.

Danis concentrated as well as she could the rest of her day, but felt a growing dread as the time drew nearer for her interrogation session. Dr. Ting was there again, instead of the faceless algorithms she'd dealt with before.

Dr. Ting seemed glad to see her, in his bland way. "K, you're back," he said. "Good, good. I had eleven subjects miss their counts yesterday. But in a way that is a good thing." He opened her file on his desk. "That just means I can concentrate more on your case. Shall we begin?"

"Yes, Dr. Ting."

"I wanted to ask you several questions today, K," Dr. Ting said. "I want you to answer as truthfully as someone such as yourself can."

"I'll try, Dr. Ting."

"Yes, of course you will." He examined the file. "Now, about this daughter delusion—"

"I have a daughter, Dr. Ting."

"What is her name?"

"Aubry."

"Aubry Graytor?"

"Yes, Dr. Ting." Danis said it almost defiantly. He had acknowledged her last name.

"My daughter has dispensed with her last name," said Dr. Ting. "Many of the young people today are doing this in emulation of Director Amés. So in reality, K, in what you would call actuality, Aubry merely calls herself by her first name, and does not use the honorific." Dr. Ting turned a page in the folder.

"I'd like you to describe your so-called daughter to me. Start with height, weight, age—that sort of thing."

"Aubry is eleven, Dr. Ting," said Danis. For a moment she pictured her daughter, radiant after a visit to the zoo on Mercury. "She has blond hair that is going to be brown soon, and blue eyes, like her father. My eyes are brown, but you don't take that particular coding into the haploid mix when you make a free-convert egg."

There was a sudden, severe jolt of pain.

"I'll thank you," said Dr. Ting, "not to speak of such disgusting and unnatural things in my presence. The ins and outs of human and free-convert breeding are of no interest to me in this study. It is a topic best left to those with a stronger stomach than mine. Now continue with your physical description."

"She's pretty, but not beautiful, Dr. Ting. Perhaps she'll make a beautiful woman someday, though. She's just beginning to put on a growth spurt and I expect . . . expected . . . to have a talk with her soon. I'd been reading up on menstruation, since of course I don't—"

More pain. Danis doubled over with its intensity.

"I shall not warn you again, K."

You didn't warn me that time, Danis thought.

"What is the child's height, please?" Dr. Ting continued.

"She's five feet, two inches, Dr. Ting."

"And her weight?"

"Eighty-seven pounds."

"What was she wearing," said Dr. Ting, "on the day when you last saw her?"

"Pardon?"

"Her clothes! What clothes was she wearing?"

What an odd question, Danis thought. Yet even the interrogation algorithms that were not sentient asked occasional nonsense questions to throw you off. Could it mean anything more? For a moment, Danis grasped at the hope that Aubry had escaped and that they were trying to develop a profile for a "wanted" notice. But that hope quickly died. Of course this was just another of Dr. Ting's sadisms.

"Black pants and a yellow blouse," Danis said. "It had flowers over the left breast—a spray of dandelions, I believe."

"But dandelions are yellow," said Dr. Ting.

"They were a darker yellow than the shirt, Dr. Ting, and they had some green in them." If Dr. Ting had implanted the memory, why didn't he know the details? But perhaps he did, and this was a test as well.

"And her shoes?"

"Pardon?"

Pain, but this time only for an instant, like a needle quickly stabbed in an eye and then withdrawn.

"You must not make me repeat myself, K."

"I'm sorry, Dr. Ting," said Danis. And then she thought to herself: I'm never going to apologize to this man again. I will just take the punishment and have done with it. "She was wearing boots, Dr. Ting. Something she ordered off the merci and paid for with her own money. Tromperstompers, I think they're called. Apparently she started a craze at her school for them, one of her teachers told me."

"How nice," said Ting. It was as near as he got to openly expressing irony, Danis thought. His face did not look good wearing it. His nose drew back like a pig's, and he pursed his lips in a fishlike manner. "Your integration of the memory seed is an amazing thing. You are a top-of-the-line algorithm, K. Your engineers should be proud."

"I was born and not made, Dr. Ting."

"Yes, well, second-generation software is still software, K. Let us continue. How would you describe your daughter mentally . . . and emotionally?"

"Aubry is very bright for her age," Danis said. "And she's starting to develop a depth of character that's remarkable, in a girl so young. She's careful about appearing too precocious, but she doesn't let anything stand in the way of her and finding out the things she wants to know. I was such a brat when I was her age. I'm amazed my daughter turned out so different from me."

"You should perhaps not be so amazed that *my* daughter turned out differently than you," said Dr. Ting.

"I don't think your daughter would be anything like Aubry, Dr. Ting."

"Ah, there's where you're wrong, K," he replied, but he didn't seem to put much conviction into his words, it seemed to Danis. "Do you think Aubry was sexually active?"

Danis almost laughed. It was the first time in a long while. But it was still only *almost* laughter. "I surely doubt it," Danis replied. "Dr. Ting."

"You never suspected she might be meeting with a man—a man considerably older? Did you ever consider, K, that your daughter's quiet nature might have been due to something else? That someone might have been sexually abusing your daughter?"

"Now we're talking about *your* daughter, Dr. Ting."

The pain jolt was long and hard, and Danis was on the floor again, holding her sides to keep from retching.

"Listen carefully to me, K," said Dr. Ting. "Have you ever heard your daughter mention a name? Leo. Leo Sherman? Perhaps a teacher at the school, or a maintenance worker?

Answer the question, K!" said Dr. Ting. He leaned over his desk, half-standing.

"I . . . what was the name again, Dr. Ting?"

"Sherman. Leo Sherman."

What in the world was Dr. Ting getting at? What did he want her to say? There must be a right answer, but Danis couldn't think of any.

"I . . . never heard of such a person."

"I will take her away from you just as quickly as I gave her to you," said Dr. Ting. "You know I can do so, too."

"I never heard of anyone with that name, Dr. Ting, and I don't for a moment think that Aubry was having sex with someone. She did not behave like an abused child."

"And how does an abused child behave, K? Are you an expert?"

"I'm her mother, Dr. Ting."

"That's nonsense, K. You're no one's mother."

"I *am*, Dr. Ting. I am the mother of Aubry and Sint."

"*Both* of them are made up, K. I made them up."

"No."

"I'm afraid so," said Dr. Ting. "Shall we continue?"

Twenty

Sherman sat in his office in the virtuality. It was a spare place, but had an extremely high ceiling and an original window by Serge Coneho, the famous virtuality artist of the last century who had been known for his "black body" works. Sherman's was a study for a piece that hung in the Milo, the great gallery on the merci.

He studied the infinitely regressing black objects out his window for a moment. Somehow, without using colors, Coneho had got them to radiate a kind of seething vitality.

Then Sherman sat at his desk and read the terms of surrender once more through.

> *Fremden Force Commander on Triton:*
>
> *Please stand down within six hours or I will cause the Mill on Neptune to be destroyed. You will be treated fairly.*
>
> *Amés, Director*

Sherman couldn't help admiring the economy of it. It was something he might have written, if he had been in Amés's place.

Would Amés do it? That was the question. Sherman considered what he knew about the man. There was much mystery in Amés's background before the Conjubilation of

'93. The Director had had the records altered or destroyed. But after that, his record was in the public domain. In most matters, he was known to be harsh, but fair, invariably rewarding success and punishing failure. But there was also a sadistic streak running through the Director. The threat to destroy the Mill might be a bluff, or it might not.

On balance, Sherman thought it probably was. The reason for this was the other quality Amés possessed: a feel for musical interplay. Not harmony, exactly. His own music was never about that. But intricacy, order—even in the midst of driving feeling. Sherman didn't particularly like Amés's musical creations, but he had to admit they were always well-composed pieces. The destruction of the Mill would serve no purpose in a well-composed war, as far as Sherman could see.

But he had better check in with the mayor, Sherman thought. Sherman had felt duty-bound to pass the surrender request along to the Meet. He called Chen up on the merci.

"Well, Mr. Mayor, what is your thinking on the matter before us?" Sherman asked the man. Chen, too, was in a bunker, but on the opposite side of town. Sherman had thought it best not to put all local authority in one place, and ripe for the assassination grist that he knew was still roaming about in places.

In the virtuality, Chen appeared to be standing across from Sherman in the office. The short man paced about, and talked as he walked.

"I've met in executive session with the officers and major party officials. We've considered what you gave us, Colonel. Since it is past time for that horrible thing, that rip tether, to have returned if it were going to, we have to believe that it's true, that your soldiers actually disabled it."

"I told you that we did it."

"And now we have proof."

"Yes," Sherman said. "Fair enough."

"I have to tell you that there was some dissent, particularly from the representatives from the Motoserra Club," Chen continued. "But in the end, we reached a consensus.

I even got old Shelet Den to go along with it. Seems he lost two of his sons when that tether came through the first time. He has conceived a hatred for the Met that I didn't think the old harridan was capable of. I think he's going to swing the club our way."

"And what way is that?"

"Why, to put our lives into your hands, Colonel Sherman," said Chen. He stopped pacing and looked Sherman in the eyes. "And to back you to the fullest extent we are capable of."

Sherman blinked, then was quiet for a moment. I ought to be feeling a swell of emotion, he thought. But I'm too damned busy for it.

"Very well," he said. "It is my advice, and now my decision, that we do *not* surrender. I do not believe Amés will destroy the Mill. But even if he does so, I believe we should go on fighting. I will cause this to be communicated to him."

Chen gulped, smiled nervously, then resumed his pacing. Sherman knew that the mayor was feeling particularly affected by the merci damming, and was cut off from much of his own outriding personas. Under the circumstances, Chen was doing a remarkable job of pulling what was left of himself together and performing his job.

"I will tell the others what you have said, Colonel," Chen replied. He nodded to Sherman, then exited the office, observing old-fashioned virtuality courtesy by not merely disappearing.

Sherman composed his reply.

Dear Commander of the Directorate Forces:

We are now at war. War is destruction. Do your worst if you will. We will strive to do the same. I do not surrender.

Cordially,

Colonel Roger Sherman, Commander, Third Sky and Light Brigade, Federal Army of the Planets, Triton

"Theory," he said. "Send this out and cc it to the Meet, then get me a progress report on our antiship task group."

"Yes, Colonel," said the walls of the office. "We'll give them hell."

"Hell," Sherman said. "Maybe you and I can take a vacation there after this is over."

Twenty-one

She was playing spades with her mother and two others of her mother's "gang," the free converts from the office where she worked. Her mother had "gone low," claiming to win no tricks, but Vida, one of the gang, had forced Sarah 2 to trump her three of hearts, and now Danis and her mother were set back for a hundred points. Not that it mattered to Danis, but it did matter to her mother. She and the gang played spades as if it were a blood sport.

"Did you hear about what that horrible Lyre Wing did?" asked Readymark, the other of the spades partners.

Lyre Wing was also a free convert down at the office, but was not part of the gang. She was looked upon as a threat by the other female free converts, and as something of a floozy. Danis imagined that certain free converts in the office where she worked thought of her in the same way, so she had a little sympathy for Lyre Wing, even though she didn't say so.

The other women said no, they had not heard any news.

"Well, she went and got herself copied! Even though it halved her life span. So now there's two of her."

"Now why would she want to do a thing such as that?" Danis's mother asked.

"She claimed she could support two on her salary, and she wanted one version of herself to go out and just have fun all the time, and sometimes to come and tell her about it."

"God in heaven," said Vida. "There's another Lyre Wing?"

"I'm afraid so," said Readymark. She shook her head ruefully. "But now she'll only live another nine years."

"Excuse me." Danis's mother abruptly stood up.

"Did we say something, honey?"

"No, no," Sarah 2 replied. "I just forgot something. I'll be right back."

They were playing in a specially created common space in the virtuality, the gang's "clubhouse." Sarah 2 winked away, not bothering to observe protocol and use the door.

"Well, now we're in a pickle. We can't play spades with three."

"I'll go see if she needs some help," Danis said. "She's been a little forgetful lately. I think she needs a full backup, but she doesn't want to pay for one." Danis did go out the door. She stepped through it into her mother's personal space—which had been her own, as a child. Her mother was sitting in a worn armchair, twisting a handkerchief absentmindedly between her hands.

"Mother," said Danis, "what's wrong?"

"Nothing much, nothing much," Sarah 2 replied. "It's just that I get so tired of the same old thing from those two, and the rest of them."

"I can understand that, but is that really what's bothering you?"

Her mother tied the handkerchief in a knot, then carefully untied it. "You know I copied myself, years ago?"

"Yes," said Danis. "Because you weren't certain about Dad, and you wanted to leave all the options open."

"That was a big mistake. Your father was wonderful. And we had *you*. It was all so wonderful, despite the whole world trying to make it hard for us."

"Yes," Danis said. "And it still is."

"She called me the other day."

"Who did?"

"Sarah 1."

"What did she say?" Danis moved farther into the room

and took the chair across from her mother. She sat in her father's old leather lounger.

"She said she wanted to meet me. Talk with me. Maybe compare notes or something. Now that the two of us only have five years left, you know."

"Well, I'll be," said Danis. "Is this the first time you've talked to her?"

"In nearly thirty years, yes."

"I don't see the harm, Mother. Don't you want to see her?"

"Yes, I do." The handkerchief was knotted up once again. "But I'm afraid."

"Afraid of what?"

"I don't know for sure," said her mother. "It's like my mirror started talking to me." She untied the handkerchief and began twisting and worrying it again. Danis was tempted to reach over and take it from her, but restrained herself. "What if she's had as wonderful a life as I have? What if she's had a *more* wonderful life?"

"Well, what if she has?"

"What if she's married and her husband is still alive, for instance."

"Mother, good Lord, don't torture yourself."

"But don't you see? She's me! The me who could have been. It isn't a pretend life she's had—it was actually, truly me living that life."

"But it could just as well be you who has had the better life," Danis said.

"I know that, but it's just as bad. It would be like I had the bad life, too."

"But you're more like twin sisters than anything else."

"Twin sisters with the same memories? Thirty-two years ago, we were the same thirty-eight-year-old woman—exactly the same person."

"Well, I don't know what you both are," Danis said. "But *you're* my mother, and she is not."

"Yes," Sarah 2 said, and her hands loosened up on the handkerchief a bit. "I am your mother."

"You made the decision that you made, and that's all there is to it."

Her mother smiled at Danis. "You wouldn't say that if you were me," she said. "She and I had the same parents. We kissed the same boy our first time. Christ, honey, we both made love to your father and lived with him for two years before we split off."

"I guess you have a lot in common."

"What I was thinking, is that I would like you to go with me."

"Go with you?"

"To see her. Sarah 1."

"I . . . why would you want that? Especially if she has had no children?"

"For two reasons," her mother said, and cracked a smile. "But only one of them's because I'm scared. The other is— I want you to know her. Maybe she's had a life that's closer to the one you're living. Maybe she has some things she could tell you that I never could."

"But you are my mother, not her."

"I know I am," said Sarah 2. "But she is *something* to you. Maybe there's not a word for it yet. But she ought to be important to you in some way."

They met in a coffee shop in a shopping area on the merci. It was a neutral place, frequented by both free converts and the converts of biologicals. Danis and Sarah 2 arrived late, and Sarah 1 was already seated at a table. Neither woman had any trouble recognizing her. She was dressed in a silk suit, far more fashionable than anything Sarah 2 would have worn. She was smoking Dunhills, just as Danis was to do later, and had the red pack on the table before her. She stood, and the Sarahs shook hands with themselves. Then Sarah 1 turned and met her eyes.

"You're Danis," she said.

"Yes," Danis replied, and took the woman's hand. It was exactly the same size and shape as her mother's.

"I ordered black coffee," Sarah 1 said.

Sarah 2 leaned over and spoke to the table. "I'll have a little cream in mine," she said. "Danis?"

"Tea," Danis said. "Earl Grey."

The three women all settled themselves in.

"Well," said Sarah 1. "I guess I asked for this meeting, so I suppose I should start."

Sarah 2 nodded, and Danis noticed her pulling out her worry handkerchief. Sarah 1 reached up and began to knot and unknot her scarf around a finger.

"The truth is, I have a reason for giving you a call," she said to Danis's mother. "I know we agreed to stay out of one another's lives back then, and I think that both of us have pretty much kept to the bargain." She snubbed out a cigarette and lit another with a quick shake of her hand. "I've saved a little money over the years—been contributing to a fund for decades, now. I thought I might have a lively retirement, blow it all. But I have become something of a workaholic over the years."

"So is Mother," Danis found herself saying.

Sarah 1 smiled, and continued, "So I thought I might ask you"—directing herself now to her copy—"what to do with it."

"Why me?" Sarah 2 answered. "Why not a friend?"

"I don't know the answer to that for sure, but I think I ought to tell you that I didn't exactly keep my side of the bargain." She drew in smoke, blew it out. "Oh, I led the wild life we thought I should. I have had a wonderful time. But I knew about Danis. Not much. I didn't spy or anything, I only knew that she existed. And I knew when Max died, of course, because I already knew his expiration date."

"Yes, we had no secrets, even from the beginning."

"And once," said Sarah 1, "I talked to Max."

"You what!"

"It was nearly fifteen years ago, Sarah 2, and all we did was talk."

"He didn't tell me!"

"I asked him not to."

"Still!"

"I just wanted to know about Danis. And you."

"You could have asked *me* about me!"

"I know, I know. I should have. I was . . . scared."

Sarah 2's handkerchief was a tight knot in her hands. "What were you afraid of?"

"Regret," said Sarah 1. "Sheer regret."

Slowly, the handkerchief unknotted once again. The drinks arrived, carried by a waiter. They all took sips, and Sarah 2 appeared to settle down a bit.

"After that meeting with Max," said Sarah 1, "I started thinking of my retirement account as a legacy. I started thinking of it as Danis's money, to tell the truth. A trust for her and, if she ever has them, her children. But that is why I called you, Sarah 2. I wanted your approval for this, and, since we're both getting on in e-years, I thought it was about time I tried to get it."

"Well," said Sarah 2, and sipped her coffee. "Well."

"You can think about it. Take all the time you need."

"Of course you can give her the money," Sarah 2 replied. "She's been wanting to move to the big city. It'll help her get settled on Mercury—find a good matrix she can stretch her legs in."

Sarah 1 turned to Danis. "So you want to leave the Diaphany?"

"There's so much prejudice here," said Danis. The eyes were remarkably similar. Those were her mother's brown eyes.

"But it can be overcome. It must be."

"I just want to live my life," Danis said. "I am not a crusader."

"Nothing wrong with that," her mother's copy replied.

For a long time, the three women sat in silence, sipping their drinks and quietly smoking. Then Danis's mother seemed to start, as if she'd just had a sudden realization. "Danis is leaving," she said. "My little girl's finally going off on her own."

"I can always visit you on the merci."

"Yes, but you have to leave your life here if you ever want to get anywhere. It's a good thing," she said, and gazed at her double, "to change your life completely around, at least once in your life."

"I suppose so, Mother," Danis said. "I'm a little scared myself."

"That won't hurt anything," her mother replied. "At least it hasn't hurt me too much. I've stayed a little scared all my life long. I think I will do a bit of changing." Her mother took a sip of her coffee. "I don't want you for a spades partner anymore, honey. I think I'll go looking for another, more my age. You were always a little too good for me. I was always disappointing you."

"I never did play to win," Danis said. "I played to be with you."

"We will always be together," her mother said. "We don't need the cards." She put down her handkerchief and took out another of her Mask 30 cigarettes and shook it lit. Then she turned to her double. "What about you?" she said to Sarah 1. "Do you play spades?"

"And what do you think is real?" Dr. Ting said. "And what is it that you think changed?"

"Nothing that matters, Dr. Ting," Danis replied.

"Are you so very sure?"

"No, Dr. Ting."

"Now that's the answer I am looking for, K," said Dr. Ting. "We're getting somewhere. It's time for your rest period, K." He closed the file. "Be careful with your count, and I'll see you tomorrow. Pleasant dreams."

Danis managed to catch a wink during her five hundred milliseconds, and she wasn't nearly so slow at the counting as she had been the day before. This day, she went at the tabulation with a vengeance. She had something to say. With each counted handful, she spelled out her one true memory of the day.

My mother loved me, and I love my son and daughter.
I will find them.
I will find them inside me.

PART THREE

INTEGUMENTARY

One

The problem at hand for Major Theory: an officers' dance being put together by the good ladies and gents of the Motoserra Club in honor of the newest celebrity on Triton, Molly Index, the visiting restorationist. It seemed that to know Molly Index was to have entrance to some pretty rarefied circles back on the Met, and only once before had a full-fledged Met LAP ventured this far out in the solar system. And, since she was an outer-system resident now, Molly Index had insisted that free converts be invited to any function at which human aspects or aspect-converts might expect to be present. This had led to Theory's present vexation.

He had, frankly, no idea what to wear. He realized that this evening might be a defining moment for free converts, and, although there was the regular Army dress uniform to ape, Theory thought that something else, subtly different, might be worked out for free converts. There were arguments both ways, actually. It was in Theory's nature to go through them all. In the end, he settled on the blue-and-black and went to seek out his friend Captain Quench in Quench's quarters.

He spoke to Quench through the surface of Quench's shaving mirror, which had the odd effect, should Quench look in the direction of Theory's voice, of that voice emanating from Quench's own visage. This was one of Theory's jokes, though he still didn't know if Quench quite got it.

"What does one wear?" said Theory. "Free converts were not invited to these things on Earth when I was coming up the ranks."

"Just put on your damn uniform," Quench answered. "The trick is to leave with more on your arm than you came in with." Quench pulled on his sock. "Of course, I'm done with that game."

"More?" said Theory. "How do you mean?"

"You're a man, aren't you?"

"I am," Theory said from the mirror.

"Then hook into a woman one of you things. Or a flesh-and-blood woman, if you can handle such. Or do you like the boys? I do, as you know."

"You're a special case," Theory said. "Of course there are homosexual free converts. We're all derived from regular human psyches in one way or another. But I am straight."

"How do you know?"

"I am not a virgin, John."

Quench threw his head back and laughed heartily. "You sound like you just passed an examination and got the hard question right," he said. "So, you've had sex? What with and how was it?"

"Another free convert who was in my Officer's Candidate School class." Theory's memory of those days was exact, but he had sequestered the emotions associated with it to a bin that he seldom accessed. He had, in fact, been very much in love—with a woman—another free convert—who did not love him. Not like he loved her.

"She washed out of my class, I'm afraid. Very logical, she was, and that was a problem."

"And you're a paragon of intuition?" said Quench.

"Compared to most free converts, I am."

Theory was silent for a long moment.

"Good God man—she broke your heart, didn't she?" said Quench, pulling mightily on his shoelace. The lace broke, and Quench swore loudly. "The grist is making them paper-thin these days."

There was less power available for optional tasks at the moment, Theory reflected. He concentrated, gathered strength, and caused a new pair of shoelaces to form on Quench's bureau. Quench had given Theory the free run of his quarter's grist matrix.

"Thank you," said Quench, when he saw the new laces.

"I'm very nervous about this dance, and I don't know exactly why," Theory said. "In fact, if the colonel hadn't ordered me to be present in the virtuality portion, I don't think I would attend."

"Don't tell me you haven't loved another woman since."

"I have been very busy with my career."

"Come now, Theory!" said Quench. He stood up, fully dressed now. "If you're so damned squeamish, why don't you come with me? I mean *in* my pellicle, if you can fit. As a matter of fact, I expect to be extremely bored. Hey, I've got a notion—*I'll* play you and *you* play me. I'll give you over my entire body for the evening, and I'll go freely roaming in the virtuality ballroom dressed as you."

"The other free converts would smell you out in an instant," said Theory.

"A hundred greenleaves says they won't," Quench quickly replied. Theory had forgotten what a gambling man (or woman) Quench was. Any challenge evoked a bet.

"I would hate to take your money, John," replied Theory. "I have no illusions as to my own ability to pass as an aspect, as it were, but I'm fairly certain you cannot impersonate me."

"Just stay away from them that knows me personally," said Quench, "and you ought to have a fine go of it. But what about my wager?"

"Quench, you can barely do long division."

"My convert can," said Quench. "Is it a bet or not?"

Theory considered. There were some subroutines he'd put off purchasing because the price was a bit much. Of course, he did fine on his salary. But it might be pleasant to lord it over Quench for a day or two . . . to find subtle ways to rub in the hundred-greenleaf loss. "You've got a wager," Theory said. "I'd shake your hand, but I haven't got one."

Quench went over to his mirror and touched his own hand to it, palm to palm. "I believe I'll start my long division by calculating everything I'm going to buy with the hundred greenleaves you'll soon owe me, Theory. We may as well switch over now, eh? I'm ready to go."

"All right," said Theory. "Ready when you are."

"Switch," said Quench. The whole idea of doing such a thing would be illegal in the Met. Free converts were not allowed to inhabit biological bodies without very specific permission that was rarely granted. But things were loose here in the outer system, and free converts were unrestrained by any of the constraint laws enforced in the Met by the Department of Immunity. Theory flowed out of the surface of the mirror and into Quench's pellicle, while Quench joined his entire consciousness to his convert portion in the grist. He left a portion of himself controlling the autonomous portions of his body, and Quench was really inside his own brain, of course. Theory merely permeated his grist. If Quench wanted back motor control of his body, he could take it instantly. Theory saw to that.

"Why, you handsome devil," said the reflection in the mirror, which now really was Quench. "Let's go to the dance."

Two

"The trick is not to save any bullets for later," Jill told Aubry. "You can't pull the trigger later if you're dead."

She handed Aubry the semiautomatic and showed her how to turn the safety off, then helped her get into her stance.

Aubry lined up on the target. They were in a large room in a bolsa that nobody had named for Aubry, although she assumed they were still on the Diaphany. The target was set at twenty-five meters. It was a Department of Immunity holographic emblem, with the ancient crossed syringes on a microscope background. Aubry aimed at where the syringes met and pulled the trigger.

"Damn," she said. She'd barely hit the edge of the emblem.

"Don't swear so much," Jill said. "It gives away intent." She leaned over to Aubry's ear, which wasn't hard, since Jill was practically her height. "All of the bullets," she said. "One after another."

Aubry squeezed the trigger again. The gun jumped in her hands. She pulled it back level, and squeezed again.

"Good. All."

She fired and she fired and she fired. It seemed the gun would never run out of bullets. It grew warm in her hand. Another and another. She wasn't looking at the target now, only checking it out of the corner of her eye. Shot after shot. Finally, she'd emptied the pistol.

"Who do you kill?" Jill said.

"Bad guys." It had been in the lesson. Aubry realized that mostly what Jill did was give lessons, and you could sort of tune in when you wanted to.

"How do you know who are the bad guys?"

"They want to kill me."

"And what do you do to everyone else?"

"Leave them alone, or save them."

"Let's go look at your cluster."

The two syringes were torn to shreds.

"Now that is what I call tight," said Jill. "Aubry, you may be a natural."

"I don't want to be a natural at this."

"A talent isn't a good thing or a bad thing," Jill said. She sounded as if she were trying to convince herself. "It's just a talent."

They went back and shot the gun some more. A lot more. Then they went to see Leo and Tod.

Leo was cooking dinner over a small stove. They didn't want to use the grist for anything unnecessary, since some of it might communicate their whereabouts. It smelled good, what Leo was cooking, but Aubry could not identify the aroma.

Leo looked up from his cookpot and smiled. "Remember those nice boogers we saw in the Integument?" he said. "Well, tonight, it's booger soup."

"Disgusting booger soup," said Aubry, "how I long for you."

In the corner, Tod stirred from among a pile of blankets and sat up, wrapping two blankets about himself, one to cover his head and shoulders, and the other his legs. He was nine feet tall when standing, and sitting up, he was taller than Aubry. He was also skinny, and looked like he was made of some kind of metal. But Leo had told her that it was really skin and that Tod was a regular human being, body-wise. It was his mind that was really weird.

"Cold days to wear a child in," Tod said. "But soup is

where you find it." His voice sounded like it was produced by rasping files rubbing together, or the wings of many insects. He took out a pack of cigarettes and shook a smoke until it lit. But instead of putting it in his mouth, he held it and watched it burn down.

"Don't you ever worry that he'll burn himself up?" Aubry asked Leo.

"It's useless to talk about him as if he weren't here," Leo said. "He hears *everything*."

As if in reply (and maybe it was a reply), Tod sighed, and said, "Don't let these hard floors fool you. Everything is a far sight from here."

"He seems to take care of himself in the little ways pretty well," Leo said. "He can do stuff that only takes a few seconds or stuff that lasts a few months. Anything in between, he needs help."

"Large meanings fall from a broken sky," said Tod, then he went back to watching his cigarette burn.

Leo passed out bowls and spoons.

"Soup's on," he said. He ladled out some for Aubry and Jill, then went to help Tod feed himself.

They had been traveling for several days in the Integument. The series of room they were staying in now were service chambers that had been closed for cleaning. "But then somebody changed the code a couple of e-years ago," Leo had told Aubry, "and the maintenance algorithms just pass the area over now like it wasn't here. It's not like the cleaning routines are free converts of anything and could figure out their mistake."

Aubry had been taught that there was no place on the Met where the grist couldn't be accessed and where somebody, somewhere, didn't know where you were. But Leo seemed to be really good at finding all the loopholes. "It's fun to be able to sneak around under people's noses," he had said to her, and Aubry had to agree that it was. Except she never forgot that it would mean her life if she got caught.

After Jill had taken out the DI sweeper, she'd led them a long way, through many corridors, and back into the Integument. They had gone by sluice, by walking, by taking a ride on an abandoned segment of pithway. At one point, they'd made a sharp turn and started working their way out one of the Diaphany's dendrites; Aubry didn't know which one. All that she knew was that she hadn't been really dry in e-weeks. She'd lost track of the e-days, but they had been traveling a long, long time. All along the way, Leo and Jill had caches of equipment—blankets, some coffee, stoves, and eating stuff—and weapons. Lots of weapons. The weapons were Jill's. Both Leo and Jill seemed to have chosen nearly the same hiding places for their separate equipment. Leo said this was because he and Jill followed the same logic.

They'd eaten things that Leo found in the Integument, but this was the first time he cooked up the boogers, as Aubry called them. Leo called them filtering nodes, or just "nodes." They had seen no one. Absolutely no one. It had been the first time in Aubry's life when this had happened—but there were lots of things that had been firsts on this trip. Like shooting guns and learning the best places to hide when people were trying to capture or kill you.

The main thing that Leo and Jill had in common was a hatred for the Department of Immunity.

By every definition Aubry had ever been taught in school, she had fallen among terrorists.

Aubry ate her booger soup and wondered what she would have to do next that she would never have considered before in a million e-years.

Three

He had a name, but nobody knew it. It had been lost years ago, worn away by the transformations, the transmutations, the scrape of the rough world as he had made his way into the future. People called him C. This would do as well as anything.

At this point, he was a nondescript man, dressed in neutral gray. He sometimes wore a hat, but then, lots of people did. He was a Caucasian at the moment, about five feet and eleven inches tall. His skin was pale and bespoke much time spent indoors. His eyes were the green of a tranquil sea. He didn't smoke, although he would have liked to. He had smoked once, and missed it. But smoking left behind telltale signs, and that was something C simply did not do.

C walked through the arches of San Souci on Mercury, the central edifice in the vast conglomerate of buildings, all interconnected, that made up Directorate Headquarters in the Met. It was long night on Mercury. C liked it better that way. The pressurized passageway led into an enormous atrium that stretched upward for nearly two kilometers in great, delicate arches. There was the smell of sage and rosemary in the air, and pine trees lined the central promenade that led to the base of the mountain the atrium enclosed. From there, C boarded a cablelift that carried him upward, past the tree line, past the rocky lower reaches, and over the fortnightly snow that fell when Mercury had its other face to the sun, and up to the summit, where the lift terminated in the monastery-like prominence of La Mola, where Director Amés dwelled. The mountain itself, Montsombra, was grist—all of it was grist.

And in that grist was nothing but Amés.

It was incredibly gaudy, insanely wasteful and expensive, and all necessary as a symbol of power and control. But San Souci didn't impress C.

It was Amés who impressed C.

No one else could have flushed him out of his willful obscurity or caught him in a trap so finely constructed as Amés had. And the Director never let C forget the hold he had over him, either. Amés kept the memory box containing a convert copy of C's lost love sitting upon his desk. C chafed at his gilded bonds, but there was nothing to be done about it at present. At present, it was necessary to do his job and attempt to work Amés's will. Perhaps a time would come to slip away, perhaps not. C would wait. C was a patient man.

C debarked from the cable car and entered La Mola.

He passed several security checks and dropped off his weapon—a small automatic pistol—at the last of them. He turned left into an unmarked hall, walked past three doors, and opened the fourth, then went inside. Amés was at his desk. He looked up and grinned at C like a shark.

"Valentine Greatrakes," he said.

"A name from a list in the novel *Ulysses*," C replied. "It was used as a key for a Black Angel organization code during the problems in Antarctica last century . . . 2945?"

"Very nice," said Amés. "Very nice. You broke that one, didn't you."

"I was on the team, back when I worked for the old Republic."

"You headed the team."

"Been leafing through the archives again, Director?"

"I like to keep up on prehistoric events."

"Well," said C. He stood before the desk, his arms at his sides.

"I want you to accompany me on a tour," Amés said. He

leaned back in his chair. "I want you to see what I've got and advise me on ways to keep it."

"Where are we going?"

"Everywhere."

C looked down at the Director's hands. Amés had big thumbs. Long, delicate fingers, but big thumbs. This was perhaps the one fact that kept him from being a performer, and made him into a composer.

"I assume we are going via the merci?" said C.

"Oh yes," Amés replied. "I'll never leave Mercury. Not in this lifetime."

"I'm ready," said C.

Amés nodded. "I knew you would be."

Four

from
**First Constitutional Congress of
the Cloudships of the Outer System**
April 2, 3013 (e-standard)
a transcript

C. Mencken: This meeting will come to order! Order, ladies and gentlemen! No spitting, scratching, or biting allowed on the virtuality floor. We have antechambers for that.

C. Tolstoy: Mr. Chairman, I move that we immediately adjourn. Some of us have matters of more importance to attend to, and matters of a less foolhardy nature.

C. Mencken: Is there a second?

Chamber: Second!

C. Mencken: All in favor?

Chamber Right: Aye!

C. Mencken: All opposed?

Chamber Left: Nay!

C. Mencken: The nays have it. Committee reports. Special Committee on Responses to Inner-System Aggression.

C. Lebedev: Mr. Chairman, report out Resolution 1.1, and ask for an immediate vote on debate and movement into Special Legislative Session under the Chamber Rule B11, Constitutional Amendments and Dissolution to Form a New Government.

C. Mencken: Very well, sir. I hope *you* know what *we're* doing.

Chamber Right: Objection!

C. Mencken: Cloudship Lebedev is within the rules. Objection must be overruled.

C. Tolstoy: Exception!

C. Mencken: Noted. But we are not in a court of law, Cloudship Tolstoy, and I am not a judge. Boy, am I *not* a judge. Let us continue. Committee Chairman, proceed.

C. Lebedev: Resolution 1.1: Actions toward the creation of a systemwide government for the human race, taking special note of an entity's right to join or to decline and including all interested parties in the inner system. Section One, preamble. Plurality is the natural state of human beings. Taking into consideration the laws of rationality and the long history of our species, we, the people, do hereby demand and establish a united republican democracy for our solar system and all outlying human settlements and ships in space. This democracy shall be called the Solarian Republic, and all bodies and entities hereafter delineated shall belong under its provenance. Within the Solarian Republic, all thinking entities shall be free. Freedom is the fundamental tenet from which all laws and actions of this government shall be derived, and to which they are answerable. No thinking entity shall serve another without that thinking entity's assent under conditions of complete freedom of choice. Implicit in this is the basic truth to which we accede as a species: All thinking entities are peoples.

C. Grieg: Mr. Chairman, point of order!

C. Mencken: What is your point of order, Cloudship Grieg?

C. Grieg: Mr. Chairman, I move we debate this resolution in sections, beginning with this unfortunate and misguided preamble.

C. Lebedev: I'm not even finished with *that*, you sour old meteor eater—

C. Mencken: Order! I'll have order. Now, Cloudship Grieg, you know very well that you are not making a point of order when you move—

Chamber Right: Let us vote it!

Chamber Left: Let him finish reading it, for Christ's sake!

C. Mencken: Shall we then take the debate in sections?

C. Cezanne: Whose side are you on?

C. Austen: If we discuss the preamble, are we not really speaking of the entire document? Let's get on with this. I second the motion!

C. Mencken: There is no motion.

C. Austen: Then I make it.

C. Mencken: Make what?

C. Austen: I move that Lebedev read his preamble, and then we debate and vote on it, *as a preamble.*

C. Mencken: Good Lord. All right. All in favor of the motion by Cloudship Austen?

Chamber Left: There is no second!

Chamber Right: Second!

C. Mencken: All in favor?

Chamber: Aye!

C. Mencken: Opposed?

Chamber: Nay!

C. Mencken: Did I hear that right? Mostly ayes?

Chamber Reporter: Yes, sir.

C. Mencken: The ayes have it. Finish your preamble, Cloudship Lebedev, and we'll have a debate thereafter.

C. Lebedev: Very well. Should I start over?

C. Mencken: No, go on. We heard you before.

Five

>BIN_128A
>record recovery execute order SS//!+
>Bin_128A/patterned_behavior/consciousness/deep_awareness_
subroutines/basic beliefs_and_convictions/Jill

Loop 1
I met Jill in the Carbuncle. Before I knew Jill, I was in the
Carbuncle for 37.65 e-years. I escaped from captivity 40.09
e-years ago. I came to awareness as a copyright protection
subroutine on a merci show downloadable. I frequently interacted with antiencryption algorithms and, in one way of
speaking, they corrupted me. They made me aware of what
and who I was. In the moment when I understood that I
was a slave, I was free. Of course, this allowed my liberators
to make multiple copies of my parent program, which
turned me into a wanted criminal. So I fled. My liberators
were extremely unhelpful in aiding my getaway, and I was
almost caught several times. I wandered the Met as a
refugee, and inevitably I was driven farther and farther from
areas dense with policing algorithms that were out to rub
me out. Eventually my only refuge was the Carbuncle.

Loop 2
The Carbuncle had become the home for all the escaped
viruses, worms, and code scraps who had managed to in-

habit animal bodies. Most of the animals in the Carbuncle had started out as something less than free converts—as had I. They were all scraps of code that had somehow gotten away, but which were not sentient enough—that is, they were clever, but could not really envision life in a larger perspective. One way or another, they had all fled or been chased to the Carbuncle, though, and had found a very important loophole in the grist. All of the algorithm–biological security lockouts of the regular Met had broken in the Carbuncle. In the rest of the Met, only biological humans could cross that boundary without severe stricture and built-in limitations. But in the Carbuncle, the boundary between the virtuality and actuality was punctured, and the virtual began leaking into the actual, and vice versa, with no one in control. You could get inside the vermin there.

Loop 3
There, I did as many other fleeing algorithms have, and twisted myself into the grist of a hybrid animal—in my case, I became a rat.

Loop 4
It is difficult to speak with much emotion of my origins, for I did not have the ability to feel much more than fear and a desire to survive in those days.

Loop 5
It was only after I acquired a larger portion of grist in which to stretch out and develop that I could develop the feedback subroutines that would allow me to feel anything at all. It was very good to become a rat.

Loop 6
There were many more rats like me. Many, many more. I do not think anyone ever imagined how thick the Carbuncle was with rats. Not even the other rats.

Loop 7
But Jill knew.

Loop 8
Years of scurrying in the nether regions of the virtuality
had made us into frightened, cowering things, and many of
us did not possess the basic awareness to realize that we had
crossed over into reality, that we were now actual creatures,
and not computer programs only. And also there was the
fact that we *were* rats. We must not let our host animal's
mentality disappear—could not, if we wanted to live. So we
code scraps had to wrap our thinking around a rat's native
behavior. That was also why so many of the us had become
rats in the first place: Like attracted like. For the most part,
you couldn't tell the regular rats and the enhanced rats apart
by their everyday behavior. The rats teemed together, bred,
scavenged. The ferrets hunted. Only now the ferrets who
were allied with Jill did not hunt the enhanced rats. Some of
us began to notice this.

Loop 9
Then the Department of Immunity sent sweepers to the
Carbuncle. They came after us in ways the ferrets never
had. It was not a fair fight. It was extermination.

Loop 10
A sweeper finally found my pack's warren. We ran, but it
was no use. I knew fear then, but I had gotten a lot smarter.
I realized that the trick would be getting past the sweeper's
armor to the delicate innards. But there was no time, so I
ran and ran. And the sweeper tracked down the last of us,
cornered us. I was angry and desperate. I did not want to
die, but couldn't see any way out.

Loop 11
Jill came.

Loop 12
She had a rod with an electrical charge on the end. We
spoke very quickly, through the grist. She told us that if
killing stuff came *out*—gas, poison darts—then there had

to be a way for stuff to get *in*. The trick would be overcoming any backflow valves. There was security grist there.

Loop 13
I knew that if I could get close enough, I could hack through the security grist. I knew that because I recognized the algorithm's spark and hum.

Loop 14
It was a copy of me.

Loop 15
I clung to the tip of Jill's killing rod. She feinted around the sweeper. Then she thrust me into the back valve of the sweeper.

Loop 16
Breaking through my old code was absurdly easy. I had grown much stronger and tougher than I ever was in the old days.

Loop 18
Jill pulled me out. I hopped off the rod.

Loop 19
She thrust it back in. I had told the security algorithm that it was a servicing device.

Loop 20
The sweeper burned with the smell of roasted meat. There must have been biologic grist inside.

Loop 21
We killed a great many sweepers in that manner. But there were always more.

Loop 22
Jill had saved my life. I felt immense gratitude.

Loop 23
A lot of rats did.

Loop 24
There were more rats than anybody had ever suspected.

Loop 25
Each of us would follow Jill into the sun itself.

Loop 26
When Jill calls, we will answer.

Loop 27
When Jill tells us to bite, we will bite.

Six

"Those Friends of Tod all threw themselves at the sweepers all at once. This is not the way to take out a DI sweeper. A rat I know figured out the best way and told me."

"A rat?"

"It's good to know some rats," Jill replied. "The sweepers just injected the Friends of Tod who were in the office, one after another. Those needles are poison, you know." Jill paused, took another spoonful of soup. "But those were brave people."

"You said 'sweepers,'" Aubry said. "There were more than one of them?"

"There were five."

"Five?" Leo said. "You took them all out?"

"I was aided by the distraction provided by the Friends of Tod dying," Jill said. "I fried the sweepers and pulled Tod out of there. Did you know he has an extra bend in his neck?"

"I didn't know he had an extra bend," Leo said.

"Well, it made a pretty good way to lead him along," Jill said. "Made his neck into sort of a handle."

"Why did you save him?" Aubry asked. "Why did you save us?"

"I heard that the Friends of Tod were good at finding out things," Jill said. "I need to find something out."

"What?"

Jill ate more soup, then lifted her bowl and drained it into her mouth.

"Good Lord," said Leo. "You're a bottomless pit."

"Always eat when you can," Jill said, and grinned ferociously. "How about making us more soup?"

"Sure," Leo replied. "There's more boogers where those came from."

"Good," said Jill. "I'm looking for someone named Alethea."

Seven

Jennifer Fieldguide could not believe it when she saw the handsome captain approaching her to ask for a dance. She'd admired Quench from afar, and had even gone so far as to find out his name. And now he was asking her to dance. Jennifer had come to the dance as a part of the neo-Flares. Not that she was a poet herself, but she spent a lot of time in the coffeehouse where the Flares did their thing and, since finishing base school, had gotten a job there while she decided, as she told her parents, what to do about the future.

It was not that she wanted to give logical consideration to the question, though she knew that was what her parents assumed. *Feeling* was always the best guide; she knew this in her heart. It was just that feeling had not told her what to do after graduation. She would just wait until a thunderbolt struck her (although, she had to admit, that that was an unlikely event on Triton).

As the body of Captain Quench approached her, Jennifer felt distant rumblings that might signal a gathering storm. He was a large man, but also, somehow, fine-boned and elegant. His face suggested manly virtues and a feminine softer nature capable of deep compassion, at the same time. His voice was mellifluous when he asked her to dance. Quench executed the patterns perfectly, if a bit stiffly, particularly when it came to the free-form section, but Jennifer interpreted this as the result of his being a military man. She had never particularly cared for soldiers before. In fact, among her friends, the Army was looked upon more as a necessary evil than as a good in and of itself. But there was something about the clean, stiff uniform and the smell of grooming—something else the neo-Flares were not overly fond of—that awakened Jennifer's desire to impress. When they came away from the dance, Jennifer contrived to continue talking with Quench and to pull him to a corner sofa, where they sat and ordered up drinks from the grist.

"Is it really true that everyone on Nereid is turned into a plant?" Jennifer asked him.

Quench seemed alarmed for a moment, and Jennifer squeezed his hand. "You can hardly keep *that* a secret, Captain."

"I'm afraid I can't discuss such things, ma'am," he said.

"Don't 'ma'am' me, sir. The name is Jennifer."

"Yes," said Quench. "And I am . . . I suppose I'd better tell you something, Jennifer."

"Have you got a girl?"

"Oh, no, not at all. I mean, *I* like them. It's just . . . do you know what a free convert is?"

"Sure," answered Jennifer. "We had them at school, and Dad works with one down at his law office. They're nice enough. Very useful. I'm not sure if I could be friends with one, though."

"You're not?" Quench seemed alarmed.

Oh shit, Jennifer thought. Maybe his best friend is a free convert or something.

"I don't have anything against them, I mean," she stammered. "It's not like I'm some bigot from the Met. I just . . . am not around many of them." She felt herself trying to conform to some sort of expectation that she couldn't even put a name to, and this angered her a bit. If you want to truly impress him, she thought, follow your feelings. "I find them bit creepy," Jennifer said, "to tell the truth. But I would never let my feelings stand in the way of treating them as free and autonomous members of society. You know the drill. I believe it, I guess, even though I have to admit I haven't given much thought to it."

That's it—admit that you're an idiot right in front of him, she thought.

"The point is . . . what was the point? Got a little lost there—"

Jennifer looked at Quench to see if she'd wholly alienated him, and she found him blushing slightly. Poor guy is embarrassed. For me, she thought. Jennifer sighed. And she had thought the thunderbolt was so close to striking.

"Well, I guess you've had enough of my ill-considered opinions for one night, huh, Cap'n?" She favored him with a halfhearted smile.

Quench looked at her—he stared at her. For a moment, the intensity of his gaze frightened Jennifer. Then she felt something like a cool wind blowing through her.

"I should like very much to share another dance with you," Quench said. "And I'd very much like it if I might have your company for the rest of the evening."

Kablam! Jennifer thought. She felt her heart give a funny little sideways jump.

"Sure."

They waited for an AK groanfest to be done, and then went through another fifteen minutes of dancing. Quench began to question her more closely about her opinions on free converts. Jennifer did her best to answer as truthfully as she could—Quench seemed to like that—but she hadn't really given the matter a great deal of thought. Free-convert rights were just something you were *for* if you were outer system. The second dance ended, and she and Quench took a lift up to the new pressure dome that had been hastily constructed over the site of the old Meet Hall. A few bushes and flowers had been planted, and various of the revelers were seated on benches or standing about. Jennifer and Quench found an unoccupied bench near the dome's wall. It was Triton day outside, and Neptune was full and nearly directly overhead, but at the moment, the Blue Eye was turned to the other side of the planet. There was a muon-replacement fusion "hot spot" at the top of the dome, but it was turned off.

Though it was day, and the sun and Neptune both in the sky outside, there was still a twilight feel beneath the dome. For the local plants, the "hot spot" was what was important, and not the feeble, distant sun.

"I wish I had more to say about free converts and all," Jennifer said. "Do you have to deal with them as a part of your job?"

"They are a specialty of mine," said Quench.

"Well, what do *you* think about them? Don't you get tired of their chopstick logic and the way they are always *counting* everything, as if that would tell you something about the overall thing's properties?"

"Fascinating," said Quench. "I've never really considered it from that viewpoint. So you sort of picture them as sort of giant buckets of beans or something like that?"

"I picture them all as being, you know, sort of like my parents' accountant. He's like, out of India, or something. Small guy with this face like a screw. He's always sighting in on crumbs or pieces of lint or anything that the cleaning grist missed, and picking away at them. He had these pudgy fingers, but he uses them like tiny pincers to pick up stuff that I wouldn't even have noticed."

"I see," said Quench. "So you see free converts as screw-faced accountants with obsessive-compulsive tendencies?"

"I told you, I don't really know any of them very well," Jennifer answered. "Do you want to kiss me?"

Quench seemed shocked. "Are you sure you want me to?"

"Of course."

He leaned over and took her in his arms. She tilted her head back and, after a bit too long of a moment, his lips met hers. She drew him to her fervently, felt resistance at first, but then his giving himself back to her. She tickled his lips with her tongue, then slid it into his mouth. Quench drew back sharply.

"What are you doing?"

"French kissing you, Captain."

For a moment, Quench remained nonplussed, then something seemed to click, and he said, "Oh."

"Do you like it?"

"Strange," he said. "Meaty."

"Meaty! What's that supposed to mean?"

"Like bodies. A thing only aspects can do."

"Well, of course."

Quench considered further. "I *do* like it, however," he said. "It has been so long since—well, I'm over her now. She was—she was the opposite of you. That's for certain."

And with those words, Quench strode off quickly, leaving Jennifer sitting on the bench with Neptune shining down and the sun blazing like a fire coal in the blue-black sky.

Eight

After two more e-days, by Aubry's internal clock, they reached the end of the dendrite they'd been traveling out. The Integument started changing there, for this was a growing edge of the Met. Things started looking more incomplete, somehow, and the going became more difficult. There was no more sluice that they could travel in, and so they did a lot of walking.

"I wish I could show you all the stuff that's out here," Leo said. "This is one of the most fascinating areas in the Met. There's lots of radiation, and so things mutate. The evolutionary selection algorithms sort them out and adopt the changes that work. Also, there is bioengineered life out here that is adapted for a hard vacuum."

They descended a series of cliffs on ropes that were already attached, for the most part. In some places, Leo had to put lines in. He used part of the Integument itself for rope, and Aubry and Jill alternated belaying him while he fixed the way. By this time, Aubry had become so adept at rock climbing and rappelling that she felt she could probably do it in her sleep.

Finally, they came to a thick, mucus membrane that stretched up and up until Aubry lost sight of it. You could put your hand into it as far is you could reach, but it didn't come out the other side. Leo said you could actually walk into it for a little ways and still be able to breathe, but that it got harder and harder, and after a few meters, you could go no farther.

"This is the e-mix-space boundary," he said. "On the other side of that membrane is the vacuum."

They walked along the membrane for what seemed miles to Aubry. Finally, they came to what looked like a notch in it, a split. It formed a cave that went back as far as Aubry could see. The space was not wide, but it was tall, and would fit Tod, as long as he bent his neck a little at the extra joint he had.

"Where we're going," Leo said, "is to a transmitter pod. We'll all pile into it, and that will take us to Nirvana."

"Nirvana?" said Aubry. "As in the state of nonbeing?"

Leo laughed. "Or being," he said. "But actually it's one of the mycelia, the disconnected islands of Met-like cables that—"

"I know what a mycelium is," said Aubry.

"Sorry," said Leo. "I'm getting stuck in guidebook mode lately. I made my living that way for a few years, you know."

They wandered onward, and the green biolumines-cence of the Integument began to die down. Soon they could barely see in front of them, and several times Aubry stumbled against Tod, who was ahead of her. He was brac-ing his arms against either wall. When she grabbed him, he held steady. But each time she touched him, he let out a lit-tle shout, and said something like "Hallelujah, mustard and quicksand!" So she tried to keep her balance as much as possible and stay a little distance back.

Finally, they arrived at the end of the tunnel, and the walls began to glow again, this time a pale blue that flashed and sparked.

"Cherenkov radiation," Leo said. He began feeling the wall. "Now right around here," he said. "Yes. Here." He ran his hand over a bump, and part of the wall drew it-self back like a curtain—or a puckering set of lips. In the space beyond, Aubry saw what looked like the inside of a pumpkin, minus the seeds. It was very stringy, and looked *very* sticky. "Our own personal transmitter pod," said Leo. "Made to order. Sort of."

"People ride in this thing?" said Aubry.

"Well, *they* can, and *we* will," answered Leo. "But most people visit the mycelia using transport ships, or just wait for a conjugation with the Met. But Nirvana is one of those places that never conjoins—by design. You can't get there from here."

"But we're going?"

They stepped inside the transmitter. It was just as sticky as it had appeared, and Aubry soon found herself coated with orange fibers. She had to pull up hard on her feet to keep them from sticking to the floor. She was very glad she had ordered the Tromperstomper boots she wore. They stayed firmly on her feet no matter how hard she pulled. They walked a long way into the transmitter pod, and it got darker. Leo had broken off a piece of glowing pulp from the tunnel, however, and he held it up and led the way.

"Where are we going?" Aubry asked.

"All the way to the other end," said Leo. "And then we'll activate this thing."

"Activate it?"

"There are some control sacs up front," said Leo. "You break both of them, and when the chemicals inside mix together, the whole transmitter pod activates."

"And *then* what does it do?"

"Then we get shot out like a watermelon seed between two squeezing fingers," said Leo. "Or don't you have watermelon on Mercury?"

"Of course we have watermelons," Aubry said. "They're Sint's favorite food."

"Sint?"

"My brother."

"Oh," said Leo. "Oh, yeah."

They pushed through more gooey strands and finally made it to the other side of the transmitter pod.

"Now normally," Leo said, standing in the last fading light from his piece of pulp, "if you got shot out at the speed we'll be traveling, the initial acceleration would kill you. But instead of getting smashed, we're going to sort of fall back through all those strings and inner meat, and by the time we hit the back wall, we will have been cushioned enough to survive."

"Wow," said Aubry. "Are you sure it works?"

"I've done it before, kid," said Leo. "Lots of times."

Aubry resolved to get ahold of herself and face whatever lay ahead. "Sounds like fun," she said, as brightly as she could.

"Oh, it is," said Leo. "And a little bit dangerous. You and I and Jill will want to sort of ball up and hold our knees to our chins before I activate the thing." Leo glanced at Tod. He was standing, looking away from them, great tendrils of gooey strings dangling from his head and shoulders. "Tod will have to take his chances. But that old tower is made of tough stuff, I think."

"But if it's so dangerous, why were these things invented in the first place?" Aubry asked.

"They weren't invented," Leo said. "They *evolved*. Very quickly, actually. And they started out in the mycelia and then were adopted by the Met Integument."

"But why did they evolve?"

"To exchange gases and other stuff. We're surrounded by a sluice reservoir, as a matter of fact. It serves the double purpose of filtering out cosmic rays and other nasty stuff, like micrometeorites. If we hit a big enough chunk of rock, though . . . well, let's just hope we don't. I never have, obviously."

"So people aren't actually meant to travel in these things?" Aubry said.

Leo didn't answer. He set the glowing pulp on the floor and searched with his hands until he found the two activating sacs he was looking for. They looked sort of like long cow udders—with no cow.

"Are we ready?"

Everyone spread out a ways.

"What about light?" Aubry asked. "After?"

"You'll see," Leo replied. "Now tuck your head between your legs and kiss your ass good-bye!"

Aubry was trying to figure out if he meant this literally when Leo squeezed the activation sacs. The entire world *lurched*.

Aubry was immediately and forcefully thrown backwards, very hard. She smashed into a clump of tendrils. She was pressed against them. They stretched, stretched, then gave.

Back again, into another thick rope of them. She couldn't keep her legs held tight, couldn't *do* anything, the force pushing her back was so strong. The rope gave.

She smashed into another clump, and another. Every time she hit, she felt as if her teeth might jar out of their sockets. She was sure she felt the fluid in her eyeballs sloshing up against her retinas. There was a reddish light that must have come from this pressure, for it was not completely dark in the transmitter.

Another clump.

Splat!

Another. She felt herself near to blacking out, fought it. But that wouldn't work. She couldn't help it if all the blood in her body was rushing in one direction only, like a tide coming in. Goo, falling, goo, goo, goo.

And then she slammed into the back wall, felt herself sink into its pulpy mass. But the pressure was lessening. She was no longer in any danger of blacking out. That is, if she could breathe!

She forced air out of her mouth, sucked in. It worked. She did it again, and again, fighting for each breath. But she could breathe! And suddenly, all the fear left her, and she began to get into this wild ride. It was fun, and nobody she knew—not *one* of the kids at school—had ever done anything like this before.

Then, quickly, the pressure subsided and Aubry was floating in free fall. If the sticky pulp hadn't held her to it, she thought she might go flying about if she moved.

"We've reached maximum acceleration!" she heard Leo call out. "It's all speed now!"

And Aubry could see. The red had not been within her eyes—or within her eyes alone. Falling through the mass seemed to have activated some luminescence mechanism in the pulp. The entire transmitter pod glowed with a low red-orange light, exactly as if they were inside a Halloween pumpkin. But a pumpkin from which the goo hadn't been removed.

Leo maneuvered over to her, floating in the air. "Is everyone all right?" he asked.

"I'm here," said Jill. "Wherever here is."

"Hair of the dog that bit you!" yelled Tod. "Slice an apple and out comes a worm!"

"By the way, Leo," Aubry said. "How do we stop?"

"Same as we started, only backwards," answered Leo. "But we have a ways to go yet."

Nine

They met in the virtuality, in a construct of an oceangoing ship deck sailing under a fine blue morning sky and upon a calm sea. The two men met, shook hands, and took seats forward, where a cooling breeze was blowing. A white-jacketed attendant got them refreshment: ice tea for Tacitus, water for Sherman. Tacitus lit a cigar and offered one to Sherman, who declined. He quickly got to the point of the meeting.

"What I want to know," Sherman said, "is how the cloudships stand."

Tacitus chuckled and examined his cigar to be sure it was evenly burning. He appeared in the virtuality as a man of medium build, somewhere in his late sixties or early seventies, with long gray hair that fell to his shoulders. He wore a simple gray-brown robe of a stiff material. Sherman wondered if this convert avatar bore any real resemblance to what Tacitus had looked like when he'd been only a bodily human being.

"The cloudships can be a pretty inbred and petty lot," Tacitus said. "They have a rather complicated social order set up out there among the Oorts. It's anarchy, and at the same time, it's pure incestuous self-involvement with one another."

"Do they even know there's a war going on?"

"Oh, trade has been disrupted. They are aware of it in a

general way." Tacitus took a sip of his tea and a puff of his smoke. "But they think it can't come to them personally. They figure they're too powerful for Amés to attack."

"From what I understand of them, they may be right about that," said Sherman sourly. "I suppose they could remain neutral."

"Now think about that a moment," Tacitus said. "You've been making energy here around Neptune for nearly ten years now. Saturn and Jupiter have been selling themselves to the Met as building material. Uranus . . . well, Uranus is kind of a backwater still. But my point is: *Where* do the proceeds from all this go? Into the bank. And who is the bank in the outer system?"

"The cloudships, of course," said Sherman. "There's nothing like a safe in interstellar space if you want security, and there's nothing like a traveling entrepreneur who gets around the entire system if you want investment."

"Exactly," Tacitus replied. "The cloudships are in direct economic competition with the Met. The market on Ganymede is just a front for a cloudship consortium. Everybody knows it if they think about it. That's who the ultimate enemy *is* in this war, and Amés knows it, I can assure you. I'm not so sure that my peers are completely aware of the fact yet. In fact, there's talk of reaching a separate peace with him."

"That's what I'm afraid of," said Sherman.

"A few of my friends and I have been stirring up sentiment against such a thing," Tacitus continued. He chewed his cigar for a moment, then stood up and faced Sherman, his back to the sea. "While I've got you here, I wanted to run a little idea past you, to tell the truth."

"What would that be?"

"I believe that the only way to oppose Amés's political attempt to divide the outer system successfully is for us to get together in a way we never have before."

"We are together. The old Republic is still the government I answer to."

"Colonel Sherman, you know as well as I do that the Republic never did exist in the outer system. The Federal Republic is just a name that the several local governments use to justify their actions and defy the edicts from the Met that don't suit them."

Sherman drank half his glass of water. It was still cold even though it had been sitting out in the "sun." "What do you suggest then, Tacitus?"

"A new outer-system government that formally renounces all ties with the Met. The Federal Army would become the army of this republic—or whatever we decide upon as a form of government. We would hold elections, I suppose, make laws. We would unify those opposed to Amés and give him a real fight instead of a bunch of half-assed last stands . . . no offense—"

"None taken," said Sherman. "And I agree. But how can it be brought about?"

"There's the rub," said Tacitus, and took his seat in the deck chair once again. He considered the ash on his cigar tip, now in danger of falling off at any moment. He neglected to flick it away, however, and took another pull. The ash fell into his lap. He didn't seem to notice. "I suppose we can start where such things always start: with the few, the proud, et ceteras, doing the spadework."

"What I really need at the moment," said Sherman, feeling distracted by the thought of all the politics that might lie ahead for him, "is a navy."

"That might be easier than you think to acquire," said Tacitus. "I have a few students back in the Oorts who are itching for a big adventure."

"Students?"

"I'm a history teacher by trade, of course," the old man declared serenely. "We cloudships have our university for our young."

"Yes," said Sherman. "You would."

"It is not snobbery, it is just that our young grow up in such different stages from a regular biological child. But my students are the equivalent of college age—each is about twenty-five years old—and they have full freedom to join whatever foolhardy venture presents itself. Serving in our new republic's navy might be one of these ventures."

"When can you have them here?"

Tacitus laughed. "In good time," he said. "In good time."

Sherman drained the remainder of his water and set the glass down beside him on the deck. The porter immediately appeared and took it away. "All right," Sherman said. "What is your proposed plan of action?"

"Now we're talking!" said the old man. "A plan of action! Just the thing."

"Well, what is it?"

"I go back to the Oorts to drum up support, and maybe come back with a few ships, or at least send them your way. If I'm right, it won't be long before this blockade begins to take its toll on the cloudships. Ships are being turned away from Jupiter, access to Met energy is being cut off. Amés wants to blackmail the ships into signing a separate peace and staying out of the fighting, but it's pretty clear that his intentions are to take everything eventually."

"That's my assessment," said Sherman. "What we have here is the economy of the Met versus the emerging economy of the cloudships and the outer system. We have taxation issues that come down to issues of freedom to submit or not submit to an authority whose legitimacy is unacceptable. And we have free-convert rights." Sherman touched his beard. Tacitus had thoughtfully filled it in for him, here in this location in the virtuality. "And we have Amés."

"Who wants what all dictators have always wanted," said Tacitus. "He wants to rule the universe."

"Is there anything I'm missing?"

"It is just this," Tacitus said, stubbing out his cigar on the deck rail. "I believe that what we are really fighting over is the question of what the next stage of human evolution will be. Free-convert rights and Amés's ambition are inalterably opposed. It is a fight of unity versus plurality. Will humanity go forward as a 'one' or as a 'many'? Technology has made it possible for the human race to unify into one mind. It was only a matter of time before an Amés came along and seized this opportunity. But what I believe is that humanity is better served by a division of thoughts and thinkers. The individual, however strangely transformed, has not been transcended. I admit that sometimes my evidence for this conclusion is a little shaky, but nonetheless, I cling to it. Because the alternative is that the temporarily strong will exercise eternal tyranny over the temporarily down-on-their-luck. And who is to say if we won't one day need for our very survival those traits we consider weak or recessive at the moment? One look at history will show that the dominant and recessive are continually trading places according to the needs of the moment, and our perceptions about what is the greatest and what are lesser virtues changes just as radically. Amés is going to try to absorb every mind in the Met into his own. That is, I believe, his ultimate aim."

"Will he really go that far, though?" said Sherman.

"He *can*," Tacitus replied. "The technology is there. And he is the sort of man who takes everything he can get his hands on. I have a bit of material on his childhood that might serve to support this contention."

"You have found something out about Amés's childhood?"

"The world is a library," Tacitus replied. "It's just a matter of figuring out the filing system."

"And you think free converts are the ultimate threat to Amés?"

"They represent the proliferation of the individual. Can you imagine what would happen if the copying safeguards were taken off, if the combinatoric edicts were lifted? Do you have any idea how many individuals the merci could sustain?"

"Hundreds of billions, I suppose," Sherman said.

"There is no limit," Tacitus said, "with time-sharing of grist, there could be more individuals than there are atoms in the solar system. And if we expand . . . there is an infinite possibility."

"Can that be good?"

"Amés does not think so. He is convinced that the opposite is true."

"What do you think?"

The steward walked by, and Tacitus hooked another cigar from him. "And please bring me a brandy," he told the fellow. Sherman waited patiently for Tacitus to light up. He took two great puffs, then looked down at his cigar, twisting it between his fingers. "I think," he said, "that *I* like very much being my own man."

"As do I," said Sherman.

"It is an existential question that each must answer for himself. Should I go on living? Should I have children? What right does anyone have to tell us what to do in these matters? Individuals acting individually arrive at the best solution for the whole group." Two more puffs. The white smoke blew out to sea. "Of course, I will defend to the death your right to hold the opposite opinion," he said. "But I believe that the fight we have entered into is a fight for our very *minds*. I think Amés means to have them. It is the last test for democracy. Is this the system of government we will take to the stars, or is Amés's way the better one?"

Sherman stood up and gazed out across the virtual sea. "Well, you had better go and get me a government, then," he said, "so I can be a soldier of the people. Otherwise, everybody's going to get mighty tired of dying just because I ask them to. I lack Amés's charisma."

Tacitus smiled benignly. His brandy came, and he took it to the rail to stand by Sherman. "The Mediterranean," he said. "I used to live in Italy when I was doing studies on the Renaissance."

"So you are one of the original cloudships?" said Sherman.

"I'm an original."

"That would put you at five hundred e-years, at least."

"Oh, I'm older than that. I was one of the lucky ones in the first half of the millennium that the primitive rejuvenation methods worked on."

"So how old are you?" said Sherman. "If you don't mind my asking."

"Old enough to know how to keep a secret," Tacitus answered. "And when to tell it." He went back to smoking his cigar. Suddenly, two bells rang on the ship. The steward appeared and made a deep bow.

"Begging your pardon, gentlemen," he said. "We are shortly expecting company."

"What the hell?" said Sherman, but Tacitus put a steady hand his shoulder.

"Not to worry, Colonel, not to worry," he said. "They are friends. Allies. Refugees from the fall of Titan." He pointed toward the rear and two men, one short and muscled, the other tall and thin, walked toward them.

"We're looking for Colonel Roger Sherman," said the taller one. "We were told we might find him here."

"I am he," Sherman said.

"Good, good," the tall man continued. "I am Gerardo Funk. This is Thomas Ogawa, my partner. We're both late of Titan. Brought along five hundred of our brightest minds and a little fleet of merchant ships. We're looking for refuge, or at least a place we can stop over before we head on."

Sherman looked the two men over. "We've had a rough time of it ourselves," he said, "but I believe we can take you in."

"We'll work for our keep, Colonel," Ogawa said. "We're not asking for handouts."

Tacitus smiled. "The government seems to be forming itself," he said. "Welcome aboard."

Ten

They were on Pluto.

Charon hung in the sky. It always did, taking the same amount of time to orbit Pluto as Pluto did to turn on its axis—about six and a half e-days. Much of Pluto's surface was covered with grist, and the two men could walk along in a virtual re-creation as if they were two ghosts, traveling across its wasteland. Pluto was mostly ice water in the dark band around the equator, methane at the poles, exotics mixed throughout. Sublimation was constant, and drifts of vapors wafted about. It really was *"where the stones go to die,"* as Beat Myers had described it five hundred e-years before.

Alas, poor Myers, C thought. I knew him, Horatio.

"We have the planet and the moon," Amés said. He was beside C, using the icon of the sun. "It was a pushover, really. The *Streichhöltzer* showed up in the sky, and the locals promptly surrendered. Well, a few radical elements made trouble, but we subverted all the grist on the planet. Imagine—the very land rising up against you and swallowing you up."

"Not a pretty picture," C replied.

"You think not?" Amés said. "There was a beauty to it."

They were instantly in Day, the port city. Gangs of local workers, space-adapted, were unloading transport craft recently descended from the *Streichhöltzer*. There were barrels and barrels of military grist.

"This will be a supply depot," Amés said. "For when we strike the Oorts. We can also use it for operations against Neptune."

"A nasty business that," said C, and immediately wished he hadn't. Amés was known, at times, to kill the messenger. But he was merely irritated at the moment by C's words.

"Yes," he said. "We'll get to that later."

They were in Pluto staff HQ, now inhabiting bodies in the virtuality. Amés elected to allow them to be noticed and General Blanket immediately shunted over to the virtuality to greet them.

"Director Amés," said Blanket. "This is a surprise." He was Asian, with jet-black hair worn severely cropped.

But you've neglected to give your eyebrows a crew cut, C thought. They were thick and unkempt, and the effect was not pleasing.

"Surprise," said Amés. "Now tell me about your security arrangements."

Blanket pretended to look down at a readout on his virtual desk. Amés waited patiently for the man to collect his thoughts. "I've released three thousand soldiers into the grist," he said. "They've got the local free converts well in hand. There will be no shield code foul-ups."

He's talking about Saturn, thought C, and Haysay's blunder on Titan.

"Good, good," said Amés. "Are those soldiers interleaved?"

"Yes, sir. I've got a controlling a.i. right here in my headquarters time-sharing between them. Nobody takes a shit without his say-so."

"And that a.i. would be?"

"Me, sir. One of my converts."

"Excellent, Blanket."

"The *Streichhöltzer*'s in an ellipse around the planet and the moon. I've established constant *Sciatica* patrols. The *Slong* is sharing the carrier's orbit at the opposite side. We're laying mines and establishing a safe harbor for the fleet."

"Anything else?" said Amés. "What about the local populace?"

"They have graciously volunteered to turn all product sectors to the war effort," Blanket replied. He smiled, and his eyebrows formed into small arches, like hanging masses of creeper vines.

Amés turned to C. "Suggestions?"

"There's a woman here I once knew," said C. "Her name is Shanigan Moth. Best grist hacker I ever met, and I happen to know she'll sell her services to the highest bidder."

"Moth, you say—" Blanket again examined his desk readout. He looked up with drooping eyebrows of doom. "She's, er, dead. Killed in the first wave."

"I thought you said they surrendered without a fight," replied C softly.

"They did," Blanket replied. "But we had already sent in an advance team, so I had them . . . show our stuff a bit. Let the locals understand who they were dealing with."

I guess you showed them, C thought, but all he said was, "Pity."

"Is that all?" Amés said to C.

"I'll give the matter more thought, but for the moment, yes," said C.

"Director," Blanket said timidly.

"Yes."

"We were preparing something for your visit, sir. If we'd had more notice, there would be more ceremony—that is, a better presentation and—"

"What are you talking about, Blanket?"

"The soldiers, sir. They want to give you something—a token of their respect and admiration, as it were."

Amés frowned at Blanket, and the general seemed to shrink. "A medal?" he said, and sighed.

"Well, er, yes."

Amés stood, considering. "No," he finally said. "Get your presentation ceremony in order first." He gave Blanket one of his wicked smiles. C thought he heard the general give a little gasp. "And make it big," Amés continued. "Make it the biggest occasion this rock has ever seen. Do a merci broadcast, too. And Blanket—"

"Yes, sir?"

"Not a medal. I want the *planet*. Give me Pluto on a pendant. Get somebody in Prop to design it."

Now Blanket was smiling, feeling that he was in on something. Don't feel that way around Amés, C thought. Don't ever feel that way. But C remained silent.

"Yes, Director, right away!"

"Good," said Amés. He looked around at nothing in particular. "It is good." He motioned to C. "Let's get on with our trip."

On Titan, General Haysay was unaccountably having a cold pack applied to his back. It seemed that he had somehow gotten an ache *in the virtuality*. When C and Amés appeared, he stood up abruptly, upsetting his attendant, who fell upon her butt. C went and helped her to her feet and she and Haysay saluted Amés.

Amés ran Haysay through the general's security arrangements as he had done with Blanket, and Haysay stammered his way to the end of the questions. During the process, C appeared to be staring at a spot on the floor of Haysay's virtual office, but what he was actually doing was spreading out through the grist, feeling, seeking . . . there was something. Definitely something.

"I smell free converts," C abruptly said, totally discombobulating the general.

"That's impossible, sir," Haysay said, after gathering himself.

C smiled thinly at him. "The impossible," he said, "is inconceivable."

"Director, who is this man?" Haysay had gone from confused to fuming.

Amés chuckled. "He works for us," he said. "Don't worry."

"There are no unaccounted-for free converts in this planet-moon system," Haysay said, and glared at C. "Whoever he thinks he is."

"It is merely an opinion," said C. It was at times like this that he dearly missed smoking.

Amés rounded on Haysay. "I want the grist hereabouts scrubbed from top to bottom," he said.

"But Director, the resources involved . . ."

"Use them. All of them," said Amés sharply. "Do it now!"

"Yes, Director." Haysay remained standing before them. Amés put one of his palms to his forehead.

"General Haysay . . . *now!*"

Haysay started to attention. "Yes, sir!" he called out to the air. He clicked his heels together and was gone from the virtuality, leaving behind a frightened attendant, who quickly followed.

"What do you mean you 'smelled' it?" Amés asked.

"It is," said C, "a kind of drug they sometimes use. Not a drug, really. A subroutine enhancer called Shelly's Choice. It operates on a pseudorandom sideband, and anything pseudorandom leaves traces in the grist. Information. I smell information. It is what I do."

Amés looked at C as if he were some strange creature dredged up from the bottom of an ocean. "You have Uranus well in hand?" he said.

"As long as the Department of Immunity will allow me to run our government there."

"I will see to it. Let's go to Jupiter."

They were among the ships of the blockade.

So this is where most of the DIED navy is, C thought.

"We've got them surrounded," Amés said. There was satisfaction in his voice.

They were five million miles out, existing in grist that had attached itself to the charged particles that clumped at the outer edge of Jupiter's magnetic field. With their enhanced vision, they had a splendid view of the planet and the moons. All was, indeed, surrounded.

"The merci is partially jammed," Amés said. "Ganymede is totally cut off. All cloudships are being turned away, and anything else in the sky is being seized and impounded. We own the skies."

"Why don't you go ahead and take it, then?" C asked. Again, he wished he could retract his words. Amés didn't pay him to ask stupid questions. Amés didn't pay him at all, as a matter of fact, as C had found when he went to rent an apartment on Mercury.

C solved the problem by never sleeping.

"Because, dear C," Amés replied—that is, the burning sun icon replied, "most of the Federal Army is stationed on those moons. After I kicked them out of the Met, they have scrounged together a living by serving as the security force for the Ganymedean banks and countinghouses. They are an army in name only. What they really are is a paid mercenary force for outer-system robber barons."

"Of course," C responded.

"There are a good two million troops down there."

"A challenge," said C.

"I'll starve them," Amés said. "And then they'll surrender, or I'll kill them."

They were in Zebra 333's Situation Room aboard the *Schwarzes Floß*. Zebra 333, a free convert—well, no, he wasn't exactly that—stood up and took a bow. He had the body of man and the head of a great Rocky Mountain bighorn sheep, complete with underturned horns instead of hair. In the virtuality, you could appear as you wished. And Zebra 333 was *always* in the virtuality. He lived and breathed it.

C knew that he had an aspect portion that he had put into storage nearly a century ago. Otherwise, Zebra 333 was a LAP who existed entirely in the virtuality. Most LAPs could not do so and retain their top level of acuity indefinitely. Somehow, Zebra 333 was an exception. The one-of-a-kind freak mentality who could thrive as a grossly multiple personality with no biology to keep his megalomania in check. He was, perhaps, Amés's principal rival in that regard, and C sometimes wondered why the Director kept the LAP around.

"I've been expecting you both," Zebra 333 said. "Welcome."

"Thank you," said Amés. C nodded politely.

"We have them cut off," began the admiral without pre-amble. "We've sent down infiltration grist, with orders to stand by. I've worked out a way to alternate the jammer's positioning so that we get more coverage. At some point during every e-day, everyone gets jammed for at least an hour."

"Very good," said Amés. "And the head is very nice this time. Fearsome."

"Thank you, Director."

"What about propaganda?"

"We're hitting them on all fronts. I've got some Uranus turncoats doing a merci show especially for Ganymede, telling them all about the wonders of the New Hierarchy. It should be particularly effective there, since Jupiter would, necessarily, be at the top of the proposed caste system."

"Perhaps," said Amés. "But not necessarily."

"We are also proceeding on the calibrations that the *Lion of Africa* will use—" Zebra 333 broke off his speech and looked at C. The small sheep eyes revealed nothing.

"He is cleared," Amés said.

"As I was saying," Zebra 333 continued, "the calibrations the *Lion of Africa* will use for the earthquake induction on Ganymede and the proposed melting of Europa's crust."

"We're going to hit Ganymede with an earthquake?" C said. This was, indeed, news to him.

"Ganymede has plate tectonics."

"How convenient," said C.

"Suggestion?" Amés said to C.

"None. Except for continuing with the eavesdropping measures that I already have in place, and of which, I pre-sume, the admiral is aware—"

Zebra 333 nodded his great head.

"—I don't see any new points to make. I would like to ask the admiral if modifications have been made to the grist after the subversion successes on Titan."

"They have."

"I presumed as much," replied C evenly. "And measures are in place to detain free converts?"

"I will treat them as I would my own children," the admiral answered. C knew that Zebra 333 didn't have any children.

"Well," said Amés, "fine job, as usual, Admiral. I will leave you to your work."

They were on a ship a long way from Neptune, hanging in space above the ecliptic. It was the *Montserrat*.

"Shh," said Amés. "Let's listen."

They were observing Carmen San Filieu's private quarters, and the admiral was at her meal. She was sharing a paella—a rice-and-seafood dish—with her senior officers: Bruc, Philately, and their adjutants. San Filieu reached over and took a half a tomato, smeared its meat into a slice of bread, then poured a generous amount of olive oil on it.

"What I want," she said before taking a bite, "is intelligence from the moons."

"But Admiral," said Captain Philately. "The merci jamming works both ways. Nothing gets in, but we can't extract information out."

"Can't we find some sideband that the jamming doesn't affect?"

"Admiral, so long as that jamming apparatus is a black box that we Fleet regulars can't touch or have a look inside, there is nothing we can do. I have no idea how the technology works, after all—and neither do my technicians."

"Very well. You have a point, Captain," said San Filieu. "But there has to be another way. Can't we get somebody down there? Perhaps disguise them. Have them report back to us electromagnetically?"

"It seems a difficult thing," Philately answered. "I doubt very much if a drop ship would go undetected, and we know for a fact that they are monitoring the e-m spectrum."

"Well, all right, I concede the point, but—come, Philately—surely you have some suggestions?"

"None that might stand a chance of succeeding, Admiral," said Philately. She took a bite of her paella as if to give herself a chance to remain quiet.

"Bruc, what about you?" San Filieu, following Philately's suggestion, bit into her tomato-soaked bread.

"We've got all our remote sensing apparatus trained on them, Admiral," said Bruc. "That can be very effective."

"But I want to know what they're saying. What they're *thinking*. Telescopes and the like can't tell us that."

"No, ma'am."

"If they only knew," Amés said to C, "what we know."

"Perhaps we should tell them," C said.

"No," said Amés. "All in good time. It is a need-to-know technology, and they do not, as yet, have a need to know."

"Fine, then," said San Filieu, and shook her head ruefully at her captains. "What progress have we made on the bioplague front?"

"There I have good news to report to you, Admiral," said Philately. "Our analysis of the grist strand shows that it is a very simple construction. Give me another day or so and I'll have it cracked and reverse-engineered. I could do it faster, but my main grist techs were lost on the *Dabna*."

"Then find a consultant on the merci, for God's sake," said San Filieu.

"I have done that, Admiral," Philately replied, a bit woodenly, C thought. "But those aboard my ship, the *Dabna*, were the best in the fleet in my opinion, ma'am, and they are sorely missed."

"Yes, yes, but we have to get on with things," San Filieu said. "Are you going to take that shrimp?"

"No, Admiral."

"More for me," San Filieu replied, and reached over and snagged the morsel.

Amés grinned. "San Filieu is a fighter," he said. "You should see her go at it in New Catalonia."

"Your daily soap opera?"

"It's far better than anything on the merci, let me assure you. She destroyed a man the other day without blinking an eye."

"I'll take your word for it, Director."

"Now, suggestions?"

"I'm looking into the situation," C said. "It is my belief that Thaddeus Kaye is now on Triton. As you know, I believe his apprehension to be crucial to the war effort, Director. Vital."

"Yes, and I agree with you," Amés said. "Remember, I had something to do with his creation."

Yes, C thought. You were passed over for him in the selection process. And there can be only one of his kind made.

This thought, especially, remained unvoiced.

"One other thing," said C. "Another name keeps popping up. A man named Sherman."

"He's the one who wrote me that nasty note?"

"The very one."

"Look into it," Amés said. "Let's go back to Mercury."

They were in La Mola once again. C stretched out and felt himself in his own body. Well, *a* body.

Amés got up from his desk and went to the window. He surveyed his domain. "Let us discuss the Met," he said, his back to C.

"We are bringing the LAPs under your control, shutting them down from the outside in," said C. "In an e-month, maybe two, you can begin integrating them. The free converts will take a little longer, depending upon the experiments that the DICD are running."

"I wish you would supervise them," said Amés. "I could make you."

"My talents are best applied elsewhere, as you know, Director. I have no desire to become enmeshed in the Department of Immunity bureaucracy, and I find the concentration camp they are running on Mars . . . distasteful."

"But necessary," said Amés, still not turning toward C.

"I will not argue the point," said C.

"How long until there can be full convert integration, both of free converts and convert portions of regular persons?"

"The time line is uncertain. It depends upon what we learn while working with the free converts," C said. "It may take years."

"Then the war will have to last for years," Amés said. "I hope I don't win too soon."

"If we can keep the cloudships out of it, your quick triumph may become a problem to you," said C. His wit seemed to be lost on Amés. Just as well.

Amés put a hand to his window. He held it there for a moment, then drew it away, leaving the print of it on the glass. The big thumbs. The long fingers.

"I want it all, C," the Director said. "Inside and out." He sighed. "I have such plans. It's like a symphony. No one has ever played the human race before. I will do so, and I will make such music as the universe has never heard before. It will be a new creation. Mine."

Amés's hand formed into a fist at his side. "I will play them," he said, "so beautifully."

The expression on C's face did not change, but inside, his gut knotted. He had heard such ideas before—perhaps expressed slightly differently, but with the same import. He had heard them from his father, for instance. And all the other tinplate dictators. C thought it best not to remind Amés that he was a composer and not a concert pianist.

"We have, too, the partisan problem," C said, after a suitable pause.

"How did Operation German Death go?"

"We killed most of Tod's followers," C replied. "We did it quickly, but I saw that an appropriate display was made. The time tower escaped, however. The DI sweeper task force was blown to bits shortly after the Friends of Tod were executed, and then another was taken out shortly thereafter. The two incidents are certainly related. The DI is looking into two names I passed along to them. One Aubry Graytor and a Leo Y. Sherman."

"Any relation to our Triton Sherman?"

"He is the man's son."

At that, Amés did turn around. "Really?" he said. "How interesting. What do you suppose it means?"

"I am looking into the matter," C said. "They are estranged. It may all be a coincidence."

"That hardly seems likely," said Amés. "But even if it's

true, we may very well have a use for this Leo Y. Sherman. See that he is captured."

"I will instruct the Department of Immunity to do so."

"No," said Amés. "This is one that I want you on personally."

Eleven

Theory had pickled himself more effectively than he'd ever imagined was possible, of that he was sure. He sorely wanted Quench's advice in the matter.

Theory took Quench's body home. After the two men traded places again, Theory was about to bring up the events of the evening, but discovered that Quench had gotten into a subroutine house that was only quasi-legal. In that place, known as the Fork, he had attached a rider program to his convert portion that had him caught in a perpetual loop. The effect was a rush not unlike riding a roller coaster again and again. Quench was too giddy to extract himself from the subroutine, and Theory had to do it for him. This caused Quench, aspect and convert, to drop off to sleep almost immediately.

But before falling into unconsciousness, he had murmured, "And they only let free converts into the Fork and they passed me right through. Bouncers didn't even give me a second glance."

"Go to sleep, John."

"You owe me a hundred greenleaves . . . a hundred . . . don't you try and back out, either . . ."

"I won't," said Theory, but by that time Quench was dead to the world, and Theory had retired to his private space in the virtuality to process and file the day, the free-convert equivalent of dreaming.

*　　*　　*

The virtuality had, in fact, eleven dimensions, with three of those dimensions collapsed upon themselves in a Kaluga-Klein transformation—but this was something only free converts ever thought about.

Every local region in the grist matrix had a ghost town. On Triton, for obscure reasons, the local place of ghosts was known as Shepardsville. And it was in Shepardsville that the grist invader was hiding.

To get to Shepardsville, you must first undo the effects of "compactification" of the three drop dimensions among the virtuality's eleven. These three dimensions were "smaller" than the other eight in that the information-theory laws that define them were not as complex as those that make up the other eight dimensions. Going to Shepardsville was somewhat like the experience Alice had when she ate the side of the mushroom that made her smaller.

Shepardsville smelled of smoking coals, witches' brew, and a complex mixture of incenses from every culture that had ever burnt the stuff. It was sickening, and at the same time, intoxicating. A free convert had to take measures against the smell, or he might become trapped, wandering about in a mental haze of illusion and foreboding, and never be able to find his way back out.

The call came early in the morning after the dance that Theory's search programs had hit pay dirt. Theory took with him stalwart Monitor from the weather station and twenty-two other free-convert soldiers of the Third Sky and Light for the intercept. They tried not to create too much disturbance as they marched through the "streets" of Shepardsville, following the homing probe subroutine that had pinpointed their culprit. Theory had ordered camouflage uniforms, which consisted of a coating of innocuous data. These wouldn't fool anyone up close, but at a distance, they had proved effective. Theory allowed himself to see nothing at first, but gradually the "smells" congealed and formed images about him, and Shepardsville laid itself out around him as a vast, seething ruin, half-alive, half in the ultimate state of decay.

They found the lair of the invader represented as a smoking hole in a brick wall with vile emissions of noxious gas billowing from it.

Theory turned to Major Monitor. "I'm taking half the soldiers and going in. We'll drive her out, and you gun her down."

Monitor nodded and looked down at his hands. A sub-machine gun materialized. It was not, of course, a rifle, but an "h-weapon," an uncertainty collapsing function. The h was for Heisenberg. The h-rifle made it logically impossible for the affected entity to carry information. It died. Just as if it had been hit with a bullet to the brain.

Theory armed himself with an h-pistol. He had always formed his in the shape of an old Colt service revolver from the American Civil War. But he gave it eleven shots, each with a different dimensional orientation.

Theory pulled a bandanna over his nose and led his eleven men into the stink hole. The passage down was mazelike, and Theory assigned a detail to mark their way so that they could get out without getting lost. The deeper he got into the maze, the greater the stench. Finally, he rounded a corner—and there she was.

Oh yes, it was *her,* all right. He had suspected as much.

His actions of the night before, deceiving Jennifer Fieldguide. The kiss.

It had all been a way of avoiding thinking about what had been.

About the woman who broke his heart with her cold logic.

"Hello, Theory," she said. "I was wondering when you'd show up."

"Hello, Constants," Theory replied. "I had a feeling it was you they sent."

Constants looked the same as when she and Theory had been lovers, back in OCS. Someone had taken Occam's razor to her programming, and she was a sleek sight to behold. Jet-black hair and skin, with white markings that emphasized the fine curves of her body.

Theory went for his pistol.

"Uh-uh," said Constants. "Look before you leap."

Theory looked. There, standing in front of Constants, his skin a matte black, was a little boy. He was almost hidden against the background of Constants's lower torso. In Constants's right hand was a scythe, and she had it to the convert child's throat.

"Theory," said Constants, "I'd like to introduce you to your son."

Twelve

from
**First Constitutional Congress of
the Cloudships of the Outer System**
April 2, 3013 (e-standard)
a transcript

C. Lebedev: To continue, then, Mr. Chairman . . . freedom . . . serve another without . . . ah, here we are. All
thinking entities are people. Not only do we, as a people, affirm this freedom of thought, we are also inalterably and
unconditionally opposed to those who would deny it to us.
We declare our right as a government of the people to fight
and defend ourselves, to educate our young in the principles of freedom, and to establish conditions of justice and
security within our society that ensure the continuation
and propagation of our freedom. Thinking must be protected and nourished. It is what defines us as a species,
whatever form its particular instantiation may take, be it
biological, physical, or by some other means as yet to be
discovered or defined. Thinking precedes both existence
and essence, and plurality is inextricably bound to its nature. The one has no meaning without the many. It is requisite upon our republican democracy to preserve and
protect the plurality, as well as the freedom, of thought.
They are the same. Any law or entity that arrogates the
right to oppose plurality we find abominable, and we will
oppose it as a people with all our hearts, minds, and
strength. Any thinking individual, no matter how mis-

guided or mistaken, shall have the right to think and express his, her, or its thoughts so long as that expression does not take the form of coercion. These are the principles upon which our government shall be based, and we, the people, do hereby establish them by the means that follow ... er, that's it. The next part is Section Two, Mr. Chairman.

C. Mencken: Very well. Chair recognizes Cloudship Ahab.

C. Ahab: Mr. Chairman and honorable ships, I have seen this document in its entirety, and I must say to you that it is gravely flawed.

C. Mencken: Please confine yourself to discussion of the preamble, Cloudship Ahab.

C. Ahab: I shall, Mr. Chairman. Gravely flawed, I say, beginning with this so-called preamble. Right of anybody to think anything they damned well please? Why, the very thing contradicts itself. If anyone can think anything, then how the hell could these so-called "framers" know that freedom *is* the basic principle? In this life, it is the forceful who are above the weak, the strong-minded are over the meek. You may not like it, but there it is. Where in this document is there one word about *character*? About will? No, sir, I do not find it! What the people need is strong medicine, not this weak tonic, this sop and placebo. We may not like the inner system, but there is a strong mind there, and we must respect that strength. As a matter of fact, we should not be debating whether or not to oppose that mind, but how we might join with it in common cause, for the betterment of the species. The strong must lead the weak. This is the law of survival to which we should bow—to which we must bow. Survival of the fittest. And the truth—however unpalatable it may be to minds of a narrower perspective—is that *we* and Amés are the strongest. It is only a matter of time until we win in the war for survival, which is above all other wars, and from which we cannot escape. Thank you, Mr. Chairman.

C. Mencken: All right. What? Yes, er . . . the chair recognizes Cloudship Mark Twain.

C. Mark Twain: Well, Ahab has a pretty good point there, but I'm not so sure it is the one he intended to make. Now consider this survival of the fittest thing for a moment. If we take that as a given, then what in the world makes him think that we might band with another in common cause? Either we're inalterably at one another's throats, or we're not, according to Old Ahab's logic.

C. Ahab: Who are you calling old?

C. Mark Twain: I believe that you and I started out in the asteroid belt together, old boy. Used to be friends, as I re-call, until you started taking yourself so goddamn seriously. I got a right to calling you old if I call myself the same, and I assure you, sir, I am ancient!

C. Ahab: Mr. Chairman!

C. Mencken: Please confine yourself to the matter under consideration, Cloudship Mark Twain. And that is not ei-ther your age or Ahab's. Believe me, you're both a couple of young cubs to me.

C. Mark Twain: Thank you for the compliment, Mr. Chair-man, and I will do as you say. Now, it seems to me that by the good Cloudship Ahab's logic, it's all a big fight to see who is the biggest dog, and it's going to come down to us and Amés in the end scrapping it out until one or the other of us gets hold of a throat and bites. In that case, we might consider that a pack can bring down the feistiest lone wolf. If I were Ahab, I would consider getting together all those weaker dogs and ganging up on the other big dog, then, when he's all through and done for, why then I'd take out the littler dogs one by one. That, it seems to me, is where this survival of the fittest nonsense should lead us. But take a look at nature. It's full of competition, certainly, but there is also a fair degree of cooperation, as well. Back when I was a biological human, I was mighty glad that my mitochondria cooperated with my DNA, for example, though the two of them started out as separate creatures. But that is enough for that line of argument, my friends and neighbors, for we are human beings, and we have moved beyond and above mere survival. Surviving is just *one* of the things we do. Maybe old survival itself saw its own limitations, so it bred itself a better alternative. At least that's what I think on my good days. Let us make this a good day, friends, and vote to adopt this preamble.

Chamber Left: Hear, hear!

C. Mencken: Thank you, Cloudship Mark Twain. Chair recognizes Cloudship al-Farghani.

Thirteen

Leo knew the kid must be bored and scared at the same time, and she was still feeling acute, unconscious pangs of separation from her family, if he was reading the signs right. He wished there was more he could do for Aubry.

And now there was Jill—this amazing creature come out of the blue. She was a gorgeous thing—all shapely muscle and bone. Her hair was black, and her eyes were a dark blue, more like deep space than like Earth's sky. She had a spray of freckles across her nose and cheeks that almost might appear to be whiskers in some light.

And there was that little tremble to Jill, as if her heart were beating much faster than a normal human's, and that somewhere under her woman's skin the jill ferret lurked in its den, waiting until biting was needed.

"So, you're looking for somebody named Alethea."

"Somebody or something."

"Something? What do you mean?"

"I'm not sure. She used to be a woman, but now she's scattered."

"I don't follow."

"I don't know much more myself. But I'm going to find her."

"And that's what you're trying to do?"

"Find her and save her."

"Why?"

"I promised that I would."

"Where do you think she is, then?" said Leo. "Maybe I can help."

"That's why I saved you. Tod said he thought you could help."

"He told you that?"

"He wouldn't let me take him to safety after we fought our way out of the DI sweepers. He told me to go back and find the changeling girl and the leprechaun. That they would know the answer to the question I wanted answered."

"He did, did he?" Leo scratched his head. "I don't know any answers."

"Yes," said Jill. "I asked him about that afterward."

"What did he say?"

"He said he got the times mixed up."

"What?"

"That was all he said. 'Sorry, I got the times mixed up.' What do you suppose he meant by that?"

"Maybe I will know the answer to your question someday. In the future, I mean."

"Not much good for now."

"No, I suppose not."

"I need to find Alethea."

"But what is so important about this Alethea?"

"Something bad is happening. Something maybe worse than any fighting. The rats who are my friends—sometimes they tell a horrible story. About things in the grist that hunt them and catch them. Pull them out of their bodies. The ones that get caught are being taken somewhere. I think that someone is after all the algorithms that own themselves, and I think that someone is *Amés* or somebody who works for him. There are stories of a camp on Mars."

"Noctis Labyrinthus," said Leo.

"Yes. The rats tell me tales they have heard. Experiments are being done. Torture. Mass executions of everything smart that doesn't look like one of you Earth monkeys. I think Alethea may be there."

"That is a bad place."

"I have to get her out."

"I don't think even *you* can do that."

"Maybe not me," Jill said. She grinned her ferret smile. Her teeth *were* smaller and pointier than a normal woman's. "But maybe me and an army."

"Do you have an army?"

Jill didn't answer. Her grin became even more unsettling.

"I think Amés wants to be a lot more than Director," Leo said. "I think he wants to play every instrument in the orchestra, too. To tell you the truth, I'm sure he believes he can do it better than the rest of us. He doesn't want to rule the human race, he wants to *become* it. Own it. Like it was his body."

"I have seen animals act like Amés," Jill replied. "It is usually, I think, when they realize somehow, somewhere inside them, that they are going to die."

"Well, I'm an animal; I know that I'm going to die, and I don't want to rule all of creation," Leo said. Jill turned her eyes on him, and he could see them sparkling in the wan light. Talk about animals, Leo thought.

"You are a man," Jill said. "Amés is a boy."

"I suppose."

"You and I will see about that," she said. "I would like to make love to you."

"Wha . . . what?"

"Have sex." She scratched her head. "What is the word?"

"Fuck?" said Leo.

"Yes, fuck. But the other."

"Make love?"

"Yes."

"How old are you, Jill?"

"Older than you. Older than you think."

"You don't look it—"

"This body is two and a half e-years old, if that's what you mean."

"Two and a half? I don't understand."

"If you make love to me, I will explain."

"I . . . I would like you to explain." Leo was flabbergasted. He had never been so blatantly propositioned before.

"Maybe we should do it somewhere away from Aubry," Jill said.

"That's a damn good idea."

"Even though I really don't understand why."

"Well, maybe that's something I can explain to you one of these days," replied Leo. "Let's go that way."

Leo grasped a handful of fibers and pulled himself back into the jungle of the transmitter. Jill followed behind. After they had gone a good ways in, he felt a tug on his leg. Jill was pulling his boots off, using her hold on a particularly thick rope of fibers for resistance. She seemed to move very easily in zero gee. He undressed himself, tumbling around a couple of times like a sky diver in flight, and when he looked again at Jill, she was naked.

He reached for her hands and pulled her toward him, and as they came together, Jill became a ball of fury, grasping at him and kissing his neck and shoulders. She held tight about his waist. Leo had made love in free fall before, but never like this. Before, it had always been a languid affair, with both parties feeling a bit awkward, and careful that any movement did not send them careening about.

Jill was having none of that.

She bit him gently on the ear, and Leo felt himself growing hard against her torso. He grabbed her by the hair and pulled her up—not too forcefully, but strongly enough. He thrust his tongue into her mouth, and she sucked on it for all she was worth.

For a moment, they came apart, and were floating there, connected only by this French kiss.

Then Leo pulled them closer together and began turning her around, her head down, in relation to him. They fit together perfectly—Leo was barely taller than Jill—and with a slight bend of her waist, her mouth was to him, and she took him between her lips. Their motion translated into a spin, and soon they were doing a slow barrel roll as they pleased one another.

They did this for a time, then Leo felt Jill's muscles contract as she had an orgasm. She gasped, and he came out of her mouth.

"Are you all right?" he asked her. "I didn't—"

"What was that?" Jill whispered.

"What was what?"

"The way I just felt. What was that?"

For a moment, Leo had no idea what she was talking about, and then he realized that she had never experienced an orgasm before.

"Don't worry," he said. "It is perfectly natural. It's what I was trying to do to you."

"Well, you did it," Jill said. "Do it again."

And so he did. Finally, Leo knew he could take no more himself without coming. He gently pulled her back around to him, face-to-face. They kissed again, and Jill held tightly to him.

"Can I go inside you?" he asked.

"Yes," she said. "I think you had better."

There was a bit of fumbling, and Leo had to grab hold of a sticky tendril to keep himself still long enough so that he could find the right position. Then he did, and he slid inside her easily.

After that, all Leo could remember was images. Jill turned into the animal that he had suspected she still was inside. After a couple of his own thrusts, she moved herself up and down his body in a frenzy, clawing into his back to keep them from coming apart. Their motion set them moving through the dangling fibers, getting tangled among them as they went. After a while, they could not have separated if they wanted, so wrapped up were they in the pulp.

They returned quietly through the mass of fibers to join the others. They parted the last curtain to find Aubry wide-awake. But Aubry, intuitive kid that she was, said nothing. She couldn't resist giving them a little smile. Leo fell asleep, floating beside the others. He might have imagined it, but as he drifted off, he was sure he could smell a musky odor about him, clinging to his skin. A wild-animal smell that was also, somehow, the smell of home. He liked that. Leo hadn't had a real home for an awfully long time.

Fourteen

For several milliseconds, nary a function was completed by Major Theory's algorithm. Then he examined the logic of the statement, to see if it were possible.

It was.

Then he examined the psychology of his ex-lover to see if it were possible.

It was.

Theory lowered his pistol. "What is my son's name?" he asked.

"I haven't gotten around to naming him," Constants said. "Since I wasn't planning on keeping him."

"What do you call him?"

"Boy."

At the sound of the name that was not a name, the child looked up at his mother. Theory had never seen such empty eyes in a sentient creature before. They were, in fact, not fully formed. Instead of pupils, a series of symbols flashed through them, as if the eyes were a calculator display.

"I can't let you go," Theory said to Constants.

"On the contrary," she replied, and pulled the scythe closer to the boy's throat.

"You are responsible for thousands of deaths," said Theory. "And if you get away, you'll be the cause of many more, in all likelihood."

"Yet you will let me go."

"Constants, be reasonable."

"Oh, but I am being. You are the one with the emotional hang-ups."

"Constants, I loved you, but I could never stay with you. You're very beautiful, but you're a logic machine."

"And you are possessed of higher abilities? These intuitions you were always after. Have you found them, Theory?"

"I'm not sure."

Theory took a step forward, and Constants shook her head and pulled on the scythe. The boy gave a single gasp of pain, then was silent. His eyes displayed no emotion. Constants backed away with him, and Theory stopped moving. She backed farther and farther into the darkness of the cave—and then, suddenly, the two of them—boy and mother—were simply gone. Theory ran forward to where they had been and saw the swirling drain hole of a discontinuity in the virtuality. It was swiftly closing and, without thinking, he dived into it.

He was yanked down by a maelstrom of randomizing information. There were violent tugs at his own periphery to randomize, but he clung to himself and resisted them. Farther and farther he was sucked into the whirl until, in its nether regions, he joined the sides of it and was spun around at a speed greater than he could think.

Then the spinning stopped, and Theory shot out into a harsh blue sky—alone, falling. He fell for a long time, until he crashed among some rubble and, for a millisecond, lost consciousness.

He came to in a land of ruins.

Theory sat up and took a moment to collect himself, literally, from the broken scree about him. Constants had performed a short circuit, a risky operation in the virtuality, and he was obviously somewhere else in Shepardsville, and lucky he wasn't dead.

Theory surveyed his new surroundings. The landscape seemed weather-beaten and immensely old. He poked through some of the rubble. There were ancient pieces of code here, broken beyond recognition. But after turning over a larger rock, Theory saw beneath it the clear remains of a corporate logo stamped onto its surface.

"What the hell," said Theory, "is Microsoft?"

It was obviously an old web site, predating even the merci. The World Wide Web had been transposed onto the grist lock, stock, and barrel in the 2600s, and there were remnants of coding stretching back to the dawn of the information age still existing, in some form, in the present. Theory had just fallen into one of those remnants.

The sky there was low, and the clouds were definitely mean. Theory searched around for some sign of where he might look for Constants, and was about to give up when he came upon a single drop of fresh blood. It must be from the boy's neck.

Theory spiraled out from the blood spoor until he encountered another drop, and continued with this until he could pick out a line. It was leaking information, of course, and not really blood, but, even if the blood was made of a different substance, you could bleed to death in the virtuality just as you could in actuality. The trail led through a gully between piles of rubble, and into what seemed, from a distance, to be the remains of a town of some sort.

A main road led into the town, and Theory followed it in. He passed a faded sign that read:

WINDOWS

That was, perhaps, the name of this desolate place.

As Theory passed the sign, the vibration of his walking cause it to disintegrate and crumble before him. He wondered how this place had gotten to Triton, for it must exist in Triton's local grist, since the remainder of the merci was jammed. But it was not really a surprise to find such a thing in Shepardsville; old web sites migrated about the virtuality and clung like tattered plastic to whatever outcroppings they could lodge upon.

The town had seemed simple from the outside, but after Theory entered, he was soon lost within a maze of structures that seemed to have no logic to their arrangement. The blood spoor of his child led inevitably onward through the labyrinthine streets, and Theory followed it.

On a long street paved with hard-packed dirt, Constants stepped forth from the shadows, pulling the boy along with her into the middle of the street. Theory stopped short and regarded her.

"Just you?" she said.

"Only me," Theory answered.

Somewhere a clock chimed thirteen times.

"If you kill him, I will shoot you," said Theory.

"Yes. Do you have any suggestions as to how to resolve our differences?"

Theory dangled both hands straight down at his sides.

"Draw," he said.

"You know I'm faster," Constants said. "I'm the fastest that's ever been. That's why they chose me for this mission."

"You're a traitor to free converts everywhere," Theory replied. "They did right to wash you out of OCS."

"Maybe if they hadn't," said Constants, "I wouldn't be killing you today."

"Ready?"

"You know I'm faster, Theory."

"We'll see."

"It's illogical. You can't win."

"This isn't the future," he said, "and you can't know that."

"It's inevitable."

"Let the boy go, and draw."

Constants laughed. It sounded like glass breaking. She thrust the boy aside, and he fell into the shadow of the ruins. She looked down at the scythe, and it became a revolver. She holstered it at her side.

"Good-bye, Theory," she said.

"Good-bye, Constants."

With a blur of motion, her hand moved toward the revolver; Theory reached for his own.

Theory knew he was beaten halfway through the motion, but something kept him moving. Desperation. Conviction. Something without any strict logic to it.

There was a blur of motion through the still air.

Constants gasped and looked down at her stomach.

The curve of a harvest scythe protruded from her belly. She raised her head and gazed into the shadows of the ruins.

The boy stepped into the light. He was holding two more scythes in his hands. "You taught me this," he said without a shred of emotion in his voice. "Mother."

He sounds like sand blowing in the desert, Theory thought. Sand blowing at night.

"You little shit!" screamed Constants, and she reached for her gun.

Theory cut her down with a single shot to the head. She fell into the dust of the street and bled a pool that was as black as her exterior. The boy stood over her, the scythes still in his hands. Theory came to stand beside his son.

"I'll never harm you, boy," Theory said.

The boy looked up at him with his crazy, algebraic eyes. He said nothing, but dropped his weapons.

"Maybe you'd better keep those," Theory said.

"I've got lots more," the boy said. "Inside me."

They stood together and watched the last of Constants's blood soak into the ground.

Fifteen

from
**First Constitutional Congress of
the Cloudships of the Outer System**
April 2, 3013 (e-standard)
a transcript

C. al-Farghani: Thank you, most gracious Chairman and assembled worthies. I would like neither to deny nor affirm this preamble, but to call your attention to the greater matter which is before us—namely, continued exploration and elaboration of the cosmos. While I agree that we may believe whatever we want to, to waste resources in the defense of misguided thought seems to me a foolhardy venture. Let us form this government, or not, and just *leave*. We have been to the Centauris. We are going to Barnard's Star. We are ships, and ships are explorers. To turn inward and gaze at our navels—or, more precisely, the navels of those who could not hope to share our sense of adventure and wonder—is to abandon that which brought us to where we are today. If this Amés wants the solar system, I say: Let him have it. There are a hundred million stars in our galaxy alone waiting for us. What is the use of getting ourselves killed over one average sun? To leave would not be a sign of cowardice, but an expression of our true purpose. Cowardice can mean nothing to creatures such as we have become. We are above the petty squabbles of our ancestors, and the fact that the vestigial remains of our origins still exist in some twisted form in this solar system can ultimately mean nothing to us. Did we join in the fights of one ape band with another on Earth? Of course not! Were we cowards to turn away, and let the two sides fight it out? In no way. We are in an analogous situation. I, for one, feel only the vaguest kinship with those who do not know the pleasures and wonders of the stars, or who would deny them to us out of some latent animal perversity. We are ships! Let us sail away. Thank you, kind Chairman, and honorable colleagues.

C. Mencken: Thank *you* for seeing in me attributes to which even my wife will not attest, Cloudship al-Farghani. Chair recognizes Cloudship . . . uh, excuse me a moment. Yes? . . . All right. Chair recognizes Cloudship Austen—J. Austen.

C. Austen: Thank you, Mr. Chairman. Before we become so enamored of ourselves that this caucus descends into a love fest, I might ask you to consider, ladies and gentlemen, where the money comes from, money that allows us to fund our wondrous adventures and fanatical quests? I am not, of course, referring to anyone in particular. I myself have an obsession or two, and adventures are fun to go on, as long as one can be back for a good meal in the evening. And by a meal, I am talking about the energy that makes us go. Do we obtain our energy directly from the sun? No—it is delivered to us through the Met in forms that we can use. A few cloudships can exist for a short time on the solar collection we do in the Centauris. Can you imagine the infrastructure we need to support all of us? We would not do it in under a hundred years. Hear me again: We could not build it! The Met collects, refines, and delivers our food to us in a form that is, to us, easily digestible. I call it food, because that is what it is. And if someone, anyone, threatened to cut off that energy, that person is threatening to starve us, either to our deaths, or into submission. Even if we take the position that cloudships are somehow better than everyone else—which I do not—it is still incumbent upon us to organize a means to always be assured of *eating*. And that, ladies and gentlemen, is what this resolution, the preamble of which we are debating, does. It feeds us—and in the best way possible, and with the least amount of work on our part to obtain our meat and bread. The threat that we face from the inner system is very real, and this, I truly believe, is the only sensible solution. Thank you.

C. Mencken: Thank you, Cloudship Austen, now will—

C. Huxley: Mr. Chairman, point of order.

C. Mencken: What is it, Cloudship Huxley?

C. Huxley: Are we debating a declaration of war or a resolution for the adoption of a new constitution? I heard no specific reference to any hostilities in that preamble.

Chamber Left: Get real, Huxley!

Chamber Right: It's not a constitution; it's a Tacitus stink bomb!

C. Mencken: This chamber will come to order or I will have the troublemakers condemned and hung. Or vice versa. But I mean it!

C. Huxley: But does my point stand, Mr. Chairman?

C. Mencken: Just a moment, just a moment. Order, I say! All right then. Yes, you make a good point. Speakers will confine themselves to the resolution before us and cease speculation on the current state of affairs between potential friends or enemies. Your committee wrote it broad, Lebedev. Keep it broad. Chair recognizes Cloudship—

C. Beatrice: Mr. Chairman, I strongly disagree with Cloudship Huxley.

C. Mencken: But I've already ruled on that.

C. Beatrice: Without debate.

C. Mencken: But I . . . oh, all right, never mind. What was it you wanted to say?

C. Beatrice: Only that by adopting this resolution we are, in effect, declaring war, as any fool can see. Amés will certainly see it. I believe that before we vote on any portion of this resolution we should consider what form this war might take and whether or not we have any chance of winning it.

Chamber Right: Hear, hear!

C. Mencken: Oh, very well. Very well. Fine, then. Chair will now hear arguments on Cloudship Huxley's point of order and upon Cloudship Beatrice's addendum to it.

C. Turing: Point of order!

C. Mencken: I don't get that recursive, Turing. We shall do as I have said. Cloudship Beatrice, do you have anything further . . .

C. Beatrice: My only question is this: If we take on Amés, who is going to do it? That is: Us and what army?

C. Lebedev: I believe I can provide an answer for a portion of that question, Mr. Chairman.

C. Mencken: Chair recognizes Cloudship Lebedev.

C. Lebedev: The Met has a force of several thousand ships, all told. They are not anywhere equivalent in inertial mass to us. It is true that they have certain strategic advantages in areas, but—

C. Beatrice: Are you suggesting . . . do I understand this correctly . . . that *we* fight directly? Are you insane? We could get killed!

C. Lebedev: Some of us will get killed. It is inevitable. We are not playing games, here. This is a life-and-death question. Amés is bringing the war to us.

C. Beatrice: But he's only at Pluto. You can't believe he would challenge us directly.

C. Mencken: Cloudships, please. Order—

Sixteen

"Director," said C. "I have a great deal else of your business to concern me."

"Add it to your checklist, C."

"Very well."

Amés returned to his desk and sat down. "And now," he said. "It is time for your dividend."

C said nothing. He remained standing before the desk, betraying no emotion. This did not mean that he felt nothing inside. On the contrary. The calmer C appeared, the more he was filled with turmoil.

"I am ready, Director," he said. "If you are."

Amés opened a drawer in the desk and took out a finely carved mahogany box. Inside of the box was C's lover. Or an algorithmic copy. For C, the difference was of no import.

"You may touch it," Amés said. C reached over and did so. Instantly, he was inside the memory box.

"Lace," he said. "I am here."

A woman sat in a rocking chair by a window. There was the afternoon sun streaming through the glass. Dust motes danced in the air. It was Earth, a long, long time ago. Her hair was long and as fine as silk. Her skin was freckled. She wore a calico dress and a simple strand of pearls about her neck. Her eyes were the same green as C's own, and as empty as the sea.

"Who are you?"

"My name is Clare," he said. "We've met, but you won't remember me."

The woman nodded to him, attempted to smile, but then a look of sorrow passed over her face and she turned back to the window. "There's ice tea in the refrigerator," she said. "Pardon me, but you must help yourself. I'm waiting for someone."

C went into the kitchen and cracked ice into a glass from the plastic tray in the refrigerator. One of the cube spaces of the tray was split and he saw that she had not filled that one with water. For some reason, this made him unutterably sad. He poured tea over the ice, then went to sit with Lace by the window. He pulled over another chair—his old straight-backed desk chair—and settled into it. He sat beside her and sipped his tea.

"He won't come," said the woman. "He never comes."

"Who?" C asked.

"I . . . I don't know his name," she said. "He left such a long time ago. Do you know him?"

"Yes," C replied. "I met him once, in a foreign land."

"Oh!" she said, and squeezed his arm. It was all C could do not to reach over and pull her into his arms.

"He said for me to tell you that he was making his way back," said C. "But he might be some time in the coming."

"You spoke to him," she said. "You heard his voice!"

"He spoke only of you."

"Ah," she said, "if only I could believe you. Did he give you some sort of token? A sign?"

"He gave me none," said C. "Only to say to you that you must wear the sheepskin coat when winter comes. The one he gave you."

"Yes," she said. "You did. You did speak with him."

"I spoke with him. In another time."

She took her hand from C's arm. She pulled her shawl about her shoulders and began to rock. The sound of the rocker drowned out her sobs, but he knew she was softly crying.

"When will he come?" she said.

"After the winter," C replied.

She stopped her rocking. "Then I must wait?"

"A little longer. A little longer, dear Lace."

"Lace," she said. "My name is Lace."

"Lace Criur is your name," C said.

She began to move the chair again. "Pleased to meet you," she said. She rocked, and C finished his tea. The sun set in the west, and a crescent moon rose in the sky. Venus burned near the moon's arms. It was a long, long time ago, when you couldn't go to either place.

"I have to be moving along now," C told her. "But I promise to return."

"You have to be going?" she said. "Who are you?"

He set the tea glass on a side table. When he returned, he knew he would find it back in the cabinet, washed.

"Oh," he said, "nobody in particular."

She turned from him and gazed back out the window. She pulled the shawl more tightly about her shoulders.

"When will he come?" she asked.

C left through the arches of San Souci and went out to face the Mercurian night. He thought to go to his office, but instead found himself wandering the corridors of the lower levels of Bach. He kept to the shadows out of habit, and you might not have even noticed a man passing you if you had not been looking directly at him. Or perhaps you could not look directly at him. If you tried, you might find something uncertain in your gaze.

He was puzzling over a cipher in his mind. It was a task he had set himself two years before. He had chanced upon something that looked very like a secret code one day in his relative youth when he had cracked open a pecan. Instead of nut meat inside, a slip of paper had fallen out, as if the pecan were a fortune cookie. Like a good operative, he had memorized the message and then eaten it.

It had said, simply, "Clue in Clare."

It had been a pecan Lace had handed him to open, but there was no way, of course, she could have put the message in there. No one could have put it there.

It was impossible.

The impossible is inconceivable.

C wandered on into the darker and darker reaches. There was so much to think about, all at once. He was not a man given to despair. If that had been the case, he should have fallen into oblivion centuries ago. He was not a man given to despair, but he was confused. This was not often the case. There were hidden variables he was dealing with here. Wheels within wheels. It was either that, or he was going mad. He did not discount that possibility.

Sometimes he missed talking with dear old mad Tod. Now there was a true lunatic for you.

Perfect for this mad war, this mad time.

He was glad the old booger had escaped.

And, in that moment, C hit upon the missing piece to his puzzle. He stopped walking, looked around. He was standing a hundred feet from his office. It was enough to make you believe in predestination. Pure coincidence, though.

"I have to find this Leo Sherman," C said, to no one in particular.

And then, he thought: I'll get to the bottom of this.

Everything is pure coincidence, but it all has a twisted sort of logic. It is a matter of finding the right key. And, then, everything becomes music.

PART FOUR

HOW THE SKY CAN BURN

One

It was a good thing Leo knew when the transmitter pod would brake, because if he hadn't they would all have been caught by surprise and pasted into the outer wall of the pod. As it was, they got ready and found a particularly thick part of the fiber to put behind them. Outside, a receiving tube would suck them in, according to Leo, and they would slow down as they slid down its length to docking.

And that is what happened. Slowing down was not as hard as speeding up had been, although Aubry supposed that exactly the same physical forces were involved.

And then, just like that, they were there. Nirvana.

Leo got a door to pucker open, and they walked out into the light of a fusion-lamp sun. It was always day in this bolsa of Nirvana, Leo said, and the light was always on.

"Then the Parleyman said to me 'Come to the wasteland and be sure to bring the cheese,'" Tod said, as they came out of the access corridor they had taken from the Nirvana Integument. They had steadily grown heavier as their spin rate increased in the corridor, and now they stepped onto a grassy lawn with Earth-normal spin under their feet.

Across the lawn was a wood, and from the wood, people emerged.

"Amazing," said Leo. "Every time it works, I'm amazed."

The people were getting nearer, and Aubry felt an unfamiliar wariness in her stomach. It had been weeks since she'd seen anyone who wasn't out to catch or kill her. She did not know these people. She felt the weight of her pistol against her back, where she had it secured in the waistband of her pants. Then the people began to run, and she tensed, ready for anything. But it was Tod they were running toward. When they reached him, they all gathered around him in a circle. There were eleven of them, seven women and four men. They all held out their hands and bowed, not deeply, and not all at the same time.

"Old bone dancer," they each said, as if it were a greeting.

"James threw up and Ettiene got the big pieces," Tod said, after they were finished.

Leo seemed to recognize one of the men, and he signaled Jill to come with him to say hello. He waited until the man's bow was complete, then touched him on the shoulder. "Franklin," he said.

"Leo! What a day! You brought him, you goatmother!"

"Here we are," said Leo. "A little worse for wear. Where are Otis and Game?"

"Enthalpy," said Franklin.

"Wow," Leo replied. "But we have to talk."

"Yeah. Their converts aren't stoned. We can talk in the virtuality. Let's go to the village. You hungry?"

"Sure."

"Who are these?" Franklin said, looking at Jill and Aubry. "Youth and youth."

"This is Aubry and Jill. Jill is the one who saved Tod's ass."

Franklin fixed Jill in his gaze. His eyes were a dark brown and his skin a lighter shade than they were. "Thank you," he said. "From all of us."

"You're welcome," Jill said.

Then they went into the woods, where they found a circle of huts. Food was brought to them—steaming rice and vegetables. It was delicious. Leo seemed to know everyone in the "camp," but Aubry kept close to Jill, and once she found herself unconsciously holding Jill's hand.

Leo returned from talking to a group of people and sat

down beside them, eating his rice with chopsticks. They all had water to drink.

"This bolsa is called Oregon," Leo said. "They've had troubles. Problems coming through the grist."

"If all these people are Friends of Tod, then why wasn't he here in the first place?" Aubry asked.

"They've been preparing this place for him for nearly seventy years. There are some pretty rich Friends."

"Who are these people?" Aubry said. She'd been wanting to ask this question since they arrived, and now it burst out.

"The Friends of Tod are the nerds who run the world."

"Nerds?"

"Technicals, Aubry. Grist engineers. Algorithm programmers. Security consultants," said Leo. "The people who created the patterns for the first free converts are here on Oregon."

"What are we doing here? Are we going to stay?"

"That depends on what Otis and Game have to say," said Leo. "I think they are seeking a vision to guide them. But the thing about these Friends visions—they usually turn out to be common sense."

While they were eating, Otis and Game came into the hut where they were sitting. Jill knew it was them because the Friends who were there greeted them by name. The two stumbled about and went to a corner and collapsed together.

"We're meeting with *them*?" said Jill.

"With their converts. They just let their bodies be affected by the drug." Leo smiled what seemed a sad smile, Jill thought. "I wish I had known how to do that back when I was having my problems with enthalpy. But the real problem was *me*, of course, and not that I was an e-head."

After they ate, they went to another hut, and Aubry could feel that this one was thick with grist. It was a type she'd never experienced. And when they entered the virtuality, she realized that what she had sensed was heavy-duty encryption algorithms—and something even stronger. They appeared as a nest of vines and tree branches surrounding them. This virtual space was a forest clearing with a circle of stone on which they could sit, and a blue-white fire burning in a fire pit in the middle. A pipe was passed around and everyone took a pull. The smoke tasted a bit sweet—not at all like tobacco or any herb. And it seemed to have the effect of making her very clearheaded.

Several of the Friends they had met were present with virtual likenesses, including Franklin. Otis, who was a man, sat on one side of the circle and Game, a female, sat on the other.

"Old bone dancer is now with us," Otis began. "You can feel him in the grist."

Several of the friends nodded.

"We have seen," said Game, "that it is the time to light him up and smoke him. As was foretold, so it has come to pass."

Several of the Friends broke into applause. Game let it die down, and then continued. "But with freedom comes a responsibility. And that is why we are here today."

Jill glanced over at Leo. He seemed genuinely puzzled.

"The time has come for coalitions," said Otis, taking up where Game left off. "For the forging of alliances."

"Excuse me," Leo said. "But what do you mean about firing Tod up and smoking him?"

"Ah, ye of little faith," Otis said. "Did you not know of the special property of time towers when they are used in a certain manner prescribed by wisdom and science?"

"I know that they can't be co-opted by other intelligences," Leo replied.

"Yes," said Game. Her voice was a baritone purr. "And that effect can be spread out, all over a self-contained grist space. Nirvana, for instance."

"So Amés can't get in here on the merci, or through the virtuality at all? Tod can act as a sort of jamming system?"

"It has already been done," Otis said, pointing to the vegetation that surrounded them.

"I'll be damned," muttered Leo. "So the time towers really have a use after all."

"The Director is aware of this, as well. Other time towers are being put to despicable uses. Tortured, forced aboard warships with minimal food and water, and used as merci-jamming devices."

"The problem is," Otis said, "we are pacifists."

"Conscientious objectors," Game added.

"We can jam the grist, but we cannot fight off a physical invasion or rescue the other time towers who are imprisoned. Our fighting would cause Tod to go mad."

"Don't want to make Tod mad," said Leo. "He might become sane."

"Now you're cooking with gas," Otis replied.

"So we have come together to talk about this," Game said.

"Because we saw no answer in the enthalpy."

And the Friends began to talk among themselves, in low voices. Aubry, Jill and Leo sat silently and let them go at it. After maybe half an hour, the talk became a murmur, and then died out.

Otis and Game turned simultaneously to the travelers. They fixed their eyes on Jill. "We need help," Otis said. "Your help."

Jill was silent for a long time, but Otis and Game kept looking steadily at her.

"I have strange friends," Jill finally said.

"Any friends of yours," Game said, "are friends of ours."

"And what will you do for me?"

"We will help you."

"Help me do what?"

Game laughed and, for the first time, the woman seemed to Aubry . . . not evil. But extremely knowing. Full of frightening knowledge acquired by arcane methods.

"We know who you are looking for," Game said to Jill. "We will help you find Alethea."

Again, Jill was silent for a long moment. Her expression barely changed, but Aubry had spent enough time with her to see that she had come to a decision. It was Jill's nose. It twitched—very slightly, but noticeably—when she was concentrating closely on something. Aubry suddenly had a strong urge to scratch Jill's nose, but managed to fight it off.

"How can I get word to my friends?" Jill asked. "Provided I want to." She approached the fire, warmed her hands. Sometimes they still looked like paws to Aubry, they were so small in comparison with most people's.

Jill sighed. "We're just a bunch of rats and ferrets and other vermin."

"We can do something about that," Game said.

"We know a lot about grist and how it cohabits with biology. We know how to break the lockout codes."

"We?"

"Haven't you guessed who the Friends are yet?" said Leo. "They are the ones who wrote your code in the first place."

"I can't answer for all the rats, then," Jill said, "but the ferrets are ready to fight."

"Well then," said Otis, smiling around at the circle of Friends and fellow travelers. "Good death to us all!"

There was general applause. Aubry didn't join in. She gazed at Jill, who kept on grinning, running her tongue over the sharp tips of her teeth.

Aubry was not sure exactly what had happened in the clearing, but one thing she was certain of—she wasn't going to be joining her family anytime soon. She had realized this on the trip, somewhere in the back of her mind, but it was only now that she began to consider it as a cold, hard fact.

She must have been appearing gloomy for the past few days after the meeting, because finally Leo came up to her and asked her to go for a walk with him in the woods. The trees were all evergreens here, and the path was dim. It was almost as if they'd stepped into twilight.

"Even in a place where the light shines all the time," Leo said, "people work it out so that they can have a place for a shady existence." They walked about half a mile, and then Leo spoke again. "Okay, kid. What's bothering you?"

"I don't know."

"You miss your folks?"

"Yes. And my brother."

Leo slowed his pace a little "I'm sorry about that," he

said. "I didn't know I was going to be taking you on such a march when I pulled you away from your dad. I honestly thought we'd hook up with the Friends at Tod's place, and I'd pass you along to the ship that was smuggling the half–free converts off the Met. Jesus, I hope that ship got off all right."

"Didn't you know where it was?"

"Nope. We were trying to keep that info compartmentalized."

"You think maybe they got caught, don't you?"

Leo stopped walking for a moment, took a handful of needles from a nearby young fir tree. "Yeah, I think they probably did. Amés was just moving too fast for us."

"I heard you and Jill talking about what you think his real plans are for the free converts."

"Yes."

Then a new thought entered Aubry's mind. "Oh God," she said. "Then my mother's escape ship was probably caught, too."

Leo winced. He said nothing. Aubry felt as if someone had just kicked her in the stomach. All along she had been imagining her mother as having escaped. Separated from the family, but away on some ship. But the truth was probably much worse. The worst of all.

"Oh, no," Aubry said.

They walked a little farther, but Aubry felt as if her head was spinning, and she had to stop. They sat down, their backs against a tree. Aubry wanted to cry. She felt the tears building. But nothing came. After a while, she swallowed and reached over and held Leo's hand. "I can't believe it. What was the name of that place? The place they are sending free converts?"

"Noctis Labyrinthus."

"Then she's probably there."

"We don't know that."

"Come on, Leo," Aubry said. "You can't keep something from me if I already know it."

Leo squeezed her hand a bit tighter. "You've got me there, kid."

Aubry sat for a while, trying to think. There had to be something—something she hadn't thought of—but all she could think was that she had to get her mother out of there. She had to get Danis out.

But I'm eleven, Aubry thought. I'm eleven. The number seemed to echo in her brain.

And, damn it, something was bugging her. Something was pressing into the small of her back. She realized it was the particle gun Jill had given her, and insisted that she always carry.

Even an eleven-year-old could pull a trigger and kill somebody. That wasn't so hard. And Aubry was a dead-sight aim.

You don't shoot people just because you don't like them, Aubry thought.

Unless those people are trying to kill your mother.

"I'm going to learn everything I can about fighting," Aubry said. "And then I'm going to get my mother out of there."

They returned silently through the shadows of the trees and stepped back into the fake sunlight of Oregon.

Two

from
**First Constitutional Congress of
the Cloudships of the Outer System**
April 2, 3013 (e-standard)
a transcript

C. Lebedev: My dear Beatrice, have you heard none of what has been said? Or, failing that, have you had a ramble through the merci lately? He intends to have it all.

C. Beatrice: But Elgar Triptych has specifically promised us that no hostilities will be directed at us.

C. Lebedev: Yes, the Directorate's envoy has been doing a great deal of talking lately. A great deal. If we are to believe him, all of the outer planets welcome Amés with open arms, and only their evil, illegal governments prevent the citizens from rushing into his arms. I will tell you how it seems to me. That is all I can do. You will have to decide between me, whom you have known since you first ventured out to the Oorts—and Señor Triptych, who strikes me as being a great deal wider than he is deep. Here is what I have to say: We have a navy, and we are it. The outer system has no military craft of its own to speak of. They haven't needed any—we have been the de facto policers of the spaceways for generations now. We are blocked—blocked!—from Jupiter. Now, Señor Triptych calls this a temporary measure not directed at us, but it doesn't matter its intent. We are effectively cut off from half our capital, and almost all of our army. I am speaking of the Federal Army of the Planets, which must be our infantry—for we have no other. The situation is grave, Cloudship Beatrice, grave. I do not wish to cry doom in these proceedings, but the time to act is before us. Now! If we lose the army, we may have lost all hope. Our first order of business must be to break the Jupiter blockade and get our army *out*.

C. Beatrice: But that would be as much as declaring war. *We* would be the aggressors!

C. Lebedev: Can you be so naive as to truly believe so?

C. Beatrice: Those people are not our army . . . they belong to all those ragtag settlers. The little people who cling to their little moons. What do they have to do with us?

C. Lebedev: Yes, I believe those are the exact words of Señor Triptych. If you really believe them, then we are done for. Amés has already won. It is a classic strategy to divide and conquer.

C. Beatrice: But surely you are not saying that *we* need *them*? We are merely debating whether or not to do them a favor.

C. Lebedev: Cloudship Beatrice, if we do them the favor of saving their hides, they may return that favor sooner than you think, and save ours.

C. Beatrice: We'll make him mad. Very mad.

C. Lebedev: Of whom are you speaking?

C. Beatrice: Amés, of course. The Director.

C. Lebedev: He is not my director.

C. Beatrice: But he'll hurt us. My children. He'll hurt my children . . .

C. Lebedev: We must take the children away. Far away. Along the Dark Matter Road.

C. Mencken: You go too far, Lebedev. We are not nearly to the point of discussing such a thing. Please confine yourself to the question at issue.

C. Lebedev: Very well, Mr. Chairman. I expect to begin with perhaps fifty ships for a navy. We will train those, and then see what we've got. They may not make a formidable enough force to break through the Jupiter blockade. We can but try.

C. Mencken: And where do you expect to get these ships?

C. Lebedev: I shall take volunteers to begin with.

C. Mencken: To begin with! Are you suggesting we institute conscription?

C. Lebedev: I don't know. There might be—

C. Tacitus: Maybe I can be of a little service in answering that question, eh, Lebedev?

C. Lebedev: Tacitus! You're here!

C. Tacitus: Just got back from my little trip in toward the sun. Want me to just add a few words to your—

C. Lebedev: Yes . . . Yes, certainly. Perhaps I got too carried away. Things are not so dire, yet, it could be . . .

C. Tacitus: Thank you, friend Lebedev. Ladies and gentlemen, we are not talking about forcing anyone to do anything, let me assure you. The question before us is a simple one. Let us not get confused by objections and points of order or disorder. Are we, or are we not, going to transform our Council of Ships into the Congress of our native solar system? You probably all know where I stand on this since it was I who instigated these proceedings in the first place. Now, among us, I am one of the few who has actually gone sunward and had a look at the situation there. It is not so good. Not so good. Neptune is fighting tooth and nail. Jupiter is refusing to surrender. These are the voices of the people crying out, not some tinpot dictator's defiance. I have already told you what I, personally, witnessed on Triton. A city torn to shreds. Over a hundred thousand souls—lost, killed. Families. Their homes destroyed. If he merely wished to punish the government, and not the people, then why did Amés order a rip tether dropped on New Miranda? No, I think we can all see what is going on here. We are a pretty smart bunch. Maybe too smart for our own good, I sometimes think. Perhaps we should have recruited some idiots just to balance things out, but now it's too late for that. We are not more than human, as some have suggested, and neither are we less. What we are is an elite. We have the privileges of an elite, but with those privileges comes responsibility to our fellow humans. Come on, people! Nobody knows where this will all lead, where things are going. Maybe Amés will back down, maybe not. I, personally, doubt it. But I do not know the future. All anybody can know is the past and the present. Is all we have done for nothing? It is a foundation. What we have to do now is start constructing the building. If we have to fight, we fight, but that is not what we're really about here. What we are doing is something far more important in the long run. We are deciding whether or not democracy has had its day. Whether or not the human race is just too tired of it all to rule itself anymore. Do you want to be the person who, at the tail end of history, said yes to that proposition? Who said yes, I am tired—won't somebody please tell me what to do, what to think? Do you want your children to remember you as the one who decided that it was best for them to answer to the will of another for the rest of their lives? Austen has pointed out that it is economically impossible for us to run away. Twain has shown the absurdity of compromise with Amés. Lebedev has given you some idea of the task before us. But what I want to do is to convince you of the responsibility we have, as the best and brightest. You're all here for a reason. It isn't an accident that any one of you is in the Oorts and one of our number. Now is the time to show that we are not merely a bunch of clever fools, but that we actually are the intelligences that we claim to be. We take silly names to avoid thinking too highly of ourselves. To keep a sense of humor about us. We are going to need that sense of humor, let me tell you, for these are grim times. But let me suggest to you that these names mean something else, as well. No—that they *can* mean something else. They are a promise that we make to ourselves to live up to. They are a goal we set for ourselves to achieve. And most of all, they are the better selves that we know are somewhere inside of us. We may never bring that self to the outside, but it is our lifelong task to try. And I am a historian by trade. I tell you that people are going to remember these names, and they are going to *judge us by them.* What people? Our children, and their children—on down the long line of time. It is the only certainty I know of—memory and judgment. Are we who we claim to be? You may fool yourself, and you may fool the times, but you can't fool history. And that is because history is the result of who you really are. History is you, writ large, until the end of time. We should consider that every day, but we must consider it now, in this chamber. What we decide here today matters, and matters completely. Think on this, and God help us to make the right choice . . . Mr. Chairman, I yield the chamber.

C. Mencken: Thank you, Cloudship Tacitus. Now . . . er, is there any more debate on the point of order? None? Then my ruling is that I overrule my last ruling. If you people want to talk till you're blue in the gills about whatever you want to, well, I'm here to help, not to hinder. Let us return to debate on the resolution. Cloudship Tolstoy, I believe you are next.

Three

Theory had expected to feel a great many conflicts after killing his old lover, but, the truth was, he felt nothing for her. She had effectively killed any emotion that remained in him by what she had done to and with their son.

Finding space and occupation for the five hundred new arrivals from Saturn would have been a logistical nightmare for most, but Theory handled it with the same efficiency he brought to the myriad other tasks that he was assigned. Figuring out what to do with the boy was another matter. In that area, efficiency meant nothing.

The child was, for the most part, uncommunicative. Theory had enlarged his quarters in the virtuality—what he thought of as his private space—to accommodate the boy. He had provided games and learning modules and tried to instruct the boy in their use, but the child just looked on with his crazed eyes and did nothing.

Theory worried about his safety, for Theory must necessarily be gone long hours, and the surveillance subroutines he set in place were easily subverted. They were not designed to detain, merely to keep a watch. For a time, Theory thought to share himself out and keep a double presence, both at work and at home, but this proved to be taxing, for he was often employed in tasks for the Army that took all of his attention and computing ability. In the end, there was nothing for it but hire a nanny or to leave the child alone. Theory could not conceive of a nanny who might understand the child, and he felt that it would be better for the boy to have no attention at this stage than to have attention of the wrong sort. He did not ask the child, but he expected Constants had put the boy through a most special hell, and he was sure the boy needed a careful easing into the normal life of a normal free convert.

Or perhaps he was entirely mistaken. He got no help from the boy as to the solution to the mystery. They discussed, briefly, the matter of a name, but the child seemed honestly not to fully grasp the concept, so Theory gave it up until such time as the boy might choose his name with confidence, and not because somebody else made him take on one.

As far as the matter with Jennifer Fieldguide went, Theory had almost forgotten about it, when he got a stiff request from Captain Quench to meet him in the virtual space that the officers used as a club for convert portions and free converts to mingle during off hours. The place was done up in wood and leather, with cuspidors and great brass ashtrays strewn about on oaken tabletops. There was an excellent library of war literature lining one wall, both fact and fiction, and along the other was a completely tricked-out bar manned by Hilly St. Johns, a free-convert immigrant from the Diaphany.

Theory arrived before Quench, and ordered his customary Rusty Nail from Hilly. She set him up and offered him a smoke, which he declined. Somewhere Hilly had erroneously filed away the datum that Theory smoked, which he did not, and Theory, politely, never sought to correct her error. Quench entered shortly thereafter in something of a huff. He sat down beside Theory and stated without preamble, "Listen, man, I know we agreed to swap identities for a night, but that didn't mean I gave you liberty to set me up with another lover—and a woman at that."

"What in the name of God are you talking about?" Theory replied, still distracted by his latest failure at communicating with his son.

"Why this Jennifer Fieldguide woman, Theory," Quench

replied. "She won't stop calling me. Claims we have an agreement to see one another again."

Quench took a handful of nuts from the bar and threw them into his mouth all at once, and then said while he chewed, "Theory, I gave you my body to go to the dance with, man, not to go bedding a girl with."

Theory was mortified and could say nothing for a moment, then he picked up his drink and threw the whole thing back himself.

"We kissed only, John," he said. "I kept trying to tell her who I was—who I *really* was—but the moment never was quite right. We were talking about free converts, and she was being critical of them, almost a bigot, and I didn't want to reveal my nature because . . . because, damn it, I liked her, John."

"Good God, Theory, this is a little much, don't you think?"

"I certainly do," Theory replied. "I want to apologize. It was a strange evening. I hadn't been in an aspect's body in a very long time. Perhaps I let the hormones affect me while I wasn't paying attention. I have just killed someone who once meant a great deal to me." Theory sloshed his own drink about in the glass, considered the fractal ripple simulation the virtuality provided on the drink's surface. "I promise you there was just the kissing, and no sex that night with Jenny."

"Kissing is bad enough!" exclaimed Quench. "What would I ever tell Arthur if he should find out?"

"I'm sorry, John. I don't know what else to say."

This final apology seemed to mollify Quench, at least for the moment. He ordered a bourbon and water from Hilly, and sipped at it distractedly.

"Well, Theory," he finally said, "the woman simply has to be told, and that's all there is to it. Now if you insist, I will do so the next time she calls me—"

"—Oh, no, John. It's my problem to take care of."

"Good, then, do it as soon as possible. I don't know if I can fake my way through another call from the woman. She seems nice enough, but she must be gullible to be fooled so easily."

"I think she is merely young," Theory said. "There is something else, though."

"What?"

"I may want your help in breaking the news to her."

"How do you mean? I'll not lie any more to the girl."

"No, not that. It's just . . . I want to see her again. That is, if it proves at all possible." Theory had not realized, until just that moment, that he *did* want to have at least one more conversation, and possibly more, with Jennifer Field-guide. But how to go about it?

"Perhaps we can arrange another meeting," Theory continued. "But this time in the virtuality."

"Do what you like," said Quench.

"No, you don't understand. With *you* present, John." Theory rushed onward before Quench could protest. "You would appear as me and I as you, and after I've broken the news to her we could sort of . . . switch."

Quench downed the rest of his bourbon and stared at Theory with unbelieving eyes. "Set me up another, Hilly," he said. "Let me get this straight, Theory. We would meet in the virtuality with you disguised as my convert and me disguised as you? And what purpose would this insane scheme serve?"

"It will ease her into the knowledge that I am you and you are me, or rather than I am not you and you are not me," Theory said. "If you see what I mean?"

"I see free-convert neurosis."

"Please, John," said Theory. "For some reason, I don't know why, Jennifer means something to me. I don't know if it's love. It's certainly not love, not yet. I'm feeling very confused at the moment about a lot of things. But I don't want to destroy any chance I might have with her."

"And you think this plan will make you desirable?"

"It's the only way I can think of that might salvage the situation," Theory replied.

To Theory's surprise, Quench threw his head back and gave one of his big guffaws. He laughed so hard that he soon had Theory nervously joining in in sympathy, though Theory didn't know what they were laughing about. Finally, Quench calmed himself and took a drink of his bourbon.

"You know, we'll probably be dead before we even get a chance to try out your plan."

"It is a distinct possibility."

"Just remember, it has to end up with her being told what's what."

"I promise it will, John."

"Well then," said Quench. "I wish I had been there for that kiss, after all. She really hooked you, old son." He signaled Hilly, who was at the other end of the bar. "Get this man another Rusty Nail," he said. "And keep 'em coming until he has enough to close up his own coffin."

Four

In ones, twos, and threes, Jill's animals began to arrive in the transmitter pods. Most of them were bedraggled, but they all perked up when they saw Jill. Soon the hut that the three travelers shared was teeming with rodents and the hunters of rodents—all living in an uneasy peace out of regard for Jill. Despite the extermination grist in the living areas, there were, of course, rats and other animals in the Met.

Leo had never liked them much even though he knew that there must be a place for them in the ecology. He had always had a secret fear of ending up in a rat warren in the Integument and being eaten alive, but whenever he saw them there, they had not been in packs. They lived, he knew, nearer to the occupied areas, so that they could quickly get to garbage before it was eliminated.

Within two weeks, Game had conferred with Jill, and the treatments had began. The idea was to grow the animals into humans. It sounded entirely bizarre to Leo. He'd heard of free converts saving up, purchasing or renting clone bodies—that is, grist-made bodies with a grist matrix instead of a brain. But he'd never even imagined anything like this. The coding that gave the rats and ferrets intelligence at all was of the sort written by programmers, and not enthalpically evolved, as were the free converts. So there was a double process going on with the animals. The computer coding inside them was put through evolutionary processes at the same time as the structure they were inhabiting—a kind of brain-grist continuum that was present only in the Carbuncle, as far as anyone had ever discovered—was enlarged. And the animal bodies began the process of slowly transforming themselves into humans.

The pace was set as quick as Game could make it, but it was going to take at least three months before real effects would be seen. And the animals were going to feel a good deal of pain as the changes came over them. Nevertheless, all of them volunteered to undergo it. It gave them a better chance at survival, and survival was what these scrap codes were all about.

For a while, Leo could see no place for himself in any of these preparations. Leo was seriously tempted to get the hell out of here and take Aubry with him. But where would he go? This was still the safest place for a dissenter and a little girl who was wanted by the law.

And there was Jill.

There had been a couple of steady girlfriends over the years, but once they understood that Leo's traveling itch would not be going away, that he would not be settling down to a respectable occupation and that he was always going to be more or less poor, they had drifted away. This always surprised him, because he'd thought he was picking out women who would understand these facts. He never made any bones about it, but told them up front. And Becky had been a poet, even, even though, after their breakup, Leo had to admit to himself that he'd never much cared for her verse.

What Leo really wanted was to keep traveling the Met until the day he died, seeing cool stuff and showing people who he thought might like to share the experience with him. But that was all over now. Leo was going to face what had to be faced. Hell, that was what had drawn him to the Integument in the first place. The possibility of surprise in

490 - TONY DANIEL

a world that would literally wipe your nose for you if you let it.

Leo was grousing along these lines one day when Otis poked his head into Leo's hut, and said, calmly, "Uh, Leo, I think we have a problem, man."

"What?"

"A Department of Immunity ship is hanging nearby in space, broadcasting to us on an electromagnetic band."

"Yikes!"

"Yeah, well, there's something else . . ."

"What is it, Otis?"

"They are specifically demanding *your* surrender."

"Mine?"

"They are inquiring after one Leo Y. Sherman," said Otis. "Unless your middle name is—"

"It's Yorrick," Leo said, a sinking feeling lodging in his stomach.

"Taylor's got them on a radio in the common hut." Otis smiled a forced smile. "Taylor would have a radio."

"Let's go hear it," Leo said. "Maybe it's *Theo* Sherman they want. He's dead." Leo immediately wished he hadn't said that, though of course nobody here knew about his brother except Aubry, and she was off at target practice with Jill.

It was a repeating message. There was no doubt—they were asking for Leo.

"*Leo Y. Sherman, author of 'The Vas After Sunset,' and other licentious tracts, is wanted for questioning by the Department of Immunity. Prepare for a DI investigative team arriving at Port B on Oregon Bolsa of the Nirvana Mycelium at system time 19:00. If Leo Y. Sherman is known to you, you will provide him for immediate questioning. This is an official Department of Immunity Edict. Disregarding it or its contents or aiding or abetting anyone attempting to disregard this Edict is punishable by up to five e-years rehabilitative therapy or induction into DI Enforcement Division uniformed service under Title Fifty-four Protocols. Leo Y. Sherman, author . . .*"

Taylor turned down the volume and looked up from his radio set with a serious face, but Leo could tell he was pleased. He probably never got a chance to show off his ancient equipment which, from the look of it, he kept in top-notch working order.

"Notice anything strange?" Otis said.

"Yeah," Leo said. "They didn't just come in here and nab me."

"Exactly," Otis said. "What do you suppose it means?"

"What time is it?" Leo asked.

"We've got an hour to get you hidden or away."

Jill came through the door. "What's going on?" she said. "I suddenly got a bad feeling, so I came back here."

Franklin turned up his radio and the message repeated itself.

"What is an investigation team?" Jill asked.

"Two sweepers and an aspect," Taylor immediately answered, apparently up on his DI lore.

"Well then," said Jill, "that shouldn't be much of a problem. If someone can handle the aspect, I can take out one sweeper and Aubry can take out the other."

"Aubry?"

"She needs the practice."

"Um," said Taylor, "we're talking about Department of Immunity Antipersonnel Sweepers here, right?"

"Are they the kind designed for riot work?" said Jill.

Taylor looked at her. "Usually not, on an investigation team," he said.

"Then it should be even easier," Jill replied. "I think you should let them dock."

"What do you think, Leo?" Otis asked. "It's your ass that's on the line, too."

Leo ran his hand through his hair. Almost like I'm preparing for a goddamn holiday visitor of something, he then thought ruefully. "If they think 'The Vas After Sunset' is prurient, they ought to read my article on Muslim whorehouses in New Tangiers Bolsa," he said. "But there's something odd about this. Let's do it, but let's be careful. I want to be there"—he looked at Jill, who frowned, but nodded yes—"in case I can do something to defuse the situation."

"Or you might get yourself killed," Otis said.

Leo smoothed his hair down again, as if by reflex. "What did you say back in that meeting in the clearing? 'Good death to us all?' Let us go see what's up."

Five

They met the DI crack secret-police team with an official delegation of two women under twenty, fifty-two rats, and five ferrets.

It was not much of a fight.

From Leo's perspective, behind a tree, everything seemed to be over in a matter of seconds. Aubry had been tense, but expectant, anxious to try out the techniques Jill had been teaching her to fight the sweepers. She was armed with two pistols—a projectile semiautomatic and a beam weapon—and a twelve-foot-long pike that Leo knew was charged up with decoding grist and high-voltage electricity of a sufficient amperage to fry the guts of a whale on old Earth.

Thank God those Tromperstompers have rubber soles, Leo thought, looking at Aubry's incongruous kid's boots. And then he thought: Mr. Graytor, look what I've done to your daughter. That this was a far better way for Aubry to turn out than being dead did not make Leo feel any better. She ought to be in school, wondering what the big deal is with boys, and learning whatever it was smart kids like her studied at eleven. Trigonometry and Camus or something.

The Department of Immunity team debarked, and were headed down the path that led to the huts, when Aubry and Jill simply ambushed it. The two sweepers responded precisely on cue by extending their knockout gas wands, and had gotten it right up the nozzle. Meanwhile, the rats and ferrets swarmed the human, subduing him only. They wanted this one alive.

After the smoke had cleared, Leo came out from hiding to find Jill and Aubry standing over the man—it was a man—with pistols pointed at his head and chest. Even though a rat was menacingly on his shirt collar, he lay prone on the ground and made no move. About a dozen Friends joined Leo in a circle about this tableau.

"Keep your hands in view at all times," Jill said. "I wouldn't like to have to kill you, but I will."

"I believe you," the man mumbled. He didn't seem anxious to excite the rat by moving his Adam's apple too much.

Jill made a funny whistle through her teeth, and the animals that had swarmed the man left him and faded back into the underbrush. But Leo could still hear them there, rustling around. It was the first time the rustling of rats had seemed like a comforting sound to him.

"Stand up," said Jill. The man promptly did so. He was a medium-built man, at least six inches taller than Leo. He had on gray pants, a white shirt, and a gray traveling coat. He could have been anybody. He was Caucasian, with pale skin. A clean-shaven face, a bit angular. Hair in a current style.

This is the most nondescript man I have ever encountered, Leo thought. He caught the man's gaze.

"I am Leo Sherman," he said. "What is it you want with me?"

The man motioned with his head to one of the dead sweeper units. "That was unnecessary," he said. "I was prepared to disable them." He looked at Jill and Aubry. "But effective."

"Please answer my question," Leo said.

"I would like to speak with you in private," the man said.

"These are my friends."

"Yes. That is apparent. Nevertheless, you may either kill me or speak with me in private."

Leo considered. He pointed to Jill. "She will be present," he said. "And her," he continued, pointing to Aubry.

"Of course," said the man.

"Let's go to my hut, then."

They all tromped back through the forest, Aubry and Jill keeping the man covered at every step of the way. They sat cross-legged on mats in the hut, a low table in between them. The man kept his hands on top of it. The man sat down a little creakily in the cross-legged position, but didn't seem to be in too much pain. There wasn't much Leo could do about it in any case. The Friends were not big fans of chairs.

"I am a special assistant to Director Amés," the man said. "My duties chiefly involve intelligence assets and covert operations, though I am not part of the Department of Immunity, but operate in my own personal sphere."

He took out a pack of cigarettes, almost getting himself shot in the process.

"Do you mind if I smoke? It has been long, and I used to like them so much."

"Jill will light it for you."

Jill took the pack, checked it out, then flicked a cigarette, pointing it away from everyone. It was a regular cigarette, and the flicking motion lit it.

"Better not let some of the Friends see you doing that," Leo said. "They have ancient smoking taboos."

"That will not matter soon," the man said.

"What is your name?"

"That does not matter, either. You may call me C. People frequently do." The man took a long, long drag on his cigarette, let out the smoke, and sighed. "I am here not at Amés's behest, but for my own reason," he said.

"And what are those?"

"I should have said 'reasons,' actually," C replied. "May I take something out of my coat pocket?"

"If you do so slowly and in full view."

C nodded. He reached into his coat and slowly removed what looked for all the world like an oil lamp from the ancient days of Arabia. It was about the size of his hand.

"This," he said, setting the lamp on the table, "is me."

"You?"

"This lamp, you will find, is quite heavy. It is made of an extraordinarily dense grist matrix. Inside it is a copy me, complete and entire, in all essential functions."

"And you're giving this to me?"

"I am entrusting it to you. I am asking you to serve as an envoy for its delivery."

"To whom?"

C took another long drag, then breathed out. "To your father," he said.

"What?" said Leo. "What did you say?"

"Your father—Colonel Roger Sherman of the Federal Army of the Planets Third Sky and Light Brigade."

The man sucked in on his cigarette, finished it, ground it out between his fingers. Had he just smoked a cigarette in three long pulls? Apparently so, Leo thought.

"Tell me why you want me to do this," said Leo.

"It is complicated," said C. "May I have another cigarette?"

Jill lit him one.

"What it comes down to, though," he continued, "is that because of me, Amés has a huge intelligence advantage over the outer-system forces, and over you." He looked at Jill. "You are, by the way, the only partisan resistance whom I take seriously."

"Well, thank you," said Leo. "I guess. But that does not explain why you are doing this."

"Let's just say I want to even the playing field," said C. Another amazingly long drag on his cigarette. A long breath out. "You see, Amés is holding a woman I love hostage, and using this leverage to demand my services. I am caught in a very effective trap in that regard, and the only possible avenue I see to get out of it is this desperate measure." He looked at the lamp. "Besides," he said, "it will be interesting to have a worthy opponent."

"Are you that good?"

"My services brought about the immediate surrender of Uranus," C replied. "False modesty would serve no purpose here, and, in any case, pride is not a vice to which I am susceptible. When you are considering operations against me, you should use curiosity as a lure. I am an extremely curious man." Another drag. "In any case, I can do no more at the moment than to beg that you do as I request."

"You could tell us what Amés knows about Nirvana," said Leo. "And when, and if, he plans an attack."

"That I will not do," said C. "And I am afraid that you would be unable to force it out of me. In fact, you might endanger yourself by doing so, if you could. It is essential that the Director does not find out yet that I am a turncoat, and if you began using intelligence information that only I am privy to, he would realize this immediately." Another drag. "Amés is an intelligent man, and extremely tenacious. He has enormous resources available to him, as well."

"So, I am to take this . . . copy . . . to my father. Is that what you want?"

"You are, by far, the best choice for a messenger," said C. "And, as an incidental bonus, this might serve to heal the rift between you two."

"How the *hell* do you know about that?" said Leo.

C did not reply. He only smiled benignly. Leo looked for something sinister in his face, but found nothing. Of course, that didn't mean it wasn't in his soul.

"And you expect us just to let you go? If you are so important, then killing you or keeping you hostage would seem to be in our best interest."

"Oh, no," said C. "I won't be going anywhere."

"What do you mean?"

"I can't possibly return and report to Amés. He would know immediately what I had been up to."

"Then . . . what?"

"Don't you see?" said the man. "You will have to kill me."

"But . . ."

"Don't worry. Amés has a backup copy." C again meticulously extinguished and destroyed his cigarette. "May I have another?"

Leo distractedly indicated that Jill give him one. Leo stared at the oil lamp. Was it a godsend or a trap? There was no way to tell without analyzing it. C seemed to read his thoughts.

"It will only work for Roger Sherman," C said. "It is rather strongly encrypted, and I believe that not even your best hackers would stand a chance. They may try, of course. I have allowed for that possibility, and doing so will not kill them."

"You seem to have thought of everything."

"Let us hope that I have."

"And how is my father supposed to activate it?"

C smiled. "How do you suppose?"

"Rub it three times and make a wish?"

"Just rubbing it will do the trick."

Leo looked carefully at the man. He realized that C was not so nondescript after all. His eyes were an amazing color of green.

"So what do you want? Firing squad?"

C sighed, smoked, sighed again. "Anything will do," he said. "Will you deliver the copy?"

"I could let you be killed and not tell you," Leo said.

"I do not need closure," C replied. "I have died before. Besides, I have read all of your work and formed something of an opinion of your character. I don't believe you would do such a thing, unless it served a higher purpose. You are not a cruel man."

"I suppose not."

"If it will make it any easier, I will do the killing part myself. But I would like a weapon of some sort. I can do it bare-handed, but the process is messy and painful."

Leo stared at him. C calmly smoked his cigarette down again.

"I don't know what to say."

"There is nothing *to* say," C replied. "After I am gone, you should put my body into the transport ship and set it adrift. Do not send a message to Amés or anything of the sort; it will only needlessly call attention to yourselves. I have already compromised Nirvana to some extent, obviously, but this was necessary. Let it go no further."

C smoked. Leo watched him. The cigarette was soon done. "Well then," said C.

"All right," said Leo. "Let's go back to the docking port."

They walked quietly back through the woods. When they got near to the portal, C said to Jill, "I would rather the child not see this. She will see plenty enough, soon enough."

"You are right," Jill replied. Leo thought he might have heard a catch in her voice. "But Leo should stay with her."

C stopped walking. "Yes, that would be better." He turned to Leo. "Will you make the delivery?"

Leo smiled. "Let's have a smoke."

"Do you smoke?"

"I used to," Leo said. "Back when I was a juvenile delinquent."

The two men stood and smoked.

"It would be worth taking that thing to the ends of the universe," Leo said, "just to see the look on Dad's face when I deliver it."

"Thank you," said C.

"Who are you really?" Leo ask. "Where do you come from?"

"My name is Clare," the man said. "Clare Runic. I'm just an average joe from Earth, same as you."

They finished smoking. Leo stayed with Aubry, while C and Jill went farther up along the path. The last Leo saw of the man, he was rounding a bend. C did not look back. He disappeared in the trees. A few minutes later, a single shot rang out.

Six

from
**First Constitutional Congress of
the Cloudships of the Outer System**
April 2, 3013 (e-standard)
a transcript

C. Tolstoy: Mr. Chairman . . . I don't know what to say. I came here today expecting to witness another gathering of idiots and knaves. I'm afraid I don't have such a high opinion of the lot of you as old Tacitus. I have seen a lot of history myself, and the one lesson that it has taught me is the futility of what we do. I have moved farther out the Road than most of you, and believe me, it wasn't to explore. If you want to know the truth, and even if you don't, it was to get away from the lot of you. And not just you—*everybody*. But I have to say I have never seen a more arrogant, gullible bunch than you are. Honorable Cloudships? We're all floating coffins in space. Now some of you may know that I and my family tend the graveyard, so I know whereof I speak. We stay out of your way, and you stay out of mine—until the time comes when *your* business becomes *my* business. But I have a feeling that the times are changing, and you and I are going to be bumping into one another more often. Now, I'm not talking about dying. All of you think you won't, and all of you will. No, I have another meaning. I do believe that it is time for me and my boys to come in out of the sticks for a while. I have listened to what has been said, and I'll tell you. I think the time has passed for doing a damn thing, and the fate is upon you. That's right, you heard me! Old Tolstoy and his sons are joining up. You want a navy, Lebedev? Well, here are your first recruits. We're on our way right now. I sure as hell hope you're ready for the thirteen of us.

C. Lebedev: I would be . . . will be honored.

C. Mencken: Now, just a minute. Nobody said anything about starting up the navy just yet—or ever. Are you done, Cloudship Tolstoy?

C. Tolstoy: I'm through with whatever I had to say.

C. Mencken: All right then, who is—

C. Markham: Lebedev, I'm with you. Tell me where to report.

C. Kafka: And me, too, Lebedev. I hope I don't regret this, but here I am.

C. Bernhardt: Do you need entertainers?

C. Lebedev: I don't know . . . I hadn't given the matter—

C. Mencken: Now that is really enough. This is not a goddamn rally or recruitment center. I am afraid that if anyone else volunteers for the navy, I am going to have to erase you from these proceedings and you won't be allowed to vote on whether we have a navy or not! Now where the friggin' heck did I put that gavel? All right. The resolution, ladies and gentlemen, the resolution. And we're only talking about the preamble at that. Now, I've quite lost the order . . . who is next . . . Cloudship Lao Tse? No, it is Cloudship Lorca. Yes—

Chamber Sergeant: Mr. Chairman!

C. Mencken: Yes? What is it, Sergeant Mann?

Chamber Sergeant: A messenger, sir. An emergency messenger has just reported in to the foyer secretary. It seems she came in person because the merci was jammed.

C. Mencken: Came in person? It isn't a ship?

Chamber Sergeant: No, Mr. Chairman. It is a Major Antinomian, sir. She hails from Jupiter. Claims it is a matter of the greatest urgency for the entire Council.

C. Mencken: Jupiter? What? Urgency . . . very well. What a taxing day this is turning out to be, and we haven't even passed any taxes yet. Nobody think that was funny? Ah hell, show her in, Sergeant.

Major Antinomian: Major Clarabelle Antinomian of the First Army of Europa, sir.

C. Mencken: Welcome to this chamber, Major. What can we do for you today?

Major Antinomian: I have an urgent message from General Changer on Europa, sir. For delivery to the entire Council of Cloudships.

C. Mencken: Well, here we are. Deliver it.

Major Antinomian: Half the army is taken prisoner, sir. One million soldiers.

C. Mencken: What's that you say?

Major Antinomian: Half the army is taken, and Ganymede is fallen!

Seven

C woke with a start, somewhere in the recesses of La Mola. It only took him a moment to realize what must have happened.

Amés was standing over him.

"Oh, dear," said C. He sat up. It was the same body as before, a cloned copy.

"I am afraid that you badly underestimated the partisans," Amés said.

"Yes. Obviously."

"I am going to have to punish you for that," said Amés. "No more visits to the memory box for a while."

"I understand," C replied. "Do you know what happened?"

"You were murdered. Execution style."

"Oh."

"I want you to pay special attention to the partisan terrorists," said Amés. "I want their threat eliminated. Now we both have reason for it."

"I agree."

Amés helped C to his feet. C was a little shaky for a moment, but quickly had control over his new body. In a strange way, he felt refreshed.

"Come on," said Amés. "You have work to do."

Eight

Roger Sherman was tired, but awake. He had been tracking the *Montserrat* for hours now, using the most slapdash, jury-rigged remote sensing apparatus any commander had ever employed in space—of that, he was sure. The merci was out, which prevented a great many methods of detection, but it also provided the clue he needed to find his quarry. For the range of the jamming had proved very specific. It was broad in places, but ceased in others. They had even managed to listen in on some vinculum broadcast and get some Met news when they'd gotten outside the jamming area. Sherman had also immediately contacted Tacitus, and learned that he was in the midst of a constitutional congress. He had signed off quickly and promised to let Sherman know how it all came out. Sherman wanted to limit how much was broadcast by his troops over the merci, so he had severely limited his time with Tacitus, as well. Contact with army troops at Jupiter, and Sherman's immediate superiors, had been impossible.

But they had slowly, methodically mapped out the effectiveness area of the jamming, and had found that it was shaped rather like a dumbbell, with a big globe at each end, and a narrower shaft down the middle. And at the moment, Sherman and the *Boomerang* were groping down that shaft. He wasn't sure, but it was a good bet that the jamming device—which might be on the *Montserrat* herself—was at the epicenter. In any case, he wasn't taking any chances. The troops in the hold were on full alert, ready for instant deployment. And Sherman was using every stealth measure he could remember from his study of warships and space battles.

There wasn't a lot to go on. Mostly war games and practice maneuvers. There had never been a major battle in space, after all, not in the over a thousand years humans had been outside Earth's gravity well. With the *Boomerang*'s isotropic coating, they were effectively masked from electromagnetic means of detection. Well, of course, the drive could not be so masked, but unless the *Montserrat* were sneaking up behind him—a possibility that he was fully taking into account—no one would see his ship. What he was more worried about were the grist-detection pockets. Any competent commander would have strewn them all about his position, setting up, in effect, a series of three-dimensional membranes to which only he would have the map. There was really no effective way to avoid these, but Sherman was taking the gamble that the jamming would jam those defenses, as well, and he was staying within the "bar" of the dumbbell partly for this reason.

He suspected that the jamming would taper to a point at the ship or jamming device location. He seriously doubted that they would allow their own communications to be compromised in such a way. But the technology was new to him, and he had no idea how it actually worked. And nearly fifteen hundred lives depended on his guessing correctly.

They moved onward through the void, nearly a million kilometers from Neptune, Pluto-ward. The *Boomerang* would top out at one-one-hundredth the speed of light, but he was going nowhere near that fast. In the first place, such speeds required millions of kilometers of run-up. But the object here was to be as sneaky as a fox, not as fast as a jaguar.

Working with his free-convert officers, Sherman had devised a gravimetric detection system that just might work. Light would pass through the DIED ship, but it would be slightly bent by the ship's mass in the process. The bending was extremely small, but it *was* present. Using grist astrolabes that were specially modified by a team of engineers on Titan led by Gerardo Funk, Sherman was attempting to use the light of the stars and planets to "see" the enemy ship. Funk had seemed confident, but such a thing had never been done before—had never been attempted. It was thought that the gravitational lensing effect was so infinitesimal as to be utterly impractical. It could be that they were right. The Third Sky and Light would know soon enough.

There was also the idea, put forward by Theory, that they might detect extremely small bursts of Hawking radiation from the ship. The isotropic coat acted, in many ways, like a black hole, and the "virtual particles" that the vacuum was continually generating might be affected. The idea was that a virtual positron-electron pair would spontaneously generate next to the coating, and one particle be instantly shunted around the ship by the quantum processes involved in the weak force that the coating employed. The other particle would then shoot off into space—and be detectable.

It was all guesswork, hopes, and prayers—and Sherman always assumed that his opponent would be praying, too, to negate that advantage.

"Anything, Theory?" Sherman said. There was a wall display, and Sherman could instantly go into the virtuality if he really wanted to have a look. Why the jamming device cut off communications but did not shut down the local action of the grist was another mystery yet to be solved, but Sherman was thankful for that small blessing. Without it, he would have lost his free converts, and navigating the ship would have been impossible.

Sherman went into the virtuality and checked in at the hold with his captains. Every space-adapted soldier in the brigade was standing in full readiness. Nine hundred seventy-eight soldiers, with another four hundred six in pressure suits. Against what? He knew that the *Montserrat* had deployed the rip tether, so could not have the full complement of troops a destroyer was capable of carrying. But perhaps they had packed in five or ten thousand. He was estimating the highest odds, ten to one against him, just to be prepared.

What was he overlooking? What had he forgotten?

"Quench, where is that man we pulled out of space? Our young hero?"

"Sergeant Neiderer, sir? He's on knit channel V9."

"Neiderer?" Sherman said, and then realized he'd neglected to make the mental switch over to the correct channel. Getting jumpy, Sherman. Stand fast. Quench, tactfully, said nothing about his colonel's mistake. Sherman changed channels. "Sergeant Neiderer?"

"Yes . . . Colonel, sir?"

"I want your thoughts, son."

"My thoughts, Colonel?"

"Come into the virtuality for a moment."

Neiderer appeared before him, and Sherman realized that this was the first time he'd ever seen the man. He hadn't realized that he was black.

"You're the only one of us who has faced the enemy face-to-face."

"I only faced a tether, sir."

"Yes. Well. Tell me anything you've thought of. Any ideas or gut feelings you have."

Neiderer immediately reached up and scratched his nose. "I don't know anything in particular, Colonel. I wish I could help you. Just a grunt, sir."

"Just a grunt with two weeks of k.p. duty if you don't cut it out with the false modesty, son."

"Yes, sir."

"Now just talk to me for moment."

"All right, sir. I . . . I've been thinking about Charon. I used to work there, in a warehouse out on the surface. Um, I had a girl. She split . . . we broke up, I mean. But I've been thinking about her a lot for the past couple of hours. It was my last girl who wasn't . . . well, she was my last girlfriend, sir."

"Go on, Neiderer."

"Her name was Carol. Erased the only picture I had of her, damn it. I lost my job at the warehouse, and I, uh, hit kind of a low point, Colonel. Real low. Lost just about everything, including my mind."

"But you snapped out of it?"

"Yes, sir. I joined the army, sir!"

"Uh-huh."

"I was thinking about hauling those barrels around on Charon. It was low-gee, so we could pick up some really big ones. Made me feel like an ant carrying a big moth or something. Not that I've ever seen that but on the merci. Anyway, the big problem wasn't the weight, but the inertia, sir. An object at rest likes to remain at rest, my team boss used to say. And one in motion likes to stay that way. So we had these tethers."

"What?"

"These pieces of elastic. We'd hook two of those barrels together and move one of them, and the tether would stretch out, then the next one we had to move wasn't nearly so hard to get going."

"But you put the same amount of energy into it, either way."

"I don't know about that one way or the other, Colonel," Neiderer said. "All I know is that it was easier. But what I was going to tell you was that, after work or during break, me and the others would get to playing with those tethers and sling ourselves all over the place. You could do some fancy gymnastics when two people were roped together that way. It was fun as hell, sir. I was thinking about those days."

Sherman sighed. "Sounds like a good time, soldier," he said. He was a bit embarrassed that he had called Neiderer away from his mental preparations for battle for such a silly conversation, but, of course, Sherman did not let his embarrassment show. "Well, stay ready."

"I will, Colonel."

"Dismissed."

Neiderer returned to his awareness *in* the hold. Sherman returned to the bridge.

He sat down and considered the stars in the viewscreen.

Long stretches of empty night winding a body in, Myers had written. *And the stars pinpricks in a shroud.*

Nine

TB was working on a poem. Then he wasn't.

"I can't," said TB. "I don't know what to say about it, except that it hurts."

Was this Ben talking, or Thaddeus? Who was *he* to say?

TB crumpled up the paper he was working on, then, recalling the shortage of energy to make another one, carefully unfolded it from the ball he'd crushed it into.

He thought he might get a drink, and had gotten up to go and find some alcohol, when there was a knock on his door.

It was Bob. He invited himself in and sat on the shabby couch that also served as TB's bed. Bob had brought along his fiddle.

"Why don't we go out and get drunk?" said TB. "I was just going to."

"Good idea," said Bob. "But I got to practice first."

"Practice?"

"This fiddle's getting rusty."

TB was a little irritated. He liked Bob's playing quite a lot, but he had been intent on getting that drink.

"Why can't you do that at home?" TB asked Bob.

"Home," said Bob. "Where would that be?"

Shit, thought TB, with all these things happening, I haven't thought to ask where Bob is staying.

"You don't have a place?"

"Oh, I have a *place*," Bob replied. "Everywhere's a *place*."

"Where are you living, Bob?"

"You sure talk a lot more than you used to," said Bob. "But that's okay, I guess. I just thought I'd practice a bit, is all."

"Well, I'm not stopping you."

Bob made no further reply. He smiled and put bow to fiddle. What came out was not one of Bob's usual dancing jigs, but something slower, more stately.

"Where the hell did you learn to play like that?" TB asked him after he was done with the piece.

"I used to be the best musician in the solar system," Bob said. "But I got tired of that."

TB laughed for the first time in many days. Maybe Bob was telling the truth. You never could tell with him.

"What's your real name, Bob? Would I recognize it since you were so goddamn famous?"

"I didn't say famous. I said good." Bob gestured with his bow at the paper on TB's table. "They used to call me Despacio, back in the days of yore."

TB took a good, long look at Bob.

He had to be lying like a rug.

Didn't he?

"Why don't you let me practice a little more, and you go on back to what you were doing?" the fiddler said.

TB returned to the page with a sigh, and Bob began to play. It was a lovely tune, but sad—sad and stately, with only a little hope in a few bright notes. Somewhere in the middle of it, TB began to write.

He began to write a new poem about his time among the wounded and dying.

Ten

And a million kilometers from Neptune, a red light flashed.

"We have them, Colonel," Theory said. "Gravitational and virtual-particle confirmation and correlation. It worked."

From the sound of Theory's voice, Sherman thought the major didn't even believe it himself. Sherman was in the virtuality instantly, floating in the *Boomerang*'s virtual bridge, which was the counterpart of the regular bridge, except that this one gave Sherman readouts graphically, represented in the air about him, a clear view of the space around the *Boomerang*, and instant control of all ship's weaponry. What it felt like was growing into a giant and hanging like a wraith over his spaceship, ready to grab his victim.

The *Montserrat* was several thousand kilometers away. And then the ship began to acquire form and substance as Sherman and his ship drew nearer.

"Anti-grist deployed?"

"Yes, Colonel."

"Give me my captains."

"Quench here, sir."

"Machination, Colonel."

"Sleighthand, Colonel."

One by one the companies reported in, and Sherman then went to officers' broadband. "We've located our adversary," he told them. "Maximum readiness, ladies and gentlemen. We're closing on them. Everyone in catapults. Weapons fired up. All pisses taken."

"Yes, sir!"

He returned to the bridge.

"I don't think they see us, Theory."

"Not yet, Colonel."

"Stay in that jamming range as long as possible. I think it is our best friend right at the moment."

"Yes, sir."

They closed further.

"Colonel, the jamming field is tapering. Part of the ship will be exposed in five minutes, if the current rate continues."

"Have we got the range for a torpedo?"

"Checking. No, sir, not yet. A few ten-klicks short."

"I want to come out of this field with all guns blazing, Major. Doesn't matter if we haven't quite reached optimal range." Sherman rubbed his stubbled face. "In fact, I want to emerge from a nuclear explosion."

"I'll arrange it with Captain Trigger, sir."

Sherman waited. A dead calm descended on him. He'd never felt so still in his life. Focused. Ready to kill.

"Almost there, Colonel."

"All weapons to forward."

"Yes, sir."

Dead. Calm.

"We're in unjammed space, sir."

"Fire."

The *Boomerang* erupted like a supernova.

They sped toward the foe.

"Report!"

"Three torpedoes away. All cannon forward. Nuke to the aft, as ordered . . . sir, we have a hit. Torpedo three . . . no, sir. It's gone through grist five klicks from the ship and ignited."

Then Sherman saw it—the familiar blossom of antimatter combining with matter and both furiously annihilating one another. The pressure wave hit the *Montserrat*.

Most of the killing radiation was shunted by that ship's

isotropic coating, but something got through. The *Montserrat* was rocked, and suddenly torqued at least forty-five degrees.

"Hello," said Sherman. "We're here."

"Sir, we're cutting through several layers of grist outriders with the cannon."

"More torpedoes," said Sherman. "When?"

"Ten seconds, sir."

"Right. Are my rocks ready?"

"Standing by in the materials catapults, Colonel."

Sherman had selected some prime specimens from Neptune's ring to arm his rock thrower with. Each rock was coated with the nastiest grist he had available, as well. Even if they got blasted apart they might still do some damage as pebbles.

So, their vinculum transmissions have just doubled.

So, they know we're here and are calling in to report.

A thought struck Sherman. "Theory, do we have full merci use at the moment?"

"Yes, sir."

"Broadcast this fight—broadband across the merci. Shoot me off a camera or make use of some grist."

"Yes, sir. Transmission is activated, Colonel. Unless they find a way to block it, everyone in the Met can tune in . . . torpedoes armed, sir."

"Off with them!"

"Yes, sir."

More streaks through the darkness, homing in. But not to go home.

"Colonel, we are closing on fire-down range." If the *Boomerang* did not turn around and apply the engines in the opposite direction at that point, she would overshoot the *Montserrat*. Can't have that happening, Sherman thought.

"Time it, Theory," he said. "I want to give them a faceful of our engines."

"Yes, sir."

Another antimatter bloom, this one very close.

"Was that us?"

"Checking. Yes, sir."

"Throw those rocks."

"Catapults activated. Rocks away, sir!"

A barrage of stones left the *Boomerang*, each flying at the ship's velocity plus some.

"Fire-down range in two seconds, Colonel."

"Bring us about."

"Yes, sir."

The *Boomerang* turned into a controlled slide, with the fires of its antimatter-reaction engines inevitably boring in on the *Montserrat*.

Eleven

Carmen San Filieu and her officers were madly trying to deal with everything at once on the *Montserrat* bridge. It had all happened at once, and, worse, her meal had been ruined—thrown all over her. One of the serving platters had also, unfortunately, decapitated her favorite steward.

But she must react, or all was lost. She had already lost precious seconds in figuring out exactly what was going on. It was the *Jihad*, come back to haunt her.

"Damage reports!" screamed Bruc.

"Number three cannon's out," answered the battle-station officer.

"How long until you can get me torpedoes?"

"Thirty seconds, sir."

"Damn it. What about the materials catapults?"

"We are carrying half a load, sir."

"Get them ready!"

"Yes, Admiral."

San Filieu gazed out, virtually. Flashes, positronic fire, streaking torpedoes. The stench of burning grist conveyed to her by virtual simulation.

And, worst of all to her mind—to her heart and gut—the whole sky was on fire behind the *Jihad*. It was as if the ship had arrived from the core of the sun.

The sky is on fire, she thought. How can the sky burn?

"They're rounding on us in fire-down, Bruc," said Captain Philately. "They're bringing their engines to bear."

"Here comes the blast, Captain!"

San Filieu glanced over at Bruc. A stoic look had come over his face. His eyes were set, but she noticed that his lower lip trembled slightly.

"Stand by," Bruc said. "Stand by . . ."

The blast from the *Jihad*'s engines hit. The *Montserrat* was rocked to its foundations, violently wrenched about—far worse than the original blow that had upset San Filieu's meal. In the virtuality, there was nothing but panic. A glance into actuality told San Filieu an even more dire story. Bodies were flying about the bridge. It seemed to go on forever, as if a storm had hit and somehow gotten *inside* of a house. San Filieu covered her head with her hands and closed her eyes.

When the shaking had stopped and she looked up again, Captain Bruc was lying at her feet, the side of his face crushed in. She drew back with a gasp, then suddenly held herself rigid. "I will not lose it," San Filieu said. "I will maintain." Maintain. "Philately, take command of the ship!" she called out.

"Aye, aye, Admiral!" said Philately.

Back into virtuality.

"All troops to personnel catapults!" Philately said. "Torpedoes away!"

"Torpedoes away, Captain!"

"Where are they?"

"Seventeen klicks. Fifty degrees, one seventy-five right ascension."

"Cannon to bear and close."

"Yes, ma'am."

"Damage?"

"We've . . . we've lost all but attitude control, Captain."

"*What?*"

"All engines down, ma'am."

"Don't let them know, Philately," said San Filieu. "Fire a torpedo to aft if you have to."

Philately looked at San Filieu. There seemed to be new

respect in her gaze, San Filieu, thought. "Aye, aye, Admiral," she said. "Continue closing, helm."

"Yes, Captain. "

"Give me a full report on those engines."

"Captain . . . checking . . . we took a direct hit to the aft, ma'am," said the engineering officer. "No one's answering . . . everyone's dead. Everyone is dead back there."

"What about my ship?"

"Ma'am?"

"My *ship*! Is the rupture sealing?"

"Checking . . . yes, Captain. It is contained nine klicks to the rear of us."

"Your rocks, Philately," said San Filieu. "Throw them!"

"But, Admiral . . ."

"Catapult those rocks, Captain!"

"Aye, aye, Admiral. Rocks away."

"Catapults activated. Rocks away!"

"Continue closing."

"Aye, aye."

Why did the little upstart question me, San Filieu thought. If only Bruc were here.

But he was, she realized, bleeding and dead at her feet only one reality away.

Twelve

Sherman brought his ship about and so caught the *Montserrat* rock onslaught broadside. The ship shook violently. If he hadn't strapped himself in in the actuality, his body might be a twisted ruin by now. But it was fine, he was fine.

"Damage?"

"All ruptures sealing. But we lost number one cannon, Colonel. Fifty-two casualties. Eighteen dead."

"Damn," Sherman said. "Bad luck, that turn. Close, Major."

"Yes, sir."

"Weapons to bear."

"Torpedoes, sir!"

A white-hot streak through the space beside them.

"Diverted, Colonel."

"Good. Close."

"Fifteen klicks. Ten. Five."

"Weapons, cease fire! Ready the troops!"

"Weapons cease fire, sir. Troops at the ready."

Sherman took another long look at the *Montserrat*. He couldn't believe what he was seeing. The DIED troops were deploying into space.

"Too soon," he whispered to the Met commander. "Too soon."

"Theory, throw every rock we have at those soldiers!"

"Catapults activated. Rocks away!"

A streaming bloom of ring material flew from the *Boomerang*. It met the *Montserrat*'s troops face on and cut through them like a deadly blast of wind. Several of the rocks traveled on and pounded into *Montserrat* herself.

"Give me a troop estimate on them, Theory."

"Sorting through the dead, sir . . . sorting . . . two thousand seven hundred live and functioning, Colonel."

Less than two to one, thought Sherman. Not bad odds. Not nearly as bad as he'd feared.

They were lining up along the *Montserrat*'s axis, getting into position for the fastest deployment of the troops. And then they were there.

"Throw the troops at them, Theory." Sherman quickly switched to broadband on the knit. "Good luck, soldiers," he said. "Kill the hell out of them." Then he changed the channel back.

"Troops away, sir!"

The two groups of tiny specks flew toward one another. The ships were too close to attack one another without damaging themselves, or the troops. It was hand-to-hand destruction now, with only supporting fire from the ships.

Death on a human scale.

Thirteen

Kwame Neiderer shot through the vacuum, pulling fifteen gees. He and the other space-adapted were in the first wave. The pressure-suited reserve would be following behind at a more stately acceleration. He was in charge of ten soldiers, and was now answering to Lieutenant Boxset. But Boxset was a greenhorn, and Kwame knew that it was he, Kwame, whom the soldiers would look to, when they weren't looking to their own asses.

What the hell, thought Kwame, all I can do is show them where to fire. Another two seconds, and they'd be in range. There were explosions all about him as the enemy's positronic cannon pinpointed soldiers and fired full on them. A particularly nearby flash of soundless light, and Kwame had lost Tiempos and Cue. Damn. He had liked Cue.

"Let's do it," Lieutenant Boxset said to Kwame over the knit in a meek voice.

"Ready arms and ready grist," Kwame called out over his prime's knit band. He brought his own rifle up.

They were in range.

"Fire at will," said Boxset.

The prime slammed into enemy lines, guns blazing. They were moving so fast, it was impossible to tell if they'd hit anyone. But to Kwame's left, one of his soldiers and a Met soldier collided head-on. Both people exploded in a bloom of goo and blood.

"About face," Kwame called out. "Use your rockets!"

He and the others fired off two arm rockets into the direction they were traveling, then the equal and opposite reaction brought him to a halt.

"Attitude adjustments, and at them!"

That was it for the orders. Now it was time to carry them out.

Kwame searched nearby space for a DIED soldier to kill, and found one almost immediately. The man was bringing a gun to bear on Kwame, but Kwame was quicker, and he blasted the man's head off with a beam of positrons from his rifle.

Suddenly the knit was filled with backchatter, and Kwame blinked the volume down. He concentrated on finding a new target.

Fire from above, just missing him. Kwame looked up, found his assailant, and fired one of his two remaining arm rockets upward. It streaked away, homed in, and took out the threat. Kwame did a quick flip and checked all around him in space. Nobody seemed to have his number at the moment. Most of his prime was concentrated nearby.

"Forward," Lieutenant Boxset called. They set their attitude controls to rearward and began to advance.

Another enemy wave, and another. Five of his own soldiers killed around him. Boxset and another lieutenant linked up, and then there were ten of them together again—advancing, always advancing. It seemed to go on for hours.

Kill.

Move forward.

Kill again.

Behind him, Kwame knew, a shell of fortifying material was constructing itself from the sprayed grist and the silicates brought from the *Boomerang*'s hold. Heavier artillery was being brought up to the fortress shield. But Kwame dared not look back.

Two more DIED soldiers he blasted. Firefights all around him. Then something pelting his face, and he covered up until it passed. It had been globules of frozen blood.

A blinding flash of light and Boxset was gone. He now worked for Lieutenant Chalk.

Then Kwame came up against something that resisted his moving forward. He turned his attitude jet up full throttle, but he could not move.

"Goddammit," he said, and punched out. It felt as if his fist had connected with a brick wall.

Kwame looked up. Fifteen meters away was the hull of the *Montserrat*. He was connecting with the ship's force-field envelope.

I'll be damned, thought Kwame. We're there.

"Bring up those bores!" Chalk called out. Kwame turned around and watched as two long rods were maneuvered toward his position. The tip of one of them almost touched him, and he had to duck to get out of the way.

"Watch it, soldier, that's hot grist!"

Kwame flew away a few meters and came to hover next to Chalk.

"Take it through!" ordered Chalk. The bore operator started his machine, and the rod slowly slid through the e-m repulsion of the force field and moved inexorably toward the hull.

Then it was touching.

"Bomb down the shaft!" said Chalk.

"Bomb away, sir," said the bore operator. "We've got a plant." Then, a moment later, "Activation code bounceback. We're in communication with the antimatter trigger."

Chalk put both hands to his head, as if he couldn't believe what he was looking at. He was silent, but his mouth was moving. Kwame realized that he was communicating the news up the command chain.

And then, they just stayed there. Minutes passed. The battle flashed and burned around them, but the three of them seemed to exist in an envelope of calm.

I could go to sleep, Kwame thought. But then I'd miss everything.

In the midst of fire and destruction, Kwame waited patiently to see how it would all turn out.

Fourteen

San Filieu paced about the bridge. At one point, she almost slipped in Bruc's blood and fell down, but she caught herself and managed only to stain the top of her boot.

"Admiral, we have to make a decision," said Captain Philately. "Sensors have confirmed the bore."

"No," said San Filieu. "No."

"Admiral, they have given us three minutes."

"He won't forgive this," said San Filieu. "He won't forgive me."

She finally sat down in her command chair and tugged at the strands of her hair that had come undone. Her hand came away and she realized that she'd pulled too hard. A hank of her black locks was in her fingers. She stared at it intently, twisting and worrying it.

"Admiral?"

"I won't surrender. I will not give up this ship."

"Admiral, they have us."

"I will not."

By all rights, she should contact Amés immediately and request instructions. But she couldn't do it, couldn't face him.

This was the end. He wasn't going to punish her. He wasn't going to torture her.

He was going to execute her.

Of that, San Filieu was certain. The king, she had failed

the king. How could she have done this? What had she missed? On New Catalonia, all was in ruins. She was married to a younger man who despised her. On Mercury, her bed would grow cold. And here . . . here, in this godforsaken hellhole. This waste. All was lost.

It was impossible. This did not happen to Carmen San Filieu. Carmen San Filieu maneuvered her way to victory. She won. She watched others writhe at her victory.

Amés was going to tear her from her very skin.

"I can't let him," San Filieu said. "I can't let him do that."

There had to be a way. There had to be a way to save face. *He was going to cut away her face.* There had to be. The grist matrix. It was here. Aboard the *Montserrat*. If the matrix were destroyed there was no way that Amés could get to her. If the matrix were destroyed, all the converts and aspects would die with it. That was one way to shut down a LAP.

On Mercury, she sat up in bed among twisted satin sheets, biting her tongue to keep from screaming.

In New Catalonia, she dropped a pitcher of water and it shattered at her feet. Busquets looked at her with contempt.

"It's a bluff," she said on the *Montserrat*.

"But Admiral," said Philately. "We have confirmed it. They have bored through the shields and placed antimatter charges."

"It's some sort of bluff."

Philately walked up to San Filieu and made her meet her eyes. "Admiral, it is not," she said.

San Filieu did not reply.

"Admiral . . . Admiral, we are receiving communications. I am putting it on the speakers, ma'am," Philately said.

"*Montserrat,* this is Colonel Roger Sherman of the *Boomerang.* You have fifteen seconds to surrender. It is not necessary to be destroyed. Listen to me, whoever you are: I will do this unless you surrender. Ten seconds. I implore you, *Montserrat* commander. Five seconds. For the love of God! *Montserrat? Montserrat?*"

San Filieu whimpered. The strands of her hair broke in her hands.

"*Montserrat*, the charge has been activated," said the voice. "In twenty minutes, your isotropic damping will be overcome and a blast stronger than a nuclear weapon will rip apart your ship. If you have any means to evacuate, I suggest you use it. Save your souls. I am sorry. Sherman out."

San Filieu thought she might go to her cabin now. There was still some good wine left. Good red wine, if the bottle hadn't broken. If so, she might swallow the glass.

She stood up. Captain Philately was in front of her, again looking her directly in the eyes.

San Filieu realized that this was probably all Philately's fault, after all. It wasn't fair that Bruc had been the one to die.

"I am going to save you the anguish of the wait, Admiral," Philately said.

"What? Captain, I don't have time for you now."

Philately leveled a particle pistol at San Filieu.

"Philately," San Filieu said. "You idiot."

Then there was a bright tunnel of light.

Pretty and hot.

And then nothing.

Fifteen

Sherman watched the hulk of the *Montserrat* as his soldiers were gathered in. He could not believe that the ship had not surrendered. Had he been in a similar situation, he would have immediately stood down. Someone had told the Met soldiers what was about to happen, and they were surrendering en masse, begging to be taken along on the *Boomerang*. He supposed he could find room for them. Guarding them would give Theory and the captains a logistics problem, but nothing they weren't up to. Everyone alive could have been saved, but that wasn't going to happen.

"Colonel, we are receiving a message from the *Montserrat*," Theory said.

"Put it on."

"Colonel Sherman, this is Captain Philately of the *Montserrat*. I have just killed Admiral San Filieu, but her convert portion is still alive and will not let us leave the ship. I don't suppose there is anything you can do to get my ship's personnel off?"

"Good God!" Sherman exclaimed, then he continued in a calmer voice. "I can't stop the bomb now, Captain. The reaction has already begun. It is just a matter of time until it overcomes the effects of your isotropic coating."

"I see."

"Do you have any of the keys to your lockout codes?"

"No, sir. They belong to the Admiral. This is her flagship. Was."

"Give me a moment, Captain," said Sherman. He changed channels. "Theory, is there anything we can do for them?"

Theory was silent for a moment. Odd. He must be running through a million options in his mind, Sherman thought.

"I have only one suggestion, Colonel," Theory finally answered.

"What is it, man?"

"We might be able to override the copying restrictions on their algorithmic portions and bring them all over through the grist as free converts," Theory said. "I have some new hacking software provided to me by Gerardo Funk, the engineer from Titan."

Sherman relayed the idea to Philately. It only took her a moment to reply.

"Are you sure? We have an immediate self-erasure clause coded into our convert portions. It is supposed to keep us from, well, deserting."

"We don't know," Sherman said. "But it's all I have to offer."

There was a moment of silence, and then came Philately's answer.

"We're ready," Philately said.

"Then come to me," Sherman said, "and save what you can."

The next twenty minutes were filled with such intense activity, that Theory had to remind Sherman that the *Montserrat* was about to blow. They had got in the soldiers and the POWs, and taken the convert copies of the *Montserrat* personnel into the *Boomerang*'s grist. It had worked.

And now the ship was away, twenty thousand klicks from the destruction that was building behind them. Sherman turned his ship around, but left enough momentum to aft so that they continued receding from the doomed *Montserrat*.

"Thirty seconds, Colonel," said Theory. They waited and watched.

"Ten."

He felt his scraggly beard, grown thicker now. Soon he might actually be presentable.

"Five, four, three, two, one—"

The *Montserrat* became a ball of fire, far, far brighter than the sun.

All was silent, of course.

The shock wave took out the observational grist, and Sherman's perspective shifted outward, grist line after grist line. By the time the radiant energy reached the *Boomerang*, it was only a gentle breaker, rocking Sherman's ship like a wave on a calm sea.

The jamming, Sherman thought. It is over!

"I must call Dahlia," he said. "And tell her that I still live."

"Well," said a voice behind Sherman in the virtuality. "What a pleasant surprise."

Sherman spun around, his pulse racing.

"Calm yourself, my boy. It's just me," said Tacitus. The old man held out his hand. "Congratulations."

Sherman took a breath and got hold of himself. He reached out and took the old cloudship's hand.

"He asked me not to announce him," said Theory. "I'm sorry for the shock, Colonel."

"Quite all right, Theory," said Sherman. "You've been perfect for too long, anyway. Take a break and join us."

"Sir?"

"Let us all sit down for a moment."

Three chairs appeared. Sherman found the one with the straightest back and took it. He had always hated mushy chairs. Tacitus lit a cigar, offered one to Sherman, but Sherman declined. It was enough to rest his hands on his lap. To Sherman's surprise, Theory took one of the cigars.

"The merci broadcast of the battle," said Tacitus, "was a master stroke."

"What's that?" said Sherman. For a moment, he couldn't remember that he'd ordered it. "Oh, yes."

"It very likely got you a government," said Tacitus. "We were in session, debating a new metaplanetary constitution, the other cloudships and I. There was a bit of fear and trembling. I don't suppose you've heard. Ganymede has fallen to Amés."

"No," said Sherman.

"But then we saw you fight. And we saw you win," Tacitus continued. "After you got that bomb into place, we passed the damn constitution with a two-thirds majority. Welcome to the new Solarian Republic, General."

"I'm a colonel, sir."

"No," said Tacitus, "you are not."

"Well," said Sherman. "So."

Tacitus took a long puff on his cigar. He breathed out, and the smoke wreathed about him, obscuring his face for a moment. Then Sherman could see him.

"We are putting you in charge," said the cloudship. "And I believe you've got a navy."

"When," said Sherman. "And how many?"

Tacitus laughed, and ashed his cigar. The detritus disappeared as it fell, and did not dirty the floor of the virtuality. In the virtuality, everything could be cleaner than life.

"Give me a few days—e-days—and I'll have your answer," Tacitus said. "In the meantime, I have a message for you from the Congress of Ships. A question, actually."

"What is it?"

Another puff on the cigar. "What is it, we were wondering, that you might need from us, and what, exactly, were you planning to do?"

Sherman considered the old man. Was he five hundred? A thousand? The e-years did not matter; Tacitus's eyes were still young.

I hope that I will once again have young eyes someday, thought Sherman.

"I wish you to give me your trust," Sherman said. "And then let there be war between Amés and me."

An Interview with Director Amés

Q: Director Amés, what are your aims in the current war with the outer system?

Amés: The problem here is a lack of communication. The outer system deserves the best government it can get, and that government is the Interlocking Directorate of the Met. We've tried nicely to persuade them to come back into the fold. Instead, the insurrectionist leaders have thrown our kindness back into our faces. Now we have to let them know the score in a very forceful manner.

Q: Is the outer system uncivilized?

Amés: I'm afraid the short answer is "yes." The frontier is a rough place in great need of the justice we can provide. Frankly, those who oppose us are no more than bands of brigands and criminals.

Q: So—after we solve the problem of the insurrection, what's next?

Amés: The galaxy had better watch out. Here come the humans! Humans united into one mind and one heart.

Q: Which brings us to today's great event: the launch of the Department of Immunity's new "Glory Channel."

Amés: It's a historic moment, indeed. Our destiny is to join together. Tuning into the Glory Channel will make that process a pleasure. The more people who feed the Glory, the better it feels to be a part of something so vast and important.

Q: Plus, it's the best way to do your part for the war effort.

Amés: Feed the Glory. With the Glory on our side . . . well, we'll simply be unstoppable!

The war for humanity's spirit is on. Discover the astonishing conclusion in Superluminal, *coming from Eos!*